SINS OF THE ANCIENTS

Book Three of *The Lies of The Guardians*

Copyright © 2021 by Herman Steuernagel

1st Edition

ISBN: 978-17771777-8-2 (hardcover)

ISBN: 978-17771777-7-5 (paperback)

ISBN: 978-17771777-6-8 (ebook)

https://www.hermansteuernagel.com

Cover by MiblArt

Edited by Novel Approach Manuscript Services

1

WIL UNDERWOOD'S arm reverberated as he blocked the swing of his opponent's sword with his own. They had been locked in a battle of wills for the past thirty minutes.

He wouldn't let her get the better of him. Not this time.

The mountain air was cool and crisp. Even during mid-summer, the elevation cooled the temperature down overnight, and the sun had yet to bring warmth to the day.

That didn't bother Wil, though. He welcomed the coolness as a reprieve.

The energy it took to keep his attacker at bay was all-consuming. The only sound heard throughout the mountain pass was the echo of steel on steel. That, and Wil's grunts as he moved to counter the blows coming at him.

He still hadn't mastered the art of grace as he swung the blade at his opponent. Finesse was a secondary skill yet to be learned; his focus, for now, was fixed on the dance required to stay fluid during the fight.

However, as Ella continued to remind him, you couldn't achieve one without the other.

Wil was impressed at himself at how far his training had progressed in just over a week. His sword arced in a show of strength, his footwork measured and his posture solid.

But it was all for nothing: Ella Torres countered and used the momentum of his swing against him. Wil went flying past her, but recovered before he completely stumbled, barely dodging the swing of her own weapon.

Only a few days ago, Ella would have been going easy on him, engaging in light banter while teaching him moves she was only half paying attention to. Now, her quips had dwindled as she focused more on his actions—and, it appeared, she was breaking a sweat trying to keep up. Wil was grateful her chit-chat had slowed; he needed to focus, and her banter was a distraction.

Ella was still better than him—*far* better. No matter the angle he attempted, she was always one step ahead of him. Wherever Wil put his sword, hers was already there, or she was dodging out of the way. He was growing tired, and though Ella grew quiet in focus, she didn't slow; it was clear she had much more stamina than he did. That would take months to develop, or so Ella had told him, at least. Wil questioned if he'd ever have the strength.

As they sparred, Wil kept his end goal in mind: to bring down the bots. Every *clank* of his sword on Ella's was another dent in a bot's paneling. Each echo of metal on metal represented one less bot in the world.

One less murderer.

Sweat dripped from his brow, down his face and to the ground below, but he barely noticed—his entire focus was on the woman before him. Seeing an opening, Wil advanced on Ella, forcing her to take a few steps back to regroup.

"A few more days of this and I'll need Liz to train me." He smirked.

"Oh, you think so, do you, Bot Killer?"

Ella unleashed a fury she had apparently been holding back. Wil could barely hold his ground as she pushed into him, one assault after another, blade ringing upon blade. He shifted his feet furiously, trying to adapt to her increased aggression. It took all of his concentration to prevent her blade from striking him.

But Wil had misjudged her reserve strength; the grin on Ella's face let him know she had plenty more if she needed. Wil, however, barely had the strength to react. With no more left to give, he stumbled backward, tripped over a rock, and earned the edge of a sword pointed toward his throat.

"You've only been at this for a week, Bot Killer," she said, irritation cutting her words. "Don't get cocky. A real opponent won't hold back —and they'll use your over-confidence against you."

Wil's face flushed. He wanted to crawl underneath the rock he had tripped on, but all he could do was try to laugh it off.

"Glad to see I haven't bested you yet." He winced as he stood, his bruised tailbone and an even more damaged ego getting the better of him. "I didn't really think I'd catch up to you in a week."

"Save it," she snapped. "If you want Liz to spar with you, I'm sure I could talk her into it, but she'll leave you with a lot more bruises than I do."

"I have no doubt about that," Wil replied.

Elizabeth was the leader of the western arm of the Resistance. Without a clear explanation, the band they traveled with had taken to calling her 'Liz' once they'd begun their journey.

Under her command, their small force had fought to defend the city of Vegas from the onslaught of the oppressive Guardians.

The Resistance, led by Liz, had arrived just in time, just as the protection offered by the Silent Zone—or SZ—had fallen. The source of its power was unknown, but it was widely accepted that the ancients had done something to the land which stopped technology from functioning within its borders. Its protection had lasted for two hundred years and had allowed humanity to avoid extinction at the hands of the bots they had created.

While she towered over Wil, a light sheen glistened on Ella's forehead, but the sweat on her brow was negligible when compared to Wil's soaked attire. The woman was slightly older than Wil's eighteen years, and she was a commander in her own right. Until a couple of weeks ago, when they had left Vegas, Ella had been a trusted advisor of Malachi Riley, the leader of the Community, a group aiming to better humanity's plight in the world through cooperation, rather than stabbing each other in the back.

Ella had been methodical in training Wil in combat techniques, giving him enough patience to learn but also pushing him to the next level. It was something he appreciated, but it also meant he sported his fair share of bruising. Despite his jests, Wil didn't doubt there'd be no contest if they put their skills to the test.

"Maybe I've been too easy on you." Ella smirked, but her brown eyes conveyed the truth of the statement. "You've done well. But don't think I'm giving you all I've got. You'll know you're at that point when *I'm* the one on the ground." She put her practice sword back on the rack behind her. "Maybe."

"Point taken." Wil refrained from rubbing his backside.

"Besides," she said, "I don't want to face Liz's wrath if you're unable to walk. We're already further behind than she'd like as it is."

They had left Vegas ten days ago, with few stops, and this was how Wil and Ella had spent every bit of daylight they'd had to themselves. The evenings had been much more pleasant.

After the battle for Las Vegas had ended, Liz had gathered the members of the Resistance who were uninjured or at least able to travel and had set out for San Francisco almost immediately. The Resistance had suffered heavy casualties, and according to Liz, their benefactor would be awaiting the news of their campaign. She hadn't explained exactly who had funded their expedition, but she had seemed eager to gather the remnants of their party and return.

Twelve. Only *twelve* Resistance members remained. Wil had gotten to know nearly all of them to varying degrees over the past week. Each of them shared his burning hatred of the robots, just as each of them had a story of losing someone close.

Only twelve had survived out of the fifty members that had made the journey to Vegas. The Resistance had embarked upon a mission to learn more about the strength of the Silent Zone. Instead, they had arrived just as it fell.

The presence of the Resistance had saved many lives, but the battle had cost the group dearly. If Sierra hadn't activated that device, they would all have been slaughtered.

Courtesy of his efforts, the Resistance had offered for Wil to join them on their journey. Once he'd had a chance to observe their movement, he could make a decision on whether he wanted to become an official member or not, and fight for their cause.

There had barely been time for Wil to say goodbye to Sierra once she had awoken from her coma, induced through detonating the blast that had ultimately saved Vegas. Part of him felt a twinge of guilt for having left her so quickly. The journey that had taken the two of them outside the Sphere had formed a bond between them.

They had believed that the dome the Guardians had built held the last of humanity, protecting their species for two centuries from the toxic wasteland the Earth had allegedly become. But it had all been a lie. It had been a means of controlling them, a means of separating them from the larger outside world, where life had continued and the fight to survive, despite the best efforts of the bots, had carried on.

Wil and Sierra had been classmates, but they had barely known each other and had had little interaction before leaving the Sphere, which had made their friendship unlikely when they were both thrust into the supposedly toxic outside world. Together, they had discovered the Guardians weren't who they had claimed to be, and they had each suffered the loss of individuals close to them as a result.

Their time together had been brief, but Sierra was his last connection to the Sphere. As much as Wil owed her for leading him into this world, he decided he couldn't stick around merely to satisfy some sense of sentimentality.

Despite their common origin, their goals remained worlds apart. Sierra had decided to stay back to help those the Resistance left behind. Her newly discovered power had been responsible for disrupting the Guardian assault on Vegas and had also released those who lived in the Sphere from their prison. Sierra was determined to help the Spherians integrate into the real world. She had decided to return to her home, find them, and help humanity to rebuild.

Wil, on the other hand, wanted the Guardians to suffer for their centuries-long stranglehold over humanity. He had agreed to follow the Resistance as a means of fighting against the bots. His allegiance seemed the perfect route to gain vengeance over the murderous machines.

Their conversation prior to him leaving still echoed in his mind.

"Just promise me I'll find you again," Sierra had said to him.

He'd looked into her purple eyes, wide and striking. Though she'd been lying on the MedCenter bed, her gaze had been fierce and determined, her eyes hinting at something else. In them, he'd noticed a change from the scared girl that had been on the run from the pursuing Onyx. A week prior, they had ventured out of the Sphere, unsure of anything that lay before them. That frightened girl was gone; in her place, a confident woman remained.

She'd need that determination when the time came to take down the blasted bots and end their stranglehold on humanity.

"I promise," he'd answered.

Wil had held Sierra's hands as he'd said goodbye. There was nothing romantic between them; it was intended as a simple gesture of not only friendship, but newfound family. Her hands had been soft, which made him chuckle. The contrast between Sierra's and Ella's hands was night and day; an unforeseen reminder of how different life was outside the Sphere. Wil had realized how easy their lives had been; how unprepared for the outside world they were after being catered to by the bots their entire lives.

Ironic, when Wil came to think about it, as the bots had always claimed they wanted the people of the Sphere to be ready for when the time came for Earth to be habitable again.

All lies. Nothing but lies.

Wil shook himself out of the memory. He had meant his promise, and he was convinced fate would bring them together again. There was much work to be done, but he couldn't wait around to see what would happen to the city; fights between residents had already broken out over the spare bits of metal and circuitry scavenged from the fallen bots.

Though the Resistance members had taken some items of value in exchange for their assistance during the battle, Wil wasn't interested in the bits of tech. They could stay in Vegas for all he cared.

The thought gave him pause. Merely a few weeks ago, the treasure trove of ancient artifacts strewn across the city would have enamored him. He still had a passing interest in the contrasts between the Sphere and the world outside its confines, but the allure of the ancient world was less appealing when humanity's future was under threat.

Wil had left that evening with the Resistance. They'd headed west for another city; the one Ella had called San Francisco. They needed to regroup, determine their next steps and precautions, and prepare plans in case more Silent Zones fell. Not every city had a Sierra or a dormant ancient device to save the day.

More Silent Zones. More Spheres. Wil had stopped asking questions about the extent of the outside world. His brain hurt with the sheer scope of how much world there was. He had grown up in a bubble that he could travel from end to end in a couple of days, and now it seemed as if he could walk forever in any direction and never find the world's end.

Once on the road, Wil had asked Ella for some basic sword training. She was hesitant at first, but he had convinced her that without being able to consistently use powered weapons, he needed to be well versed in hand-to-hand combat if he was going to survive.

He had been lucky with his power so far—its appliance represented a crucial turning point in the Battle for Vegas—but Wil still didn't know how it worked, or why, so he couldn't depend on it. All he knew for certain was that the energy discharged from him had the ability to deactivate the bots. The sudden, unintentional destruction of a scanner by Wil's hand had caused the Guardians to murder Marco, just as it had forced Wil to follow Sierra out of the Sphere.

Even if he could, it would be useless against human attackers. Which, according to Liz, it wouldn't be long until they were forced to face.

Wil was still trying to figure Liz out. She kept mostly to herself and didn't want to linger in the city at all after the bots had fallen. Liz felt the Resistance would be at its most effective when it was on the move, but the Resistance's losses had been heavy, and she had given her people a few days to bury their dead and to mourn.

A few days. Nothing more.

Vegas had been almost completely destroyed. The bots—the *Guardians*—had all but crushed its residents.

Guardians, Wil scoffed to himself. *Their designation couldn't be further from the truth.* It was why he refused to address them as such—they had caused so much death and suffering, they didn't deserve the title.

The Resistance had sworn to seek an end to the senseless killings, promising an end to a life under the oppression of machines. Why did so many others accept this was how it had to be? Sierra and her friend Terre had shown that they could take these beasts down.

"What's holding you back is your anger." Ella's voice brought him out of his daze. "Let that go, or you're bound to make a mistake. You must focus on the opponent in front of you, not the one in your head."

Wil rolled his eyes. Anger wouldn't destroy him; it was what *fueled* him. The hope of tearing down the machines drove him forward. To destroy those who had taken so much from him. From *all* of them.

Ella placed a determined hand on his shoulder. "I have lost too many friends, consumed by their rage. I don't want the same to happen to you."

Ella had been great company on the trip west. There were nights where it had been just the two of them left beside the campfire. They had joked and laughed, mostly about what life in their Spheres had been like and their shock once they had discovered there was an outside world. But Wil was now tiring of her lectures on his need for justice. Surely, of all people, Ella could understand? She had lost so much herself. Wil didn't know how she wasn't at least as enraged as he was, if not more so.

"Don't you dare assume I'm not angry," she had said to him one night when he had called her out on it around the campfire. *"It's one thing to use your anger to seek vengeance; it's another to channel it towards things you can control. Don't let your anger drive you to a void you can never satisfy. Focus on what you're able to do in the here and now. Don't get so*

wrapped up in the past that you destroy your future as well. Blind rage doesn't solve anything."

Wil had tried to see her point, to convince himself that channeling his rage would equip him better in the war ahead, but he was unable to control the roiling fury the bots had left him with.

A pair of gray orbs flew overhead, catching Wil's eye. That was the third pair he'd seen that morning—unless the same pair had been circling the camp.

"Are they looking for something?" he asked, shrugging off her concern, eager to change the topic. "They've been flying close all night."

"This is where the road meets the mountains. They know we're here, but until we leave this valley, they won't be able to get a lock on us. The bots will eventually give up and move on to their normal patrol vector."

The alcove where they sparred was removed from the rest of the camp. Their companions knew how to hide, and there was no reason to panic on account of the presence of two orbs.

It would have been more concerning if they hadn't seen *any*.

Their current downtime was a rare break in the hurried pace the group had kept. According to Ella, they were about to embark on the final and most dangerous leg of the journey.

Liz appeared, rounding a corner from the main campsite. Wil was getting used to her choice of outfit. It seemed to be the accepted style among the Resistance, but it was unlike any fashion he had seen. Wil was used to the drab, commonplace colors of grays and browns, both in the Sphere and in the desert; the faded greens and yellows Liz wore were both unsettling and beautiful to him. The colors were intended to blend in with both the desert landscape and the dying greenery of the land they had traversed along the way.

Her black boots rode midway up her calves. Tucked inside were her dark green leggings, below an armored green bodice and a yellow coat. The others in the Resistance wore similar outfits, all in a mismatch of colors that Wil had been unaccustomed to seeing on clothing.

Following close behind her was Cali. The two women couldn't have been more different if they'd tried. While Liz was closed off, short and in command, Cali was timid and sweet. It was hard to picture her as a fighter, but she was as agile with a bow and arrow as anyone he had ever met.

"I thought you two would have been done training by now." Liz's commanding voice gave them both pause. She eyed both Ella and Wil with disapproval. "Get this gear packed up. We need to follow behind those orbs. If we don't leave now, we'll have to wait hours for the next window."

Liz was something of an enigma to Wil. Ella had informed him that Liz had taken great interest in him, where he came from, and the power he had called upon to defeat the bots in battle. She had apparently asked Ella extensive questions about both him and Sierra, but she had never quizzed him directly. She offered him praise for his role in the Battle for Vegas, but otherwise she kept her distance.

Wil could tell something about him made Liz uneasy, but he wasn't sure what that was, and it bothered him. He had practically volunteered his life to the woman and her cause, and she barely gave him more than a few moments of recognition.

According to Ella, Liz had also enquired about their Sphere, likely wondering how two people with such strong and extraordinary powers were born of the same place, but Ella hadn't been able to give her any answers. Wil had offered to answer questions Liz might have had directly, but he had yet to be taken up on his offer.

Liz left them to finish packing, while Cali lingered to assist with the clean-up.

"You don't have to help," Ella said. "We've got this."

"It's no bother at all." Cali smiled in the sweet way she always did, her long brown hair bouncing as she grabbed an armful of practice weaponry that had been scattered throughout their training area.

Wil and Ella packed away the rest of the sparring equipment, and the three ventured up the path to the main camp. They crested the rise and discovered their tents and gear had already been loaded onto the cart.

Each of them would bend over backward to accommodate the other. Cali had been a prime example of that. Though she had the sweetest demeanor, her eyes had carried a hint of sadness throughout the duration of the trip. And yet, despite this, she was always the first to volunteer to help.

"I'm going to help with the horses now," Cali said. "Let me know if you need anything else."

Only two horses had survived the attack on the city: Stepper, who Wil had ridden to the city before the attack, and Che, Liz's personal steed. The two animals had pulled the entire Resistance encampment through the mountains each day, rarely slowing until nightfall.

T'al, another of their group, led Stepper to its place in front of the cart. The man's arms were muscular but not as large as the guards Wil had seen in Vegas. T'al spoke gently to the horse, stroking the horse's neck calmingly while hitching it to the cart.

T'al was perhaps only a couple years older than Wil and had a surprisingly quiet demeanor for one so fierce in battle.

"I got your tent packed, Bot Killer," T'al smiled as he finished hooking Stepper up. "You owe me."

"I'll clean yours tomorrow," Wil suggested.

"We won't be camping tonight," T'al replied. "At least, I hope not. There's no respite between here and the city. We walk for two days out in the open, no stopping. In about six hours, we'll take shifts sleeping. Three at a time will sleep in the cart in six-hour intervals. We won't stop until we reach the safe house in the Middle Ring. If Liz can get us entry, then we'll head into the City Center in the days that follow."

"Oh? I thought we'd head right into the city."

"The Rings form *part* of the city, but the City Center is a whole other world. They don't let just anyone in, either. Liz has connections, but she'll need to negotiate our entry."

"She has to pay to get us through the city gate?"

"It's not quite that simple." T'al grinned. "But we'll cross that bridge when we come to it. San Fran is going to blow you away, my friend."

The Resistance members continually talked about San Francisco as if it were a marvel, but nobody had quite explained to Wil why. Ella had grown up in a Sphere near there, but even she had never been to the city itself.

"Let's move!" Liz shouted over the buzz of the fighters, and the chatter quieted down as a couple of members finished tightening the straps on the carts. And with nothing more to do than venture west, the horses once again led the party toward the city of San Francisco.

2

THE GROUP CONTINUED to move throughout the day, and Wil hung back with Ella and T'al. The mountain path the cart currently rolled along opened to an undulating hillside that flattened and stretched out to the west. Wil had already seen more magical landscapes throughout their journey than he had ever dreamed were possible: crooked streams that ran off the heights of enormous mountains; giant trees wider than he was; and a world so green he would never have believed it to be real if he hadn't seen it with his own eyes.

The land before them had turned brown. Other than the rolling landscape, it reminded Wil of the desert that surrounded the Sphere. Brown grasses and muted dirt hillsides emphasized the parched earth. It seemed as though decades had passed since it had last seen rain.

"Drought has ravaged this place since long before the wars," T'al explained, confirming Wil's suspicions. "Only once we get closer to the coast will you see the land come to life again."

Ahead of them, two other Resistance members, Ice and Buzz, walked alongside Stepper and the lead cart. Though Wil had gotten to know them since they had left the city, he hadn't yet learned their proper names. When Wil asked T'al about it, he was told it would be best to leave the topic alone; they'd tell him if they wanted to. Those who took on new identities, T'al warned sagely, were often trying to leave behind a past they'd much rather forget.

Both men were fit, though not as large as T'al, and both wore capes intended to fight the morning chill that now rustled with the breeze coming off the mountain. The dark green capes complimented the lighter green outfits they wore, though the color against Buzz's pale skin made him seem almost sickly. Ice's warm beige skin suited the clothing much better.

Liz walked beside Che as the horse pulled the second cart. Voth, a petite but agile woman, walked with her. Both of the women were silent.

Wil had also come to know Voth over the past week. She was a close companion to T'al, and where you found one, you could usually find the other. A force to be reckoned with, Voth was even more confident than Ella, quick-witted and even quicker with a blade. A pair of daggers were sheathed within her belt at all times, and Wil prayed he'd never be on the receiving end of them. He'd never see them coming.

A foot shorter than Wil, Voth's jet-black hair made her fair skin appear pale and ghostly, and her eyes were so light that they were nearly white themselves. She was friendly enough with Wil and had been willing to share a drink and a laugh with him as much as any of the others, but she kept her past close to her chest. Any time Wil asked a question that she felt bordered on being too personal, she clammed up. Wil didn't think she shared anything personal with anyone, perhaps with the exception of T'al.

The cart Che pulled held fewer supplies, leaving enough space for them to sleep comfortably. Three beds slid into the cart's side like drawers, part of a hidden shelf toward the front, designed for this specific purpose.

Just as T'al had mentioned earlier, six hours into the journey, the group stopped to let three of the members stop for a break. It was midday, and Wil doubted any of the team were ready to sleep just yet. Those who were the first to sleep now would also walk the entire night. It seemed like the short end of the stick, but perhaps after traveling in this manner for some time, the Resistance had grown accustomed to sleeping when it was necessary to do so. Wil certainly wished it was a skill he possessed.

"How did they decide who has to stay up all night?" he asked, more to himself than to anyone.

"They drew straws," T'al answered. "Because you and Ella are guests, you'll get the sleep quarters overnight. Midnight until sunrise."

"That hardly seems fair," Wil replied. "We decided to come on this journey, which means we should be treated the same as everyone else. No special privileges."

"That's just how we operate, Bot Killer. If you officially join our movement, you can walk through the middle of the night like the rest of us." T'al shot Wil a grin as he shifted his pack. It was only then that it crossed Wil's mind that he and Ella had been the only ones not carrying extra weight.

How had he missed that?

"That may be sooner than later," he mused, doing his best to ignore Ella's sideways glare.

T'al's grin widened, and he pushed ahead, leaving Wil and Ella behind. Wil watched the wheels of the cart move over the bumps in the road as they descended the last stretch of the mountain pass. From there, they would reach wide open terrain.

Wil hung back behind the others with Ella, grateful for her company.

As if she could read his thoughts, she turned to him and gave him a warm smile that extended into her dark brown eyes. Ella seemed happy just to be spending time with him, and he enjoyed being around her. Her smile alone certainly made the draining slog of travel much more bearable.

The sound of scraping metal caught Wil's attention, breaking him out of his thoughts of Ella. Cresting a final ridge, Wil could see a series of lower hills lay before them, topped with brown grasses and relics of a bygone era that sporadically lined the sides of the road. The road ahead forked from the path they were on and wound its way along the base of the larger mountain range, working its way back into the woods. A small crest into the forest obscured their view, but there was something moving just over the ridge.

And whatever it was sounded sizeable.

Wil and Ella had fallen back from the pack, so it was likely the others hadn't heard the noise over the sound of the carts crunching dry dirt and rocks beneath their wheels. Nobody ahead of them seemed curious as to its origin, and even Ella beside him didn't appear to have noticed it. Something familiar about the sound urged him to investigate.

He raised an eyebrow to Ella. "Stay with the others. I'll catch up."

He drew his sword and turned to follow the side road.

"What are you doing?" Ella hissed, trailing after him. Her eyes flitted back to the rest of the group.

"I hear something," he said, hoping she wouldn't say anything to give him away. "I just want to get a quick look."

"And let you get yourself killed? No chance. I'm coming with you."

"Fine—but be quiet."

The road followed the tree line as it snaked around a large outcrop of the woods. Given its condition, the road evidently saw a lot of traffic, possibly more than the one that scaled the mountains. With the forest on one side of them and the barren landscape on the other, it was as if this road was the divider between two worlds.

They didn't have to go far before the road crested the ridge and turned to a clearing within the trees, taking them out of the line of sight of their travel companions.

"What do you think you're going to find, exactly?" Ella hissed.

Wil raised a finger behind him to silence her.

Ella balked at the motion, but movement within the trees stopped her from responding.

Wil grabbed Ella and pushed her against a large pine at the side of the road. Wil held his hands at her waist as he peered around to get a better look.

"What are you doing?" Ella rebuked.

"*Shh!*"

"Don't '*shh*' me. What kind of game do you think this is?"

"*Quiet!*" He pointed to the white figures barely visible behind the brush. "Sentinels!"

Three bots stood at full attention at the side of the road. Their white-paneled bodies stood out through the brown foliage, their standard blue accent lights visible but appearing dim in the glare of the harsh sun. Two youths were on their knees in front of them, their hands bound.

Wil's mind raced. Would the detainees be led to their deaths? Or perhaps to a Sphere? The fact they were still alive suggested the latter, but Wil still didn't know exactly how the bots operated.

Only one thing was certain; they were programmed for destruction.

The youths were still, their heads down. Wil couldn't tell much else about the pair through the barrier of branches and trees, other than they were young, perhaps in their mid-teens, and that there was one boy and one girl.

"We need to help them," he said.

"We should get the others," Ella whispered. "Liz will know what to do."

"There's no time," Wil replied. His heartbeat reverberated around his skull. Wil had taken on far more bots during the Battle for Vegas, before his newfound power had stopped dozens of them. He was confident he could handle three, especially with Ella by his side.

This ends now.

Wil didn't give Ella a chance to argue—he drew his weapon and charged from his hiding spot. He desperately wished he had been allowed to carry a blaster, but typically he drained the thing just by holding it. Energy weapons weren't easy to come by, and his powers completely ruined them.

His sword would have to do.

Fewer bots in the world meant fewer people terrorized; fewer people falling victim to their ridiculous lies. Wil was ready to put a stop to it all. One bot at a time, if need be.

During the attack on Vegas, he had learned that Sentinels had weak spots that could be exploited. The neck, the eyes, and the spots that connected synthetic flesh to metal were all vulnerable. It was just a matter of getting close enough.

Though he moved as quietly as he could, Wil hadn't gone more than twenty feet before the three bots turned, their eyes fixated on him.

"Threat detected," the three voiced in unison.

Without a second warning, the bots drew their blasters and fired.

Wil dove to the ground and rolled, narrowly dodging their beams. Dust plumed from the path where their bolts struck. He scrambled forward, closing the gap without being hit, and lifted his blade into the gut of the closest bot, plunging through an exposed slit of wire and hoses that connected the Sentinel's bionic legs to its torso. His sword sliced through the connection, and sparks flew as the machine stumbled backward.

The two youths, bound beside the bots, managed to fall to the ground and evade blaster fire, though their bonds still prevented them from escape.

Wil tried to position himself between the downed bot and the other two machines, but they were no longer focused on him. Instead, they fired past him, over his shoulder.

Wil stole a quick glance behind him. Ella had her blaster drawn and continued to duck behind the pine tree where he had left her.

She was trying to draw their fire.

Ella had impeccable aim, shooting out a bot's eye with ease, causing sparks to erupt from the damaged socket.

Wil took advantage of the opportunity. He lunged at the damaged Sentinel, lifting his sword and driving its point into the mechanical vertebrae of the bot's neck.

Metal crunched, and more sparks flew from the malfunctioning machine. Wil lifted a boot and kicked the bot forward in an effort to dislodge his blade.

A cry caught his attention, and Wil turned in time to see three members of the Resistance joining them. T'al and Voth were running with a concerted effort, their blasters firing on the remaining Sentinel.

Cali had been ahead of them, but she had now fallen to the ground in a heap.

The bot's final shot had made contact.

"*No!*" Wil yelled, tripping over himself as he tried to gain his bearings.

Cali lay on the ground, motionless, as her two allies stood above her, firing at her assailant.

While Voth drew fire, T'al holstered his small weapon and grabbed a double-handed blaster from the holster rig across his back.

Voth took cover. T'al whipped around the face of the tree and let the gun unload into the middle of the Sentinel's chest, sending it flying backward into the woods.

T'al swung the large weapon, returning it to his back. He grabbed his small blaster again and hustled to the Sentinel's location to ensure it was down.

Wil briefly admired how quickly T'al could move his gigantic frame before running to assist their fallen friend.

"What the hell happened?" Voth asked, her knife out and tearing through Cali's shirt to get to the wounded flesh and to assess the damage done.

"The bots had taken these kids prisoner. We had to stop them!"

With Cali being attended to by Voth, T'al had moved to where the youths still lay helpless in the dirt and began to work at their bonds.

"Why did you sneak off by yourselves?" Voth scolded. "What the *hell* is wrong with you!"

"Hey! I just did . . ."

"Answer the question."

Liz's voice caused Wil to stop. She didn't raise her voice, but her stern tone could have cut glass. She towered over them, her face silhouetted against the sky, but Wil didn't need to see her features to know how deep her scowl went.

"I thought I had it under control," he replied sheepishly.

Cali was still breathing, but she wasn't conscious.

"I'm guessing this was your idea? Ella has more sense than this. Usually."

"She tried to stop me . . ."

"I should have tried harder," Ella confessed.

"I just did what I thought was right," Wil said defensively, his eyes still focused on Cali.

"And nearly got somebody killed," Liz rebuked. "Maybe you should leave the judgment calls to people who know what they're doing."

The damage to Cali's skin looked severe. The blaster bolt had burned a deep wound into her shoulder. It was black and oozing with pus and blood, and a horrid stench hung in the air as a result.

"How is she?" Liz asked Voth, her scowl softening into concern. Wil breathed a sigh of relief that she had turned her attention away from him for the moment.

"Not great," Voth replied honestly. "Her breathing's ragged, but at least she *is* breathing. Could've been a lot worse. I'll be able to pull her out of this, but she's going to need to rest the whole way to San Fran. It'll mean we're down to two rotating beds."

Liz sighed. "Wil! Stand up!" she ordered. He hadn't been sitting, but he straightened in response. "What possessed you to break away from the group? And then to take on *three* Sentinels without backup?"

Wil stood dumbfounded. *Did she truly not know?* They were bots, built for war, and so Wil had taken the fight to them. He wasn't prepared to stand by and let those two kids suffer at the hands of the bots.

He looked down towards his fallen friend.

Had it been worth the cost?

"If you want to be part of the Resistance, you need to learn to control yourself, Wil," Liz continued, not waiting for his answer. "Arrogance is not acceptable. If you were one of us, you'd be dismissed from the movement."

Liz studied the injured woman as Voth bandaged her wound. "Frankly," she continued, "at this rate, I'm not sure you'll ever be one of us."

His heart sank.

"What is that supposed to mean? I thought killing bots is what the Resistance does."

"What the Resistance does is work together to end the Guardians' rule. Put yourself or anyone else at risk to attack three Sentinels without a plan is helping nobody. If we accommodated every disenchanted youth who went rogue, we'd never make any progress. We have ways of doing things for a reason. Because of your actions, Cali is now injured, you've slowed us down, and there will be less sleep for the rest of us. Not to mention these Sentinels likely sent off distress beacons when they detected a threat. There will be more bots coming, thanks to you. There's a time to be a hero and there's a time to sit back and be strategic."

"I just thought . . ." he began.

"You *didn't* think." Liz paused between each word for emphasis. "You acted on blind rage. Don't think you're going to fool me with your false sense of duty. The machines have hurt us all. I've seen many like you come and go, filled with anger and little sense. They never live long."

Wil could say no more. Liz was right. He had been so caught up in his anger that he had put himself, their party, and Ella in harm's way to prove himself.

And Cali had paid the price.

He took little comfort in the fact that Voth said she'd be ok.

Ella stood silently off to the side, her cheeks flushed.

Is she embarrassed by what I've done? he wondered. *Or is she embarrassed she didn't do more to stop it?*

"Come on," Voth said, her dark hair stuck to her face as she wiped the sweat off her brow. "There will be time for this later. Give me a hand and help me carry Cali back to the cart."

"What about these two?" T'al approached the group, with the two youths who had been held by the Sentinels in tow.

Wil wiped a sheen of sweat from his forehead, grateful neither teen had been hurt in the crossfire.

Both youths had bright blue eyes and light brown hair. Wil guessed they were brother and sister. Dirt streaked their freckled faces, revealing the faint trace of tears from their earlier ordeal.

"What are your names?" Liz barked.

The eyes of the girl went wide. The boy simply clenched his jaw.

"I'm Sara," the girl answered, busying herself with brushing off some dirt from her already brown outfit. "My brother's name is Dagger."

Dagger's lips were still tight, his eyes skeptical of their would-be saviors.

"Where are you two from? Why are you out here by yourselves?" Liz demanded, as if speaking to a couple of soldiers and not two scared kids.

"We were looking for food," Sara answered. "We got lost and wandered into the path of the Sentinels."

"Why are you so far from an SZ? Where are your parents?"

"They're dead," Sara answered. "Our farm is on the edge of the Outskirts. There was a fluctuation in the SZ as a patrol passed. My parents were in the fields, about to come in for the day. The Sentinels shot them and announced we were about to be re-educated."

"How long have you been imprisoned for?" Liz's eyes appeared to soften, but her commanding voice offered no comfort.

More tears welled in Sara's eyes. Wil wasn't sure if they were the result of the memory of her parents or brought on by the woman aggressively questioning them.

"The Sentinels have marched us for three days and nights. This was our first break."

Liz nodded, turning to T'al. "Let them go," she said. "There's nothing more we can do for them."

"Wait." Wil stepped between Liz and T'al. "Where will they go? Surely we're not just going to abandon them here?"

The two youths looked at each other, wide-eyed, and Sara visibly trembled. Dagger was pretending to be indifferent, looking around as if uninterested, although crossing his arms in irritation proved he was doing a poor job.

Neither teen protested.

"Listen," said Liz. "How many times do we have to keep going over this, Wil? As long as you travel with us, you need to accept *my* orders. These two have been walking for three days without rest. We have another several days of walking ahead of us with no breaks, and, thanks to you, we only have two beds to share between us. We can't afford to be slowed down any further or make their problems our own."

"We can't just leave them!" Wil protested. "They have no way to protect themselves!"

"Not my problem. Keep it up and I'll leave you out here, too."

"Lizard," T'al said, lowering his voice. Wil had only ever heard T'al call Liz that in private. To Wil's knowledge, nobody else used the nickname, and Wil dared not repeat it.

"I'll watch over them," T'al continued. "They can be under my charge. Let them take turns sitting with the driver. The kid's right; they have no way of defending themselves. And with their current fatigue, I doubt they'll last the night. Leaving them here is a death sentence."

Liz let out an exasperated sigh. "We're not in the business of picking up strays, T'al."

"We're also not in the business of leaving kids to die. You said yourself, more bots will be coming this way. If we leave these two, they're going to be executed."

"Fine," Liz relented. She lifted a hand to her temple, shaking her head. "I'll allow it, but only because our charge put these two in this situation." She nodded in Wil's direction. "But we're not going to make a habit of picking degenerates up on the road."

"Thank you," Wil replied, lifting his eyes to meet the glare Liz cast on him.

"Just don't go off trying to be the hero again, you hear me? We can't afford another stop."

"Fine. Got it."

"I'm not so sure you do, *Bot Killer*." Liz jabbed a finger into Wil's chest. "War is coming. I need you on our side, but more importantly, I need you to get your head in the game. You can either make these dumbass decisions to let out your frustrations or you can make a real difference. The choice is yours. The path that wins isn't always the path that looks to be doing the right thing. Sometimes you must act in a way that seems heartless to ensure the greater good. One wrong decision and thousands die instead of a handful. There's only one path that rides with us, so choose wisely. Now help Voth get Cali onto the cart. We've got to keep moving before any more bots show up."

Wil quickly aided in carrying Cali back to the cart. Liz could blame him all she wanted for her injuries, but if it hadn't been for the bots, Cali wouldn't have been injured at all.

He was going to stop them. No matter what.

3

WAR IS COMING.

Wil's thoughts raced as they returned to their caravan. Humanity had been fighting the bots for two hundred years, and only *now* war was coming? What hadn't the Resistance told him?

Choose wisely.

He knew Liz's intentions were good, but why shouldn't he be able to make the bots pay for what they'd done? So many had died at their hand. Marco, his late best friend and lover, had just been one of many.

Wil sighed, looking at Cali's lifeless body as he helped T'al hoist her onto the back of one of the transport carts. He supposed he knew the reason why Liz was asking him to show restraint. Cali's limp body should have been all the proof he needed.

Ella had been doing her best to avoid his gaze. When she finally relented and looked at him, her eyes were filled with both concern and embarrassment. It was no secret to Wil that he meant more to Ella than she did to him, but that didn't mean he didn't care about her. Quite the opposite, in fact; she was the closest friend he had. With the death of Marco so recent, he was unwilling to allowing any feelings he might have had to take root. That wasn't to say he wasn't tempted; he just didn't know if he was ready.

T'al had become a good friend, too, but Wil wasn't able to confide in anyone like he could in Ella. But it could have just as easily been Ella on that cart. He'd almost gotten her killed.

A second friend the bots had almost stolen from him.

Wil wondered what Marco would do if their roles had been reversed; if Marco had been the one to live instead of him. Would he be standing here now, plotting revenge? Would he go to war to avenge Wil's death? Or would he have ever left the Sphere? Would he be sitting there now, waiting to be liberated by Malachi's Community after Sierra's blast knocked out the Sphere's force field?

Marco had always been headstrong. Wil, on the other hand, was always the one to hang back, unsure if they should carry out Marco's wild schemes. That had all changed the day he discovered the Guardians' lies. But if Wil had been the one who died that day, he guessed Marco would have jumped on those orbs then and there, likely getting himself killed or banished in the process.

Wil stopped. Thinking of banishment brought to mind all his fellow Spherians who had been reportedly sent into the toxic wasteland over the years. Wil now realized none of them had actually left the Sphere. The bots wouldn't have sent anyone into a habitable world to exist without them. He shuddered at the realization.

The Guardians had murdered every single one of them.

THE RESISTANCE CONTINUED their journey west. Cali lay in the cart that rolled beside Wil, wounded and unresponsive.

The result of his actions still crushed his mood. Regardless of the intended outcome, he could have handled the situation better. But the bots had to be defeated—he was more resolute in that fact than ever. Humanity had been playing cat and mouse with them for two centuries. It was time for humanity to take back their planet.

The hill the Resistance caravan climbed leveled out and the landscape opened up, revealing a seemingly endless expanse of lush green hills and fields.

Wil gasped as they crested the rise. Far in the distance, a pillar of light, translucent with a bluish-green hue, stretched into the sky and disappeared into the clouds above it. Its appearance reminded him of the force field of the Sphere. Its semi-opaque surface mimicked the way the Sphere had looked when he and Sierra had turned back to view the world they'd fled.

This was no dome, however.

From a distance, Wil couldn't be sure of its exact size, but it had to be massive—probably at least the diameter of the Sphere's base, but much taller. It stretched so far into the clouds that he couldn't see its summit. The scope of the pillar made it appear as if it should be closer, but he knew they still had more than a day's travel ahead of them.

Wil's pace had slowed somewhat, allowing him to admire the view. It was only a matter of minutes, though, before T'al fell back to speak with him.

"It's incredible, isn't it?" T'al said.

"What is it?" Wil asked, still not sure what he was looking at.

"San Francisco. Or its City Center, at least."

From where they were, the color of the pillar seemed to shift as the clouds passed by.

"Is it Sphere technology? Did the Guardians make that?"

T'al chuckled. "No, quite the opposite. The tech is similar, but the ancients built it to keep the bots out. A pocket of humanity still keeps itself locked away inside."

"So, they're their own prisoners?" Wil asked, arching an eyebrow.

"I guess you could say that. Though nobody would ever think of it like that. You'll understand once you see the Center for yourself."

"You live there?"

"Hah! No. Those who live inside rarely leave, if ever. We are fortunate enough to have favor with the city's Director. Few can travel through the city gates as freely as Liz and those around her."

Wil had never imagined humans would have intentionally separated themselves. He supposed it made sense, in many ways. Protection from the bots and having control over their own resources would be a valid enough motive for most.

"What's it like inside?" he asked.

"Come on," T'al said, waving him forward. "We still have a long way to go before we get there. It'll be much better if you see it for yourself. This is just a glimpse. It's even more impressive the closer you get."

Wil nodded and pushed forward. The air hung heavy here, a humidity Wil had rarely experienced back in the Sphere, similar to that brought about by a good rainstorm.

He shook his head at the thought.

Rain in the Sphere. The few times a year they had received rainfall, the Spherians had believed the force field eliminated the toxicity of the water. Now he realized it was yet another lie. The water was harmless; the force field did nothing to it.

He wondered where the idea of the filtered rain had come from. When Wil thought about it, he couldn't remember a single Guardian repeating the idea. The people of the Sphere had done the dirty work for their captors. It was amazing the prisons humans could put themselves into without even being asked. His people had been so brainwashed that they had come up with ways to rationalize anything that didn't add up.

Was that how humanity had survived centuries of fleeing the bots? Or were humans always so eager to believe the lies they were told? Wil thought of Vegas and those living in the Underground. Thousands of abandoned rooms sat above their heads—or at least they had before the recent battle—but for hundreds of years, those in the city had convinced themselves the Underground had been the better option. Fearing the light of day, they had lived, impoverished, below ground, hoping it would provide them with the safety their ancestors never had.

He sighed. How many of these imaginary constraints had humanity operated under without even realizing it?

As he studied the landscape, Wil noticed a lone figure running along the open plains. The individual didn't seem to be concerned whether or not he was seen, as he was making his way directly towards the party—and he was moving quickly.

It wasn't long before he could make out it was Renny, the scout Liz had sent ahead of them. His red hair was unkempt, frazzled by the wind and soaked with sweat. Wil thought it was strange he hadn't tried to hide his approach. According to T'al, Renny was one of the best scouts the Resistance had. He could kill three men before they realized anyone was close by.

His approach suggested the man had thrown his typical caution to the wind.

But, Wil supposed, there was no reason for him to sneak up on his own people.

Renny had been traveling ahead of them for the past twenty-four hours. The group only had two sets of scouts and they would both take shifts, allowing one set to rest while the other ran ahead—or at least that was how it had worked before one bed had been occupied full time by Cali.

Wil cringed. *Looks like I messed up the scouts' sleep cycle, too.*

Renny's shift wouldn't be over for another few hours, and his partner M'iko wasn't with him. As Renny approached Liz, Wil worked his way forward through the caravan so he could hear the scout's update.

"What flag do they fly?" Liz asked. Wil hadn't heard who she was referring to.

"The Flag of Mourning. They still grieve for their fallen oppressors."

Oppressors? The Guardians? Who would weep for them?

"What of M'iko?"

"She's skirting the camp to see if she can glean any more information. She'll determine the extent of danger they pose. If they are consumed in ritual, we may get lucky."

Concern flashed across Liz's face, but only for a moment; a rare break in the stoicism she typically exhibited.

"Strange they would set up camp here, of all places," Liz continued. "They're the middle of the main route. What do you make of it?"

"It's hard to say. The Order veils themselves in mystery at the best of times. Since so many of the bots fell . . ." Renny paused and shook his head. "Well, who knows how they are reacting to the news. Since we're still a couple of days from the city limits, they would know we're far from any help."

"Could it be a trap?"

Renny shook his head again, this time more emphatically. Dirt streaked his face from where sweat had run from his brow. "If it is, I can't see it being meant for us. We wouldn't be worth the effort. Besides, they don't misuse their flags for subterfuge. It'd be in breach of their oaths."

"How many did you say were in the camp?"

"At least eighty, but it could be twice that. It was hard to tell without getting closer. M'iko should be able to give us a better idea once we catch up to her."

"That's too many to take the risk." Liz scanned the horizon as if looking for the answer to her dilemma. "Do we have time to go around them?"

"If we don't maintain the pace we've been going at, the Scanners will overtake us," Renny answered. "We'll have far more problems dealing with them than with the Order."

"If the Order picks a fight, we may be dealing with the droids either way. Guess we have no choice but to carry on, do we?"

Renny stared blankly at her, as if unsure whether he should answer or just listen to her work it out for herself.

"I'd recommend going off-road," he finally offered. "Make as wide of an arc as we can without breaking course. As the Order are camped in the middle of the flats, there's no way we'll avoid being seen, but if we make clear we have no intention of interacting with them, they'll hopefully leave us be."

Liz maintained her gaze ahead of her, silent for several moments.

"Agreed," she said. Lowering her voice to the point that Wil barely caught what she said, she added, "What choice do we have?"

The caravan hadn't slowed their pace throughout this entire exchange. Wil tried to gauge the thoughts of the others within earshot and was met with uncertainty and nervousness.

Wil pushed down the burning sensation in his gut as he overheard the news. He didn't understand the implications of what they were talking about, so there was no use in getting worked up. Yet.

Ella was busy talking to T'al, and neither of them appeared to even have noticed the exchange.

"We carry on, then," Liz stated, louder so the entire party could hear. She turned back to Renny. "We'll make as wide an arc around them as time will allow. Let's hope they're too preoccupied to worry about us."

"Everyone!" she announced. The rumblings of conversation quieted down almost instantly, until the only noise that could be heard was the *clip-clop* of horse hooves and the creaking cart wheels. Liz tried to position herself off to the side of the caravan in such a way so everyone could see her, although she didn't have to. She had everyone's full attention.

"We are soon going to be approaching an Order camp. We have no choice but to pass by it, much closer than I would like. Keep your conversations minimal and do nothing to antagonize them. The Order are flying a Flag of Mourning, so if we are lucky, they will be too self-involved to bother us. We should start to see the encampment within the hour."

She turned her attention back to Renny and gave him a nod of thanks. "Head back to M'iko. Let her know we're on our way. And try not to be seen."

Without response, Renny turned and took off again at a run. Wil marveled at his pace as the man disappeared over the horizon in no time at all.

Wil fell back beside T'al and Ella, who were maintaining a steady position between the two carts.

"Learn anything of value?" Ella asked. Her dark wavy hair hung loose around her shoulders. She wore a jacket she had found made of leather, and a green shirt clung to her trim middle below it. The short cut of the jacket allowed her energy weapons to be visible, clipped to her belt. Her pants were black and also clung to her body. Wil wondered how her attire could possibly be comfortable for traveling.

"Nothing of importance that she didn't share with everyone else," he replied. "I don't understand, though. What is the Order doing here? Don't they control and run the Spheres?"

Ella looked as if she were holding back a laugh. Her eyes betrayed her amusement, but she managed to contain it as she answered, "Only some of the Order are placed within the Spheres, but their reach extends much further."

"Why are we so concerned with them? The members of the Order I knew in the Sphere weren't the most pleasant, but they didn't really pose a threat."

"They're more sinister than you realized. Their members pledge themselves to the Guardians, worshiping them as the gods they claim to be. They work to ensure others comply with their rules. It may not come as a surprise that they don't get along with the Resistance."

Wil's stomach lurched like he had been punched. How could anyone outside of the Sphere revere the machines responsible for enslaving humanity? Bile rose in his throat. He could understand those who knew no different, who could do nothing but focus on the daily struggle; he could understand those more concerned with helping each other survive in this wasteland the ancients left for them; but for anyone to align themselves with the bots?

"They recruit followers under the promise of protection," T'al continued, sensing Wil's confusion.

"I still don't get it," Wil managed. "The bots don't attack them?"

"You didn't wonder how they could be camped along our path while we've been traveling day and night to stay out of the path of the Scanners?"

There was so much to this unknown world that Wil still had to process that it hadn't even crossed his mind.

"Why, though? What sets them apart?"

"Nobody outside their cult knows," T'al continued. "But the Guardians' tolerance adds to their credibility. It's easier to convince recruits what they're saying is true if the Guardians are willing to leave them be. But, in reality, they are just as enslaved to do the bots' bidding as the people they preach to."

"I thought the bots re-educate or kill anyone they find? That's what we were told."

T'al shook his head. "Not the Order. It's one of their most closely guarded secrets. Only their Elites know the true reason."

Wil's head spun. "And they're enemies of the Resistance?"

"Sort of," Ella answered. "The Order doesn't really agree with anyone, but they'll typically leave others alone outside the Sphere. They'll try to convert them or look down their noses at them, but they mostly let other Outsiders go about their own business. The Resistance, though? Yes, the Order is openly hostile towards *them*. They'll attack without reason, simply for promoting violence against their sacred Guardians."

Ella seemed more determined than ever to separate herself and Wil from the group of freedom fighters they were traveling with.

Wil ignored her tone. "And how does the Resistance respond?"

"The Resistance holds no love for the Order, either," T'al answered. "But we leave them alone if we aren't provoked. Our fight is with the bots, not with those misguided by them."

Dark clouds loomed in the distance as the wind picked up. The cloak Wil wore gave him protection from the wind, but it couldn't stop the chill that seeped into his bones.

4

THE WEATHER HAD CHANGED without warning. What had started out as a few dark clouds earlier had manifested into a full storm by the time Wil and the Resistance had the Order camp in their sights.

Wil held his cloak tightly around him and lifted his hood to protect his ears from the brunt of the cool wind. He closed his eyes to keep out the stinging needles of its force, along with the rain which beat down on their small caravan.

Ella stood beside him. She had removed her leather jacket and had replaced it with a dark cloak which she had wrapped around her. The two of them, like everyone else, had pulled in as close to the cart as possible for the little protection it provided.

The tarps protecting their belongings flapped chaotically and had to be retied several times in order to keep them secure.

Wil didn't think he had ever experienced a rain as intense as the deluge the sky was unleashing. Each step had become more difficult than the last as water pooled in the dirt beneath their feet, turning the path they followed to mud. His feet had gone numb, and he wondered how far he could go without being able to feel his extremities.

Despite the fury of the storm, Liz didn't ease the pace. The hurried effort, at least, had been enough for Wil to temporarily ignore the pain in his feet, though he wondered how long he'd be able to maintain their speed. He couldn't help but notice Liz's continual glances to the sky.

As Wil followed her gaze, he wondered how she expected to see anything but the ferocious clouds that blanketed above them.

Though they had tried to maintain their distance, the Order camp was still visible through the gloom. Dozens of white tents had established themselves as a barricade on the road. It was clear they were attempting to impose their dominance on those who dared to travel the exposed lands between the mountains and the Silent Zone near San Francisco. Though Wil had trouble ascertaining the reason, there was no mistaking the statement.

The canvas shells of the tents flapped angrily in the wind, warning potential travelers of whose domain they were entering, while their owners dashed in a mad scramble to prevent them from blowing away.

Despite his best efforts, Wil couldn't make out anything distinguishing about those within the camp. They were still too far away.

"We'd be best not to draw any attention to ourselves from this point forward!" Liz yelled into the wind. She continued to speak, but her voice was lost to the storm.

Thunder boomed above the group. The horses, previously undisturbed by the weather, reared, shaking the carts, as those trying to obtain what little shelter they could from them scattered in fear of the carts possibly toppling over.

The handlers steadied the horses, and the travelers returned to their sides.

"Why can't we take shelter from this storm?" Wil yelled to Ella.

"The storm won't affect the Scanners," she replied. "We can't stop."

Ella's eyes were glowing again. Wil knew he wasn't one to be wary of an unusual power, but he had held back in asking her about it. Nobody else in the camp had dared broach the subject. He had deduced it somehow helped her to see better at night, like a cat or a wolf, but Wil had no clue as to how Ella came to possess such an ability. Ella had offered no explanation, either, and Wil didn't want to be the one to bring it up.

Ella ran ahead, next to Liz, shouting something into her ear that the wind carried away. Whatever information she had offered, it appeared as though Liz made a forced effort not to react.

Their pace subconsciously quickened. Whatever Ella had revealed wasn't good, but Wil was already struggling to maintain their current speed.

They continued on the path Liz had set them on. They were a few hundred yards away from the camp, and this would likely be as close as they would get. So far, the Order were more preoccupied with bracing for the storm than their approaching little party.

M'iko was suddenly beside Liz, shouting as well. Wil had to do a double take, as he hadn't seen the petite woman approach. Her dark hair and cloak allowed her to blend into the surroundings.

M'iko was furiously pointing away from the camp. Wil couldn't hear anything she was shouting over the wind, but her wild flailing and earnestness told him all he needed to know.

Liz turned to Ella, who shook her head nervously. Her glowing eyes continuing to flit skyward behind them.

With her shoulders deflated, Liz waved her wrist toward the driver of the lead cart, and the party took a hard right turn. Their arc was about to expand.

The turn brought them to face due north, and the wind no longer affronted them head-on. It was only then Wil realized how much he had been struggling to breathe against its force. He took several deep breaths, as though he had been underwater and was only now coming up for air.

M'iko stuck with the party as it altered its course. She was a hard one for Wil to read. She paced nervously beside Liz, holding her hands behind her back. In doing so, she was probably walking nearly twice as many steps as those around her. Rain dripped down her face, running from her black hair, which was completely drenched. It would have been enough to hide the fact she had been crying, if her eyes hadn't also been puffy and red.

It wasn't long before they returned to their westerly course. The camp was still within sight, but barely. Wil wasn't sure why they had ventured this far from the path if they were running out of time. Was their window with the Scanners really so narrow?

Wil squinted into the wind. The rain had either let up or he was just getting used to it. He looked back to the camp, mainly to turn his face from the gale to catch his breath, and gasped. Six men on horseback were headed in their direction.

Three at the front, three behind, each of them on a white stallion. Their horses stood out in stark contrast to the black clouds behind them. The three front men each also wore a white cloak with a glowing red crack running across the fabric, as if they were made of glass and smashed to reveal a red light inside. The three following wore dark cloaks with the same mysterious pattern, with the luminescent cracks appearing to pulse as the cloaks flapped in the wind.

Wil was so mesmerized by the patterns that he didn't think to alert the rest of the party. Ella, however, happened to look up and follow his gaze.

"We've got company!" she yelled.

The wind was silent at that moment, making it sound as though her voice had been amplified that much more. The rest of the Resistance members whipped around, their weapons drawn.

The six horsemen moved fluidly, despite the weather. Only their flapping cloaks indicated that the breeze touched them at all. It was only another moment before they stood in front of their traveling party, barring them from continuing further.

"We don't have time for this," Ella muttered, casting one eye to the sky. Wil couldn't help but look as well, but there was no way to make out anything through the thick cloud cover.

A burly man in the middle of the front row spoke. "State your business, Oathbreakers." He had pulled his hood back, and the rain beaded down his bald head. A red scar glowed down his face, displaying the same effect as his cloak. The pattern of it was more geometric, almost like a map through a lost maze; it crawled up the side of his neck, over his cheek, and back behind his ear, glowing in the darkness the storm provided.

Liz sat straight on her horse, unfazed by the man's presence. "It has been a while since our paths crossed, Oculus." The wind and rain had lightened for the moment, and Liz's voice was clear and strong.

"Not long enough," Oculus sneered. "Why are you trespassing?"

"We are merely passing by on our way to San Francisco. This is a public path—you have no claim here."

"The Guardians know what is best for this world, and we are their mouthpiece. You live only because they've willed it so."

"What do you want, Oculus?" Liz said, unfazed by his bravado. "We have no interest in disturbing the peace."

"You say you're just passing through, yet you send spies into our camp?"

"We sent a scout ahead to ensure we wouldn't come close enough to insult you."

"*Lies!* We found him sneaking around our camp. If it hadn't been for the rain, perhaps, he would have evaded our detection, but his footprints betrayed him."

"You've captured my scout?"

"Yes, I captured your spy, and now the rest of you will come with us as well."

"What would a spy uncover that I don't already know? I have no intention of . . ."

"*Enough!*" He revealed a dark staff which had been obscured underneath his cloak. He slammed its base on the ground, illuminating a ruby red crystalline bulb set into its red hilt.

"What's that?" Wil whispered to Ella.

"Not now!" she hissed, her eyes locked onto the staff.

"What are you going to do?" Liz asked Oculus, her expression unchanged. "Kill us?"

"That's for the Guardians to decide. But with the damage you've done, I think we both know what their answer will be."

Liz reached for the blaster attached to her hip, but the Order guards lifted weapons of their own in unison and aimed them at her, giving her pause.

"Do you really think that's wise?" Oculus asked, his stance unchanged. "Even if you managed to kill me, you would invoke the rage of a hundred Righteous Order members within the camp."

Wil and the other Resistance fighters all stood, holding their breath, all eyes on Liz. There were fourteen of them, including the three sleeping in the cart, plus the two youths who sat at the front of the carts, their mouths agape. The odds were seven to five in their favor. But Oculus was likely right; they wouldn't be able to get out of there fast enough with their two large carts unscathed. And then there was the question of Renny. Had Liz known they had captured him when she had extended their route? Had she just resolved to abandon him?

Oculus took advantage of the moment of indecision. He nodded to his men, who dismounted and removed Liz's firearm before collecting the weapons from the rest of them.

Wil looked to Ella for direction, but she offered none.

A spidery man approached Wil. He was skinny, perhaps in his mid-fifties, hunched over and missing several teeth, rendering him far less intimidating than his companions. The man wore a red cap which glistened in the rain. Despite his dark features, his eyes lit up, as though thrilled to exercise control over two of the younger members of the caravan.

"Weapons!" His nasal voice was the perfect match for his demeanour.

"We're not carrying any." Wil held his hands up, his cloak sleeves falling to his elbows.

The man grabbed Wil roughly, pushing his face against the cart. A bony elbow lodged in Wil's back as he was patted down, searched for the weapons the man was convinced must be there. The only thing stopping Wil from slugging the scrawny idiot was his decision not to be the one to escalate the situation. There had already been enough injury caused by him today. This wasn't his fight.

Ella had no such convictions. She hurled herself at the man, pushing him off Wil, and they both flew down in a heap into the mud. Ella sat on top of the man, her fists pummelling his face before he had a chance to react.

A large hand grabbed Ella by the hair and pulled her up with little effort. Oculus, still sitting on his horse, held her inches off the ground. She continued to struggle until a blaster rested against her temple.

Involuntary tears flowed down Ella's face. She gritted her teeth, reluctantly accepting her situation.

The man who had searched Wil stood and brushed the dirt from his cloak, his face bruised. He lunged at Ella.

Wil reacted more quickly this time. Not wanting to cause anything that might make Oculus pull the trigger, he simply stuck his foot out and sent the bony man flailing past Ella and under the horse.

"*Enough!*" Oculus yelled.

Ella had a grip on the man's wrist, trying to hold herself up to relieve some of the pressure on her scalp.

The man stood once again and delivered a quick punch to Ella's gut.

"Malfus!" Oculus barked. "Stop this! Bring these two and the others."

"But they are resisting! They refused to surrender their weapons."

Oculus's red eyes twisted and turned as he studied the pair. Wil shivered. Oculus looked first to Wil and then down at the woman he still held in his grip.

"They are unarmed, you fool! Quit playing games. Tie them up and let's get moving."

Ella's face was bright red, but Oculus had yet to break a sweat from holding her with one outstretched arm. Wil didn't believe he could match that kind of strength. He didn't know anyone who could.

Oculus released his grip and Ella fell in a heap on the ground, narrowly avoiding being trampled by the man's enormous horse.

Ella pushed herself up just as Malfus rushed over, eager to get his grubby hands on her. Wil stepped in front of him before he could get to her, extending a hand toward his friend and pulling Ella back to her feet.

Another bony elbow jabbed him in the back as Malfus collided with him. The momentum rocked Wil forward, but only slightly. There wasn't a lot of weight to the scrawny man, who looked like he had inherited the white robe he wore from someone twice his size.

"Get over there!" Malfus gathered himself before grabbing Wil's cloak at the shoulder, twisting and pushing as he led them toward where the others stood.

Wil tried his best not to smile. T'al and Voth were noticeably missing, either still asleep on their shift or pretending to be.

"What about their carts?" Malfus asked. Wil shot a glance to Liz, but she didn't flinch, staring straight in front of her, unenthusiastically, toward the camp that would be their destination. Ella, too, ignored the remark.

"Are we just going to leave them out here? Abandon them for bandits to find?"

"Grab the horses. We'll send men to come back for the goods later."

Lightning crashed overhead as the Order rounded up the Resistance members and pushed them forward into a march.

The skin on Wil's wrists burned as he fought the rough rope Malfus had used to tie them behind his back. He walked in the rain with the rest of the group, soaked to the bone, bruises darkening on his back and shoulders. Perhaps they should have stood their ground. They could have resisted the six Order members and been on their way.

Anger burned in his chest, but he did his best to keep calm, reminding himself Liz was a fighter. She wouldn't simply surrender without a reason. But if it were up to Wil, they wouldn't be headed toward the very place they had been trying to avoid.

5

WIL'S LEGS burned as they arrived at the Order campsite, so much so that he was actually relieved when they finally stopped amid the mass of white tents and robed figures. He collapsed as soon as they reduced their breakneck pace.

Wil had never been much of a sprinter, but Oculus and his allies had made them keep pace with the horses. Though they had managed to keep up in places, Dagger and Sara had been unmistakably dragged for a good portion of the journey. Wil was grateful it hadn't been far. The two youths appeared to be a little scraped up, but likely more mentally traumatized than physically harmed.

Despite the rain, or perhaps because it was now dissipating, the campsite was buzzing with activity. Any hope Renny had given Liz about the rain keeping the Servants at bay had been misguided at best. The members were eager to attend to their assigned tasks, and it was apparent not even rain would slow them down.

The Resistance and their captors journeyed to the center of the encampment. The arrangement of the Order camp was much more organized and rigid than that of the Community outposts. Tents were laid out in a grid, row upon row, with an equal amount of spacing between each canvas to allow for neatly lined paths in the spaces between.

Men and women dressed in cloaks of various colors, many with the same glowing design, scurried around the site, all of them busy. Various markings were painted on the sides of nearly every tent, but they meant nothing to Wil. The only clear thing was, even though Wil had a limited understanding of the world, he knew these people weren't in mourning.

A large wooden structure had been erected on the outer perimeter, filled with what could easily have been a couple hundred horses. The structure seemed oddly permanent for a traveling group of robot worshippers. Men and women in plain clothes, some no older than teenagers, ran between stalls, tending to the horses. Some of them met Wil's eye and quickly looked away.

Others were carting goods. It was hard to tell what many of the carts contained, but there was a lot of food. The servants had overloaded one cart with assorted weaponry, some too large to carry. Many were energy weapons, but there was also a fair number of swords, knives, and other handheld armaments. Wil watched the attendants approach a large canvas tent and begin unloading its contents.

These people aren't mourning—at least, not anymore, Wil mused. *They're preparing for battle.*

The guards split the party and escorted Wil and Liz to a solitary tent under the direction of Oculus. The tent was much like the one he had shared with Sierra in the Community outpost, except the beds and homely furnishings were missing. Instead, the tent was empty except for two chairs, a few jackets hung by the door, and several pairs of boots. Wil silently questioned what this tent was used for when the Order didn't have prisoners to intimidate.

Or perhaps that was never a concern?

Oculus pushed Wil onto a stool and allowed Liz to sit more gracefully on her own. The space within the structure was small enough for the two of them to sit and stare at the entrance, and not much more. This tent was intended for the sole purpose of questioning captives.

"Wait here," Oculus said, pushing his way back out the tent door.

As if we're able to go anywhere, Wil thought.

There was nothing to do but wait. Wil's focus wandered around the small space and across its bare walls. Only two blemishes marked its surface. The first, a large rack that took up a large part of the wall to the side of the entrance, stabilized by poles embedded in the ground. Upon them hung blades of various shapes, sizes, and designs. The second protrusion was a small black box with a blinking red light in the ceiling's corner.

It was clear nobody stayed in this tent. Whoever the few scant items within belonged to had left the tent and had never returned.

Wil swallowed as the implications sunk in.

Liz's focus remained resolute, with her head directed straight ahead at the entrance as if waiting on an invisible entity to make the first move. Her chest rose and fell as her breathing slowed and deepened. Her long brown hair had been tied back and still dripped from the storm. At least the tent provided some respite from the rain.

Wil had seen Liz fall into these trances before, usually when an important decision needed to be made. He wanted to ask her what she was doing during these spells, but he had a feeling she wouldn't have answered his query, even at the best of times.

Wil's feet squished in his boots as he shuffled them from side to side. Now that they had stopped moving, he realized how cold and wet his feet were. It was as though they had been trapped in blocks of ice, and he couldn't help but shiver as the cold seeped through his cloak and into his bones. He considered telling Oculus anything the Order wanted to know for the prospect of a fire to dry off beside. What information they were after, he couldn't even guess at.

Oculus had mentioned the destruction Liz had caused. Had he meant the three bots on the road? Or the attack on Vegas? Word of either attack would had to have traveled fast to have reached the camp.

Wil took a deep breath as he tried to collect his thoughts. Having to fight off bots was one thing; being captured and held by humans was entirely another.

"Why did they keep us together?" he whispered.

That Oculus had separated him and Liz from the others had struck Wil as odd. Liz was the leader of the Resistance, and he was little more than a tagalong. The others in their group seemed to have been paired off as well. Was it done at random? Or was there a connection he didn't see?

"No questions," Liz snapped. "When he comes, let me do the talking."

"I don't understand. What's happening?"

"If you're lucky, I'll explain it to you later," Liz said. "But for now, keep your mouth shut!"

Wil blinked in confusion and shook his head, even more bewildered by their situation. He let his eyes wander, wishing he could rub his tender arms and legs, and he gently tested his bonds. He didn't think he'd be getting out of them on his own. Not that he had anywhere to go if he did.

The small black box, placed at the point where the wall met the ceiling, caught his eye again. It was reminiscent of something he would have seen in the Sphere.

He knew instinctively it was a camera.

"They're watching us, aren't they?" he asked, mostly thinking out loud.

"Yes," was all Liz said.

Wil nodded to himself. So much of his interaction in this world had been within the Silent Zone. As a result, he knew little of the level of technology that existed beyond its reach. It wasn't all swords and torches.

Liz's eyes were still locked onto the entrance to their prison.

"What are they hoping to see?" Wil probed.

Liz clenched her jaw. *"No questions!"*

Wil sighed. The woman was infuriating.

"They're waiting to see if we give something away," Liz relented, her voice lowered but the ice remaining. "Every question, every comment, every hint of body language has the potential to give them information. When Oculus returns, keep your mouth shut. Let me do the talking."

Wil didn't have the strength to question or to argue further, so he resolved to sit in silence. His eyes were heavy, desperate for sleep, but the breeze that found its way into the tent continued to chill his bones, and his thoughts raced at what the Order might use the blades which hung on the wall for.

Wil shivered. The cold night air penetrated him, and he knew he wouldn't dry off without a heat source. He shuffled uncomfortably in his seat as the chill in his bones became ever more intolerable.

Liz's resolve impressed Wil. While he shifted in his chair as much as his bindings would allow, trying to gain an ounce of comfort, she remained steadfast. She sat straight, her shoulders back, as if nothing about this entire situation bothered her, and her purple eyes betrayed nothing.

Wil had just about resolved that the Order's plan was to let him die in his chair when the tent flap finally opened, revealing the dark of night behind Oculus as he strode inside. His red glowing tattoo was even more prominent now that the rain had subsided, and it was clear it extended its tendrils to the back of his bald head and down his short, thick neck.

The man's bushy red eyebrows matched the thick red beard that just touched the bottom of his chin, and Oculus still donned the white cloak. Its glowing red pattern still mesmerized Wil, not least because he didn't know how it could possibly be accomplished. It reminded him of the light patterns on the surface of the Guardian orbs, somehow working just below the cloak's surface. The man's tattoo produced the same effect, which was equally baffling. It was as if the Order guard had sewn a piece of tech into the surface of his skin.

It was hard for Wil not to cower in the presence of the imposing figure that dominated the entryway. In every way, Oculus was the complete opposite of the squirrelly Malfus who Wil had antagonized earlier. Even if Wil had been standing, Oculus would have stood more than a foot taller than him. It was hard to tell beneath the sleeves of the cloak he wore, but Wil could tell Oculus's arms were like trees, thicker even than the guards Leo prided himself on. The man was a block of pure muscle.

Oculus pushed back his sleeves, confirming Wil's suspicions, and crossed his arms. His lips curled back in a self-satisfied snarl as he simply stood there.

"What is this about, Oculus?" Liz said, resigning herself to be the first to break the silence.

"You tell me." Out of the howling wind, it became clear just how deep and commanding Oculus's voice was. Nothing about this man was small.

Wil wasn't sure which of the two leaders in the room intimidated him more.

"We were heading for San Francisco when you kidnapped us without cause," Liz responded. The bite in her voice indicated she felt none of the same trepidation as Wil. "Sound about right?"

"Tell me about your Oathbreaker friend here." Oculus motioned to Wil while keeping his eyes fixed on Liz.

"I don't know what you're talking about," she replied.

"Everyone is in the mood for games today, it seems. I, however, am not." Oculus turned to the blades hanging on the wall, as if contemplating whether their use would be necessary. "We have caught Resistance spies within our camp. We have heard rumors that hundreds of Guardians have been desecrated in Vegas, and that you and a pair of Oathbreakers are behind the atrocity."

Wil's heart was beating so loudly that he could hear it between his ears, while Liz remained unfazed.

"The rumors are true. Bots *have* fallen in Vegas," Liz volunteered. "But if you are looking for the one who brought down the Spheres, she is not among us."

It took every ounce of Wil's strength for him not to cry out, never mind keeping his gaze steady in front of him. Liz had been willing to leave Renny behind. Was she going to tell this man about Sierra as well? Would she betray Wil if it was convenient? Or worse, would she do the same to Ella?

He suddenly questioned his decision to follow these people he knew so little about. For all Wil knew, Ella was likely being interrogated in another Order tent. Liz might be prepared to leave his friend behind, but he'd go back for Ella, no matter what.

"You expect me to believe that? You conveniently approach from the east, where the fires from Vegas have barely had enough time to cool. And you have this Oathbreaker here with you; from the same Sphere as you, no less. Two Oathbreakers, conveniently traveling from the same city the demons desecrated."

Wil had been trying his best not to give anything away, but he couldn't control the wide-eyed look he gave to Liz.

Same Sphere?

"Oh?" Oculus's voice raised a notch, and he tilted his head toward Liz. He squatted down on his haunches in front of her, yet somehow still tall enough to look her in the eye. "He doesn't know!"

A deep, guttural laugh echoed through the tent as Oculus threw back his head and howled. For the first time, he directed his attention to Wil. "She's as damned as you are, boy!"

Liz sat, expressionless, her eyes focused in front of her, but her breathing had quickened. There was something about the exchange that was getting under her skin.

"I knew," Wil said defiantly. He wouldn't let this man have the satisfaction of believing he was able to drive a wedge between Wil and the Resistance. "As one ancient once said, better to rule in hell than to serve in heaven."

A knife appeared in Oculus's hand. He brought the blade to Wil's face, lightly placing the tip against his cheek.

"Be careful with your words in this place, boy. The Resistance may allow your blasphemy, but within our presence, the Guardians' word is law. Oathbreakers die by the sword, unless The Holy Ones deem you fit for redemption."

Oculus traced his knife across Wil's neck and rested it just below his ear.

"The Resistance has yet to taint you, boy. I can see it in your eyes. I'd be careful which side you choose in this fight."

"Why? Who was it that tainted *you?*"

A giant backhand landed on Wil's jaw.

That's going to sting.

Oculus turned to Liz. "Control your pet better, Elizabeth! I'd be justified in spilling both your blood." He brought the knife back from Wil's face, studying it as if contemplating following through on the threat.

"But first, I want answers. A legion of the sacred Guardians has fallen; the Silent Zone has grown in size; and it is rumored two Oathbreakers are responsible for it all, possessing a magic powerful enough to disable Guardians with mere thought alone. And now, conveniently, I have two sitting in front of me, who have traveled through the mountains from where this destruction has taken place."

Wil couldn't help but swallow hard, and he did his best not to cringe at the implied accusations.

"One of them, a leader of the blasphemous Resistance. Since it seems your friend doesn't understand the gravity of the situation, I'll leave you to talk it over. I'll be back in a few hours. Decide your next course of action wisely. Next time, I won't be so forgiving."

Oculus pushed the tent flap open and marched out.

Wil unconsciously stretched his throbbing jaw.

"You should have kept your mouth shut!" Liz hissed. "Antagonizing him will get us nowhere."

"If I had been privy to all the information, perhaps I wouldn't have been surprised, 'Oathbreaker'. And when were you going to tell me you once lived in the Sphere?"

Liz took a deep breath. "It's complicated."

"Yeah, well, so is being tied to a chair, facing a man with glowing tattoos who enjoys holding a knife to your throat. What was I supposed to do?"

"You were supposed to say *nothing*, like I asked!"

"I was caught off guard."

"Of course you were! That's what he was trying to do! He didn't *know* you were from the compound, but now he does. Oculus's whole game is to gain information from us. You gave him that and managed to piss him off at the same time."

"Well, if I'm not told everything . . ."

"I only reveal what's important for you to know. That way, I can trust you won't spill secrets because someone gets under your skin. You can't expect to gain inside knowledge of those around you in a matter of weeks just because you decide to come along. You need to understand, there is much you don't know, and much you will *never* know. Oculus is a master at manipulation. He'll tell you truths, half-truths, and lies to get what he wants—and you won't know which is which until it's too late."

"That's not good enough. I've lost everything and everyone I've ever cared about. You and El . . ."

"*Shut it!*" Liz turned to look at him for the first time since Oculus had left. Her eyes narrowed, motioning with her head toward the ceiling behind her, and he suddenly realized he had almost unwittingly given up more information for the camera.

His mouth fell, and Wil turned to face forward, his eyes downcast to the ground. He had to remember that, here, eyes watched his every move. He had almost become used to the freedom from technology the Silent Zone had offered.

Through the crack of the tent door, he could see the legs of people walking by. Sounds of laughter, shouting, and muted talking could all be heard through the canvas, as the camp residents continued with whatever plans they were in the midst of arranging. It was now late evening, and Wil would have expected the campsite to have quieted down by now. The pitter-patter of raindrops on the canvas above them had disappeared, leading Wil to think the worst of the storm had passed.

Whatever the Order were doing, they wouldn't wait until morning to make it happen.

With nothing else to occupy him, Wil strained to see as much of the movement outside as he could, though there wasn't much more he could decipher besides the activity of the camp being continued late into the night.

The cramped tent emphasized Wil's discomfort. The ache in his feet had all but been forgotten after sustaining the throbbing in his face.

What did these Order members have planned? And why couldn't he get a straight answer out of anyone?

Everyone Wil encountered had either been lying about something or hiding at least part of the truth. He was getting sick of it. So far, Ella had been the only person to open up to him, and even she had her secrets. Wil had begun to trust Liz with his life, agreeing to come to San Francisco, believing he was going to be saving the world from robots, but it appeared he knew next to nothing about the woman or her intentions.

What were they going to tell Oculus? What would Liz tell him to save the Resistance? Would she sacrifice to save the others? Would she betray him? Would she tell the Order about Sierra?

If there was one thing Wil wasn't willing to do, it was to give her up. Sierra was his last link to the Sphere, and, though he didn't feel any need to be tied to his old home, he felt their fates were linked.

He'd sacrifice himself before he let the Order go after his friends. That included Ella. She had warned him not to take this journey; warned him not to be too eager to join the Resistance. She had only come along because of him. Wil at least owed her a means of escape. But how? If he offered himself in exchange for the others, would Oculus release them? Or would he just kill them once he had the information he desired?

Sierra was the one Oculus truly sought; the one who had activated the ancient machine and had brought the Onyx down mid-battle. But Wil had wrought destruction on the wave prior, bringing down Sentinels before they could wipe out the Resistance. Maybe it wasn't much of a stretch to tell Oculus *he* was the one responsible, and that there was no second party.

He jumped as a hairy hand covered his mouth from behind and hot breath whispered in his ear, "Don't you *dare* make a sound!"

6

Wil instinctively tried to bite the hand covering his mouth, but the palm turned into sharp fingers that pinched his cheeks on either side.

"Stop that!" the voice hissed as the man behind the hand whipped in front of Wil, revealing himself.

It was T'al.

The tension flowed out of him at the sight of his friend.

"Keep quiet," T'al whispered. "We're going to get you out of here, but any noise and they'll be on us in seconds."

"The cameras?" Liz asked, nodding toward the box on the wall.

"Jammed." Voth was suddenly beside them, working Liz's bonds. "You two finally sat still long enough for us to freeze the frame. It won't give us cover for long, though. We've got maybe ten minutes, at the most. Fifteen, if the guard watching the feed isn't paying attention."

Wil was rubbing his face before he realized his bonds had been severed. Between Oculus's backhand and the pinch of T'al's sausage fingers, his jaw throbbed. Blood flecked his palm as he pulled it away. The zealot's slap must have been harder than he'd realized. He touched his face again and felt the sting course through his cheek, but the bleeding was subtle and would likely stop within minutes.

Wil started to ask how they'd got into the tent before he remembered the call for silence. Not wanting to cause any more disruption, he bit his tongue. Wil stood from his chair and stretched as best he could. His feet were still numb, and he cringed at the pins and needles sensation that flooded them as he shuffled in place in order to get blood moving again.

T'al motioned him to the back of the tent, where a small slit had been cut into the base of the canvas. The opening was the perfect size for T'al to have slipped through, which was to say it was double the size of what Wil needed.

Wil squatted, trying to avoid becoming wetter and muddier than he already was. Voth and Liz had already crept through and sat crouched on the other side. The muted torchlight from lanterns set up alongside the nearby path reflected on their faces. The rain had all but stopped, but the remaining clouds masked the full moon, gifting them with near darkness aside from the small torches scattered throughout the camp. Voth's pale white skin made her appear almost spectral, T'al was near invisible, and Liz seemed to blend into her surroundings regardless of the time of day.

"Where are the others?" Liz whispered to Voth.

"They weren't as heavily guarded. They should be ahead on the trail. We're going to catch up with them."

"And Renny?" she asked. "Were you able to find him?"

"He's being held toward the center of the camp. It seems the Order doesn't take well to spies. Ella's with him."

Wil barely kept his voice hushed. "We have to go get them!"

Liz shook her head. "Too risky. We need to ensure the others are safe."

Wil would have laughed if he saw anything funny about the situation. Just as he had predicted, Liz was all too eager to leave people behind.

Wil lifted his hands in protest. "I'm not leaving her here. The rest of you can go, but I'm getting them out."

"You getting caught as well will do us no good!" Liz scolded.

"What do you propose, then? Leave them here to be tortured and killed? You may be willing to sacrifice them to save our own skin, but I'm not. I'm going in." He turned and started toward the corner of the tent. "We'll meet up with you on the road."

A massive hand landed itself on his shoulder. Wil shook T'al off but turned to look at the man.

"You can't stop me," Wil said. "If you think I'll make things worse, then just go."

"I'm coming with you," the burly man whispered. Even while trying to be quiet, his voice was deep and larger than life.

Wil softened as concern flashed in T'al's eyes. "You don't have to do that. Ella's my friend. My responsibility."

"She's a friend to us all," Liz chimed in. "But there's a balance to risk and reward. I won't jeopardize the lives of the rest of the group on the slim chance of getting them out."

T'al nodded to Liz. "You're too important to spend any more time here. Go with Voth. The kid and I will get the girl and Renny."

Kid? The man may have been twice his size, but the two were nearly the same age.

Liz shook her head. "You're both important." She sighed. "But so is the girl. Renny . . ." She trailed off and lifted her hands with a shrug and a grin.

Voth let out a squeak, and T'al stifled a chuckle. Wil raised an eyebrow in dismay before he realized Liz was kidding. Come to think of it, he had never heard her crack a joke before and he had to contain a belly laugh.

The smile faded nearly as quickly as it came, and Liz relented. "Renny's the best scout we have left. If you can get him back in one piece, do so."

T'al nodded. Liz gestured to Voth, and the two women made their way towards the edge of the campsite in a crouch.

"You know where we're going?" Wil turned his attention to T'al. He appreciated the man sticking around to help him out.

"Follow me," T'al replied. "Watch our backs."

The activity from earlier in the evening had quieted down. Many of those who had been busy while the light had held had finally retired to their beds. T'al and Wil made their way stealthily between the tents. T'al attempted to choose the dimmest paths for them to follow, but on occasion, they had to duck back into the shadows to avoid being seen.

The rows of tents grew tighter as they wound their way toward the center of the campsite. The tents were grouped closer to one another here, and increased in size the further they went. Symbols adorned the flaps of six of the largest tents that circled what appeared to be the center of the site. Now was not the time to ask T'al what they meant, but Wil made a mental note to find out later. Each symbol was painted in a different color to the next; red, green, blue, orange, purple, and gold each adorned the canvas doors. The one painted red resembled the tattoo Oculus sported, though, unlike the tattoo, none of these colors glowed. A solitary guard stood in front of each of the colored tents.

A shout in the distance broke the silence of the evening, and the crash of a loud cymbal echoed through the evening air.

"The alarm," T'al whispered. "They've discovered we've jammed the feed."

The two crouched in the shadows of a tent, a small bush aiding in their disguise as guards raced past. While Wil and T'al had been inching between tent rows, the guards made use of the roads, enabling the two to remain out of sight. The guards were expecting them to flee the campsite, not be inching towards its center.

In a matter of minutes, the center of the camp had nearly been vacated, except for the guards who hadn't moved from their posts outside the elaborately decorated tents.

"Come on." T'al tugged at his arm. "This buys us some time, but not much."

Where the painted tents encircled the campsite's center, a large fire pit separated them all. In between these tents rested several more, which were undecorated and unguarded. Off to one side stood an even smaller, less impressive tent, with no flare other than the four torches that lit its entrance. Two guards remained in front of this tent, trying their best to remain resolute.

Wil eyed their destination as he and T'al crawled through the wet mud and brush. Freeing Ella would be trickier than he thought. Each guard had direct line of sight of the tent, never mind the two who stood at its entrance. Even if they were able to pass them undetected, the guards would hear anything amiss within.

Each step proved harder to remain in the shadows than the last. Every stick Wil stepped on seemed magnitudes louder than it should have, and every ragged breath was like a beacon to those looking for them. Wil tried to time any noise he made with the chime of the alarm, but it was impossible to sustain. For every noise he made during the drum of the alarm, he made two more in the beats between.

Wil soon gave up and focused on reaching their destination, following T'al closely. They had approached the tent they were intent on entering from the rear. A patch of bushes rested a few dozen feet away, and the two men made for them before stopping. There would be no more cover between them and their friends now. Wil hoped T'al was right, and that Ella and Renny were inside with no other soldiers. All they'd have to do was free them and get themselves out of there.

"Will there be cameras in there as well?" he asked.

T'al nodded. "Their resources aren't infinite. There may be cameras, but there's enough chaos in the camp that they might not catch us in the act. Either way, we're heading straight into the fire."

They maneuvered themselves until they could no longer see a guard within their field of view. Wil hoped the torchlight would blind them to most movement in the surrounding darkness. They just had to find the path with the least amount of light. But as he eyed the tent, he didn't see a way that was going to work.

An explosion rang in the distance, from the direction in which they'd come, followed by a burst of flame that shot into the sky. An orange glow lingered, reflecting on the clouds above.

"Let's go! *Now!*" T'al was a few feet ahead of him before Wil could even react. The remaining guards left their posts and raced toward the plume of smoke.

Wil broke from his hiding spot and caught up with T'al. "What was that?" he asked. Trying to catch his breath, he leaned on the canvas for support. The hairs along his arms stood on end.

T'al seemed unaffected by the sudden distraction. "I don't know, but the timing couldn't have been better." His eyes rested on the back of the tent, ignoring whatever questions he might have had himself. Wil resisted the urge to glance beyond the tent to watch the chaos unfold. One problem at a time.

T'al produced a curved blade from his belt and tore at the canvas, etching a slit barely long enough for him to peer into. He stuck his face through the canvas for a few moments, and once satisfied, he brought the knife back up and widened the hole, making it nearly identical to the one they had escaped through moments earlier.

Wil followed T'al in and was greeted with a blade pressed to his neck.

His hands shot in the air as he slowly rose from his crouch. A shadowed figure pointed another blade at T'al.

"What do we have here?" Shadows danced on the face of the short, stocky guard, his sword held at T'al's chest.

"I think we've found the runaways." The second guard was a woman with a short blonde haircut. She snarled as she spoke. "Guess they caused the explosion trying to free their spy and ol' Demon Eyes here."

It was only then Wil noticed the two figures who sat in chairs at the center of the tent. Renny was slumped over, tied to the chair and sporting several cuts and bruises across his face. Ella was next to him, gagged and with her clothes torn. Her eyes glowed with a greenish-yellow tint, while tears flowed down her face as she tried to scream through the gag. Ella's muffled yells tugged at Wil's heart and only strengthened his resolve.

"Oculus is going to be pleased," the stocky man chuckled. "Maybe we'll be granted an extra ration of brandy! What do you say about that, Lory?"

Lory scoffed. "*Pfft.* It's not like what you're rationed ever holds you back."

"What are you saying?"

The fat man sweated profusely and briefly moved his sword to wipe his brow with his sleeve. T'al took the opening, jabbing an elbow into his gut, followed by a punch to the guard's pudgy throat.

Wil tried to take Lory's legs out from under her, but missed and toppled over onto his back. The fall was fortuitous, as the motion caused him to evade the jab of her sword. With nothing to break her momentum, Lory then tripped over him. She fell on her blade, impaling herself, her legs resting against Wil's chest.

T'al removed Ella's gag. "You two are ridiculous!" she said in stone-cold seriousness, before pausing, and then bursting out in nervous laughter. "I appreciate the rescue, but I don't think you could have been less graceful if you'd tried."

Wil was grateful for the darkness hiding his red face as he stood. Though Ella's eyes were still producing their yellow glow, and he wasn't sure if that enabled her to see the flush of his skin or not. He hardly felt like laughing. The guards had nearly run him through with their swords.

"Just be grateful the sweaty one was incompetent," T'al said.

"You don't know the half of it," Ella agreed. "I probably could have freed myself if they hadn't knocked Renny out first."

T'al finished untying the thin redheaded man. "I'm going to have to carry him," he observed. "Did they hurt you, Ella? You're okay if we have to run?"

Wil had been so distracted by the yellow glow in her eyes that he had failed to notice the dark bruise which marred her cheek.

"I'll survive," she said, rubbing her wrists. "I've been through worse."

Ella's eyes rested on him, their glow fading in and out as she lifted a hand to Wil's arm. Tears in the blood-stained fabric of her shirt revealed fresh scratches beneath. "Thank you for coming back."

Electricity raced through Wil's skin.

"Leaving you here was never an option," he answered. "But don't thank me yet. We still need to get out of here."

Wil moved to embrace her but thought better of it. There was no time, and chances were good he would end up hurting her. Instead, he settled for a pat on her arm, which earned him a disappointed frown.

"That explosion won't keep them distracted for much longer. Time to move!" T'al warned, grunting as he picked Renny up and swung him over his shoulder. T'al stuck his entire head through the tear in the canvas, making certain to perform a thorough scan of the area beyond the tent before ducking through with the man under his arm.

Outside, T'al hoisted Renny over his shoulder as if he were a rag doll. Was the man even still alive? Wil pushed the thought aside.

T'al pointed wordlessly to the edge of the camp, in the opposite direction to where the explosion happened. A haze lingered in the air, visible where there was light to see it. The smell of smoke hung heavy. Wil stole a glance behind them. The smoke was so thick on the far side of the camp that he could not see much more than the movement of men and women still scrambling to minimize the aftereffects of the blast. The fire looked to be nearly out from what he could tell through the smoke.

Wil tried hard not to choke on the stench. They needed to remain absolutely quiet if they were to escape the camp undetected. He counted themselves lucky the winds of the storm hadn't yet cleared the haze; it served their purpose well. Even though visibility was riskier in the direction they headed, the smoke hid their escape from most of the camp.

The guards near the decorated tents had returned, but they gathered on the road that ringed the center of their posts. The mayhem still distracted them enough to give Wil and his group of absconders enough of a window to move into darker, less guarded areas.

Once more, they made their way between their tents. The patrols had lessened, their efforts focused on the explosion.

"I want to know *who* set that canister ablaze!"

A voice echoed through the night, ahead of where they walked. T'al lifted a fist, signaling for them to stop. The group crouched as low as they could, hovering behind the closest tent. Wil brought up the rear, but maneuvered so he could see around the obstacles in their way.

Oculus stood beside the adjacent tent, his back toward them, the red glowing tattoos and the markings on his robe shining through the darkness of the evening.

"This is the doing of the Oathbreakers," Oculus continued. "They must still be in the camp. They couldn't have gotten far."

"Our men swarmed as soon as we could get close and have been combing the surrounding area since. There is little chance they would have escaped our reach."

"Yet somehow they all have!" Oculus barked. "Your incompetent guards couldn't keep a single *one* of those heretics contained! Not even the spy and the demon eyes remain—and they were surrounded by the High Scribes!"

"Sir, I . . . They were all bound. There was no way they could . . ."

"And yet they did!" Oculus bellowed into the night. "You are no longer commander of the guard, Ithius! This is the last time you've failed us!"

A metal sword scraped its scabbard as it was drawn, and the squelch of its blade entering flesh was all Wil could perceive of the man's sentence. The action was out of view, but the thud of the man landing on the dirt below was enough of a sign as to what had unfolded.

Wil's nerves jumped as the body hit the ground, but he forced himself to remain still.

"Should I send out a party after them?" a second quivering voice asked.

"If they don't turn up in the search of the camp, then leave them for now. See that this mess gets sorted out. We'll catch up with them in the Guardians' time."

7

ONCE WIL and the others were out of sight of the camp, the party's pace shifted from a scurry to an all-out run. It would still be hours until the sun crested the horizon, so, for Wil at least, it felt as if they were running blindly into darkness.

The chirping of crickets was the only noise they could hear over their own heavy footsteps, as shouts from the Order members had faded into the distance.

Even though they had heard Oculus instruct his men not to pursue them, Liz didn't want to take any chances. Besides, there were still the bots to worry about. The Scanners they had been worried about previously would have passed them by long ago, but there would always be another patrol sweeping through. They had to make as much ground as they could.

Despite the pain in his feet and the ache in his muscles, it surprised Wil that he had no problem keeping up. His training had served him well over the past couple of weeks, and in the cool evening air, the group's pace was something he felt confident he'd be able to maintain for hours.

Dagger and Sara, however, were not finding the journey easy.

Dagger was maintaining the pace, but his breathing was heavy and labored.

More than once, Dagger had to encourage Sara along. She consistently lagged behind the others and wasn't going to last much longer.

Wil knew Liz wouldn't be willing to slow down. He suspected she was already holding back, naturally wanting to push the group even faster, but despite the strength of her team, she had to know they had their limits. Better to keep at a pace where they could cover the most ground.

But Wil had no doubt she'd leave the youth behind in a heartbeat.

What in this woman's past had left her so cold and calculating? It wasn't selfish ambition—Liz thought of those under her command above all else. But if the best interest of the entire group was to leave a person or two behind? So be it. She'd sacrifice one person to save ten. It wasn't personal.

If it hadn't been for T'al's intervention, Liz would have left Sara behind in the first place. Perhaps this was a chance for her to be proven correct; for her to prove picking up strays was an unnecessary burden.

Wil was merely speculating, of course, but if there was a shred of truth to his observations, it would be far more heartless than even he had initially thought. If the Resistance wouldn't help two youths who needed them, what good was it to try and make a difference against the Guardians? The bots wouldn't tolerate weakness, either.

Wil hoped they would stop for a break when they caught up with T'al and Voth. The pair had taken Stepper, Che, and the carts and had journeyed ahead, adding as much distance as they could from the Order camp to their supplies. And with Cali.

Wil surveyed the rest of the party. It was a wonder they had all made it out of the camp.

Wil thought back to what T'al had told him of the escape. T'al and Voth had awoken when the caravan had stopped, and they had heard the entire exchange between Oculus and Liz. They had waited for a while after the group had been captured. If it hadn't been for the storm, the Order would likely have brought the carts into the camp as well.

After laying in silence for what felt like the right amount of time, the two had covertly made their way to the camp.

The Order had split their group into pairs, hoping they could learn more by separating them. With the exception of Wil and Liz, the Order had, without fail, beaten one in the pair, hoping to encourage the other to talk.

T'al had systematically gone from tent to tent, releasing half of the crew and slaying a half-dozen Order Guards before anyone could sound the alarm.

Buzz and Ice had been the first to be found. Once free, the pair had known they had to create a distraction. A torch tossed into the camp's alcohol reserves had lit up the night sky. The act created enough of a diversion for everyone to get out undetected.

With the camp in chaos, Buzz and Ice had managed to free Che and Stepper, after which they'd galloped back to the carts where Cali still lay unconscious and waited for the others to catch up. It wasn't long before the rest of the Resistance had joined them.

They loaded Renny onto the cart, a second person injured to ensure the rest of them would get little sleep.

During their escape, the scout had let out several audible groans, which had thankfully been covered by the cries in the campground. A gash on his forehead marked where Renny had been struck. Other bruises showed the guards had been impatient with his unwillingness to answer questions.

Unlike Che, Stepper had appeared to be as nervous as Sara and Dagger, his hooves shuffling back and forth with unease.

"The explosion spooked him good," Ice had commented as she'd tried to steady the steed.

That horse was always fidgeting anyway, Wil thought as he recalled the first time he rode the animal.

The horses departed with T'al and Voth astride them, leaving the rest of them to try to increase their distance from the camp on foot. Liz was seemingly unconcerned about a potential pursuit, her eyes instead warily watching the sky. He didn't dare ask how much time they had before the next wave of orbs was upon them.

Now, Wil focused on the hard slog ahead of them, covering as much ground as they could, their enemies nowhere to be seen and yet ever present in their fears.

Ella was at the front of the charge with Liz. She rarely revealed the glow in her eyes when among others, but this evening, she had either thrown caution aside or was having difficulty in restraining the ability. In the past, she had even tried to hide it from Wil, but she wasn't as good at controlling it as she thought she was. He had been hesitant to ask her about it, but that was going to change after tonight. She could clearly see into the darkness better than anyone he had ever met.

Wil and Ella had gotten to know each other well over the past weeks of travel with the Resistance, and he felt a level of comfort with her now that he hadn't at the beginning. Ella adopted a tough demeanor while others were around, but when it was just the two of them, she softened. He didn't understand her reasoning, but she had liked him from the moment he had arrived at the Outpost with Sierra. Something about them connected as he helped her stitch a wound in the infirmary that evening.

Ella had tried to kiss him that night, but it had been too much, too soon after Marco's death. But, as the weeks wore on, it was getting harder to ignore he was developing feelings for her as well.

It was difficult to explain his attraction to Ella. She was everything Marco wasn't, other than being strong-willed, but she was also reasonable and level-headed. Despite her strength and her ability to lead, Ella also provided Wil with comfort and reassurance and was more likely to pull him out of trouble than get him into it. He couldn't think of someone more the opposite of Marco in that regard.

And as he seemingly couldn't resist getting himself into tough situations, Wil supposed he needed that.

He just wasn't ready to open up to someone again yet. Not in the same way. Not when the same dangers that had taken Marco from him threatened to take anyone else he cared about. He had stopped the bots from hurting Ella in Vegas, but what if he couldn't stop them the next time? The last thing he wanted was for her to be hurt because of his actions.

Dagger and Sara began stumbling more often, tripping over jagged rocks and gasping. Tears streamed down Sara's face as she struggled to keep up with the rest of the group. Dagger was beside himself, wondering how he could help his sister but was unable to do so.

They maintained the hurried pace for over an hour. Dagger and Sara appeared on the verge of collapse when, through the darkness, the carts appeared, waiting for the rest of the group to catch up.

Liz lifted a fist, signaling the team to stop.

"Finally," Dagger gasped. He doubled over, fighting to catch his breath, his hands on his knees. "I thought we weren't ever going to stop! Were you planning on running us to death?"

The youth had done fairly well, considering. Being bound by Sentinels for days on end, they would likely have received little, if any, food or water.

"We saved your skin, lad. Show some respect," Buzz chided.

As if in response, Sara fell face-first into the dirt with a grunt, her torso raggedly heaving for more air.

Buzz rolled his eyes as Dagger jumped to his sister's aid. Pulling her up, he dusted off her cloak. "My sister can't walk any further. You may have saved us from the Sentinels, but the Order nearly flayed us, and now we're driven to exhaustion!"

Fury filled the kid's eyes. Wil couldn't help but notice the fresh bruise on Dagger's face. He must have taken the brunt of the beating while his sister had been made to watch. It was doubtful the two teens would have been able to tell the Order anything of importance, but the zealots weren't to know that when they'd set about torturing him.

"Dagger," Sara whispered, trying to gain some semblance of herself back. Mud streaked her face, and the dust from the ground she had fallen on mixed with the sweat on her brow. "Don't be an idiot. These people are helping us. We'd be dead if it weren't for them."

"We might be dead all the same!" Dagger spat. "They haven't told us where they are taking us or what their plan is for us! They could be planning on selling us, for all we know! Why else would they have taken us on?"

Wil raised an eyebrow at Ella, but she wasn't paying attention to him. She watched the youth, open-mouthed, as if trying to decide if she should respond.

"If you think you'll do better on your own, then leave," Liz said. "You're only here because Wil insisted on helping you. Scanners will be upon us soon. We're going to move with or without you. But if you want your sister to survive the hour, I suggest you help load her onto the cart. We have no extra beds, but you can sit with the driver if you can't keep pace."

Dagger's face could have been drawn in stone.

"It's still a long way to the SZ. I suggest you choose wisely," Liz cautioned. She directed her focus to the rest of those with her. "And quickly. Everyone has five minutes to drink and to piss and then we're on our way. Whether you're on board or not."

Dagger looked dumbstruck at the woman's words, but Sara jostled her brother and he quickly appeared to shake off his anger. Despite his reservations, the boy seemed to realize he had no other option but to lead his sister to the cart, with one eye to the sky.

Ella stepped to Wil, putting a hand on his arm. "I never thanked you for rescuing me," she said. Her eyes, still yellow, reflected the moonlight that had broken free from the clouds above them.

"I only did what any of us would have done," he said.

Disappointment reflected on her face. She dropped her hand, and the pins and needles left Wil's arm.

"Yes, I suppose," she answered.

Wil cringed inwardly, realizing the sentiment she had hoped he would express. He would get to that point with her, but he needed more time to sort through his feelings. The warmth of her hand on his arm had felt nice in the cool evening air, and he was disappointed as she withdrew it.

"What do you make of the kids?" he asked. "Dagger is ballsy to chide Liz."

"Dagger's hardly a kid. Out here, anyone over fourteen is pushed out on their own, sometimes younger if they're orphaned. It's likely he has had to take care of himself and his sister for a long time. His misplaced bravado is a product of that, but it's also an act. He's more scared than anything."

"I'm surprised Liz didn't just send him packing."

"Liz understands better than anyone what it means to be forced into this world alone at a young age. She won't put her people in danger, but she's not blind to the situation they're in."

"It certainly didn't seem that way back on the road," Wil responded.

"You have much to learn about Liz."

"I suppose I'm learning a bit about everyone tonight," he said. "We wouldn't have made it out of the camp without your vision."

Ella cocked her head to the side and furrowed her brow, as if he had mentioned something he wasn't supposed to know about. The light in her eyes dimmed, their dark brown returning, reflecting nothing more than the moonlight. She turned and walked away without saying another word.

Wil brushed a hand to the back of his head and watched her join Liz. She grabbed a waterskin and drank her fill. Her eyes never returned to his.

What had he said that would have upset her? It wasn't as if she had been hiding her ability. His mind raced with possibilities of how Ella might have taken offense.

T'al walked up beside him and placed a large hand on his shoulder. "Women," he said. "Don't try to understand them. You'll drive yourself mad."

"I meant it as a compliment . . ." Wil replied.

"Doesn't matter. My guess is, she's been self-conscious about her ability for so long, any remark sounds like a jab. I wouldn't stress about it too much. You two are close. Give her space, and she'll open up when she's ready."

Ella was whispering something to Liz, who nodded in agreement.

"What choice do I have?" Wil asked.

T'al didn't answer, so Wil decided he might as well change the subject. "What's the plan for the carts?" he asked. "Will they be keeping pace with us or run up ahead?"

"I think we're going to press ahead. The quicker we can get them to the SZ, the better. That way, we can get Cali and Ren to a MedCenter as soon as possible. It's not looking good for either of them right now."

His stern words were broken by a command from their leader.

"All right, crew," Liz called out. "Time to move."

8

FIRST LIGHT DAWNED on the horizon. The Resistance had been mobile all night, and Wil's legs were burning from the effort. They hadn't been going at an all-out sprint, but Liz had seemed to grow impatient as the group's pace inevitably slowed with fatigue. They moved steadily enough, but Wil knew his body was going to give out sooner rather than later.

They hadn't stopped for water since they had parted ways with T'al, Voth and the carts, and that was hours ago. He was feeling light-headed, likely from dehydration and lack of sleep, but he had also never run for this long in his entire life.

As Wil surveyed the crew, he wondered what kind of super-humans he had aligned himself with. Though it felt like it had been in another lifetime, he used to hike the Red Mountains within the Sphere frequently and had been in the best shape of his class. Yet those around him now seemed to be barely breaking a sweat at the effort of their run.

Even Ella, at the front of the pack, was moving smoothly and gracefully, with little sign of physical fatigue.

Wil had long given up on feeling his feet. The Resistance team had been kind enough to gift him the boots he wore, but they had been crafted for durability and not for speed. Their construction was solid, crafted by some artisan within the Resistance, but they were also much heavier than the shoes he was used to. It felt as though he were lifting weights with every step. He was sure blisters had formed hours ago, but the numbness in his feet ensured he was only vaguely aware of their presence. Knowing the suffering they would cause him once his feet thawed only added to his misery. He was sure they'd open and bleed before their trek was through.

With the early morning light, Wil could now make out objects that lay next to their path. Rusted vehicles driven by the ancients dotted the landscape, overtaken by vegetation years ago. The shells of a bygone time offered only hints at a past filled with tragedy, and the plants that had claimed them boasted the world no longer belonged to humans, acting as a reminder that the Guardians hadn't been the only thing to take advantage of the downfall of humanity. As he studied the greenery and focused on what lay beneath, Wil could tell the relics were endless. There were so many dotted along the way that Wil could barely comprehend how many people there must have been to have driven the vehicles. Treasures would likely rest among them, unless they had all been picked clean ages ago.

Occasionally, human remains also littered the road, indicative of more recent tragedy. Piles of scattered bones rested at the roadside, yet to be hauled away by animals. Whether bandits, the Order, or bots had taken their lives, it was impossible to tell.

The picked-clean bones weren't as bad as the fresh carcasses. Though not nearly as many, the remains of men and women Wil estimated had been killed within the past few days were frequent enough to make him want to retch, especially as it was impossible for him to hold his breath while running. Feral dogs feasted on many of the deceased, and ravens and other wildlife were also drawn to the corpses. Each of the bodies was covered with flies, attracted by their horrendous stench. Wil pondered why anyone took the risk to venture this road at all, but it drove home why they had to get to their destination as quickly as their legs would allow.

It didn't seem right that these people hadn't even received a decent burial, left to rot, as they were, in the sun. It seemed death in this world offered no more respect than life did.

Wil was still lost in thought when Liz cried out, *"Hold up!"*

On her command, the group slowed to a stop.

Now stationary, Wil's legs shook so much that he feared they might give out. It took all his strength not to sit in the dirt beside the road and let sleep take him. He had to remind himself that in doing so, he might never wake up.

"Stepper," M'iko whispered.

The horse that had been leading one of the carts was running at full gallop toward them, kicking dust in its wake.

"What's going on?" Wil asked.

"Nothing good," Ella replied, her hand rubbing the base of her scalp.

Liz jogged to the creature, holding her arms up, motioning for the beast to slow. The horse relaxed to a trot and then came to a stop as it reached her. It shuffled its hooves as if uneasy and brought its head right to hers, as if taking solace in its owner's presence.

The rest of the group stood silently as they watched the exchange. Wil was unwilling to come to terms with what the horse's appearance meant, but he knew full well what the implications were.

"Is there any chance they would have reached the SZ?" Wil whispered to Ella as he struggled to register the possibilities.

Ella shook her head. "I don't think so."

Liz led the horse back toward the group, her eyes betraying none of her thoughts other than her usual determination.

"M'iko," she said. "Let's ride ahead and see what's happened. The rest of you, continue at our previous pace until you catch up with us. We'll return and warn you if it appears to be too dangerous."

Wil glanced at those who remained: eight, including himself and Ella. Four men and four women. Those of the Resistance were all in prime physical condition. All of them had left their makeshift battle armor in the carts, instead donning more flexible and lightweight skins for traveling. Their agility allowed them to continue on at their hurried pace, unencumbered by the bulk of their protection. But it wasn't without its drawbacks; choosing agility over armor also left them vulnerable to an ambush.

Wil hadn't gotten to know any of them as well as those who had journeyed ahead. He would struggle to even point them out with the correct names. Many of them had been quiet and kept to themselves. They were there for one purpose only: to fight bots.

The others, who he had grown closer to, had all been part of the group ahead, facing an unknown danger. Even if there had been room, Ella and Wil were considered guests rather than soldiers, but he wished they could help. Despite his eagerness, Wil was certain he'd have his fill of fighting when the time came, but that didn't make the wait to find out if his friends were okay any easier.

IT WAS ONLY a few hours before they reached Liz, M'iko, and what remained of the carts.

One cart lay on its side, partially dismantled, while the second one, though upright, was in the middle of having a wheel replaced. It appeared Liz and M'iko had taken one wheel from the dismantled cart and were applying it to the one with less damage.

T'al sat next to them in the cart's shade. Scratches marred his arms, and he sported a bruised eye. Beside him lay two bodies. One was Sara.

"You made good time," Liz said as they approached the devastation. "We've just finished repairing the cart. The other one is beyond what we're able to do for it here, but we still need to determine if there's anything worth salvaging."

"Bandits?" Wil asked, eyeing the wreckage.

"Prowlers," Ella answered as she unsheathed a dagger from her hip. She surveyed the road ahead as if expecting them to still by lying in wait.

The other members of their party didn't stop before getting to work, placing scattered goods back into the standing cart and rummaging through the last pieces of the second.

"Sara and Dagger? Are they . . .?" Wil couldn't finish the thought. Sara lay completely still on the dirt path, but Dagger and Voth were missing.

"Dagger is unconscious in the back of the cart," M'iko answered. "He's a little beat up, but he'll be okay."

Wil's eyes wandered to Sara's lifeless body.

"She wasn't as lucky," T'al said, still seated in the shade, his gaze downcast. "They tried to take her, but Dagger wouldn't have it. They already had Voth tied and loaded. Sara tried to make a run for it, but she wasn't a match for their horses. Dagger launched into an attack. They kicked him in the head, but not before he pulled his sister out of their hands. Their horse trampled her in the process. Dagger was left on the road, unconscious but alive."

"She might have been luckier this way." Ella eyed the young girl's body, tears forming in a rare display of emotion. "There are times I still wish I had died, rather than have had to experience what they put me through." Ella crossed her arms over her chest and walked away from the wreckage. Wil knew better than to follow her. She'd be okay with some space.

"You couldn't stop them from taking Voth?"

T'al sneered at Wil, as if it was the dumbest thing he could have said. "There were half a dozen of them and only two of us. They took us by surprise. Knocked Voth off of Che before she knew what was happening. I tried to reach her, but I got clubbed over the head. I was lucky they didn't use a sword." He nodded to the body of an unkempt stranger lying on the side of the road. "We got one of them. But they had the upper hand."

Something about T'al's story didn't make sense to Wil. Voth was one of the best fighters the Resistance had and wouldn't have been easily surprised. He had seen a few Prowlers when Ella and himself had been captured; they were nothing more than sniveling crooks looking to make quick coin. Wil couldn't picture them being able to hold Voth down.

"They took Voth but left you and your cart in one piece?" he asked.

"They'd just finished stripping the other one when we showed up,"

M'iko answered. "If Stepper hadn't managed to escape, I think they would have just taken the carts. They saw us coming and fled."

"And Cali and Renny?" Wil asked.

"They're unharmed, in the back of the cart with Dagger." M'iko nodded to the cart.

"Enough questions," Liz said. "We already are risking too much here; we need to move."

"What about Voth? Surely we're going after her?" Ella said.

Wil didn't think he had heard his companion question Liz's orders before.

"I think if we should feel sorry for anyone, it would be Voth's kidnappers," Liz answered. "They won't be able to hold Voth for long, and we'll have worse things to deal with if we don't move now."

No sooner had she said the words than a familiar hum sounded behind them.

M'iko rushed to Stepper and worked to harness the horse to the remaining cart.

"T'al, M'iko, get on the cart and head for the SZ; get the injured to the MedCenter. If we get out of here, we'll meet you at the safehouse. Hurry."

"I should stay and fight," T'al said, standing from his place in the shade. "I am one of the strongest fighters here."

"Normally, I'd agree," Liz said. "But you took a nasty blow to the head that needs to be looked at. I won't have you enter this fight if you're not up to it. No more arguing. If they overtake us, they'll be after you next, and even Stepper can't outrun a band of Sentinels."

T'al appeared hesitant but nodded. Wil gave him an apologetic look before joining M'iko on the cart.

"You and Wil should leave as well," Liz said to Ella. "Take Che and follow M'iko."

Wil was about to protest when Ella spoke. "Not a chance," she said. "We're able, and we're not going to leave you behind."

Without waiting for Liz's response, M'iko called to Stepper, and they wheeled off down the road. Liz merely grimaced and turned her attention to the incoming threat.

The hum of the Scanners grew steadily louder as they approached. They would have detected their group long before being seen. Having no firepower themselves, their role would be to alert other, more militant bots to their presence.

Wil could make out a group of four Sentinels running toward them against the horizon. He unsheathed his sword and braced for the worst, knowing he likely wouldn't get close enough to the bots to use his weapon, but he was without a blaster and he vowed to be ready, just in case.

If nothing else, the crew had to hold off the attackers long enough so M'iko, T'al, and the others could make enough distance to escape.

"Get into position!" Liz called out.

The remaining Resistance members assembled behind the fallen cart. Wil and Ella followed suit. It wasn't much, but it would at least provide the group with some protection.

Ella had her blaster drawn, ready for the onslaught.

"Surely we can take out four," Wil said.

"It's the ones that will come after you should worry about," Liz said. "These were just the closest. More will come, especially once we take these down."

Wil sighed as he stood his ground. The Scanners circling above were too high for them to hit effectively with their blasters, and the machines would be broadcasting everything going on to any Sentinel within range.

Wil dove for the ground as firepower met the edge of the cart, splintering a wooden beam.

"Easy now, Bot Killer!" one of the Resistance members laughed.

Wil dusted himself off as he got back to his feet, more embarrassed than injured. He remained crouched, but his face had reddened.

Ella lifted a hand to his shoulder, but he couldn't help noticing the smirk on her face.

The others were already returning fire. Wil poked his nose through an opening in the cart's frame. The bots were closing in quickly, taking on blaster rounds. The Resistance's blasters were less than effective at this range, but they wouldn't be for long, and one lucky shot would mean the difference between a downed bot or another to deal with when it was on top of them.

One of the Sentinels flopped into the dirt as blaster fire landed true on its knee joint. Typically, the legs were poor targets, made of reinforced metal and designed to take heavy damage. The one weak spot they contained was the partially exposed wiring at the connecting knee joint as the leg extended during its run. To hit it required a perfectly timed shot.

That left three, closing in fast. Wil could tell the shots were landing solid now, as sparks flew off the reinforced shielding. Significant damage to the head unit would also take the bots down. Though far more protective than human skin, the Sentinel's synthetic faces and necks were made to be aesthetic rather than protective.

Blaster fire whizzed past Wil's head. A cry came from a Resistance member Wil hardly knew, Alek, as he fell backward. Smoke rose from a burn mark on his temple. A direct hit.

Without thinking, Wil bent over the man to disarm him of his blaster. Alek wasn't going to be using it, after all.

A rough hand ripped the weapon from his grasp before he could celebrate his gain. Liz scowled at him as blaster fire continued around them.

"I don't think you realize how rare these are!" she shouted above the sound of firepower striking the underbelly of the cart. "We can't afford you to be draining them!"

Wil rolled his eyes and resigned to watching the action unfold as he questioned why he didn't leave with the others. During the exchange, the group had taken two more of the bots down, leaving only one.

The remaining Sentinel was almost on top of the party before it collapsed, crawling to the overturned cart before it finally shut down. Its face had been completely peeled away, having received the brunt of the attack. The damage revealed circuitry and electronics underneath, sparking as it fell into the dirt.

Wil curled his nose in disgust at the silver skull, one of its blue lit eyes still glowing from its inset bulb. Blaster fire had melted the other.

The bot's frame twitched, and T'al stepped past the cart and placed a foot on the Sentinel's sternum while yanking its artificial spine from its body. The spasms stopped as T'al hurled the dismembered frame to the ground.

Smoke rose from holes pierced through the overturned cart by blaster fire, their charred edges sparking before igniting the entire vehicle in flames.

Wil jumped, but the rest of their party seemed more annoyed than concerned about their already trashed transport. Green fields stretched across the horizon as far as he could see, offering no protection. Far in the distance, it appeared as if there might be a forest, but it was far off and not in the direction in which the Resistance intended to travel.

A plume of dust rose on the path ahead of them.

"Sand!" he cursed as he watched the frames of several white bots appear through the cloud.

"What do we do?" one of the Resistance members asked.

"We fight," Liz answered.

Wil ran his fingers over his sword hilt, feeling the ridges marking its grip. His breath was slow and controlled as the wind blew over his skin, prickling the hair on his knuckles and cooling the sweat that had formed on his brow.

Ella's gaze focused on the incoming threat. Ash and debris soiled her face and sweat glistened off her bronze skin.

"There's too many," Ella said as she cocked an eyebrow to Liz. "I'm all for standing our ground, but how do we take them all on?" Her fierce demeanour waned, but only slightly.

Wil didn't blame her. Their hands had been full with four. Over twenty Sentinels were now coming their way, and with the cart engulfed in flames, they had no protection.

"Do you see any other options?"

Wil had one other way in mind, but he hadn't been able to get it to work since they had left Vegas. He had only willingly done it once, but if there was going to be a chance for any of them to make it out alive, he was going to have to try again.

"I need to use my power," he said, half to himself.

"It's too risky," Liz said, shaking her head. "It takes its toll on you every time you use it. If we take these out, there will be another group headed our way, and what then?"

"What do you propose?" Wil asked. "We can't possibly take them all on and make it out of here."

The bots were drawing nearer. The rest of the Resistance members lifted their weapons, bracing for a fight.

"How far are we from the SZ?" Ella asked.

"Likely an hour at an all-out sprint," Liz answered. "Longer if we have to carry someone. And that's only if we avoid more bots."

"I think we've got to try," Ella said, uneasily eyeing the group fast approaching.

Liz sighed, then closed her eyes. The wind picked up, tossing her brown hair, and her chest lifted as she breathed deeply.

Time was running out.

"Liz?" Ella pressed.

Liz raised a hand, flashing her palm at Ella and Wil, but her eyes remained closed.

Shots came from the direction of the bots. They weren't yet close enough to hit their targets, but they'd ensure the group didn't push closer.

"I want you to know something, Wil," Liz said, her eyes still closed. "You are unlike anyone I have ever encountered. Sometimes—not often, but *sometimes*—I can see a person's future. Their destiny. I can see the great things they will achieve or the horrible things they will bring about. Consistently, when I see these things, they are around events of great magnitude. Usually, there is nothing I can do to prevent what I see. Occasionally, I can alter events, but more often than not, it makes things worse."

Wil monitored the approaching bots. It would be mere moments before they would be under their fire. Whether or not Liz gave him the okay, he would try. He wouldn't allow them to be overrun if there was anything he could do to help it.

"Your future is of great importance, Wil. Perhaps more important than any, but one that I have come across. Yet you stand on the edge between light and darkness. Every step you take pushes and pulls you in one direction or the other."

The approaching Sentinels faded as his vision narrowed on the woman that stood before him. Even Ella and the rest of the Resistance members blurred in his periphery. What was she talking about?

"Why are you telling me this now?" was all he could manage to ask.

"I don't know which choices will lead you down which path," she answered. "But I know this power of yours is related. Each time you use it, the chance to sway your path increases."

She opened her eyes and met his gaze.

"But you're right. We have no other choice."

Wil's awareness extended to the surrounding chaos that had erupted; his gaze shifted from Liz to the bots coming toward them.

Her words buzzed in his mind.

Liz took her weapon and returned fire at the bots as she yelled above the noise, "Whatever you're going to do, Bot Killer, *do it now!*"

9

ELECTRICITY COURSED through Wil's arm as Ella grasped it. He turned to meet her brown eyes, now locked onto his. Concern and confusion were reflected on her face. If she had any thoughts about Liz's prophecy, she wasn't volunteering them.

"I need to try," he said.

"Quit standing around then!" she said, a smirk forming on her lips.

Wil nodded. He knew he was stalling. The last time he had felt the burning in his gut had been during the Sentinel attack on Vegas, when Ella had been put in harm's way. He hated any life being lost to the villainous bots that seemed hellbent on wiping out humanity, but he wouldn't lose another close friend to them.

Nothing had changed now.

He just doubted his control.

Wil put his arm around Ella and pulled her in. His chest warmed as he did so, and he had the sudden desire to put his lips to hers in a farewell kiss, but he stopped short of doing so and instead embraced her in an intimate hug. He had admonished Ella for kissing him in Vegas in the same scenario. He wasn't about to complicate things further now.

Instead, he pulled her body close to his and pressed it into him.

Wil's hand rested at the small of her back, and he couldn't help but marvel at how smooth her skin was. He had held her hand on more than one occasion; it had been dry and calloused from the desert air and the tasks she had performed within the Community. Her back, on the other hand, was soft, and the contrast emphasized how rough his own hands had become.

Ella nuzzled his neck and started as if she was about to whisper something to him but thought better of it. She released the embrace first, put a hand to his shoulder and gave him a nod and a smile.

Wil sighed as she stepped aside. He had nowhere to go but forward.

Nothing but the dirt road stood between him and the bots programmed to fire on the small remnants of their group.

Heat radiated off the cart, still engulfed in flames behind him. The sun had reached its zenith, a white halo surrounding it, and its white-hot strength licked his skin, which had reddened over the course of their journey. Beads of sweat dripped down Wil's forehead. A warmth flooded his chest, but he believed it to be from the embrace he had shared with Ella. If he survived, trying to determine his feelings for her might drive him to madness. The path ahead of him would likely be a lonely one—and a dangerous one. It wouldn't be fair to bring her along. She was more than capable, but this was his fight.

Hiding behind the feelings for Ella was the heat of his power coming to life. The sensation came as a surprise to him; he had done nothing to summon its force, yet there was no mistaking what was happening. The sensation was so similar to what had bubbled inside of him because of the intimacy with Ella that he had nearly missed it, except this was raw and spread to his extremities, like a gritty fire coursing through his veins that desired to permeate his skin, as though it had taken on a life of its own.

All of his life, technology had malfunctioned around him. Wil had assumed it had merely been bad luck until the day he had been forced to leave the Sphere. The taunts he had received as a boy when datapads malfunctioned around him and automatic doors refused to open for him had been crippling. His superiors had always assured him these follies were coincidence—technology glitched all the time.

But that hadn't stopped the pain of being different, of thinking something had been wrong with him. Wil had cried himself to sleep cursing himself and his stupidity, wondering why he couldn't get something as simple as a datapad to function correctly in order to complete a simple assignment.

As it turned out, there *had* been something wrong; something far more powerful and destructive than a few burned out computer screens. Wil wouldn't discover the full extent of what hid within him until it destroyed a Guardian scanner by mistake. That devastating action had led to the death of Marco, and the events that followed had led him Outside, into a world that wasn't supposed to exist.

Since then, while faced with the dangers of the Outside, the same power had awakened within him more than once, but he hadn't been able to call it at will since. Wil had no idea what it was or why he had been given this ability. It had already saved him and Ella at least twice, and now, it seemed, it might do so a third time.

Wil continued his stride toward the Sentinels, ignoring the blaster fire swarming around him, his companions drawing much of the fury.

If the Guardians had discovered the full extent of his strange abilities while he had lived under the Sphere, he would likely have been killed. And yet, somehow, others around him seemed to share his luck. Sierra possessed the ability to activate tech, even in places where it should not work, as well as seeing visions of the past. And even though she didn't want to talk about it, Ella had some sort of heightened vision, allowing her to see at night. And now, perhaps, Liz had manifested abilities as well.

Sierra and her sister both possess unexplained powers.

It couldn't be a coincidence.

His mind drifted to the words Liz had spoken, and Wil tensed at the implications. Did she have the ability to see into the future? Or was she speaking in riddles? *On the edge of darkness.* What did that mean? Could this power of his turn him into something he didn't want to become? Each time he had harnessed the power, it had taken a toll on him physically; twice he had passed out from its use. The impact seemed to correlate to how big of a target it affected. When one small orb fell from the sky because of him, Wil had barely felt an impact, but when he had knocked out seventy Sentinels in one hit, it had left him bedridden and weak.

Could the power affect his mental state as well? Did its use affect his judgement? His morality?

There was no way for him to know, but Wil had to complete the immediate task ahead. His companions were depending on him.

Wil stopped as the force built within him. The monstrous bodies of the Sentinels flowed over the ground like a wave. They weren't elegant by any means, but their movements were smooth; they had been built to run. Though their legs were solid metal, the features of their bone-white synthetic skin were exact replicas of human complexions, albeit with a haunted look to them.

A hollowness that screamed of their artificial design.

Cries echoing behind him indicated one or more of the Resistance had been wounded. Blaster fire surrounded him now.

He had to act.

Wil tried to grab onto the power that coursed through his veins, searching for a way to guide it and control its impact. Perhaps he could minimize the effect it had on him. It pulsed as though a part of him, and yet it eluded his consciousness as though it were a separate entity that had taken residency inside him. He had no control, not in the same way he did over his arms or legs; it was more like trying to control his heartbeat. He could feel around its edges, as though control might be possible, but it ultimately evaded his grasp.

The fire pushed its way to the surface of his skin, building pressure until he felt like he would explode under its force, before unleashing itself, and everything went black.

WIL AWOKE TO DARKNESS. As his eyes slowly began to focus, he made out stars winking in and out above him. The dry stab of dying grass did little to cushion the hard-packed dirt he lay on. He attempted to move his limbs, but the weight of them kept him pinned to the ground.

He concentrated on the simple act, and it still took several moments before they responded to his command, but even then, there wasn't much he could do with them.

"Easy now," Ella's voice broke through his senses. He could feel the warmth in her approach as she sat next to him, her voice calming and reassuring. If nothing else, he had protected Ella.

She took the hand he had found so hard to lift and held it in her own, reminded again of its roughness. Her hands had spent years training with swords and weapons that had caused them to callous. It spoke to him of her strength and determination. He didn't mind, but it always made him wonder what Ella saw in him. Despite the recent blisters he'd developed, his hands, in comparison, were soft, the result of a peaceful life. The bots had made those in the Sphere reliant on them for manual labor.

"Where . . ." He struggled to speak, his own hoarse voice sounding as if it belonged to someone else. "Where are we?"

"We're inside the border of the SZ. Liz decided to set up camp here to allow you and the others to rest."

Wil couldn't help but smile. "It worked, then?" he asked. He could feel some of his mobility slowly returning, and he managed to lift his head.

Shapes were blurry, but through hazed vision, he could make out a small fire flickering at the center of the camp. Resistance members had made their beds around the fire. T'al and M'iko had joined them, wrapped in blankets as they lay on the ground, finally able to rest. Their cart was stationed at one side of their circle, and Liz stood near it, at full attention, standing guard against bandits or Prowlers who might try to chance their luck.

"Yes, but you need to rest," Ella answered. "We won't be going anywhere now, at least until morning."

Wil put his head back down, but flexed his toes. His mobility was coming back, albeit slowly.

Ella ran her fingers through his hair, before heading for bed herself.

Wil lay still, but only because he had to. Despite the stillness of his body, his mind raced.

He had been successful in his attempt to bring down the bots, but the power had still reacted on its own, still moving through him unaided and unguided. It was as if he were merely a spectator to its will, a vehicle through which it could be channeled, and it seemed to draw as much energy from him as it desired. This time, he had knocked out fewer Sentinels, and it had left him incapacitated. Would it draw so much that, eventually, it would kill him? The emptiness in his veins told him it would. If he couldn't control its release, and it needed to draw more strength from him than he had, could this ability become his undoing?

He shivered as the thought manifested. He didn't have an answer, and for the first time, the power he possessed sent chills of fear down his spine.

Until that afternoon, his inability to control whatever it was had only concerned him to the point that he might not be able to activate it when he needed it the most. The power seemed to come at random, though he was now starting to see a pattern.

Twice now, his ability had called to him when Sentinels had surrounded him and he had no means of escape. During the attack on Vegas, he had intended to protect his friend, and even when the orb fell in the Sphere, the case had been the same, though Wil hadn't realized it at the time. The ability appeared to manifest itself when he needed protection.

When Wil had confronted the Sentinels that had kidnapped Dagger and Sara, he had felt no sign of the burning fire that usually accompanied the pulse, nor had he done so while they were hiding behind the cart. Somehow, the power seemed almost sentient, knowing to materialize only when there was no other alternative.

But how far could he trust it? And how coincidental were these events? Wil was hesitant to believe it would always appear as he needed it.

How he drained the power from smaller items when he touched them was another question. Wil had been plagued by that question his entire life, and he had always assumed he was unlucky. Perhaps he was, just in a different way.

As he lay still, another concern found him: Liz's words of his potential future.

You stand on the edge between light and darkness.

Did the key to his demise—or victory—rest on a power he didn't understand and couldn't control?

He needed to talk to her and discover more of what she had seen in him.

Wil flexed each of his muscles as he was able—at first, that was all he could do. Wiggling toes turned into calf flexes, which turned into fluid movements and pushing himself over onto his hands and knees. Once he had a range of motion, the rest steadily returned. He sat kneeling for a few minutes, allowing his strength to creep back into his arms and legs.

Liz hadn't changed her stance. The rest of the camp lay asleep, including Ella, who was already snoring. She had likely stayed awake to ensure he'd return to consciousness.

A full moon provided plenty of light over the campsite. The size of their group had noticeably shrunk since they had left Vegas. He assumed the three injured still rested within the cart. From where he was, he could make out M'iko and T'al, as well as a handful of others. By his count, they had lost three in the latest encounter with the Sentinels, which meant only a half dozen of their group now remained.

Was every trip through the Interzone as treacherous? The bones lining the road suggested it was.

He stood, his legs shaking beneath him as he pushed himself to his feet. Wil gained his balance, testing the strength of his legs to ensure he wouldn't topple over.

The moonlight cast shadows across Liz's face, which emphasized the feeling that something felt familiar about the woman. Ever since they had met, something about her had reminded Wil of someone, but he couldn't quite put his finger on who. She mostly avoided him.

Despite her affability with Ella, Liz rarely sat and chatted if Wil was in the group, and he had yet to determine why.

Liz's eyes shifted toward him. She was unsurprised by his approach, but she met his gaze with caution.

"I'd like to know more about what you said to me back there," he said.

"It's nice to see you've come around," she said. "But I have nothing else to share with you." She remained focused, watching the surrounding shadows with suspicion.

"Are you worried bandits might take us while we sleep?" he asked. "I'm surprised you are the only one standing watch."

"Bandits are always a worry, but here, animals are a bigger concern. The drought has affected them as well, and if they come across a camp of unsuspecting travelers, it could mean an easy meal. This is Resistance territory; bandits and Prowlers are rarely so bold as to attack a camp here. It never works out in their favor."

"How big is the Resistance?" Wil asked, thinking of the larger number who had helped to defend the city.

"Thousands, likely, though similar movements exist elsewhere under other names. We're not organized enough to keep an accurate head count. We gain new members and lose old ones every day. Several hundred occupy San Francisco."

"You had a premonition of the attack on Vegas, didn't you? That's why you made the journey."

"Partially, yes," she answered coldly. She left the words hanging.

They stood in silence for a few minutes, the sound of crickets chirping filling the silence.

"I have had these premonitions for ten years," Liz eventually offered, perhaps realizing Wil had been waiting patiently for more. "Since I was a teenager. They usually bring me more heartache than good."

"My friend, Sierra, saw visions," he said. Grasping at a way to get Liz to talk, he needed to learn more. "She had visions of the past, which led her to activate the device that brought the Onyx down. It seems there are others who share abilities similar to yours."

For the first time, Liz broke her concentration and turned to Wil. Light from the campfire danced across her face, and the moon highlighted the purple in her eyes. Whether it was the way the shadows highlighted her features or the topic of conversation he had chosen, he suddenly realized why Liz seemed so familiar.

He nearly stumbled backward, his legs having not quite returned to their full strength.

"You're . . . Izzy," he said. "You're Sierra's sister!"

Liz looked around, agitated. "Quiet!" she hissed. "I don't know what you're talking about."

In so many ways, the woman that stood before Wil was the exact opposite of the teenager he had escaped the Sphere with. Liz was confident, strong, in peak physical condition, and in charge. Sierra, on the other hand, though determined, was soft, more caring than bold, and more curious than confident. It was no wonder he hadn't put it together before now.

Liz seemed a natural leader, while Sierra had fallen into her role by what seemed like happenstance. But both sisters seemed to have an insight into the past and the future.

"Why did we leave Vegas without you saying anything? Sierra talked about you nonstop. We left without you even seeing her!"

"*Enough!*" she barked, her eyes flitting back and forth around the campsite. "I don't have to justify myself to you."

Wil took a step toward her, suddenly feeling bold. "You asked me to join you. You've given me a cryptic warning about my future. I think it's only fair that I ask for an explanation as to why you don't want anyone to know who you are."

Liz looked back into the night, as if she hoped the answer to Wil's query lay somewhere in the ether, and sighed. "It's hard for me to explain," she began. "The fall of the SZ was only part of why I returned to Vegas. If I never had to step foot in that part of the world again, I would be happier for it. But fate, it seems, is not kind to me. I had to return then, as I'm sure I'll need to return again before this war is over.

"The SZ's collapse enabled me to bring men and supplies. It helped save much of the city, but as you know, most of the populace died. But I can rarely change the path of what I foresee."

The wind picked up and brought with it the humidity from a water source nearby. *The ocean*, Wil surmised. *That's what Ella had called it.*

"The Director of San Francisco granted us funding and supplies to venture east to discover what we could about the SZ's fall," Liz continued. "I had worked hard to convince him of the dangers if the SZ around the City Center fell. I convinced him to fund our expedition to learn more about the weakening field in Vegas. I knew it was coming, though I hadn't realized it would fall before we even arrived."

"But why did you come? Most of your people were slaughtered. If you foresaw what was to happen, you could have prevented their deaths."

"Though we lost people, the cost of me staying behind was far greater. We saved far more lives than we spent, but my real motivation for coming had nothing to do with the SZ's collapse. It had everything to do with both Sierra and yourself."

Wil arched an eyebrow. "It did? Then why didn't you tell Sierra you're alive? She thought you died ten years ago!"

Liz sighed. "I've told you more about your future than I should have. Nothing good comes when I share too much, no matter how good my intentions might be. And the higher the stakes, the worse the effect becomes. All I can tell you is what I said earlier. Your decisions, along with the ability you have been gifted, will either cause great accomplishment or great ruin. I don't know enough to tell you when, how or why, only that each time you use it, it brings you closer to that reality."

Liz's words were not reassuring. How would he know if its effect was bringing him closer to the right outcome?

"And Sierra?"

"The longer I stay away from my sister, the better," she replied grimly.

"What's that supposed to mean?"

"I don't know the reason, and I don't even know the cause, but everything I've seen indicates that the sooner Sierra and I are together, the worse the devastation will be."

Wil furrowed his brow. "Devastation?"

Liz sighed once again. "Ever since I was a girl, I have had glimpses of war and destruction you could not begin to imagine. You're going to have to trust me when I say that, for whatever reason, the longer Sierra and I stay apart, the better it will be. For everyone."

"She thought you were dead," he said. "I know how much it would mean to her to know you're alive."

"I imagine now that she's out of the Sphere, she'll learn the truth about me soon enough. No matter how much it hurts that I can't be there for my sister, I have to keep away from her."

Liz finished the thought with a hint of sadness.

"What happened?" Wil asked. "In the Sphere? Sierra told me there was an accident."

"It was no accident," she said. "The Guardians and the Order tried to kill me, but I escaped. And I spent the next ten years learning how to live in a world that should never have been."

Liz sighed again, and Wil felt he had pushed the matter as far as she was going allow for one night. Reluctantly, he nodded and turned to head back to the others.

"This stays between us, Bot Killer," Liz said, still keeping her voice low. "I'm sure I don't have to remind you that, in this world, possessing special abilities puts a mark on your head."

10

Their journey into the Silent Zone lasted for the better part of the next day. It amazed Wil that despite the vast distance these areas appeared to cover, they were largely uninhabited.

Unlike the SZ surrounding Las Vegas, the terrain here appeared to have been lush with life, at least at one point in time. The grass that had been green as they had left the mountains had now turned brown and lifeless, and green weeds poked through, as if uncaring that they hadn't been watered in decades.

Drought had affected much of this area for a long time. Trees grew, but they were gnarled and stunted and appeared as if they constantly struggled against the harsh conditions.

Perhaps the area being uninhabited wasn't so strange, after all.

The Resistance's path had turned to the south. A large bay separated them from their destination, and there hadn't been a direct route to cross it since the time of the ancients. Ella had patiently tried to describe the difference between the ocean and the bay. The water all came from the same place, so he didn't quite understand, but he knew he still longed to see the ocean.

Wil inhaled deeply and smiled. They were still several hours from the shore of the bay. The smell the wind occasionally brought to them was unlike anything Wil had experienced before, in that it was both fresh and sour. It surprised him there could be so little water available to the life here, considering how close they were to such a massive supply of it.

According to Ella, if it hadn't been for the body of water separating them from the city, the trip would only take a matter of hours. Despite them being close, the hilly terrain prevented them from seeing it, but occasionally Wil would get a glimpse of its green force field rising high into the clouds. The field rose high enough that it appeared to taper off in the distance. Even from where they were, miles away, he had to crane his neck to follow the mysterious field into the sky.

Ella had told him the Resistance had claimed most of the territory on this upper lip of the SZ—not that they had much competition. Other than the farms that lined the eastern bank of the bay, nobody was interested in the territory. It was too far from the city to be a worthwhile base for trade, and most of the trading outposts were established to the south. Few traders were willing to make the journey eastward for the little they'd get from the inhabitants of Vegas. It usually went the other way. Only Prowlers and traders from Vegas hoping to make a living with the limited resources they had would brave the journey. They had far less to lose.

But despite its drawbacks, the area had its upside. Plenty of coastline meant there was enough fish to go around, and since it was away from the main road, there was little traffic. The Resistance could easily keep to themselves.

Sierra had often talked about one day seeing the ocean. Growing up in the middle of a desert, an endless body of water had sounded like a fairy tale; like desert monsters, or men flying into space among the stars.

It was still hard for him to comprehend that the woman he traveled with was Sierra's sister. Although, now he thought about it, perhaps it wasn't as incomprehensible as it first seemed. Both were strong-willed women. With a little more time outside the Sphere, Wil had no doubt Sierra would gain the same confidence Liz possessed.

And both possessed mysterious powers. Powers that could potentially aid in defeating the Guardians.

In contrast, though, Liz was jaded in a way he hoped Sierra would never become. She possessed a hard edge that was the product of a difficult life her younger sister had yet to experience. Hopefully, with their combined efforts, they could bring down the bots and build a new life from them all on the Outside.

Wil wasn't sure if he should be concerned about Liz's prophecy about the two of them meeting. He knew Sierra would be ecstatic to know her sister was alive and well. If he believed Liz gave any credence to his words, he'd try and convince her to return to Vegas as soon as they could. But he knew that even though Liz saw him as a valuable asset due to his power, she thought him foolhardy and irrational. His insistence to return would likely cause her to dig her heels in deeper and stay clear of Sierra. He'd have to wait for the right opportunity to present itself, though the war they faced was likely to do the heavy lifting for him.

Early that morning, several men and women had appeared as if out of nowhere while the crew had been dismantling the camp. They wore the makeshift armor Wil had seen other Resistance members wearing during the Battle for Vegas. Liz's shrinking group had since removed the bulk of their gear in favor of lighter garb more suitable for travel.

Wil had almost forgotten how clean and fresh the armor had looked at the beginning of the group's expedition. The new arrivals appeared as though they had spent hours polishing the makeshift gear, fashioned from pieces of plating from fallen Sentinels and other bots. Metal armor hung in chains alongside swords of such a size that they rivaled anything Wil had seen or imagined.

Those they had met with had been saddened, though not surprised, at the small number who had returned. Most of the returning members were excited to be back in familiar territory and to rejoin the larger group, heading back to wherever their main base of operations was located.

The newcomers took much of the excess weaponry and supplies that had been salvaged from battle and fallen members. Much of it would be restored and refurbished, to be reused another day. They also took Renny and Cali as well, who would be well taken care of at their MedCenter.

Dagger, on the other hand, had awoken with the dawn. One of the field medics had given him a quick inspection and determined he wouldn't have any lasting physical effects from his injuries, but the look in Dagger's eyes told Wil the pain of losing his sister would far surpass any physical trauma the lad could possibly have obtained.

Somehow, the group of Resistance members talked Liz into keeping Dagger with them, whereas Liz had initially seemed intent on sending the boy on his way. Something about his presence made her uneasy, and Wil thought there was more to it than just an extra person to slow them down.

Mostly, the group had been eerily quiet for the duration of the journey. The continued death of their companions was taking its toll.

Even those accustomed to this world had their limits.

Ella seemed to have forgiven Wil's comments about her eyes and had spent the majority of the trip by his side. This had been the third time he had awoken from an episode to discover her taking care of him. Wil was grateful for her loyalty; he didn't think anyone else he had encountered in this world had offered him that, with the exception of Sierra.

T'al was his next closest companion, but he had kept mostly to himself since the Prowlers had kidnapped Voth. His big, happy-go-lucky bulk had been replaced by a brooding, introspective persona. Everyone handled loss differently, Wil supposed.

Voth had been T'al's closest friend, and they had been so familiar that Wil had assumed they were a couple when he'd first accompanied the Resistance. They had been inseparable; where one went, so did the other.

T'al likely would have fared better if they had killed Voth in the skirmish, but being kidnapped by Prowlers was something else. Death on the Outside appeared to be commonplace, though Wil didn't think he'd ever be able to grow accustomed to its normalcy. He knew everyone had their time, but in the Sphere, he had never once woken up wondering if that day would be his last. Ever since the Onyx murdered Marco, he did not have that same luxury.

According to what Ella had told him of the Prowlers and her own confinement at their hand, Voth's kidnapping wasn't anything Wil wanted to imagine or dwell on for too long. It still gnawed at him that humans could treat each other in such a ghastly way, especially when the bots were the ones at the root of humanity's misery.

That Voth may have succumbed to a fate worse than death was something T'al didn't appear to be willing to accept.

WIL FOLLOWED Liz through an unassuming wooden door which led into the Twisted Serkhet pub. He didn't know what a Serkhet was, but an image on the sign that swung above the door suggested it was some sort of gray scorpion. Ella, T'al, M'iko, and Dagger followed close behind.

The difference between this part of San Francisco and the other parts of the city they had passed through was striking. How these two distinct realities could coexist so close to each other was puzzling.

On their journey into the city, Wil and the others had passed farms with lush green fields that surpassed even the growing areas the Sphere contained. Beyond the farms, they'd passed makeshift communities where villagers had sat on the street in groups, huddled around small fires, cooking what Wil could only assume, based on the smell, was cabbage, along with some of the oversized rodents he vividly remembered from his time imprisoned with the Prowlers. Their homes appeared to be haphazardly constructed from a combination of ancient and modern debris. The buildings showed permanence the further they ventured, and by the time they reached the pub, brick had become the construction material of choice.

The torchlit room now before them revealed those who frequented the Twisted Serkhet were much better off than most of the city. Its patrons were well dressed, so much so that Wil felt out of place in the grubby tunic he had been wearing since they had cleared the mountain pass. The smell of delicious meat wafted from where it was being cooked in one of the back rooms. Wil would have guessed pork.

Those sitting at the tables were jovial, and most appeared to be well fed; a stark contrast to the gaunt faces lining the streets outside.

"What is this place?" he whispered to Ella.

"Welcome to the Middle Ring," she replied, her lips parting as she surveyed their place of respite.

"Find a table," Liz said. "Enjoy yourselves. I have some business to take care of. We'll head to the safehouse afterward."

Wil exchanged a questioning look with Ella, but nodded regardless.

A couple of staff members made their way from table to table, taking and fulfilling orders. Two large guards stood at the end of the bar, silently watching the patrons as they conversed. One of them had their eye on Wil and his party. Wil shifted uncomfortably.

An odd sense of the establishment came over him, like it was a place that shouldn't exist in this world. Plenty of food and drink lay on the tables in front of its patrons, who were all laughing and enjoying themselves.

Liz made her way to the back of the room without another word. Two more guards stood before a blue curtain that separated a section in the back of the tavern. Both gave Liz a familiar nod as she dipped through.

"What's that about?" Wil asked.

"With Liz, you're better off not asking too many questions. There are things you don't want to know, and there are others she'd stick you for if you found out."

"Are you serious?" he asked. "Would she really stab someone for something like that?"

"You have much to learn about this world," T'al said. "Life doesn't have as much value as you're used to."

You think?

"Many would kill you for less," Ella chimed in. "Liz is fierce, but at least she's just. But many of us have pasts we'd rather keep to ourselves, and pacts we need to keep hidden. You'd be best to keep your nose out of the affairs of others. If Liz wants to tell you her business, she will."

"Can we sit down already?" Dagger chimed in. "My feet are tired, and everyone's looking at us."

Wil surveyed the faces in the room. The boy was right; all eyes were on them. Nobody stared directly, but everyone watched the group in their peripheral vision, wary of the newcomers, though some did a better job of hiding their thoughts than others.

Despite them being some of the cleanest and well-dressed people he had seen since leaving the Sphere, Wil had no doubt the majority of the bar's patrons would happily slit their throats and not think twice about it.

M'iko led the five of them to a sturdy table toward the back of the establishment. Its solid wood frame wasn't elaborately crafted, but it was functional, and the heavy, weathering stains and marks on its surface showed it had withstood the test of time.

The bar matched the aesthetic and was lined with stools, set up along one side of the room. A lone barkeep stood behind it, cleaning glasses and staring off into nothing. Ancient light fixtures still hung from the ceiling, suggested the place had once had electricity. Now, sconces on the walls held torches, staining the surrounding walls and ceiling with soot from decades of use.

The group ordered a few pitchers of ale for the table.

"These folks seem to be better off than the ones we passed on the road," Wil whispered to his companions. "Why is that?"

"The city is divided into the City Center and the Three Rings, and beyond those are the Outskirts," Ella explained. "We are on the edge of the Inner and Middle rings. The Resistance has established its stronghold in the Outskirts, where we met the others. It used to be overrun by Prowlers and Bandits, taking advantage of those on their way in or out of the city, but the Resistance moved in and mostly cleared them out. That said, with the Resistance numbers constantly in decline, that becomes harder and harder to maintain.

"The Outer Ring is vast, and, as you saw as we moved through it, farms and orchards occupy most of this land. They supply produce and food for the other residents. The Middle Ring is a mix of shanty towns for those scrambling to get by, dominated by lesser merchants trading goods that serve those within the Rings. They're typically unskilled at what they do, but they've faked it well enough.

"The Inner Ring hosts high-level merchants and traders. These are usually middlemen who buy from the farmers and the Outer Ring, who mark up the goods and then resell the products to the City Center. They are crafts- and tradespeople and are well compensated and well adjusted. Typically, they never want for either food or protection."

"The City Center is the area behind the green force field?" Wil asked.

Ella nodded. "Within the field, technology still functions, and they've separated themselves from the rest of the city."

"Why does San Fran have the force field to begin with?" Wil asked. "How does it work within a Silent Zone?"

"During the time of the wars, the ancients set up the barrier before they created the SZ. The powers that be in the Center likely know the reason, but all that's been passed down outside are rumors. They say the people of the Center closed themselves off before the wars even began, barricading themselves in so they wouldn't have to fight the Guardians."

"And now the city helps in the fight against the bots?" Wil asked.

T'al nearly spat out his ale. "Not exactly, Bot Killer," he chuckled. "The City Center helps no one but themselves. You saw the people we passed on the way in. The Center won't even help those technically under their charge. Those on the inside don't care about the well-being of those of the Inner Ring, and the Inner Ring sure as hell doesn't care about the Middle Ring. Almost no one cares about anyone past the SZ boundaries. I doubt most of the residents even know the threat from the bots exists. Everyone here carries on with their own lives with no regard for anyone else."

By this point, most of the other patrons had gone back to their own conversations, no longer paying attention to their group. T'al's comments had received a few dirty looks, though, and M'iko placed a hand on T'al's arm to quiet him.

"There's no need to draw extra attention to the fact that we're Resistance," she said.

"What's wrong with being Resistance?" Wil asked.

"The Resistance is not well liked," she replied. "We're classed as troublemakers, agitating ancient settlements for a worthless cause."

"I would have thought being able to live in comfort would provide opportunity to develop a strategy to take on the bots."

"Living in comfort allows people to forget why taking on a cause is worthwhile. Most here live and die within the SZ. The bots aren't something these people fear."

"Even so, why would the Resistance cause them any concern?"

"Humans are funny creatures," T'al replied. "They don't want to see others taking up the cause, because it makes them feel bad about themselves. It challenges the order of things, and it calls into question the life they're living. Life may not be perfect here, but people have made it work, and they are content to live their lives without looking outward."

"I don't understand why anyone wouldn't *want* to fight. Who knows when the SZ here might fall, too? And they sit in comfort as if *nothing* will ever change?"

By this point, Wil wasn't bothering to lower his voice, which drew more than a few angry glances.

"Would you keep your voice down!" M'iko scolded. "We won't win any favors if we get kicked out. Liz has worked hard to get us to where we are."

"So I just have to pretend that I'm not eager to fight the bots?" He had lowered his voice slightly, but Wil was too upset at the connotations to stop speaking. "That we are safe and sound in a bubble? Just like the Sphere?"

"For now, yes." Ella rested a hand on his arm, her eyes pleading with him to calm down. The other patrons had stopped what they were doing, all eyes focused on their table once again.

He sighed. Why did he always have to make things worse?

His heart beat heavily in his chest as adrenaline coursed through his veins. "I need to get some fresh air," he said, getting up from the table.

M'iko made a move to stop him, but T'al intervened. "Let him go," he said.

Wil ignored their concern. He needed to clear his head, and the stale air of the pub made it hard to breathe. He drew the eye of more than one person as he marched back through the pub and out the front door.

Once outside, Wil took a deep breath, feeling the cool evening air filling his lungs. It was damp and chilly, but incredibly fresh compared to inside the tavern. All around him, the faint green glow of the City Center's force field reflected on the buildings within the Rings, and Wil wondered if the Ring's residents had ever known total darkness.

Now that he knew of the divide, he could clearly see where the Inner Ring ended and the Middle Ring began. An arch stood on the main road, just across the street. Four large guards stood in front of the gate, their arms thicker than his legs. The only large people Wil had ever seen outside of the Sphere had always appeared to be guarding something. *If you hold that sort of stature in a world filled with the malnourished,* he supposed, *you're going to be sought out and offered positions. And if you were apt to make a fair wage, you wouldn't refuse.*

The buildings within the Inner Ring stood in stark contrast to the Middle. While the buildings of the Middle Ring appeared to be ancient brick or cobbled together from previous structures, the Inner Ring appeared to be more recently constructed. There were some remnants of the ancients, but most of these were hidden from view among more sleek white concrete construction. Some stood six or seven stories high, while nothing in the Middle Ring appeared to be more than two or three.

"I hear you like killing bots," a haggard voice said from the darkness.

Wil turned to its source. The man before him couldn't have been much older than Wil, and he sported a thin moustache, spiked hair, and a ring pierced through his left nostril.

"I might have an offer you'd be interested in."

11

"I DOUBT THAT," Wil answered. "I'm doing all right as I am."

The man was short, spindly, and wore a suit that appeared to be too big for him; its sleeves hung over his arms and the shoulders didn't sit where they should have, like he was wearing clothes that didn't belong to him. Wil wasn't interested in hearing a sales pitch or interacting with anyone; all he wanted was to be left alone.

"You haven't heard what I have to say yet," the man persisted. Street lanterns cast long shadows across the man's face. His eyes were sunken, like he had seen tough times, but he dressed as though he were trying to prove otherwise. On account of the suit being so ill-fitting, he had to push up his sleeves several times during the first thirty seconds of their encounter. His hair was spiked, presumably in an attempt to hide that it was thinning, more than it should have been for someone of his age.

"I have no interest in buying whatever it is you're selling. I'm just passing through."

The man snickered at the comment. "Choose your words carefully. You let on that you know little of the place you're in. Nobody 'passes through' the Inner Ring. Especially when they travel with Elizabeth Runar of the Resistance."

Elizabeth Runar. Wil paused as the weight of Liz's full name sunk in, driving home her link with Sierra. It hadn't dawned on him until now that he had never heard anyone say Liz's last name, which Wil found surprising. He knew Liz had built a reputation for herself on the Outside. Ella and others in the Community had warned him that she had a reputation to be wary of, and it seemed that it extended further than he had realized.

The man had an odd way of blinking, rapid and not always with both eyes at the same time, as though he had something in them he couldn't quite seem to dislodge. He also seemed to be in a permanent squint, which added to the effect.

The man took a small card from the breast pocket of his jacket and handed it to Wil. Wil grabbed it instinctively before realizing that maybe he shouldn't have; he didn't want to be indebted to a stranger for taking something of value. The card was a small green rectangle, made from hard plastic, that had the look of something Wil recognized as a computer shard. Text, and what appeared to be a crudely drawn map, had been scrawled onto its surface.

"I'm not here to sell you anything," the man said, rolling his eyes and pointing to the card. "If you're interested in fighting bots, this is the place you want to be. It'll get you and one of your friends in."

Wil raised an eyebrow, looking at the card. The map showed the Rings of the city, with a big "X" sitting to the south of the edge of the Outer Ring. Wil didn't know the area, but he could tell one thing: that mark wasn't in the SZ.

The character before him didn't exactly give off a reputable vibe, and heading outside of the SZ felt like he was being baited into a trap.

"What is this place?" he asked, curious enough, at least, to find out what he was being offered.

"A place where people who hate bots like to meet and take out their frustrations. Don't tell anyone who's going to short circuit easily, either. Take someone who's as upset about the bots as you are, and you'll do just fine. If you want to take out your frustrations, this is the best place around. The Resistance is all talk and no action. Trust me; they don't fight bots if they don't have to."

Wil stood still, staring at the card.

What the man was saying wasn't wrong. Liz seemed a lot more hesitant to fight the bots than what he had been led to believe. Before he had left Vegas, Ella and Malachi had made it seem like revenge was all the Resistance cared about, taking down the bots at all costs. Fighting bots was what he had accompanied them to do. However, during their trip, Liz and the others had seemed much more reserved about their methods than he had imagined. Scolding him for rescuing Sara and Dagger, for example. Though the girl had died at the hand of the Prowlers, Dagger sat inside with the others, alive because of *his* efforts. Cali had been injured, but she was alive. It seemed there was no guarantees of staying alive in this world, regardless of whether you took on the bots or not.

"Who are you? And why are you telling me this?" Wil asked. "I have nothing to offer."

"Everyone calls me Fry. Let them know I sent you. I have a knack for spotting talent like you. With a nickname like 'bot killer', you'll fit right in. I'll tell the doorman to expect you. Oh, and one more thing, kid. Don't tell those women you're with, especially not Elizabeth Runar. Their methods are not as . . . *enjoyable*."

Wil smirked. Fry seemed to be about as unreliable a man as any Wil had met, but he could relate to his assessment of Liz. He could already hear Ella chirping in his ear about not going anywhere near this man. Something else told Wil he shouldn't consider it, either, but Fry had piqued his curiosity, and there'd be no harm in taking a look.

"So, I can only take one other person with me?" he asked. "What is this? A private club?"

"Precisely," the man said, continuing to blink awkwardly.

Wil ran his fingers along the edges of the hard plastic card and tapped it along the palm of his hand. "All right. Thank you. I'll think about it."

"Don't think for too long," Fry replied. "There's a meeting tonight, but who knows when the next one might be."

Without another word, Fry turned and walked down a side street into the shadows.

Wil studied the map. They had walked for hours through the Outer Ring, coming down from its northern edge. The southern border of the SZ did not appear to be too far from where he stood.

If this group was truly interested in killing bots, perhaps it was something he should at least check out.

WIL RETURNED to the pub just as Liz had finished meeting whoever had been behind the blue curtain. The group exited through the back and crossed an alleyway to a second brick building. Nothing about it stood out from the many others lining the streets of the Middle Ring. A small green door was its only entrance, and Liz waved them inside.

The door led into what appeared to be a common space, a large room which opened up to a mezzanine on the second floor. A staircase on a sidewall led to the main balcony at the back of the room. The space could easily have fit a couple dozen people.

The interior space was limited, and not much more elaborate than the building's exterior. The brick was the same rough red, and someone had decorated the walls sporadically with tapestries and a few paintings. Several tables, couches, and armchairs filled the room.

While there didn't appear to be anyone around, a fire awaited them, pre-lit as if the group had been expected. The smell of cinnamon and spice told Wil someone had also put a pot of tea on.

Wil had a close look at the paintings hanging on the walls. Many of them depicted a Guardian attack on a city, and with the ocean prominent in many of them, he could only guess it had been ancient San Francisco. Onyx flew through the sky, firing on ancient structures, as people ran for cover.

Three words had been painted in curving script on the brick above the fireplace.

Be Ever Free.

"We'll be here for a few days," Liz said. "T'al and M'iko, show Wil, Dagger, and Ella around. We've been calling in our reserves, so the safe house is quite busy right now. You'll be sharing rooms, but at least you'll each have your own bed. Get some rest. We have work to do, starting tomorrow."

"Absolutely not!" T'al said.

Despite the cooler evening temperature, sweat marked the armpits of the larger man's shirt.

"I just want to see what this is about," Wil said. "I don't want to go by myself, but I will."

"You have no idea who this man is or what could be there. It could be a trap, for all you know."

"That's why I want you to come with me," Wil replied. "Look, ever since I left the Sphere, the only thing I've wanted is to help fight the bots. Humanity deserves to be free of them."

T'al looked unconvinced.

"I followed the Resistance here because I believed they were the answer. But so far, Liz hasn't shown me she's too interested in taking the fight to the bots."

"You'd be wise to watch who's around when you bad-mouth Liz," T'al replied.

"I'm not asking you to leave the Resistance, T'al," Wil said. "And I'm not saying I don't want to join. I just want to check these people out; explore my options."

T'al rolled his eyes and shook his head.

"Anyone telling you they're going around fighting bots who isn't part of the Resistance are just vigilantes. Their anger makes them impulsive, and there's only one way that will end—with you dying." T'al prodded the end of his thick finger into Wil's chest. "I'm not interested, and I suggest you stick around here, too. As far as I'm concerned, it's fine to be motivated by revenge, but you can put it to better use than getting yourself killed."

Wil rubbed the spot T'al had poked. The guy didn't realize his own strength. As he massaged his sternum, Wil knew he wasn't going to win T'al over. He didn't really want to venture out on his own, especially this late at night, but the card in his pocket burned hot with anticipation and unspoken promises.

He resolved to wait until T'al had fallen asleep—there was no point in risking an argument and causing a scene. If Ella got wind of his plan, she'd likely tie him up to prevent him from leaving.

T'al snuffed out the lanterns before retiring to bed. Wil slipped into his bed fully clothed when his companion's back was turned, sure he didn't notice in the dark room.

It was mere moments before the man was snoring. It had a been a tiring few days with little sleep for all of them, and Wil had to fight himself to remain awake.

He waited a few minutes, until he was sure T'al was indeed asleep. He got up, ensured his daggers were attached to his belt, and slipped out the door to the common area.

The cinnamon smell still lingered in the air as Wil crept down the stairs as carefully as he could. He didn't want to make a noise and potentially disturb any of the others who would, hopefully by now, be sound asleep in the other rooms.

He slipped out of the building without incident and into the alleyway.

The alley itself wasn't well lit; only the residual light from the street lanterns reached him. The moon, however, was full, which would provide more illumination than he would need.

He reached for the card. The path from him to the "X" on the map appeared to be a straight line. He would be there and back before the others had time to wake.

"You're a special kind of idiot, aren't you?" T'al's voice startled Wil from behind.

Wil hunched his shoulders. Had T'al been faking slumber? Or was he a light sleeper?

Wil turned to face him with a feigned sheepish look. He stammered, unsure of what he could say to redeem himself or if he even had to.

"Well, if you're determined on getting yourself killed," T'al continued, "I'd better come along to keep your scrawny butt alive. I've already let one friend down today. I'm not going to stand by and lose you as well." A touch of sadness marked T'al's eyes at the hint of Voth's disappearance.

"You're not going to try to stop me?" Wil asked.

"You've made it clear you're not going to listen to reason. And I'd rather not have to deal with Liz's wrath if you disappeared."

Wil eyed the man suspiciously until T'al added with a smirk, "Besides, I can't let you have all the fun."

Wil relaxed his stance and returned T'al's grin.

"Where is this place, anyway?" T'al said. "Even with two of us, walking through the city at night isn't my first choice, and I would love to get some sleep tonight."

Wil reluctantly showed his friend the map.

"Bloody bots," T'al griped. "This is outside the SZ."

"I know." Wil nodded. "Can you think of why they would meet there?"

"Only if they wanted to use tech," T'al said. "But I don't like it. This whole thing smells."

"Let's at least have a look," Wil said. "Come on, it's not that far."

The two ventured south, back through the districts. The Middle Ring wasn't difficult to navigate, as they kept to the primary route. Lanterns lit the street as people meandered in and out of pubs that seemed to inhabit an ill-proportioned volume of real estate for the area they were traveling through.

"Why are there so many pubs here?" Wil said. There were dozens of them. They only had one back in the North Village, and even in Vegas, he couldn't think of any other than the Rio Grande.

"This is one of the major routes of the Western Shore," T'al replied. "This road sees a high volume of traffic, as it passes through the SZ and to the south, all the way to South Angeles and into the wasteland of the southeast."

They crossed under an arch that led to the Outer Ring. A bridge Wil didn't remember appeared to connect the two districts, and two guards stood on either side, though what they were policing Wil couldn't determine. Banners hung from large slabs above them; gray and yellow with a large red bird in their center. Lanterns lined either side of the bridge until it connected with a similar gateway on the other side. In stark contrast to the lit path, a wall of darkness marked the boundary of the Middle Ring.

"I got the impression there wasn't a lot of travel," Wil reflected. "The road we came in on was bustling with skeletons."

"The road east is nearly deserted," T'al said. "The Outer Ring is nearly empty in that direction, and the Interzone between here and Vegas is far too wide an expanse for meaningful trade. Only the most desperate are willing to make the journey. But there is a long line of Silent Zones if you can stand the long trip south. Life is still hard for folks there, but those in the City Center make trade worthwhile."

"Is the City Center that well off?" Wil asked.

T'al chuckled. "Look at it this way: they don't have the giant force field for nothing. If we survive tonight, I believe we might get the chance to have a look inside."

Almost as if he wasn't thinking about what he was doing, T'al turned back to admire the tall green pillar lightly glowing behind them.

"You've never been inside?" Wil asked, astonished at the revelation.

T'al shook his head.

"Why not?"

"They don't let just anyone in; there are very strict rules about those who can come and go. Liz had to get special permission for a few of us to go inside."

"Oh," Wil said, seeing his opportunity to explore the Center fading. "I guess I won't be invited along." Other than Dagger, he was pretty sure he'd be the last person Liz would take with her to somewhere exclusive.

T'al let out a belly laugh, loud enough that they got irritated looks from the few passersby sharing the bridge with them.

"*You're* the whole reason we're going in, idiot." He laughed. "Liz sought special permission just for you and Ella. M'iko and I were an afterthought."

Wil furrowed his brow. "Why?"

"You are the bot killer, after all."

"I seem to be attracting a lot of notice with that nickname," Wil said. "Aren't we in the middle of the Silent Zone? Are they attacked by bots often here?"

"Not since the wars," T'al answered. "But having you around will make it look like the Director's doing something useful."

"So, he wants to use me in order to look good?" Wil asked.

"I dunno. But the Director does nothing if he doesn't stand to benefit."

The sentiment didn't sit well with Wil. Heading toward the outskirts of the city to check out this meeting place with Fry was sounding more appealing by the minute. Wil had come out west to kill bots, and killing bots was what he intended to do. If all Liz wanted to was play political games with his powers, he might as well see what others might do with them, too.

"Liz told him about me?" Wil fumed. He wondered how much Ella knew. He guessed not much, as she had warned him to exercise caution when it came to making himself stand out. The last thing he wanted was a target on his back. He looked warily at those who passed by, but nobody was giving them a second glance.

"Liz has her reasons for doing things, and they are often her own. She rarely goes about the most direct way of accomplishing her objectives."

The two had reached the end of the bridge. If it weren't for the full moon, the edge of the Middle Ring would have been cloaked in near complete darkness.

Small fires illuminated the faces of families huddled around them. The atmosphere was heavier, despite the smiles that met them. The type of structures lining the streets steadily shifted from being finely constructed of brick and wood into makeshift homes that were crudely constructed from debris that had been collected.

The traffic along the road also lessened, but Wil couldn't tell if it was because people were more hesitant to venture to this part of the city at night or because there were fewer pubs. Those who huddled around the small fires appeared to be entertaining themselves, chatting and discussing things Wil was unable to decipher through the chatter.

Wil could feel his jaw clenching as he eyed those in the area. The poorly constructed dwellings appeared as if they were about to fall over. Perhaps he had made a mistake in venturing this far out late in the evening. He carried his daggers, but they would likely do him no good if a large group swarmed him. The chill in the air deepened, and he rubbed his arms for warmth.

"You can relax," T'al said. "The folks here won't bother you."

"What do you mean? I thought the people here were desperate."

"They are, but most of them are still good people. They may be poor, but they'll treat you better than most. Remember, these are the people we're striving to protect. These people may dream of more, but they need people around them to look after them. It's the bandits and Prowlers you have to watch out for, and they won't bother us on the main road. Not tonight."

Courtesy of the Sphere, Wil had grown up in a world where everyone was taken care of; where they were all treated more or less the same. He had a hard time imagining what life would be like in a home made of repurposed materials, though he would gladly live in a tent for the rest of his life if Marco was there as well. He'd even go a little hungry if he had to.

"If we can defeat the bots, we could improve the lives of these people," Wil said, more a statement than a question.

"Perhaps," T'al replied. "Though humans haven't done a much better job of helping each other, either."

The faces became a little sadder around the fires the further out they went, until the homes slowly became more and more isolated and then abruptly ended.

After that, dwellings popped up again, but they were much more spread out among the fields. Wil recognized they were now in the growing district of the SZ. They had left the city proper.

"We had to travel for hours to get through the farms earlier," he thought aloud. "How are we so close to the edge of the SZ?"

"We came from the North, through the Outlands. The districts circle the City Center, hence why they're called the Rings. This is the Outer Ring. The Outlands here, on the south side, are almost nonexistent. We'll be leaving the SZ soon."

No sooner had T'al said the words than a small settlement appeared in the distance, off to the side of their path. Small torches lit the buildings spreading out into the fields. It appeared to be a fair distance from the main path, but Wil knew this was the area they were looking for.

A dirt trail meandered off the highway and into the rugged terrain. If it weren't for the lights and the sounds of people laughing and cheering, the buildings would have easily been missed.

T'al looked to the sky warily as Wil charged ahead.

It didn't take long for them to reach their destination. A couple dozen wooden buildings had been constructed, complete with a quaint town square and marketplace. There was at least one pub and a few other buildings that appeared open for business, even at such a late hour.

Dozens of people walked the side streets among the buildings, dressed as though they had come from the Inner Ring, and some of which were even fancier. Many wore similar suits to the one Fry had worn. Many women wore more elaborate outfits, decorated with feathers, streamers, sequins, and jewellery, all in a mismatch of colors.

"Something about this isn't right," T'al said. "I have never come across this place. These people are from the City Center. I have never seen so many outside of the SZ."

"Everyone here appears to be quite well off," Wil said. "It looks like the perfect group to organize a fight against the bots."

"No. Quite the opposite," T'al said. But before he had a chance to explain, the sound of a crowd cheering erupted into the night.

A gigantic building in the center of the small village dwarfed everything else around it. The cheers came from within, and those who remained in the streets were pouring inside.

In that moment, Wil knew he had found what he had been looking for.

12

WIL TOOK two eager steps toward the building, overflowing with patrons. If there were this many people interested in taking on the bots, he had surely come to the right place. His mind raced with the possibilities. Why hadn't the Resistance worked with them?

T'al's large hand grabbed Wil's arm, holding him back. Wil whipped around to see what his companion wanted, and his enthusiasm waned. T'al's eyes were hard, his lips pursed. He had no intention of moving.

"We need to head back," T'al said.

"Head back? We just got here."

Wil shrugged off T'al's grip and pushed his way forward. The number of those crowded against the building was staggering. Wil hadn't seen anything like it. Hundreds of people milled about, many wearing suits and dresses, others in what appeared to be a mismatch of styles, leather vests and pants mixed with silk shirts and top hats. Some women wore feathers, and others wore slim-fitting outfits covered in belts, buckles, and buttons. Men wore monocles, a variety of hats, and cloaks of all colors. Many faces were lavishly decorated, some with light makeup accented with bright red lips, dark eyeliner, and bright teal and rose coloring on their eyelids. Others had lines and designs etched into their skin, luminous in a similar way to how Oculus's scar had been.

Many also carried what looked like pistols from the time of the ancients. Ella had told him such weapons had all but disappeared after the wars, rendered useless after the required ammunition had been depleted or lost. Their presence, Wil presumed, was likely purely decorative.

Still, the ones he could see, tucked into holsters and belts, had an impressive look about them.

The building itself was circular in shape, its size indicating it would likely hold several hundred people, and, judging by those who were gathered outside, he wasn't surprised. As they got closer, the sound of music steadily increased from within, until it was loud enough to be nearly all that could be heard.

Wil marveled at the surrounding spectacle. How could there be so many of them, yet they had slipped under T'al's radar? Those around him weren't the despondent who they had passed on the way through the Rings. These folks were affluent, which meant they would have the funds to back an uprising. Wil couldn't hold back the smile lighting his face.

Men and women dressed in uniform toured the grounds as well, most equipped with large, double-handed blasters, and looked ready to strike at any moment. Their presence drilled home that they were truly outside of the SZ. Wil glanced to the sky quickly out of pure reflex, but with the lights from the assembly shining so brightly, he couldn't see anything at all.

He was so enamored by it all, he had all but tuned out T'al's droning behind him.

"I'm telling you, Wil—this isn't what you think it is," T'al said, pushing through the crowd to keep up with him.

"Let's just get a look inside. I've never seen anything like this before."

"I don't think they're going to let us in, Wil. We shouldn't be here."

Wil shook his head in disbelief that T'al wasn't as amazed as he was. Everything about the place was incredible. He was sure even Ella would be impressed.

The smell of food wafted past him, and not the sickly stench of cabbage or fried rodent, either. He couldn't place the aroma, but whatever it was smelled sweet. It reminded him of a chocolate torte dessert served in the Sphere; something drizzled with caramel. As he thought of it, Wil's mouth began to water. He had yet to have a dessert since he'd left his old life behind.

There was a narrow opening in the crowd, in front of the building's entrance. There was no door he could see; just a mammoth opening in the wall. The odd person wandered in or out, without more than a passing glance from six armed guards who stood on either side of the entryway.

Three men and three women stood fully alert, monitoring the crowd as if expecting each and every one of them to create a disturbance.

Wil was about to walk around them when the woman closest to him raised a hand to stop him, her other hand resting on a blaster. She wasn't going to leave anything to chance. Her uniform was the same as the others: a blue-tinted green suit with a matching hat. A ponytail of blonde hair fell from behind her hat, and her piercing blue eyes told Wil he wasn't going anywhere.

"Sorry," she said. "City Center residents only. You have no business here." Her fingers danced on the hilt of her weapon. It wasn't a nervous twitch, but she was readying herself for Wil to do something stupid.

"We were invited," he said, holding up the green card. "A man named Fry told us to come."

A smirk crossed the face of the guard, as if she were in on some joke he wasn't privy to.

The smile quickly faded as she regained her stately composure. "You want the side entrance," she said. "Head around the back of the stadium, and you'll find a small orange door ajar. Give that card to the men at the table inside."

"Thank you," Wil replied.

"Good luck," she said. The corners of her mouth lifted, but only slightly.

Wil tucked the card back into his jacket and followed the wall of the stadium around the corner, as the guard had suggested. He only briefly noted T'al's confused look, and part of him now wished his friend hadn't come. The man was dampening Wil's mood, and he had no idea why. The energy of the crowd was enough to send chills of anticipation through his bones. He had never been to any sort of festivity with this many people in attendance. He questioned if there were more people here than had been present at the Battle for Vegas.

"Look," Wil said. "Don't worry so much. Look at all these people." He nodded to those milling about the grounds. "They all look like they're having the time of their lives."

"That's what I'm trying to tell you, Wil. Most of these people are from the City Center, but some are from the Higher Inner City. Look at their dress. This is not going to be a band of people looking to take on the bots."

"Just one look inside, my friend. If what you say is true, we leave, no harm done." He turned before T'al could respond and caught the tail end of his mutterings. Something about Wil being stubborn.

The stadium—as the woman at the gate had called it—rose several stories high. Towering over them, it was easily the largest structure Wil had ever come across, either inside or outside the Sphere. Someone had constructed it hastily; unlike some of the structures built by the ancients he had seen, built of solid metal and concrete, this structure was made of wood and had edges that didn't quite fit together. Despite these imperfections, it was obvious the construction had been no simple task.

Wil wondered what purpose building the stadium outside the SZ served, and why this was the chosen place for such a spectrum of people to meet. While on the road, he had quickly learned Ella and a few members of the Resistance instinctively knew where the border of the SZ rested. Wil could never tell the difference, but here it was made apparent so none could have doubts. A single line of electric lamps ran from the stadium gate to the tiny village that rested a few hundred yards away, and perhaps beyond. There were five that were lit, but the rest were dim. A row of oil lanterns ran adjacent to them, so there was no doubt where each of the lights should be.

From inside the stadium, the volume of the music increased, as did the noise from the crowd. Those meandering around the shops surrounding the arena made their way to the main entrance. Wil scanned the wall of the stadium and could make out the orange entrance the guard had mentioned.

He could hear T'al cursing behind him, but the surrounding cacophony drowned out anything else the man was saying.

Not wanting to miss out on whatever was happening, Wil picked up his pace. The chill of the evening slapped his skin as he closed the gap to the door.

The side entrance was not as grand as the main one, and it had no other guests using it. Perhaps Fry had granted them special access. Or was this for newcomers? He had so many questions, but he knew that only once he was inside would they all be answered.

Just as the guard had said, the doorway was only partially open. Wil grabbed the solid wooden door, peering inside before stepping through it. T'al was close behind, his face twisted in a scowl.

They entered a small room painted orange, with two larger doors at the opposite end leading into the facility. There were six guards in the room. Each stood at attention, even though Wil doubted anything could surprise them within such a small space. Two appeared beside them as they entered, one on either side of the door. They wore the same blue-green uniforms as those outside.

In front of the second set of doors was a small table with two people behind it; a short, stout woman and a bald, aging man with a thick white mustache. Both wore a haggard expression, as though they had been standing behind the table for hours and would rather be anywhere else.

"Can we help you, young man?" the woman asked. Her dark purple hair was cut short, slicked back in a way that reminded Wil of Fry but with its own unique flair. She wore a gray suit that clung to her aging curves, purple accents highlighting its breast. A bright pink shirt she wore underneath peaked through the buttonholes of the jacket. Her outfit, covered in sequins, casually reflected the electronic lighting that lit their small space.

The man was a couple inches shorter than Wil, but had a larger presence. His hair had lost its color years ago, and his eyes were pale, too. Wil would have described them as hollow, searching for purpose.

Wil fought his nerves as he fumbled for the card Fry had given him. His hand shook as he held it out. He didn't know why he was suddenly nervous. Perhaps it was the presence of the guards.

"A man named Fry gave me this and told me to come here. I was told this was where I should go if I wanted to help kill bots."

"Oh, you're in the right place, all right. What are your names? Do you have nicknames or anything else you go by?"

"I think there's been a mistake," T'al said. His eyes danced around the room as though he expected specters to jump out of the shadows and attack them both.

Wil furrowed his brow and exchanged a bitter look with his friend. "No mistake," he said. "My name is Wil. They call me the Bot Killer."

"How original," the woman said. Her bored expression didn't change as she made a note on the datapad she held. "And you, big man?" She looked at T'al.

"His name is T'al."

"Better than 'bot killer', I suppose," she said, rolling her eyes.

"What about the kid? This card was to register a team of two. We don't allow groups of three. You'll have to split up. One of you will have to fight solo."

Group of three? Both he and T'al turned around simultaneously.

Behind them, wide-eyed and wringing his hands, stood Dagger. Nearly a foot shorter than Wil, he was still a hair taller than the older man at the table. The way the light in the room highlighted the hollows in his cheeks made him look sickly. At first, Wil thought Dagger was scared, but he instantly realized his error.

He was determined.

"I'll go alone," Dagger said. His palms flinched around the sides of his hips. The kid had hidden a weapon. He was spoiling for a fight.

Wil thought of Dagger as a kid, but, even though he was much smaller than Wil, he was only a few years younger. And he had likely seen far more hardship than Wil could ever imagine. With the loss of his sister, it was no wonder he, too, wanted to fight.

"Very well. Guards, escort them to their positions."

"Wait!" T'al exclaimed, his eyes suddenly wide in panic. He took two steps toward the table before two guards blocked his path. "What is this? What are we in teams for?"

Wil had no inkling about what they had signed up for, but he knew Dagger would not win any sort of fight on his own—not unless these people were willing to provide him with significant training and a proper diet. And with the moneyed look of those who lingered outside, it wasn't beyond the realm of possibilities that they might do just that.

"As your friend indicated," the woman said, responding to T'al, "you're here to fight bots. You two will fight alongside one another. The kid there will fight on his own."

"Let me join the kid," T'al said, flashing Wil a dangerous look. "I'll fight with him instead."

Wil wasn't sure what was happening, but there was no mistaking the look in his friend's eye. T'al believed Dagger was in danger.

"I can go alone," Wil offered. T'al had deduced something he hadn't figured out yet, but the kid might be in trouble. Because of him. "These two should stick together."

"No," Dagger said. "I'm not afraid."

Both T'al and Wil looked at him incredulously. The kid had spunk. Dagger must have followed them from the safe house all the way out to the edge of the SZ. Wil hadn't been paying enough attention to have determined they were being followed, but it surprised him that T'al hadn't noticed.

"Idiot!" T'al yelled.

Wil nearly let out a laugh, but kept it in. It wouldn't help anything to antagonize either of them. Was Dagger being brave or stupid?

"Enough!" the mustached man declared. "The teams have been

decided. Take them to their cages. The matches will begin shortly. May the ancients keep you well."

Matches?

The six guards stepped forward, and two grabbed Wil underneath his arms. They didn't quite pick him up, but they certainly encouraged him to their intended destination and pulled him through the wooden door behind the desk.

The door opened a crack, revealing a slit of light. More impactful was the wave of noise that came crashing from whatever lay behind it. The roar of people overwhelmed them, nearly pushing them back with its force.

The room they were in wasn't exactly dark, but the light from behind the door made it feel as if they were exiting a cave. White spotlights landed on Wil as they shuffled him out the doorway.

His heart raced as his eyes attempted to adjust. What had he signed them up for?

It took a few moments, but he finally figured out the noise was coming from the crowd of people who had now filed into the expanse that opened before him.

Wil had only ever read about events that had taken place in humanity's past, where thousands of spectators would look upon some sporting event, cheering for their favorite competitor. It appeared he now had a front row seat to such an event.

Dozens of thoughts raced through his head as his eyes adjusted to the blinding light. Squinting, he could still make out the hundreds of people who filled the stands. Was this where he would learn the goal of this group? Were all of these people part of taking down the bots? Or were they benefactors of some kind?

To the baying of the crowd, Wil Underwood finally realized he had been very wrong. These people weren't benefactors.

He should have listened to T'al.

It wasn't until Wil's escort shoved them into a cage that he grasped the tragic mistake he had made.

13

THE DOOR to the small cell slammed shut behind them. The guards threw Dagger into a duplicate cell to their left. On the other side of Dagger, a third cell contained a man even larger than T'al. He appeared to be twice their age and so bald his head reflected the light from the stadium.

In a fourth cell, directly to their right, sat a woman in the shadows. Unlike their cell, she had a bench where she could rest. Her features were mostly hidden, by virtue of the stadium spotlights avoiding her. Her frame was muscular, and a golden headband rested in her short, spiked hair. Wil would have said the outfit she wore was a costume, but with the attire of everyone else in the stands, it was hard for him to tell. The red bodice clung to the woman's body and was complimented by a tight red skirt. Brown knee-high boots completed the outfit.

"What's going on?" Wil asked T'al, still surveying the crowd in the auditorium. There were two levels of stands, all roaring with fans. Their cheers were so loud, they rumbled through him, as though the entire stadium was shaking with their excitement.

Dead bodies were being dragged across the stadium floor by what appeared to be a couple of maintenance robots. Wil could tell the bodies were of two young women, possibly the same age as himself. They both had dark brown hair. One wore a white dress, while the other wore a short black one with knee-high stockings. The white dress sported a red spot on its front, which was growing. The other woman had a hole burned through her middle.

"You wanted to fight bots," T'al said, his breathing heavy as his eyes darted around the arena. "Be careful what you wish for."

"What do you mean? What is this place?"

Before T'al could answer, a loud voice thundered throughout the stadium. *"That didn't go so well for Alice and Suzi, did it?"*

The crowd in the stands erupted in boos and cackles as the voice boomed around them.

"Bots," T'al cursed.

The floor cleared quickly. Men came from either side of their cages and slid open the door to the cage of the giant.

The man lifted his arms as he exited. His head bore a black tattooed pattern that swirled on the back of his skull before forming a single line that wrapped around his forehead. His face was wide, his nose flat and square like the rest of him.

The man picked up an ax, larger than any Wil had ever seen. The blade was as big as Dagger, and even with the man's muscular frame, it appeared as though it was an effort for even him to lift it.

The crowd cheered at the man's showmanship, their volume deafening, and Wil had to consciously refrain from covering his ears.

"Now entering the arena"—the voice echoed above the noise. The cheers died down slightly, but only enough for Wil to make out the man's words—*"you're in for a treat, ladies and gentlemen. Hailing all the way from Phoenix, Cahal the Annihilator!"*

The crowd erupted. Wil's jaw dropped as he surveyed those who now stood from their seats. Men and women who had given him such hope moments ago, sporting ridiculous hats, belted vests, and embellished robes, now stomped on the wooden floor, only amplifying the noise.

Cahal, in the meantime, spun around where he stood, his arms still in the air, encouraging the crowd.

Sand. What kind of madness have I got us into?

The noise subsided once again as the announcer continued. *"Cahal has defeated bots in the Phoenix arena fourteen times! He has one of the longest undefeated streaks in over a decade! And now he has decided to test his mettle against the bots of San Francisco!"*

"What is . . ." Wil couldn't quite get the words out before being drowned out by the cheers of the crowd.

The door of another cage, twice the size of their own, slid open at the opposite end of the arena.

From within the cage, a monster appeared.

"As you know, folks," the unseen announcer continued, *"Goliath has yet to be defeated by one of our contenders. Will Cahal be the first to do so?"*

A couple of single cheers broke out, but overall the volume had quieted down substantially. All eyes rested on the metal beast that now pushed itself out from behind the bars and onto the floor, stepping into the center of the arena.

Goliath, as the announcer called it, was a bot, but it wasn't a design Wil had come across before. It had to be at least a dozen feet tall as it extended from the cramped cage. Its chest had been built like a metal wall, reminding Wil of a solid tank. Its head was a giant gray bulb, lit with deep-set yellow lights for eyes. A darker gray plate ran across its face, substituting for a mouth.

Unlike the clean, sleek, white-plated Sentinels Wil was familiar with, this bot appeared almost cobbled together. Pieces of the bot had obviously been replaced or repaired. Its original body comprised a cold gray titanium, aluminum, or some other metal compound. Someone had roughly soldered pieces of discolored textured alloy into the beast's frame. Its legs were as thick as Cahal himself.

Cahal's jaw opened as he beheld his adversary, his shoulders pushed back and his neck strained at the robotic behemoth walking toward him. Wil could feel the ground vibrating with every step Goliath took.

"What's going on?" Wil finally managed, his eyes not leaving the scene unfolding before them. He had pressed his face against the bars, and at his side, T'al was doing the same. T'al's frame filled most of the space in the cell, forcing Wil to push himself into the corner.

"It's a fight club," T'al said. "The audience has come here from the City Center. Whoever is running the show is charging money to watch people fight bots."

"They paid money?" Wil asked. "Fry gave me that pass for free."

T'al's sideways glance made Wil want to disappear into the corner of the cage completely.

"Have you really not pieced it together?"

He had; he just didn't want to admit it to himself.

Cahal had been busy bracing himself. He held his axe in front of him, as though hoping it would stop the monster from advancing. Wil had to give the man credit; despite obviously being outmatched, he held his stance. His chest heaved as he readied himself, but there was no sign of fear.

Goliath took two steps, closing the distance between itself and Cahal. The bot lifted a gargantuan hand and brought it down in a swing toward the man. Gasps from the crowd filled the arena as the man dove into a roll at the last moment, barely missing the metallic limb that swung for him. The robot's hand smacked the dirt of the arena floor, kicking up a huge bloom of dust.

Cahal lifted his ax above his head. He was just in range to strike the robot's foot, but before he could bring the weapon back down, Goliath had regained momentum and backhanded the man across his chest. Cahal sailed backward a dozen feet, losing his grip on the ax, which sent it crashing to the floor.

Cahal gained composure enough to drop to the ground before Goliath's next blow landed and somehow swung his massive frame around to kick at the back of one of the robot's legs.

The bot stumbled, only briefly before it gained its footing, but it was enough time for Cahal to grab his ax and take a good swing at the core of the beast.

The blade of the ax connected with the bot's solid frame in a reverberating thud of metal on metal. Wil swore he saw sparks fly from the connection.

The bot seemed to howl in fury, lunging for the man who had pierced its side.

Cahal stumbled, but only because his blade wouldn't break its hold on the beast. His face turned a deep purple, straining from the effort, but before he could make any progress, the mechanized colossus threw him across the arena.

Everything about how Goliath had acted until that point had led Wil to believe the bot was big, slow, and lumbering, but it crossed the distance between Cahal and itself in a flash.

The bot reached down, picked up a still-stunned Cahal, and tossed him against the boards that separated the fighters from the crowd with a tremendous crash.

Wood buckled and splintered from the impact and tore through the man. Cahal shook himself, placing a hand to his bald head. The roar of the crowd filled the stadium once again.

Are they cheering for the bot or for him?

Goliath was already pacing, calculating Cahal's next move.

Cahal pushed himself off the ground. Blood ran down his arms and back, having been scratched thoroughly by the wood he had demolished upon impact.

The man's body heaved with each breath, his chest lifting under the strain, as though he had suffered internal wounds as well.

But Cahal was not backing down.

The man grabbed a scrap of wood that had detached itself from the edge of the arena and lifted it above his head before charging full speed toward the bot.

Goliath didn't move. It stood with its bulbous yellow eyes fixed on Cahal and tilted its head. The bot lifted an arm, fist pointed toward the man, and fired a bolt of energy from its forearm.

The bulk of the man landed on the arena floor. The smoldering mound of charred flesh took one last heaving breath before releasing a cry and breathing no more.

As the crowd erupted into a roaring cheer, Wil turned his face and fought the urge to vomit.

His mind finally allowed him to accept their situation. Fry had recruited him to be a fighter in the arena.

They were going to have to fight Goliath.

Wil's heart sank, and his mind raced in a panic. He couldn't breathe as he tried to grasp the reality of what lay ahead. He had only grabbed a pair of daggers on his way out of his quarters—he had no blaster. Perhaps T'al had one, but against the cannon blast the bot had shot out of its arm, Wil suspected they were finished.

He swallowed, trying to survey the arena for any advantage they might use.

"And so it seems even the mighty Cahal is no match for San Francisco steel! Can anyone defeat the awesome Goliath?" The announcer's voice rang out once again through the loudspeaker, and the crowd quieted enough for his words to be audible. *"Well, perhaps we're about to find out? We have a special treat for you tonight, ladies and gentlemen." We have three more rounds of excitement lined up for your viewing pleasure! Can any of them overcome the arena's champion?"*

Three? Wil thought.

"Next up, the announcer called, *"from right here in San Francisco—he may be small, but they say he's feisty—it's Dagger!"*

Wil's heart caught in his chest. Every part of his being stopped.

The neighboring cage door slid open.

Wil gasped as Dagger stepped out of the cage. The youth was evidently putting on a brave face. He held his shoulders back, with his chest puffed out, but his breathing was visibly shaky, erasing the façade he was trying to portray.

One thing was for certain: he didn't stand a chance.

If the youth had known what he had been signing up for when he'd followed them into the stadium, Wil wouldn't have had to guess at his motive: revenge for his sister's death.

Wil tested the resolve of the cage door, rocking it violently.

"They're solid steel," T'al offered. "Electronically locked. We're not getting out of here until they want us to."

Wil looked on in horror. Dagger had his blades in his trembling hands, but the small knives would be about as effective against the titan before him as a pair of sandflies.

"What is the point of this? Why is this bot here?"

"Spectacle," T'al said. "There's some gambling involved, but it's mostly entertainment."

"People are being slaughtered by bots every day. How could anyone find this entertaining?"

Goliath was taking its time. The bot stood at the opposite end of the stadium, shuffling from one foot to the other, as if it was enjoying toying with its prey.

"These people are from the City Center. Most of them have never seen a Guardian before."

Never seen a Guardian before? How far removed has this place become from the rest of the world?

The catcalls of spectators taunted Dagger from the stands. He stood only a few feet from his cage's entrance, despite still holding his chest puffed out in feigned heroism. The twitch in his face made it apparent he was contemplating backing up into its protective confines.

That choice was taken from him as the door promptly slammed shut. There was only going to be one way out of this fight, and it would likely be through death.

And then we'll be next.

Cahal had at least been built as though he could have gotten a few hits on the massive robot—if the laser cannon hadn't struck him down first. Dagger, on the other hand, was a mouse locked in a box with a tiger.

Goliath's thick metal legs creaked as it walked slowly toward a shaking Dagger, the hissing of its rudimentary hydraulics marking each step.

The beast lunged. The heavy *thud* of each foot shook the ground as the machine ran full tilt. Though it was impossible, as the bot had nothing more than a solid metal plate for a mouth, Wil could have sworn it was smiling.

As Goliath overtook the youth, Dagger dove between its legs.

Goliath swung, missed its target, and tripped as its momentum continued. The bot launched into a somersault and landed perfectly on its feet, a couple of dozen feet from the boy.

Dagger's chest heaved, his eyes darting around the stadium in a silent plea for help.

Wil forced himself to breathe. T'al appeared to have no visual reaction to what was happening in the arena, but Wil was sure of what he was thinking; that it was Wil's fault for getting them involved in this disaster.

Dagger held his fists, as if he planned to cut the bot as it approached. Goliath lifted one foot and stamped it on the ground, then lifted the other and repeated the action, both legs bent in anticipation of another charge.

Then the alarm sounded.

14

GOLIATH FROZE IN PLACE. The bot's bulky head swung up and around, as if trying to determine the source of the noise. The audience didn't move. Some looked around anxiously, but most of their eyes were lit with delight. Clearly, they thought this was part of the show.

"What's happening?" Wil asked. He wasn't convinced; whatever this was, things had gone from bad to worse.

T'al shook his head. "We need to get out of here!" he shouted above the noise. He tested the walls of the cage, but unsurprisingly, they didn't budge. Wil tried his hand as well, pushing his entire weight into the cold frame. It was no use.

Those in the stands hadn't moved. Some wore worried looks, but most grinned, fanning themselves with paper fans, delighted at what the next part of the show might be.

Sparks exploded over their heads. It was only then that most of the audience realized this might not be part of the act. Grins turned to screams as wood and debris came raining down.

Dagger had managed to move to the arena wall and pushed his body against its edge.

"Dagger!" Wil yelled to the boy.

The youth glanced sideways at Wil but stood firm in his position.

"We need help getting out of here! Can you unlock the cage?"

Dagger didn't move. Perhaps he was too frightened, but Wil didn't think Dagger would let fear stop him.

A crash sounded at the far end of the arena as a hole ripped through the ceiling; a laser beam sliced through the structure and erupted on the dirt floor. The beam continued to cut its way through the wood and made its way to the stands. Spectators who had finally begun to flee scrambled to avoid the attack, climbing over each other and knocking down those too slow or too feeble to get out of the way. Those that didn't move fast enough were burned alive under the force of the firepower.

Smoke rose from the stands where the beam had struck wood, followed shortly by flames that only added to the chaos.

Through all this, all Wil could do was stand and watch, horrified at what was taking place. The crowd piled toward the main gate, pushing each other out of the way. Wil cringed as women and children were pushed down and trampled. Nobody stopped to help them; they simply stepped over them in order for those with more heft to push through.

The crowd streamed out for several minutes until there was a sudden shift in momentum and the crowd fell back into the stadium. The same people who had pushed others aside were now shoving to get back in. Pressure against the arena's outer wall caused the wall separating the arena from the stands to collapse, spilling fragments onto the floor around Dagger and Goliath.

What could possibly have sent them sprawling back inside?

Goliath, who had been motionless until this point, lifted a hand in the air and let out a metallic roar, as if it were indeed a giant metal beast. The crowd spilled out along the remaining edges of the arena, still screaming, as they attempted to avoid the now rampaging bot.

Goliath pushed forward toward the crowd of people who had invaded its space. The bot stepped through the crowd, kicking people out of its way as it moved toward the now open edge of the arena.

The ceiling above their heads creaked and groaned. The stress on the building was so loud, Wil could hear it over the screams of the crowd. A large chunk of ceiling crashed to the ground, kicking up clouds of dust as more debris rained into the arena.

Wil was getting dizzy trying to keep up with everything that was going on.

As the dust settled, people continued to stream deeper into the arena, attempting to get as far away from the entrance as they possibly could.

By this time, Goliath had made its way into the stands. The bot slapped at those trying to avoid it, tossing them across the room as if they were old trinkets. Wil thought it was strange that the bot didn't seem to be going after anyone in particular, merely bowling over those who stood in its way.

The hole in the ceiling gaped open to the stars.

And to the Guardians converging on the stadium.

Familiar orb-shaped bots flew overhead, the lights on their glassy surfaces spinning out of control. They were large and gray and firing beams of light at targets Wil couldn't see. Having blasted the hole in the ceiling, their attention was now fixed elsewhere.

Through the stadium gates marched a group of eight Sentinels. Their blasters fired swathes of light into the crowd as they entered. Those in their path scrambled desperately for safety, scrabbling around on top of one another with no thought for the survival of others. Just as many people were trampled by their peers as those being struck by the Guardians' fire.

Now that the Sentinels were inside the arena, many spectators rushed back toward the main gate, trampling each other as they clambered despairingly to clear the building. From the screams and noise Wil could hear from outside, there wasn't much more safety there, either.

Wil took no pleasure in watching those who had been eager to watch bots attacking people for sport now having to flee themselves.

There was only one way Wil knew of to stop the destruction that was going on around him.

He was going to have to use his ability.

He closed his eyes and leaned back against the cage wall. He searched within himself, desperate to ignite the warm sensation that always accompanied the burst of energy.

Wil's thoughts raced for a way to stimulate his dormant power. Sometimes it seemed eager to be unleashed, irrespective of whether Wil wanted it to or not, and other days, like right now, it was as though the ability had never existed.

That familiar warmth was absent. Whatever he had sparked in previous situations, he couldn't find so much as a trickle now.

Despair took over. He opened his eyes. The crowd had made their way to the front of the cells. Only the sealed cage doors separated Wil and T'al from the madness that had now pushed themselves against their prison. People with their buckled outfits, capes, hats, and multicolored hair stood in front of the cages. A sweet smell wafted from them, pungent perfumes as elaborate and unique in their scents as the appearance of those who wore them.

Wil had come to the arena at the word of a stranger he had met on the street, hoping to find warriors ready to take revenge on the bots. Instead, those here had no concept of the daily struggle the rest of the world faced. To them, fighting bots had been entertainment. Now, the people of the inner city were realizing how real the fight actually was.

Wil had pushed himself as far back in his cage as he could manage. T'al had crouched down, no longer paying Wil any mind.

Suddenly, Wil remembered Dagger, and he forced himself to the front of the cage, peering through the cage walls. There were so many bodies, both alive and dead. Those who hadn't trapped themselves in the wave of other spectators were still attempting to flee from the main entrance. Dagger was nowhere to be seen. Wil could only hope he had made it out among the chaos.

Wil realized he and T'al were likely in the safest place, at least for the moment, but he didn't feel like watching those in the arena die at the mercy of the bots.

Goliath was still running loose in the stands, but the behemoth had made its way to the gap in the wall the Guardian blast had carved out. The large bot seemed almost as intent to escape the arena as the people who scrambled out of its way.

Sparks flew against the outside of Wil's cage as blaster fire hit its frame. A burn mark in the corner smoldered, but it didn't appear as though any damage had been done to the cell itself. For the moment, they were safe from the attack, but it was unclear how long the cell would stand a sustained effort to blast through its wall—though it wouldn't matter if a stray Sentinel or orb blast made its way between the bars.

Another piece of the ceiling crashed onto the arena floor, flattening some who were trying to retreat from the Sentinels. Others continued to cry out as they dove out of the way.

The screaming was constant and no matter which way the crowd turned, a new obstacle threatened to kill. Between the destruction of the building, the horde of Sentinels, and the bodies lying in their wake, there wasn't enough space for people to get to the exits. Many were trying to climb walls to get back into the stands, but they quickly learned of the force field that had protected the audience from the show. Places where it had been struck by concentrated fire were now visible, revealing gaping holes, but there weren't enough of them that connected with where the walls ended.

"How did you two morons end up here?"

Wil whipped around at the familiar voice. Ella crouched in the hallway behind their cages, peering over her shoulder nervously.

"Ella!" he said. "How did you find us?"

She glanced tentatively at T'al, who had now stood and joined Wil at the back of the cage. His eyes were brighter, but he still said nothing.

"I went to your room to talk to you," she said. "And I discovered you were missing. You two leave a pretty obvious trail."

Wil wanted to reach through the cage to hug her. "Well, I'm glad for it," he said. "Can you get us out of here?"

"You should be happier I was the one to discover you'd gone and not Liz. If these bots don't scour you, she will. A robot fight club? What the hell were you thinking?"

"I didn't know what it was. I was told it would be a way for us to fight bots."

Ella rolled her eyes. "You're determined to get yourself and everyone around you killed, aren't you?"

Wil shrugged off the comment. There was no time for them to argue.

Ella bent over the controls of the cell door and punched some digits into the keypad. A monitor lit up beside the cell, filled with digits and numbers Wil recognized as code, but was unsure of the language. The cell hissed as the locks released and with a bit of effort, Ella turned a handle and pulled back the door of the cage. The hall behind them was empty. With no other access to these back chambers, it seemed the crowds hadn't made their way to them yet.

They were about to make a run for it, back down the hall, when a woman's voice called above the noise cascading from the arena behind them.

"Please! Let me out!"

15

WIL HAD NEARLY FORGOTTEN the woman in the adjacent cage. She had pressed her face against the grate mesh covering the back door of her cell, distorting her features.

"Please, don't let me die in here." Her accent was thick. Wil had never heard someone speak so melodiously.

With a grunt, T'al approached the cage and lifted the heavy metal bar sealing it.

"Thank you," the woman said. "T'al, isn't it?" Something in her eye sparkled as she spoke. Shorter than Wil by nearly a foot, she couldn't have stood much taller than five feet.

Now that she had stepped out of the shadows, Wil could see the woman was breathtaking. She appeared to be the same age as him, or possibly slightly younger. Her features were smooth, her red lips formed what seemed to be a permanent smile, and the flecks in her brown eyes danced in the light of the stadium. The outfit she wore was revealing and accentuated her features. The muscles on her arms and legs were well defined, and though it appeared she had covered them with makeup, scratches and bruises marked them. This wasn't her first fight.

The woman stretched out her limbs as she exited. Though she

looked capable of holding her own, Wil doubted she would have stood any more of a chance against Goliath than the rest of them.

"I'm Kayla."

"You already know myself and T'al, it seems," Wil replied. "This is Ella."

Ella rolled her eyes and turned her attention to Wil. "We don't have time for formalities. Where's Dagger?" she asked. "Did you pull him into this little adventure or did he follow you out here?"

Wil shook his head. "He followed us. He was called into the ring when this attack started and disappeared into the crowd. I can only hope he got out on his own."

Ella cursed under her breath. "Come on," she said. "We need to leave."

T'al gave Wil a knowing look and pointed for Wil to follow Ella to the side entrance they had come in through.

The group ducked instinctively as a blast hit the floor above them, sending dust and light debris down on top of them. Wil coughed as he inhaled the grit. Blaster fire lit the edge of the cages once again, sending sparks dancing all around them.

The cages appeared to have been built to withstand stray fire. Maybe they would have been the safest place to have waited out the attack after all.

Without warning, a giant wooden beam as wide as T'al came crashing down from the stands above. A metal coupling on the edge of its frame pierced the top of the cage he and T'al had been confined to.

Wil jumped at the noise, and his jaw dropped.

"We need to get out of this building, *now!*" Ella shouted.

The floor shook, nearly causing Wil to stumble, but he managed to keep his balance and follow Ella toward the back door. As they were about to turn down the hall and out of sight of the main arena, another large tremor caused Wil to grab onto the wall. He glanced behind him as he did so, in time to see a large section of the stands collapse, sending the dozens of people still clamoring over them crashing to the ground below. Immediately thereafter, another large chunk of the ceiling landed on top of the crowd.

The portion of the building that had fallen away was substantial enough to reveal the night sky and the handful of Orbs still firing upon their unseen targets.

Wil gained his footing once again and pushed on, T'al and Kayla close on his heels.

Ella stopped short as she pushed outside. Wil nearly collided with her, but stopped himself, grabbing her waist to slow down.

She sidestepped him and pushed him aside.

Was that intentionally aggressive? Wil thought. *Or was she making room for the others?*

She motioned for them to move into the shadows cast by the stadium.

Hundreds of men and women were running toward the city. Light from the full moon provided enough visibility to see them filling the road until they disappeared over a hillside. Beams from the orbs overhead fired into the crowd, scattering those trying to make their escape. Moonlight reflected off the glassy Guardians as they circled the area, targeting the higher concentration areas.

Flames licked the village that had stood several hundred yards away. Small groups of people stood staring at it, as if uncertain whether they should try to douse the blaze or make a run for it. Most of them looked to be joining the group on the run, but a resolute few were determined, scrambling for firefighting equipment.

"What's happening?" Wil asked.

"What do you think is happening, dumbass?" Ella shot back at him.

Wil was startled by her shortness.

"This building didn't go up overnight," he said, irritation marking his words. "Why are the bots choosing to attack now?"

Ella pointed to two rows of lights that stretched between the stadium and the village and beyond. Wil hadn't realized before just how far the row of torches stretched. When they'd arrived, only three electric lights had been lit, but now all of them were, as far as the eye could see.

"The SZ? It's fallen?" His eyes were wide as he surveyed the orbs circling above, firing into the crowd as they ran for their lives.

Ella shook her head. "No, but it's a large fluctuation. Those lights show how far the SZ reaches, a warning system, in case of a large shift in the border. A large swath dropped at once, and the bots just happened to be close by."

"This stadium has stood on the border for years," Kayla offered. "Minor fluctuations are a common occurrence, but I've never heard of one of this magnitude. A large group of people so suddenly exposed; it's no wonder we hit the bots' radar."

"Sand," Wil grumbled.

"We can't stay here," T'al said. "But we don't want to be part of that crowd, either."

"How far do we have to go?" Wil asked.

Ella shook her head. "Past that hillside, for sure. We won't know until we can see over that rise."

"What about Dagger?" Wil asked.

"Do you know where he went?" Ella said.

Wil looked back to the stadium. Screams still echoed from within its walls, accompanying those emanating from the crowd on the road. Smoke billowed from the second story above them. The entire building would likely be ablaze soon.

"Keep an eye out," she continued. "But he's more than likely already left—or he's dead. We'll never find him in this crowd. We just need to hope he's gotten out and will meet us back at the safe house."

Ella was right, but Wil hated leaving the kid behind. He sighed, breathing in the smoke that permeated the air.

Wil couldn't help but feel responsible for the boy. Dagger had joined their group because of his choices, then he'd followed Wil to this place. The kid had made the decision to fight on his own, and now who knew where he had ended up, or if he was even still alive.

T'al and Kayla leaned against the wall of the stadium. T'al's chest heaved. Kayla stared blankly into the distance, as if she was deciding not to see the surrounding devastation.

Wil detected a sweet aroma originating from Kayla's direction, like honey and lavender, mixed with leather.

"Looks like it's your call, *Bot Killer*," Kayla said. Her smile was radiant in the glow of the dancing flames which lit the village.

Ella crossed her arms with a grunt, but said nothing.

"I guess we head back, then," he replied. "Can we skirt around those lights? That way, we'll know we're headed in the right direction?"

Most of the escapees were heading down the main road back to the Outer Ring. A few appeared to be running into the open fields with little sense of direction. Their only intent appeared to be to get as far away from the bots as possible. Wil knew they would only be safe once they re-entered the SZ. The orbs which flew above the farms in the distance indicated that they might have farther to go than he would have liked.

Ella didn't respond. Something else had captured her attention.

Two children were walking among the legs of those trying to flee. Their panicked faces looked from one adult to another, appearing to look for their parents. They couldn't have been older than seven or eight years old.

Ella took two steps forward, intent on going after them, when T'al grabbed her hand, his massive palm nearly enveloping hers.

"There's nothing we can do for them," T'al said. "We need to go."

Ella nodded, but her eyes were moist. Wil pushed down his own urge to protect the children. There were hundreds, if not *thousands*, of people here needing protection. And this was just one small proportion of those in danger.

Wil probed within himself again, desperately hoping to spark his ability. He wished he could figure out its trigger; the catalyst that would erupt his inner being into a wave of destruction against the attackers.

He found nothing and instead glanced at his companions, who still watched the ensuing chaos, almost as if they were afraid to move. It had only been a few weeks since the Las Vegas SZ had fallen. Was this one about to go down as well? From what T'al had said, there were more to the south—what of those?

"Kayla, do you have somewhere to go?" he asked, realizing the woman was still sticking close to them. "Or are you coming with us?"

Kayla nodded absently. The glow from nearby flames bounced off her light skin, giving her an orange glow.

He assumed that meant she was joining them. Ella snorted, but Wil ignored her.

"All right, then. Come on." He nodded to T'al, and the two men made to leave.

Wil broke into a slow jog. He didn't want to attract attention, but at the same time, they couldn't afford to waste any time by being overly conscious about being spotted.

They hadn't gone much further than a few dozen paces when a rogue blaster bolt crashed behind them, striking the edge of the stadium. An enormous piece of the building landed where the four of them had stood not moments before, erupting into a ball of flame.

Wil blinked twice at the inferno now enveloping where they had just been.

T'al cursed quietly beside him. They were receiving more than their fair share of luck, and Wil worried it wouldn't be long before it finally ran out.

"*Whoa!*" Kayla said.

"Let's go!" Wil shouted, breaking into a run.

More blaster fire echoed into the night, targeting the mass of people on the road.

Wil and the others approached the rows of lights. They stood much taller than Wil had expected, reaching nearly three times his height.

Once on the trail and surrounded by the beacons, Wil pushed as hard as he could, glancing back only to ensure the others were keeping up. As he fought to keep his breathing in check, he remembered he had nothing to be concerned about; he was likely the weakest runner of them all.

T'al and Ella didn't appear to be breaking a sweat, keeping only slightly behind him with the effort of a light jog. Kayla was having slightly more difficulty, but it appeared to be more to do with her outfit than her athleticism. Her tight skirt restricted her stride, forcing her to take shorter, quick steps.

Further along the road, farmhouses ignited in flames. Farmers intent on protecting their property stood outside, some firing blasters wildly into the sky. Being a couple of miles into the SZ, Wil guessed some of them had never been used in anger before.

He watched one man pull the trigger on a blaster, only to have a small squirt of light come out that didn't reach anywhere near its intended target. A blast from the orb he was targeting landed on the farmhouse behind him, obliterating the man's wife and an aging gentleman who had been standing on the deck, looking on in horror.

Others stood on their property with swords or bows and arrows drawn. Upon seeing the ineffectiveness of their weapons, most ran. These farmers were not as intent on sticking to the road as those who had erupted from the stadium, and they took off through the fields. Some appeared to be attempting to free their livestock before pushing ahead themselves.

It took more time than Wil would have liked for them to reach the last few lit markers. Orbs hovered in the distance, but none seemed to be interested in them. There were only a few hundred paces between them and the last lit lamppost.

Feeling as though he might collapse, Wil wheezed between breaths. He slowed their pace slightly, forcing himself to remain on his feet. They weren't out of danger yet, but they were far enough away from the bulk of the chaos to allow themselves a reprieve. He had both run and walked enough over the course of the past few weeks to last him a lifetime. He was ready to find his bed and stay in it for as long as he was allowed. They had gotten far enough from the epicenter for the smoke to dissipate, the moon revealing itself once again.

Kayla nearly stopped completely, and the others slowed to encourage her onward.

"Let's go, Spandex!" Ella shouted.

Wil shot Ella a puzzled look that she promptly ignored. He circled back to Kayla. It was as though she wanted to linger until the last possible moment. They had merely a few dozen yards before they were once more within the safety of the SZ.

Focused on the chaos behind them, they completely missed the giant bot standing in their path.

16

WIL CURSED as he froze in place.

The bot that had pulverized Cahal in the ring stood several hundred yards from them. The moon dimly lit Goliath's bulky gray frame, its metal dull and grimy and far removed from the gloss of the Sentinels or the orbs still wreaking havoc in the distance.

"Stand back!" Ella cried, pulling her blaster from her belt. It whirred to life with a familiar hum as it charged.

The bot froze.

"No! Wait!" Kayla dove at Ella, jarring her arm and causing the blaster to fire wildly into the night sky.

"What is wrong with you?" Ella shouted, pushing back.

With Goliath momentarily forgotten, Ella wound her arm as if she were about to deck Kayla. Wil jumped to intervene, realizing the two women fighting wasn't going to help them.

The bot lifted an arm toward them.

"Look out!" he yelled, jumping at both women and bowling them over onto the ground.

Wil landed hard on his shoulder, both women falling on top of him in a tangle of freshly plowed dirt and sod. Stalks of whatever crop had been growing around them was ripped out by the impact and tangled around their limbs.

T'al was on the move toward Goliath, sword in hand, but he suddenly stopped short, perhaps remembering how the fight with Cahal had ended.

"Don't hurt it!" Kayla cried, fumbling in the loose sod to find her footing. She kicked dirt onto Ella as she pushed toward T'al.

Wil sat up, watching the girl move and place herself between T'al and the giant bot.

Is she trying to protect it?

Goliath still held an arm in front of its face. As Wil studied its actions, he realized it wasn't in the same attack stance as it had been previously. Now, its arm was raised more like a shield.

Wil stood and offered a hand to Ella, who ignored his gesture and pushed herself up.

"Please!" Kayla continued as Wil and Ella approached. "Please don't harm it. It won't hurt us."

"Won't hurt us?" Wil announced. "Did you see what that thing did to Cahal? It ripped his head clean off!"

Wil glanced at the machine, bracing himself for the worst, but the bot stood stationary and tilted its head, as if listening to the interaction between them.

"I know," she said. "But it's my bot."

"What do you mean? *Your* bot?" Wil asked. "You were locked in one of those cages next to us."

"The arena was designed to mess with its programming," Kayla answered. "Goliath is harmless outside of it."

"A bot that size? Harmless? It's obviously built for fighting," Wil said.

"It was," Kayla said, holding her hands in the air toward them. "I designed it."

"You did?" Wil asked incredulously. Her admission was the last thing he had expected, but the look in Kayla's eye told him she was telling the truth. "So, what then? You expect us to take it with us?"

Another fusillade of blaster fire behind them acted as a reminder

144 | HERMAN STEUERNAGEL

that they were still outside the Silent Zone. T'al looked anxiously toward safety, past the twelve-foot gargantuan robot standing in the way.

"Let it come; we'll be within the SZ soon anyway," T'al said. "But we can't say here arguing about it."

"I don't like it," Ella said. "We know nothing about her, and if the Guardians hadn't attacked first, that bot would have ripped Dagger to shreds without a second thought."

"I'll explain everything," Kayla said. "But not until we're within the Silent Zone."

Wil exchanged an uncertain look with Ella. He had seen what the machine was capable of. There was no reason for Kayla to lie to them, but the fact they had only just met her wasn't lost on him.

Wil fumbled for the daggers in his belt. He knew full well they would be of no use against Goliath, but he had nothing else to protect himself with. Once again, he desperately reached for some sign of the power he held, but he was still unable to summon its protective force.

Kayla confidently walked forward, her stride now bolder in light of the bot now accompanying her. Wil and Ella didn't move, but T'al eagerly followed Kayla and her impossible pet.

The hair on Wil's skin stood on end in the cool evening breeze. Part of him was beginning to question Kayla's rationality. How long had she been cooped up in that cage for? Then again, the bot appeared to be cooperating, but there was plenty of distance between the SZ and them for it to turn on them.

As Kayla reached the gray cobbled-together creature, it became apparent it wasn't going to hurt her. She reached up and placed a hand on the robot's thigh, and it squatted down so that she could rest a second on its face.

It might have been Wil's imagination, but Goliath's yellow bulbous eyes seemed to warm in color in response to Kayla's touch.

Wil hadn't realized how long he and Ella had stood frozen in disbelief until blaster fire struck a nearby farmhouse, convincing them to catch up to Kayla, T'al, and Goliath.

Only three lights remained lit before them, marking only a couple dozen yards to safety. Past that line, the Guardians would no longer be able to detect their presence.

"What's your plan from here? He can't come into the SZ," Ella insisted as they overtook the others. "And we have business in the City Center in the morning."

"I'm going to the City Center as well," Kayla said. "I'd like to stay with you this evening, if I can."

"Absolutely," Wil said.

"No way," Ella replied.

The two gave each other confused looks.

Wil stared uneasily at Goliath. Up close, he could tell the machine had been buffed by hand; marks from whatever tools had been used to finish its metal frame marred its surface. Bits of scrap metal had been attached to its gray exterior through crude welds and rivets. Someone had at least tried to find similar colored metal for most of them, but others looked as though they had been sourced from metal signs from an ancient era, like someone had used the closest thing they could find to patch a hole.

"What about the bot?" Wil asked. "It won't be able to pass through the Silent Zone."

Kayla gave Wil a knowing smile and walked to the back of Goliath's thigh. She opened a panel and tinkered with something on the inside that Wil was unable to see.

"It'd probably be a good idea to back up a few feet," she said. "You don't want to get in the way."

They all took a few steps back as Goliath sat on the ground. The bot tucked its legs and head in toward its frame until the machine resembled a large metal brick. Its frame lifted from the ground as twelve enormous wheels deployed from its underside.

"I'll have to pull him through the SZ," Kayla said. "He'll be able to move on his own once we're in the City Center. And thank goodness —I'd hate to have to pull him up those hills."

An orb made a pass close to them, the display on its frame spinning, before a gathered ball of light formed.

"We need to move, *now!*" Ella shouted, but the group was already running.

Kayla had been about to attach herself to a harness hanging from the oversized robot, but she didn't have time to get it properly secured. Instead, the curled-up bot simply moved slowly behind her.

Wil paused in his escape, turning back to help.

"No, get out of the way!" Kayla shouted at him. "Everyone get out of the way!"

Wil raised an eyebrow but didn't adjust his course. Kayla wouldn't make it if she was struggling to pull the bot on her own.

"Goliath! *Go!*"

The bot made a deep whirring sound, and its wheels briefly spun in the dirt before they gained traction and propelled the machine forward.

"Move!" Kayla yelled.

Wil barely had time to jump out of its path as it roared past him. Thankfully, T'al looked over his shoulder in time to see the wheeled machine hurtling toward them, and he grabbed Ella and rolled to the side into the field.

Goliath kicked up dirt and dust, sending Wil into a coughing fit. The cloud was so thick, they lost sight of each other, as well as the orb circling above. Wil knew the orb wouldn't have a problem seeing them, though.

Wil pushed off and forced himself to keep running towards the SZ's border, ignoring the cramp in his leg and doing his best not to choke on the dust.

The torches ahead of them licked at the haze, directing the group as the dust settled. Another laser blast struck where Wil had been standing only moments before. Wil's feet slipped as he tried to push faster in the loose dirt, nearly falling from the effort, but he gave it everything he had.

As he passed the last electric light, he nearly tripped over Ella and Kayla, who had stopped next to the first unlit lamp. The adjacent fiery torch provided enough light through the settling dust for the party to make each other out as they caught their breath. The green glow of the San Francisco force field now dominated the view ahead of them.

T'al continued on for a few hundred yards to where Goliath waited, still folded in its box-like state.

Wil shivered against the coolness of the air blowing over his sweat-covered skin. They may have passed into an area where the bots could no longer reach them, but it didn't feel like a victory. Wil tried to catch his breath as the screams of those still attempting to flee echoed on the wind. Fires littered the landscape, the livelihoods of hundreds of farmers and ranchers, who had done their best to man the farms their ancient ancestors had somehow managed to salvage and maintain, now burning. Clusters of weary people remained on the unprotected side of the line, having given up on their attempts to fight back or unable to move at a faster pace. Even those who had now safely made it to the Silent Zone still frantically ran toward the center of the city.

Blaster fire could now be seen coming from the edges of the Outskirts. Men and women on horseback emerged from the direction of the Resistance camps, doing their best to distract the bots while farmers and the arena spectators continued to flee.

"Will Liz and the Resistance in the city be coming to fight?" he asked.

T'al shook his head. "Those fighters from the Outskirts will hold them off as long as needed. The bots will move on once the people are gone. Liz needs to focus the efforts of the city in preparation of the SZ dropping completely. If this is a sign of what's to come, we'll need all of our efforts ready for the battle ahead."

"So many farms destroyed," Ella said, almost to herself, her voice as distant as her focus. "So many needlessly slaughtered."

"Shouldn't be a surprise at this point," Wil said.

"I swear, Wil Underwood," Ella scolded, "you won't rest until you've killed us all."

"You can't be serious," Wil huffed, still winded. "You can't blame *me* for this attack."

"What were you hoping to prove? That bot would have crushed

you." She nodded to the block of metal T'al was inspecting, now resting dormant on its wheels.

"That thing?" Wil smirked. "Apparently, it wasn't a threat."

Ella's crossed arms and tapping foot erased the grin from his face.

"They misled me," he said, doing his best to be sincere. "I was tricked into entering the stadium—and then they locked me up. The plan was for me to fight Goliath, but it definitely wouldn't have been my first choice of ways to spend the evening."

"She's right," Kayla said, keeping a watchful eye on T'al as he tinkered around her machine. "Goliath would have destroyed you in the ring."

"I think *you* have some explaining to do," Ella said, now directing her scorn toward Kayla. "This bot killed that man in the arena and was about to do the same to our friend Dagger. But it listens to you. Were you really being held captive? Or were you part of the game all along?"

"It's not Goliath's fault," Kayla said as she blew a sigh.

"Oh, come on!" Ella exclaimed. "It was *obviously* built to fight."

Kayla nodded. "We built it to fight, but I had meant for it to fight other bots, not humans. Things got out of hand, and once the show escalated to tonight's spectacle, I didn't know how to stop it."

"Goliath was meant to fight the Guardians?" Wil asked, hopeful about the woman's motives.

"What? No," she said, her brow furrowed. "No, nothing like that. Life can be rather . . . uneventful in the City Center. I built it to fight other bots in the arena. The stadiums used to host bot only tournaments. The winner would get the spoils of the evening and bragging rights. Now, all the crowds want to see are humans fighting the bots."

"You could have stopped it."

"Some things are easier said than done," she said, her lip curling as one nostril lifted in disgust. "Believe me, I'm just as happy as you are to be away from that filth." Kayla turned to Wil. "And it's all thanks to you." Her eyes glistened, the flames engulfing the distant fields reflected in their gaze.

"Why would anyone want to watch robots kill people?" Wil asked. "There's so much death and destruction already."

"It's just another show. The stories of the ancients tell us that humans used to challenge the bots. Things haven't always been this way, Wil. But inside the City Center, all they have are stories. Many question if there really is a threat, or if the Guardians are even real. For a price, they're promised a front row seat at a real fight between humans and bots. They're led through tunnels beneath the city to the edge of the Silent Zone. It's illegal, but people always find a way."

"People are dying every day," Wil said. "The Guardians are slaughtering hundreds and imprisoning thousands more—and all these people want is to watch an orchestrated fight?"

"Those within the city work hard," Kayla said. "All they seek is entertainment."

Ella snorted.

"They're looking for a way to relieve some stress," Kayla continued, ignoring the other woman. "The fighters usually volunteer. Most don't wander in mistakenly looking for a revolution."

Wil scowled. "But *you* go along with it. You built a bot and programmed it to kill."

"I didn't," Kayla protested. "The organizers set up a frequency in the arena to override the programming. Within the confines of the stadium, Goliath could do nothing but kill. They kept me locked in that cage so there was nothing I could do to stop it. They would bring me out as part of the show now and then, turning off the frequency so that it appeared as though the bot was showing me mercy. That way, it appeared to the punters as if Goliath was *choosing* to fight the others."

Wil shook his head. He had seen the way Goliath had butchered Cahal.

They caught up to T'al, reaching Goliath curled up into its metal box and waiting to be towed into the city. Its motorized wheels stopped as soon as it hit the invisible wall of the SZ.

"And what waits for you in the City Center?" Wil asked.

"I go home to my father. There will be so much business to attend to, and he does a horrible job when he's left to manage it himself.

There's an important event I must get ready for. If you're truly headed for the City Center, I'll look for you once you've arrived. Maybe I'll be able to show you around."

Kayla brushed Wil's shoulder with a hand before approaching Goliath and attaching herself to the bot's harness.

17

KAYLA HAD PARTED ways with the rest of the group before they'd headed back to the safe house. Wil was relieved when she had let them know she'd have to carry on to the city on her own.

It was bad enough he would have to give some sort of explanation of where they had been, and of Dagger's disappearance to Liz, and he didn't want to explain why a woman and her robot had followed them home.

The ball in his stomach also informed him he would still need to have a detailed conversation with Ella over his decision to leave in the first place.

As it stood, Ella had been too tired to discuss the events of the evening, as was he. There were precious few hours before they'd have to regroup, and he wanted to at least attempt to get some sleep before then.

They crept back into the safe house. The few Resistance guards who stood watch initially appeared alarmed as they entered, but relaxed as they recognized the group.

"Out for a nightcap?" one of them asked T'al, a grin on his face. "Showing the newcomers what the Inner Ring looks like at night?"

"We have more serious issues than late night carousing," T'al said. "Alert the Guard and Liz. We need to have a meeting."

"We heard weapons fire coming from the south," the guard replied. "Is it that bad?"

"It's beyond bad," T'al said. "Part of the SZ has given way, and the attack extends to the Outskirts and the Outer Ring. Some of our members are out there to help, but we need to ensure we're ready. Get Liz. We need a plan of attack."

T'al turned to Ella and Wil. "I'll fill Liz in on what's happened. I can explain away my absence by being out on patrol, but your involvement will be harder to excuse. Nothing will happen until morning, anyway. Get a few hours' rest while you're able."

Neither Wil nor Ella argued.

Sleep didn't come easy for Wil, though. Adrenaline still coursed through his veins from the events of the evening. His heartbeat was so strong, the mere sound of it kept him awake.

He found his thoughts drifting back to Kayla. Despite her being gorgeous, there was something else about her he found intriguing; she seemed determined and driven, and she was willing to break the rules to get things done. Though he didn't know how he felt about her pet bot; she seemed to shrug off the people Goliath had killed far too easily.

The fluctuation of the SZ's boundary also disturbed him. Apparently, variations were normal, but it was apparent an outage of this degree was out of the ordinary. Surely the bots had never caused such an extensive level of damage on the farmsteads previously?

With the attack on Vegas only weeks ago, Wil wondered if the Silent Zone around San Francisco would be the next to fall. It seemed bad luck had followed him. And there were yet more protected areas scattered in faraway places. Were they all destined to fall, too? It only intensified his goal of taking down the bots. The evening hadn't worked out the way he had envisioned, but that didn't weaken his resolve.

He had hopefully learned something of the people in this city, though. Fry had tricked him, using his desire to fight the bots as bait.

In the Sphere, Wil had never had to worry about someone deceiving him.

Except for the Guardians, of course. Everything they'd told him had been a lie.

Thoughts of Dagger also plagued him. The kid had made the decision to follow him to the arena, he had decided to enter the ring, but had he understood what he was signing up for? Wil sure hadn't. He hoped the youth was still alive. Wil assumed that if he was, he'd make his way back to the safe house. He wouldn't know where to begin if he had to try to find the youth.

Wil lay in bed, his eyes wide, staring at the ceiling. The moon illuminated his room, along with the ever-present green glow emanating from the City Center.

The morning sun soon replaced the light of the moon. Wil's eyelids drooped as he got up and made his way down to the common area with a yawn.

Liz and Ella were already seated on the room's plush chairs, and sunlight streamed in through the windows. He could only make out the back of Liz's head as he came down the stairs, but Ella's brow was furrowed in concern as the two women talked.

"We can only hope it's temporary," Liz finished saying as Wil descended.

Wil cleared his throat to announce his presence, as he didn't like feeling as though he was sneaking up on the women.

"Look who's awake," Ella said, before taking a sip from an oversized mug.

There must have been a kitchen in the house, but Wil hadn't seen it. Plates of fruit, pastries, and other delicious looking goods were spread out on a low table. He wondered where the snacks had arrived from, but he realized there must have been someone in charge of looking after the house.

"Good morning to you, too," Wil said, snatching a muffin from the table. He took a bite, pleasantly surprised by the variety of options presented. The muffin was dry, but it was one of the better tasting items he'd come across outside of the Sphere.

"What's with all the choice?" he asked. "We haven't been treated to a meal looking this good since we left Vegas."

"Liz has friends in high places," Ella said with a smirk.

Liz put a hand up in protest.

"Nonsense," Liz said. "Don't say things like that. Rumors fly faster than the truth in this city. I have worked hard for the contacts I've made. They're important to our survival and our efforts going forward."

Liz looked at Wil. Her eyes were bright, and her complexion was smooth. One of them at least had got a good night's rest. Just thinking about sleep caused him to let out a yawn.

Despite returning to the safe house together, Ella appeared to be fresh as well. She had pulled her hair back, revealing the radiant skin of her neck. Her dark eyes betrayed none of the bitterness she had expressed the night before, as if eager for whatever adventures lay ahead of them. Wil, however, felt disheveled and barely alive after such a harrowing journey. They had spent days on the move without proper rest. The previous night had been their one chance to recover, and he had blown it by getting them into trouble once again.

"Ella's been telling me about your adventures last night," Liz said, giving him a sidelong eye.

"Oh?" Wil said. He did his best to appear unconcerned as he didn't believe he had anything to apologize for.

Other than putting his friends in harm's way and potentially getting Dagger killed.

"Do you care to explain what happened?"

He didn't, but he started fumbling through an explanation. "A man approached me outside the pub last night and asked if I wanted to fight bots. I said yes, and he handed me a card with directions on where I could meet a group of people. It turned out to be something else, Ella called it a robot fight club. Watching humans fight robots for sport isn't something I ever expected to exist. I just thought it would be a group of fighters looking to take on the Guardians."

"*We* are a group of fighters," Liz said, elevating the tone of her voice. "I know you'd rather go out swinging, in a blaze of glory, but after decades of losing our best soldiers, we've learned there is a need to be more strategic."

"I just wanted to check it out," Wil stated. "I didn't expect it to escalate."

"Ella says Dagger is missing," Liz said.

Wil nodded. "He followed T'al and I. I didn't know he was with us until he volunteered to fight in the arena on his own. When the stadium was attacked, he disappeared."

Liz let out a sigh and put a hand to her temple.

"What's done is done," she said. "But every decision you make is important to how this war plays out. Never lose sight of that."

"You said every time I use my powers brought me closer," Wil said. "I wasn't able to use them, though not for a lack of trying."

Wil took another bite of his muffin and waited for an answer.

"Everything is pushing you to using your powers in one way or another," Liz said. "I have tried to warn you, but you seem hellbent on ignoring me. The path you are currently on will lead to your death. My efforts seem to push you in the wrong direction. I don't know what it will take for you to see that you're causing more harm than good."

Wil resisted the urge to throw the last of his muffin at Liz. Instead, he swallowed.

He wasn't dense, but he *had* just stepped into this world after a lifetime of being sheltered and told that humanity had been destroyed. How was he supposed to know Fry had been setting him up? If he'd known what the arena held, he wouldn't have gone. Goliath wasn't even a Guardian.

He paused for a moment and wondered if it mattered. Was a bot built today inherently better than one constructed two hundred years ago by the ancients? That was how the Guardians started out, wasn't it? Benevolent creations built to help, in the end turning on humanity. Goliath was no different. Whatever signal was being broadcast in the arena had turned it against humans all the same.

Wil suddenly wondered if he should have destroyed the bot when he'd had the chance.

Ella's dark brown eyes looked at him with desperate hope, her wavy brown hair framing the tanned complexion of her face. She studied him, and Wil froze, wondering what to expect. She smiled, as though she knew something he didn't.

"Despite my disappointment with you running off *again*," Liz continued, "the rift in the SZ is far more concerning, and that you had nothing to do with. You were simply in the wrong place at the wrong time."

Wil breathed a sigh of relief. *Off the hook for now, at least.*

"What about the attack on the Outskirts?" he asked. "Where was the Resistance? Surely you would have at least heard the attack from here? What about Dagger?"

"The boy was never our responsibility," Liz said. "But considering he evaded T'al's detection, he's more than capable. If he's alive, he'll either make his way back here or move on."

Before they could continue, T'al came meandering down the stairs with bags under his eyes. It seemed Wil's friend had slept no better than he had.

T'al looked greedily at the plates laid out on the table and reached for a pastry, also snagging a few pieces of fruit and shoving them in his pockets.

"I need to leave," T'al said, running a hand through his thick, curly hair. "I need to find Voth."

T'al stood looking at Liz, as if expecting a reaction, or perhaps waiting for permission. The man wore a sleeveless tunic which was tight against his muscular frame, and his pants were loose but not baggy. The ferocity in his eyes indicated he didn't plan on taking no for an answer.

Liz nodded, as if T'al's decision had been expected. "I'm surprised she hasn't returned on her own by now, too."

"I'll check the Resistance camps on my way out to be sure," T'al said. "I blame myself for not going for her sooner."

"Voth is resilient, and you had every reason to believe she'd escape on her own. Knowing what we do, her captors have probably drugged her to keep her subdued," Ella said.

Liz walked over to the man, who was nearly twice her size, and gave him a hug.

Wil couldn't help but smile at the gesture; Wil had never seen Liz show affection to anyone before.

T'al turned to Ella. "You're going to have to take care of this one on your own," he commented, gesturing to Wil with a grin.

"Hey now!" Wil said, feigning outrage. He wished T'al wasn't right.

They said their goodbyes as T'al stepped out the door. Wil hoped the man found Voth, and that she was all right.

"We need to leave immediately," Liz said, wasting no time. "From what Ella has told me, the scope of what we're dealing with is extreme."

"I thought fluctuations were normal?" Wil asked. "Isn't that why the lighting system is in place?"

"Slight variations *are* normal," Liz replied. "And they have grown more frequent of late. It's designed so those who are traveling know at what point they are safe. However, the city has never seen a drop of this magnitude, especially for this long. Reports are saying most of the surrounding farms are now exposed, and some swaths may go even further. If that section of Silent Zone isn't restored, many in the city will starve."

"Can't the residents bring in goods from the SZs to the south?" Wil asked.

Liz shook her head. "There are several Silent Zones on the west coast, but each is still a long way from here. It would be far too great an undertaking to transport the supplies needed. The roads are treacherous, and everyone has their own problems to deal with. Other SZs may not have enough to spare to make up for the loss here."

Wil grabbed another piece of fruit for the road. He didn't know when they'd next be able to eat.

"Can I ask why we're here?" said Wil. "Why has the rest of the Resistance stayed behind while you escort Ella and me?"

Liz stared intently at Wil, as if deciding how much of her plan to reveal. "I am working with the Director of the City Center," she said. "I'm building support for the Resistance, and as part of a deal, I convinced him to fund our expedition to Vegas to help in the fight against the bots there. I was also tasked with discovering if there was a way the city could stop the attack, and report back with something tangible."

"So, you're bringing *me* back?" he asked, shuffling where he stood.

"You were instrumental in bringing down the bots. The Director needs to hear firsthand what kind of threat we're up against."

"This Director needs convincing that the bots pose a threat to the city?" Wil asked.

"The City Center is . . . *unique*. They've been cut off from the outside world for too long. The citizens aren't supposed to leave the confines of the force field, so most live and die without realizing the threat they face."

"But you think we can convince them to assist in overthrowing the Guardians?" Ella asked.

"I believe there is a way we can, and I believe Wil is at the heart of that equation. The Resistance will do what it can, but the City Center has access to resources we do not. If the upper class can put aside their internal prejudices, they'll not only help to defend the city, but their force field can save many lives in the process."

"How?" Wil asked.

"I've said as much as I can," Liz sighed. "We're going to have to let the rest play out. But a word to the wise, Wil, be careful of your words. There are many deep-rooted beliefs held by those in the Center that will make no sense to you. Our goal is to win them over with sympathy and kindness. The Director won't respond well to threats or if he feels he's being intimidated into something."

Wil rolled his eyes and wondered how he'd mess things up this time.

18

WIL WASN'T OFTEN NERVOUS, but the walk toward the city gate filled him with an overwhelming sense of anxiety. Liz had done little to reassure him he wasn't being presented as a potential savior of the city. She had promised not to reveal his power, but she had implied his presence alone would be enough to sway the city's future.

He clenched his fists as they approached the green force field that cut the City Center off from the rest of civilization.

They were midway through the Inner Ring before he noticed the surrounding homes were becoming more grandiose and elaborate. Greenery filled terraces, windows became adorned with shutters, and the squat one or two storey buildings gained height incrementally as they drew nearer to the gate.

They hadn't walked more than a dozen blocks before the gate was within sight. The homes had now reached seven or eight stories, and though they weren't as tall as some of the buildings in Vegas had been before the battle, these were in much better condition; some were newly built, and others freshly painted. Green vines climbed pillars on the sides of homes, and other plants decorated planters resting under window panes and on porches. Someone meticulously looked after every detail.

Those in the Inner Ring lived in an unimaginably different world to those in the makeshift shacks of the Outer Ring.

"Life here seems better than in the other rings," Wil thought out loud.

"That's because it's built off the backs of others," Ella said. "Mostly commerce managers and merchants. They buy crops and goods from the Outer Ring, mark them up more than threefold, and then resell to the City Center."

That didn't seem quite fair.

"Why don't those in the Outer Ring sell directly to the City Center? They could keep the profits for themselves."

"If only it were that simple," Liz replied. "Only a select few can come and go through the Center gates. Those in the Inner Ring hold a higher status and are allowed to send a proxy into the Trading District within. You need access credentials to enter the gate and farmers aren't allowed through, therefore they need someone of higher status to sell their wares for them."

Wil raised an eyebrow. "But wouldn't it be better for the city to get the goods for cheaper?"

"There are many things that would be of benefit if people would only open their eyes," Liz answered.

Wil shook his head in disbelief at the large estates that lined the streets. Many of the houses could contain six or seven of the makeshift homes that were set up on the Outer Ring, and there was a significant disconnect between how new and pristine they appeared when compared to those on the road into the city; those had appeared to be held together by nothing but string and gravity. And that was *before* the attack.

A thought occurred to him.

"Will those in the Inner Ring help the farms to rebuild after the bot attack?"

"Hah!" Liz burst. "They'd rather starve."

The gates into the city reminded Wil of the sliding glass doors within the Sphere, though they were twenty feet high and set open.

The edges that stuck out from the door's frame were clear, but Wil doubted they were actually glass.

The sun had begun to warm the air. Carts and villagers creaked slowly to the gate under the watchful eyes of guards. Nearly all the carts were pulled by hand, many piled with food stock, but others held wares of various sorts. Those pulling the carts wore tattered coats, while nearby to each one stood someone who was much more finely dressed. Men and women stood impatiently waiting for their load to be hauled to the door, but they weren't willing to do the heavy lifting themselves.

Ella explained to him that though the commerce managers and merchants would perform the transactions, the villagers and farmers themselves were still responsible for the deliveries. Once the goods were past the gate, the managers would complete the transactions and then repeat the process with their next client.

Few appeared to be fit enough to do the work, many were elderly and frail and about to topple over from the weight of their load.

The road they had traveled on wasn't flat, either. The city streets spanned multiple hills, many of which would be nearly unperceivable until you had to pull a wheeled cart up one of them.

Wil didn't know where to look. They still had some distance to go before they got to the gates, and there were still wonders Wil struggled to see.

The buildings themselves were marvels, built on the remnants of structures from the ancients and added to over the centuries. Cement and metal boxes sat beneath many of the newer towers. *The ghosts of war*, Wil thought. There was evidence of where the ancient structures had bent and twisted and broke, before someone had come along and took what was old to resurrect it.

It was a stark contrast to the fields of the Outer Ring, where the structures had either been completely decimated or overgrown.

Similarly, every now and then, a piece of the ancient roadways worked its way through the dirt and gravel that lined the streets. Chunks of gray concrete emerged from the dirt—a memory to a wondrous time long since past.

The green force field before them dominated everything. Wil wondered what sort of treasures lay within its grasp. Wil also thought Marco would have loved to see this city. Regardless of what lay within the barrier, even the Inner Ring would have provided them enough marvels to last a lifetime. Relics and symbols from the Old World lay everywhere.

In the Outer and Middle Rings, they had constructed many of the buildings with remnants and pieces left behind from its destruction. Here, it appeared as if they built homes around these items, some incorporating faded billboards and signs into their appearance. But nothing was haphazard; everything appeared to be integral and planned.

The road abruptly shifted from uneven dirt and cobblestone to a smooth and polished surface which stretched the last few hundred yards to the gates. Liz took them past the column of traders making their way through with purpose.

Many people in line were acting as if their farmland hadn't been raided by the bots the night before. Some looked as though they had slept less than he had, and he wondered how much of what had transpired last night would change the city's dynamic.

Indeed, as they grew closer, Wil could tell there was a rumbling at the fringes of the line, from a separate group of people who were grumbling and didn't appear to be part of the queue.

Liz had made it sound like the residents of the Inner Ring would be unconcerned about the events, but Wil found that hard to believe. The bots had killed their neighbors and were closer than ever to their doorstep. How could that be ignored? Especially if their own livelihoods would be affected by the scourge.

"We're going to have to find another way," Liz said, pushing her way to the side of the road.

Wil snapped out of his thoughts, realizing the throng of people had noticeably thickened. If they didn't move soon, they would be caught amid an increasingly growing crowd.

Ella bore a frustrated look, until her eyes met his and softened. The people around them were pressing against them. Instinctively, he reached for her hand so they wouldn't get separated.

She took it and held on tight.

Was she nervous?

The mood of the crowd had changed from sleepy everyday life to urgency and desperation. Ella's face appeared as unwavering as ever, but she held onto Wil's hand with an ironclad grip.

Ella had been a valiant leader within Malachi's Community in Vegas, and she had left it all behind to follow him.

He caught her eye, and her concern quickly made its way to her face. He pulled her closer to him as they worked their way through the increasingly agitated and hostile crowd.

The flip had been so sudden, Wil wondered if there were a catalyst he had missed. The closer they got to the gate, the more congested the crowd became, though the number of bodies behind them was rapidly increasing as well.

The guards who stood in front of the gates held large shields, using them flagrantly to keep the crowds back.

Wil nearly forgot he was attempting to follow Liz and fought a moment of panic when he failed to see her. He soon caught sight of the back of her wavy hair again and pushed people out of the way in order to close the gap between them, Ella in tow, but it was enough to unsettle him.

A side street meandered its way through the Inner Ring, allowing them to break from the crowd, as it was nearly deserted. The few who did wander the road also appeared to be looking for a way around the chaos.

"Have you ever seen anything like that?" Ella asked Liz. "I haven't spent much time in the city, but I've never seen a mob crowd the gates like that before."

It was only then Wil realized Ella still gripped his hand and that he was returning the gesture. They had been through a lot together the last couple of weeks—especially the last twenty-four hours—but it seemed the brittleness between them from the previous evening was gone. She gave him a warm smile as she let go, and he couldn't help but return the sentiment.

Wil was glad her warmth had returned. It was in these moments he appreciated the woman latching herself onto him. It assured him he wasn't alone, and that he could count on her to be there for him. He just wished he could get it through his head during his more impulsive moments.

"Most of these people's homes and farms have been destroyed," Liz answered, cutting Wil's thoughts off abruptly. "If not, their neighbors' have, and they're worried they'll be next." Liz shook her head. "I wish I could say the chaos would end at this."

Wil looked over his shoulder at the crowd now spilling onto the side street behind them.

"The piece of the SZ that fell isn't going to come back, is it?" he asked.

"No," Liz answered. "It's not."

The thought of entering the glowing force field made him uneasy, but he also knew it held the key to him being able to push forward in trying to take on the bots. He didn't know who this Director was or quite understand why Liz was taking them with her, but perhaps Wil could make him see that supporting the Resistance was worth undertaking. It certainly sounded like the City Center had the resources to help.

"How are we going to get in now?" he asked.

"There are two side entrances not far ahead. We need to get to them before the crowd realizes they aren't getting in through the front. Otherwise, the City Center will lock down before we have a chance. The gates will close, and if things go south, the City Center might enter full lockdown. By then, things will be too late . . ."

Liz trailed off as she looked to the city wall, as though seeing it for the first time. Wil studied her features as he tried to ascertain what she was thinking. The shape of her jaw, the way her purple eyes set into her skull, mimicked her sister Sierra's, though time had been harder on Liz. Not that she appeared old or unattractive, but her face was more tired; wrinkles from worry had formed on her brow. That aside, she held more resolve and her stance was considerably more confident than her sister.

His thoughts wandered to Sierra and how she might be faring. What would she make of the new threat of another SZ collapsing? Sierra had been the true hero in the Battle for Vegas. While Wil had stopped a wave of the attack, she was the one that had truly ended the fight and reinstated the Silent Zone.

Sierra had always had an insatiable curiosity, and he wondered what she would think if she could see the city behind the towering green force field. Would she be apprehensive, or eager to enter its maw? He guessed eager, but despite her inquisitive nature, she also had a cautious side.

"If we can't get in before they seal the gates," Liz continued, "we won't be able to get in at all."

"The other entrances won't be just as crowded?" he asked.

"I hope not," Liz answered.

"How many other gates are there?"

"There are only two we can access," Liz answered. "One entrance to the southeast, where we're headed. The other where the City Center meets the ocean to the west."

Though their party had to travel around the bay to reach the city, Wil hadn't even had a glimpse of the ocean yet. He wondered how far the city stretched. It seemed as if it were endless.

They walked for over an hour, following the perimeter of the Center wall. Much to Wil's disappointment, they hadn't been able to walk directly beside the force field for most of the walk, instead following nearby streets to get ahead of the crowds. Liz pushed them at a swift pace, dodging in and out of back roads, sometimes cutting across properties and hopping over fences to keep on the most direct route.

The further they went, the more the handiwork of the ancients became apparent. Cement roadways, now mostly crumbled and decayed, stretched before them. Taller buildings, some as high as ten or fifteen stories and made of steel and cement, stood in various states of reclaimed use. Some looked to be abandoned altogether, others bustled with the activity of merchants, traders, and other high-ranking officials.

It was a hodgepodge of the old and the new. It was evident that humanity could not clear the wreckage of the past, so they had built on top of it or around it. Over the years, the sun had bleached much of what remained. Newer developments and add-ons rose in stark contrast, with bright colors and symbols painted onto their surfaces.

A group of men and women dressed in black armored uniforms came running down the street, passing them. There had to be nearly a dozen soldiers holding formidable-looking batons. They had strapped blasters to their backs, and their helmets with their dark visors added to the intimidation.

Wil didn't ask the question he guessed he knew the answer to.

Why would the City Center send out soldiers to control a mob, but not to keep the bots at bay?

"I'M SORRY," the guard said, his gruff voice matching the intensity of his outfit. His visor was lifted, revealing his face. "Nobody is allowed in or out until we get the main crowd under control."

The man who stood before them wasn't what Wil had expected when they approached the barricade. His predominantly gray mustache and wrinkles gave the guard's face added character, but despite his advanced years, the man appeared to have more energy than most people Wil had seen since leaving the Sphere.

People trickled down the road to the side entrance, their eager faces indicating that they hoped to have found a way to get their wares inside. Others wore scowls, possibly those who had grown tired of trying to get close to the main gate. Wil, Ella, and Liz didn't have much time before a similar chaos would engulf them.

"I'm operating under an assignment from the Director himself," Liz persisted. "If you don't let us through before the side gates are overwhelmed, you'll have to answer to him."

The man rose a bushy eyebrow and tossed a questioning look to a second officer, who merely shrugged.

"Do you have any proof?" the first guard asked.

Liz held up an arm. Wil didn't understand the significance of what she was showing the guards. It appeared to be a silver bracelet with an inscribed emblem.

Whatever it was, the guard's eyes went wide at the sight of it, and he seemed to step over himself to move aside to allow their party through.

"I'm very sorry. I didn't know," the man stammered. "I wouldn't have stood in the way if . . ."

Liz opened her palm, stopping the man mid-sentence. "No harm done," she said.

The guards cleared a path, allowing the three of them to slip inside.

"Hurry," the guard said. "If these protests keep up, even that bracelet might not get you where you need to be."

Wil was about to ask Ella about the bracelet's significance, but suspicious glares from the guards encouraged him to hold his tongue.

19

Wɪʟ, Ella, and Liz filed through a narrow corridor, barely wide enough for two people to stand side by side, a steady stream of people all around them. Liz walked in front of them, confident and purposeful.

Wil felt there was still so much mystery surrounding her. Liz was good at keeping secrets, for the most part, but at least he had gotten a glimpse as to why she had avoided him at first. After revealing her secret about being Sierra's sister, he had hoped she'd warm to him— but she had remained as aloof as ever.

Wil pushed her remoteness from his mind; as long as the Director could help take the bots down, that was all he was here for. He didn't care how it happened, but he hoped this Director, whoever he was, would be the one to help make it a reality. Otherwise, this whole endeavor would be a waste of time.

The hall smelled of body odor and sweat, and fluorescent lighting attached to the ceiling painted its occupants in a blue hue. Wil now understood why this was a side entrance; there was no way the merchant wagons with their mountains of goods would fit through the narrower hall. It appeared to have been built to serve craftspeople, or those of other professions who did not require hauling their wares.

The corridor funneled into a wider opening overseen by another group of armed guards. A scanner had been built into the wall, forming a sort of gateway that emitted a film of blue light as a person stepped through.

People appeared to be tossing weapons into a bin before they reached that point.

"Are the weapons returned when their owners leave the city?" he whispered to Ella.

Ella shrugged. "I doubt it."

Wil kept forgetting she hadn't been inside the City Center before either. Liz could have answered the question, but she hadn't seemed to be paying attention.

Words had been engraved into the gray concrete wall and painted over in bright yellow paint:

1. No talk of the Outside

2. No Outside technology

3. The city is safe.

Something about the mantras made Wil want to retch.

"No talk of the Outside?" he asked.

"The ancients built the City Center as a barrier to the problems the Guardians had wrought outside," Liz answered. "The City Center believes the world's problems are its own."

"So, the people here don't know about the Guardians? Or about the rest of the city?"

Liz sighed. "In theory, they know. But the memory of the outside world has faded with time. Some simply choose not to believe it, but most are so detached from reality that anything happening outside these walls is irrelevant to them."

Thousands of their fellow humans are dying, and they think it's irrelevant?

"Why are we here, then?" Ella asked.

"Because this is where the Director is," Liz whispered, glancing around. "But keep your voice down. Nobody else needs to know our business here."

It didn't take them long to file through the scanner. Wil wasn't allowed to carry tech at the best of times, and there had been no reason for the two women to be carrying within the SZ. After what happened the night before, Wil wouldn't have blamed them for wanting to keep their options open. Liz had indicated his daggers would be fine but cautioned Ella to leave her bow at the safe house.

Wil followed Liz and Ella through the blue beam. A bright light flashed, and nothing more. Guards, in their black helmets and green uniforms, stood expressionless on the opposite side of the machine and waved him through.

No sooner had Wil passed through the scanner than a deafening cry echoed through the hall, causing him to jump. *"You can't hold us down any longer, City pigs!"*

Wil turned sharply but couldn't see the source of the commotion. Blaster fire bounced off the wall with a flash, and a powerful arm grabbed Wil and pushed him against the wall. The force of the impact knocked the wind out of him.

As he struggled to catch his breath, uniformed guards rushed through the hall. More blaster fired echoed though the passage, and sparks flew around them as the beams bounced off the walls.

A breeze brushed past Wil's arm, followed by the sound of metal grating against the walls as a steel barrier dropped. The gate closed inches from Wil and those behind him had been blocked from entry.

Red lights blinked on the walls beside the now dim fluorescents. The result was an eerie purple glow that shrouded the tunnel.

Wil caught his breath and met Ella's wide-eyed gaze in front of him, who had also been pressed face-first into the adjacent wall. Guards circled around behind them. One pulled Wil back into the hall and pushed him forward, away from the steel barrier. Adrenaline spiked through Wil's veins, and he had to stop himself from pushing back. He had nothing to gain from picking a fight with the well-armed guard. He guided Ella more gently but had to work not to tromp on her heels with the guard's incessant shoving.

A glass window separated the hall from a small room that stood off to the side, where guards scrambled inside, grabbing their blasters and moving through doors leading to unseen destinations.

"Move!" the guard behind Wil barked.

There must have been something blocking the path at the front of the crowd. The hall had become packed so tightly, it was difficult to move, but the guard seemed insistent on using his oversized shield to push Wil forward.

Wil struggled not to trip over his own feet as he was forced forward into the assembly. He would have grabbed onto Ella, but he needed both arms for balance.

Cries of annoyance broke out ahead of them as people slammed into each other. Some poor soul tripped and was lost under the carnage, and Wil couldn't help but stumble over their body; a middle-aged man wrapped in a gray cloak, from what he could tell. He wanted to help, wanted to reach down and grab the man and help bring him forward, but it was impossible for him to do anything but put one foot in front of the other and keep himself upright.

The shields pushed them down the hall for what felt like an eternity, though Wil knew it couldn't have been more than a few hundred paces. A doorway ahead promised their journey would come to an end soon.

The horde spilled out like a pipe bursting under pressure, scattering in every direction they could, most tripping over themselves when the constraint of the walls disappeared.

Their destination was packed with people, too, and though it wasn't as tight, there still wasn't much room to navigate. Wil limped to keep up with his companions, the soreness of his heels suggesting they had been bruised from the guard's impact.

The guards had drawn together at the entrance, their shields stationary, creating a blockade. Nobody else was getting in or out.

Wil's eyes took a moment to adjust. He squinted against the daylight and inhaled deeply, securing his footing.

Despite the guards now blocking off at least two of the entrances to the City Center, hundreds of people clogged a road which appeared to circle the inner perimeter of the force field. Except it wasn't a road as much as it was a grander, more elaborate hallway that had been designed to appear as if it were outdoors.

Wil had to remind himself that people weren't being let *out* through the gates either. It was as crowded on this side of the door as it was outside the main gate, though those here didn't seem to be as angry. The people crowding the gargantuan space appeared to be from all walks of life. There were those who held empty carts, and others whose carts were full of supplies. Most of those who had exploded out of the narrow hall to join them were picking themselves up and brushing themselves off, ready to do business.

The road itself was a wide channel which curved along the edge of the force field. About twenty yards across, market stalls lined the far wall, many calling out to those in the crowd to purchase wares on their way in or out of the corridor.

The wall that stood across the channel rose a dozen feet in the air before curving into a ceiling that mimicked the sky, with clouds painted on its blue surface adding to the illusion. The upper part of the far wall below the ceiling was a large display screen that appeared to run as far along the wall as he could see, unbroken and lined with displays of advertisements. Prices of various commodities were listed, and Wil wondered if these were for the merchants to sell their wares or if they were more ads for those who wished to buy things at the extensive market stalls.

"They have power here?" he thought out loud, though the weapons scanner in the hallway should have been his first clue.

Neither Ella nor Liz appeared to have heard him. He could barely hear his own words; the noise of the crowd drowned out anything else.

Ella stood frozen, her wide eyes taking in the spectacle just as much as he was.

Liz, however, looked around with purpose. She was either trying to find a way through or was looking for someone in particular, though trying to find an individual in the sea of people would be nearly impossible.

What else are they hiding behind this wall?

Wil subconsciously reached for Ella's hand; he didn't want to be separated from her here. Streams of people pushed past in both directions, with nowhere for them to go, and the congestion on the street only appeared to be thickening.

Ella barely seemed to notice. She moved as Liz pulled on her other arm. It appeared Liz had found the person who she had been looking for.

Behind her stood a man in a black suit, a wire hanging from his ear and dark glasses sitting on the bridge of his nose. His face betrayed no emotion as he beckoned Liz over.

Ella wasn't responding to Liz's prompts, her mouth agape as she continued to stare, and when Wil caught Liz's eye, she motioned for them to move to where the man stood.

Wil squeezed Ella's hand tightly and shook her shoulder. She blinked, snapping out of her trance, and looked at Wil as though she were confused as to who he was and why he was there.

She quickly regained her bearings, though, and moved to follow Liz.

A small door stood against the wall, on the side of the corridor where the Center's force field should have been. Wil supposed the door represented another passage leading back outside until they stepped through it.

They had entered what felt like a small closet, made of solid steel. Memories of the cell at the stadium came rushing back. The only thing that stopped him from diving for the exit was Liz's calm demeanor.

Their new companion pressed a single button on a panel next to the doorway, which slid closed once he did so.

The noise of the street disappeared, and Wil exchanged a dazed look with Ella. She had let go of his hand, but their shared uncertainty comforted him.

Ella nearly jumped into his arms as the entire room momentarily shook. It soon steadied itself, but there was a distinct sensation that the entire room was moving upward.

Neither Liz nor the man expressed an ounce of emotion as the small closet shuddered. Wil saw his own bewildered face reflected on Ella's and worked hard to regulate his breathing.

He wanted to ask what was happening and why they had entered this chamber, but the man's intimidating presence suggested it would be best to save his questions for later.

For now, he had to put his faith in Liz and trust that wherever they were headed, she would know what to do once they got there.

But that was easier said than done.

20

THE MOVING SENSATION ABRUPTLY STOPPED. Wil gave Ella a stunned look of relief, and she gave him a nod and a restrained giggle in return. His heart was beating rapidly, but the trepidation he felt wasn't due to the contraption they were in. There was something about what was about to happen that didn't sit well with him. What scared him more was the feeling nothing about his life would be the same again.

He chuckled to himself. *The same as what exactly?* His life had been nothing short of a whirlwind of change for the past month, from Marco's death to being forced to leave the Sphere, to traveling across a world he had spent his entire life believing was uninhabitable. If someone told him life would be normal from now on, he wouldn't even know what that would mean. Where would he go? What would he do? He had one purpose right now, and hopefully this Director would hold the key for him to move forward.

"This device is called an elevator," Liz said, finally answering the questioning looks he had shared with Ella. "It's a means of transport to higher floors in these tall buildings."

The door slid open again, and Wil nearly fell backward. Nothing could have prepared him for the sight that lay outside.

He squinted, unsure if what he was seeing was real or if it were a projection. Ella mirrored his scrunched face of both wonder and confusion.

The four of them stepped onto a wide platform. They were now high above a city unlike anything Wil had ever seen before or had even imagined.

Massive skyscrapers lined the sky, built with metal and glass. He had seen photos of ancient cities, but he had never imagined actually seeing one in person. Flying vehicles hovered between the buildings; buildings that climbed into the sky, blocking out views of the ocean beyond. Below them, people hurriedly made their way to their destinations along sidewalks lining the streets, and more vehicles wound their way along the paved roads.

Surrounding everything was the shimmering green force field circling the city, seemingly allowing sunlight to flow in naturally. Just as it had done from the outside, the force field revealed nothing beyond the limits of the City Center other than the sun. It was a wall of green that appeared to be almost alive, as light danced vertically along its surface.

The platform they stood on was encased in glass and a white track ran from its edge, through the sky and into the city. Several more tracks branched out from the inner city to four similar platforms that hugged the City Center boundary.

A white train car sat outside the platform. They had similar rail transport vessels within the Sphere, used to travel to the Core, but it was flatter than those egg-shaped vessels. The biggest difference was how high the rail traveled through the sky; they had to be hundreds of feet in the air.

Liz and the suited man stepped inside, and Ella and Wil wordlessly followed.

The transport was essentially a glass bubble with white trim. From within it, they could see the entire city spread out before them. Although elaborate, the city itself occupied less space than Wil had imagined. Half of what lay within the force field was water.

"How is this possible?" Wil asked, breaking the silence the group had shared since entering the elevator. The hum of the transport car was light, and the ride itself was smooth, as if it wasn't touching the track at all. "How can all this exist within the SZ?"

"The City Center isn't part of the Silent Zone," Liz said. "The ancients erected the field to stem its effects. Though the bots can't see through this shield any more than they can within the SZ itself."

"The ancients had that ability? Are there more cities like this?"

"We don't know for sure, but we don't think so. You've probably figured out that it's related to the technology used to develop the Spheres. This is the only city we know that uses it."

The city moved quickly beneath them as they entered the metropolis. The polished glass and steel structures that surrounded them looked as if they had ignored everything that had been happening outside of the force field for centuries.

In a way, Wil supposed they had.

Shadows cast over the shuttle as they entered the city's core. Structures loomed overhead, higher than anything Wil would have thought was possible.

"Did the ancients build these?" Wil leaned on a banister on the edge of the pod, trying to take in everything he could.

"The wars destroyed most of the ancient city before the barrier went up," Liz said. "Earthquakes and floods took care of the rest. There's little of the ancient world left."

Wil wanted to ask more, but the expression of their accompanied guard had soured with his questioning. His curiosity was apparently unwelcome.

Liz simply nodded, her face expressionless, as if she understood his realization and agreed.

Their journey lasted only a few minutes before the hum of the pod ceased. Skyscrapers now surrounded them, casting shadows from the surrounding buildings over the faces of Wil and his companions.

The door opened, and a chill came over him.

THE COLD, hard tiled floor reminded Wil of the Sphere. He stopped, his gaze scrutinizing the buildings all around him. He hadn't thought of home in weeks—if he could now call the Guardian settlement that —but something about the feel of the surface underfoot and the adjoining sterile white walls took him back. The school, the offices of the Order, the institutional centers—all had similarly tiled floors. The smell of industrial cleaner drifted around him, burning his nostrils, just as it had in the hallways at his school on those afternoons the Order had forced him to stay late. He'd often greeted the janitors beginning their rounds, who'd smelled exactly the same way these halls did now.

Until that moment, thoughts of home had only conjured images of the bots and the suffering they had caused. Now, he thought of his family for the first time and missed them, and then he felt guilty for not having done so sooner.

His parents worked hard, and they always provided the full extent of what the Guardians had allotted them. Wil had pushed thoughts of them aside. He'd *had* to push those feelings aside. If he hadn't, they would have overwhelmed him. He did the same again now. He had to focus on why he'd left and what he could do now to help them.

With any luck, Sierra was greeting family and friends from the Sphere who had been liberated from their oppressors, as they had. When Sierra's device had taken out the Sphere's force field, it had ended centuries of lies for its inhabitants. Part of him wished he could be there to help his people, but he knew he had a much greater task ahead of them. If he was to secure their future and help humanity to survive, his path needed to take him in another direction.

Once Sierra had proven there was a way to get outside the Sphere, he knew he'd had to follow her into whatever world awaited them. If he hadn't, his family would have been a target. Then, as the Guardians' lies had revealed themselves, the magnitude of death and destruction had become apparent, and he hadn't been able to sit idle any longer.

The world that stood outside, a city he had been told shouldn't exist from fifty-two stories in the air, came into focus. The tallest building in the Sphere had only been three storeys high. Even in Vegas, there wasn't a building that stood more than a dozen floors.

According to a plaque on the wall, the skyscraper they now entered was named the Renaissance and stood out as a masterpiece, even among the other buildings that rose sky high in the City Center. Though Wil assumed more materials had been incorporated than were visible, the exterior appeared to be made entirely of glass. It also stood at least ten stories taller than any other building to grace the Center.

Their escort hadn't slowed, but Wil couldn't help but take in the spectacle. Ella and Liz had continued to match the pace of the guard, who seemed eager to be rid of his charges.

Wil braced himself against the railing that lined the windows, suddenly feeling unsteady on his feet. An entire city lay below, and the only thing that separated him from a lethal descent was a thin rail and a wall of glass. The entire exterior of the building seemed to be one big window, marked only by the seams in the glass panes. He could only bring himself to linger for a few moments before carrying on, a little disappointed at being hurried along, but the view was making him dizzy. The next hallway they turned down was solid on either side, and Wil breathed a sigh of relief.

The passageway led them down yet another corridor, which then opened into a large room that appeared to be meant for waiting. Red couches lined the walls, contrasting with the white walls that rose only part way up to the tall ceilings. Behind the half-walls, the true glass walls exposed themselves yet again.

A behemothic wooden desk stood at the far end of the open space, and behind it, deep wood paneling decorated another partial wall that reminded Wil of something he had seen from photos of centuries ago. A place and time marked by business dealings and currencies that, as far as he knew, had long since faded away.

A lone man sat behind the desk, his head down as he typed furiously on a datapad. Their escort gestured to the desk, gave Liz a shallow nod, and turned around to disappear the way they had come.

The man behind the desk had a boyish smile, light blond hair, and an odd way of wringing his hands. Wil wasn't sure if the man was young or if he'd altered his face. His complexion was so smooth, Wil was sure the man was wearing makeup. Wil would have thought him attractive, but he was flawless to the point of discomfort. He had painted his eyebrows on, and his blue eyes were so bright, they seemed unnatural. His dark hair was streaked with blue, styled with thick curls, and reminded Wil of the stadium attendees. The man tugged nervously at his dark charcoal suit jacket, which resembled Fry's in appearance, though it had blue-colored trim and fit much better on account of its higher quality of fabric and tailoring.

"Welcome back, Elizabeth Runar." The young man basically tripped over himself to say the words. Wil guessed the fifty-second floor saw few guests. "Director Sens has been expecting you for several days now. Did the mission go as planned?"

The man's blue eyes were eager with anticipation. He leaned on his desk, his hands resting on it awkwardly, and Wil worried he might jump over it and overwhelm them with an embrace. The man seemed harmless enough, just overly eager.

"That's for me to discuss with the Director," Liz replied. "Could you please let him know we have arrived?"

The man's shoulders slumped as his gaze fell to the floor, and his expression soured as he tapped a few keys on his datapad. "He's in his office," he said, his previous bounce now deflated. "He'll see you now."

Liz strode confidently through the seating area and walked around the desk. A small opening in the wall behind the desk gave way to an open chamber. Around the bend, the rest of the floor transformed into a single office. Floor-to-ceiling windows lined three sides of a room so vast Wil had seen nothing like it before.

At the far end, a larger set man stood with his back turned to them. The room otherwise held a single desk, a few couches, several potted plants, and not much else, making the room feel like a sterile, empty cavern. They crossed the cold tile floor as they approached the man, who continued to stare off into the distance.

"Did you know that the City Center used to be twice its current size?" the man said. His speech was slow and deliberate, pausing on each syllable half a beat longer than seemed necessary. Wil couldn't tell if he was talking to them or himself.

"A hundred years ago, half of the city fell into the sea. The completion of a century-long process of water rising, earthquakes, and poor craftsmanship. In the blink of an eye, our great-great-grandparents lost control of half of the most technologically advanced civilization left in existence. A century before that, our ancestors had had to fend off a plague of its own creation. Artificial intelligence had run amok, and the only way they thought they had to save themselves was to shut off the city from the rest of the world."

The man turned around, facing them. His hair was graying, but Wil wouldn't have called him old. He had bright green highlights through his hair, which only added to the crazed look he had on his face. This man, too, wore a suit, though it was gray and had little in the way of embellishment.

"We've had our problems," he continued. "But mostly it's worked for two centuries. We were fortunate enough that we could grow crops outside the field but still within the Protected Area. And now? Now what will we do?"

The man lifted his gaze and jumped slightly as if he hadn't realized they were there. He tugged at the edges of his suit jacket and straightened his posture. Wil thought the man's face flushed slightly, but it faded quickly as he cleared his throat.

Nearly a dozen chairs sat empty around an elongated wooden table, as if waiting for a meeting.

"Director Sens," Liz said. "I assume you've heard about the breach in the Silent Zone."

The man waved a chubby hand as though the news was of no consequence. "A minor inconvenience," he said. "We've had fluctuations before. I'm more concerned with the farmers trying to tear down the city gate."

"Our reports indicate this is more than a fluctuation," Liz answered. "There is a gap in the SZ that runs the entire depth of the Outer Ring. Even a few homes on the edge of the Middle Ring claim to have been affected. There have never been so many warning lights active, and it's now been over twelve hours with no improvement."

"Is this what you've come to talk to me about?" The Director's tone shifted from light-hearted grandfather to irritated in the blink of an eye. His arms crossed over his chest and he shook his head, one eye still peering out the window.

Beside them, a door opened.

"It's like I said, Father," a woman's voice said as she stepped through the doorway. "The bots were attacking homes all the way through the . . ."

The woman's face was familiar, though it was much cleaner than their last encounter. Wil almost didn't recognize her without the red leather suit.

Kayla greeted Wil with a warm grin, but she didn't acknowledge the two women standing beside him. She had replaced the tight leather outfit with a suit similar in style to the one Director Sens wore, though it sported the same burgundy tones.

Kayla regained herself and continued. "All the way through the farmland."

Though the warmth in her smile didn't fade, Kayla shot Wil a warning glare with a brief shake of her head. The smell of lavender and honey filled the room as she entered, and Wil had a hard time not staring. He had found Kayla attractive in the pale light of the previous evening, but now that he could see her features better as daylight streamed through the windows, she was drop-dead gorgeous.

And the Director's daughter, apparently.

"Kayla," the Director sighed. "Please. Now is not the time for your stories."

"But it's true!"

Director Sens shook his head, as if trying to clear his mind of what his daughter was saying. He turned his attention back to Liz. "Are these the two you spoke to me about? The ones our fate is tied to?"

"The boy is," Liz answered.

Wil shot her a confused look. How much had she told the man?

"You took long enough to return here," Sens said. "I've already had multiple reports of the fall of Vegas. I sent you out there so you could bring me back word before the event happened."

"We weren't expecting it to happen so soon," Liz said. "We didn't even arrive before it fell completely. And we were met with . . . *complications* on the way back."

"What complications?" Sens asked.

"The Order, Prowlers, bots; the usual setbacks of traveling through the Interzone. None of which I expect you to understand."

"You think me naïve," Sens replied. "But I understand the reality of the world outside San Francisco."

"Just because a messenger tells you something doesn't mean you understand it," Liz responded coldly.

Sens crossed his arms over his chest and leaned back. "Is there a point to this? Or did you come here to insult me?"

"The crux of the matter," Liz continued, "is that my vision came true. Their SZ fell and the bots attacked Vegas. If you are not naïve, then make preparations now before it is too late."

"As I've said before," Sens replied, "our force field will protect us. This is precisely what it was designed for."

"What of your citizens who live in the Rings? Have you decided if you will let them in? Or do you agree with your Council that their lives are of little value? You don't have much time to decide. Already they swarm your gates, and only a small section of the Outer Ring has fallen. What happens when it all goes? What happens when there is no buffer between the bots and your walls?"

Director Sens clasped his hands behind his back and turned to the window, his focus lost somewhere in the distance. "Tell me about Vegas," he said, sidestepping Liz's interrogation. "I granted you the funding to chase your wild claims, and yet I've heard stories coming from the streets instead of from you. I'd like to know what you can tell me."

"The battle played out mostly as I had foreseen. The Silent Zone fell, and the bots destroyed most of the city."

"Pfft," Sens scoffed. "There wasn't much left standing to begin with."

"That may be," Liz said, her voice steady, determined. "But thousands of people still call the city their home."

The Director sighed and waved the sentiment off. "The Zone, though, was restored. That tells me these failings could be temporary."

"Vegas had a stroke of luck that you will not see," Liz said. "The girl I foresaw, her actions stopped the battle, but she has other matters that need to be dealt with. She won't be able to save San Francisco."

Wil tried to put the pieces of what Liz was saying together. Had she foreseen Sierra's actions to restore the SZ? How much did her ability reveal to her?

"And what of these two? Are they of no use?"

Ella's eyes nearly bugged out of her head. "Now, wait a minute!"

Liz held a hand up, silencing the protest.

"They have a purpose in all this," Liz continued. "But not in the way you'd hope. There will be nobody to restore the SZ here."

"*Pah!*" the man balked. "If the SZ falls, it is of little concern to me. As I said, the ancients developed our force field to protect the City Center from just such an attack."

Kayla stepped forward. "Father, we should consider the scope of our influence, not only those within the City Center."

"I'm not convinced it will fall."

"You're wrong, old man," Wil said. "It's already begun."

Wil wasn't sure why the conservative leader was refusing to see the reality that had descended upon the city. Liz's diplomacy didn't seem to be getting through him.

"Elizabeth," Director Sens said. "Who is this boy, and why have you brought him here?"

"Wil is special, and it was important for me to bring him here today."

"*Pah!* You and your hunches. The kid needs to learn some respect. Guards! Please show the boy out."

Wil took a step back. He might have been a bit rude, but he hadn't expected to cause offense. That aside, he couldn't help thinking back to how he would have been treated if he'd spoken to an Order member or Guardian in that way.

"He stays," Liz said, shooting Wil an angry glare. "He has moments of rashness, but he still has an important role to play. I had to bring him here."

"What nonsense are you talking about?" Sens asked, growing noticeably frustrated.

"Wil," Liz replied, "is the only chance San Francisco has of survival."

21

"THIS IS NONSENSE," the Director stated, waving a dismissive hand at Liz.

"Is it?" Liz asked defiantly. "I told you about the fall of the Vegas *weeks* before it happened. I told you the fate of the city depended on two youths I had foreseen. And because of the recruits we deployed, we minimized the damage to the city before the girl could unleash the ancient weapon and provide the citizens with a safe space once again."

"And yet you claim the same can't be done here," Sens replied. "So, what would you have me do? I thought you were seeking information that could help."

"We can still minimize the impact. Deploy the City Guard and allow the Resistance to station ourselves in the Inner Ring. We'll be a line of defense against the bots when they encroach into the city limits."

"Why would I agree to this?" the Director countered. "It'll needlessly scare the citizens. There will be greater chaos than there already is, and the force field remains in place. It *will* stop any attack on the City Center."

"If you're so confident of its integrity, why not open the gates to those who'd seek refuge? There are a few dozen farmers who've already lost their homes. That would be a good place to start."

The Director's face reddened.

"The truth is, Director," Liz continued, "the fight is already in your backyard. I'm offering you assistance to bring it under control."

"You know it's not that easy," Sens replied. "Even if I allow your fighters to prepare for battle within the Rings, the citizens won't understand, and my opposition will use it against me. I have an election coming. I can't throw caution to the wind based on a *dream*."

Wil rolled his eyes. They were wasting their time. If the Director didn't want to allow the Resistance to mobilize, then he definitely wouldn't send guards to wage war against the bots outside the city's influence. It was a nightmare. Wil had agreed to come west because he thought he could help weaken the bots' stranglehold on humanity, but so far, he had only found people who were resigned to do nothing.

"Your people are dying out there!" Wil growled. "How will your electorate feel when they learn you chose to let them die, even when you were offered help?"

Ella put a hand on his shoulder. He tried to shrug it off but caught the warning look she was giving him. The pleading in her eyes told him he should back down.

The Director's face had turned purple. Kayla stepped in front of him, attempting to distract him.

"Dad, please," Kayla said. The Director looked to his daughter, and though his face didn't lose its newly acquired color, he disengaged.

Kayla crossed the floor toward Wil and his party, her hips swaying as she approached. Wil could feel Ella stiffening beside him.

"These people are our guests," Kayla continued. "I feel like we should at least hear them out."

"Why?" the Director asked. "Clearly they are looking to gain a stronger foothold for the Resistance. I will not allow it, not so close to the election."

Kayla stopped in front of Wil, and her dark brown eyes stared into his own. He tried to read them, tried to get a sense of what she was thinking, but she masked her intent well.

Wil struggled to reconcile the woman that stood before him with the costumed fighter who had sat dejectedly in the cell next to him at the stadium. The glint in her eyes was the same, though, as was how she smelled. The honey and lavender scent overpowering from only a few feet away.

Under the bright fluorescent lighting, Kayla seemed more mature than the teenager she was, like someone who knew their way around being in charge. She exuded a different energy to the person who had been running for her life with a deactivated robot in tow.

"I'm not convinced," Kayla said, and her expression finally broke into a knowing smile as she turned away from Wil. "The Ringers are threatening to knock down our doors. Perhaps if we give them the illusion of action, they'll be more inclined to be peaceful."

The Director's demeanor softened at his daughter's intervention, and his hand fidgeted with a corner of his graying mustache. "If the citizens judge our actions as an admission of there being a threat, then there will be chaos. I can't let that happen. As far as we're concerned, we are fortified within the force field. Stirring doubts about that fact will serve us no favors."

"Chaos will come if we don't act," Kayla suggested, her voice calm and reassuring. "These people are offering us help. If we simply turn the other way while they prepare to fight, rather than providing our own soldiers, the citizens will believe there's no merit to the threat. And while that may be good for the election, it's not good for the city."

Sens looked uncertain, but he appeared, at least, to be considering his daughter's words.

"We're having dinner with the Council this evening," Kayla said. "I think they should join us."

Sens sighed. He returned his hands behind his back and paced toward the window.

"It has been two hundred years since the ancients established the protective Zone around this city," he said. "In all that time, it has safeguarded those living in the Rings, and now, when my re-election is less than a week away, it falters." He let his thoughts trail off.

"Decide wisely, Director," Liz warned. "This could be the

moment of the city's greatest victory or its greatest defeat. And whichever happens, you'll go down in history as the one behind it."

WIL'S LEGS didn't want to cooperate. The boat hadn't even left the dock, and already he was unsteady on his feet, as if he might topple over as it bounced along with the waves.

At Kayla's insistence, the Director had agreed to invite the three of them to their dinner party, and to stay the night in the City Center. They had been provided accommodations in the Director's guest tower.

But she had neglected to mention they'd be eating on a boat.

A vessel floating on top of the water's surface seemed like a peculiar place to host a party. In the Sphere, they hadn't been allowed to venture near their only lake, never mind float atop of it. Wil wondered if there'd ever be an end to the surprises this world had to offer.

Wil shuffled uncomfortably in the suit the Director's staff had provided him, having never worn anything so constricting before. He'd opted for a less pretentious style than the bright and bold colored outfits that lined the closet of their accommodations, settling on a coral blue suit with dark trim.

Ella and Liz were both provided with formal dresses.

Wil tried not to stare at Ella, whose dress accentuated her curves in a way that her normal desert wear never could. She had avoided the brightly colored options altogether, choosing a black dress that shimmered with silver when the light hit it.

Liz had chosen a bright purple dress that was equally well fitted. *Leave it to Liz to choose something bold,* Wil thought. The dress did little to soften the woman's confident demeanor; she was now a powerhouse that looked damn good along with it.

Despite their ability to clean up well, neither woman appeared to be comfortable. The way they shifted and pulled at the edges of their skirts made it clear they were used to wearing more rugged attire, more fit for fighting than making a statement.

"Do we *have* to wear these?" Ella asked at one point. "I think I'd rather be naked."

Wil cleared his throat and pretended not to have heard, studying himself in the mirror to keep himself out of their conversation.

"Perhaps Sens would be more accommodating to our requests if you were," Liz said, and both women burst out laughing.

Wil felt utterly ridiculous in the blue suit he had decided to wear, and the way Ella smirked when she looked at him confirmed it, though he had to admit the blue made the green tints in his hazel eyes pop, and the slim-fitting nature of the shirt highlighted the 'V' in his figure. He was glad they'd be inside the boat, rather than on its deck. As fashionable as the shirt might be, it wouldn't offer any protection from the cold ocean breeze.

If it hadn't been for Kayla's insistence that they join the Council for dinner, Wil would have been looking for a way back out the city gates. There was nothing for him here, as far as he was concerned. The Director didn't want to protect the perimeter of the city, never mind launch an assault on the bots. Their time could be better spent elsewhere.

Despite the women's heeled shoes, they didn't seem to have the same struggle walking on the boat as Wil. Ella grabbed Wil's arm, but he wasn't sure if it was for affection or support. He hoped it wasn't for stability, because it was more likely he'd bring her down with him.

Ella gave a short laugh as he tried to gain his bearings.

"Don't laugh!" he said, half in jest. "I've never been on a boat before!" A short wave punched the boat up a foot, which sent him stumbling briefly before he regained his balance and was thrown into a fit of laughter.

The boat itself was the size of a building. A yacht, Kayla had called it.

It was of such impressive construction that once they were belowdecks, Wil wouldn't have been able to tell whether the craft was a boat, or a building, had it not been for the constant movement of the floor beneath him. The yacht's interior was as modern and sleek as the Director's office tower. Wood flooring lined the deck and the cabin, and large glass windows surrounded the entire vessel. The atrium ceiling was made of glass, yet there were no stars to be seen. The sun had set, but both the green hue of the field and the lights from the city blotted out any hope of stargazing. The barrier produced enough of a glow that, whether inside or outside the field, the city likely never saw complete darkness.

The technology in the city had far surpassed anything Wil had ever imagined. Every light, every knob, every button was a fascinating treasure. He'd grown up collecting artifacts from the ancients, imagining what their world must have been like, finding a button here, a coin there, occasionally getting lucky and finding a cup or a watch. Nothing could have prepared him for the wonders San Francisco offered.

Everything relied on the power of the sun. Even the yacht drew its energy from solar panels lining its roof.

Yet, despite all of the surrounding marvels, Wil still wanted nothing more than to leave and find a way to prepare for the battle that was inevitably ahead of them.

He'd prefer not to have to defend another city, but it appeared that was unavoidable—and this time, they would receive little help from those in charge.

From Kayla's blasé description of the evening's meeting, Wil had been under the impression it would be a small gathering at most. Several dozen people, however, filled the decks. High-ranking officials meandered through the cabin, in no real hurry to get to the atrium where the main event would be held.

"We need to go to the washroom," Ella said, pulling Wil in close enough for him to hear her above the noise of the ship. "Don't go running off."

"Where am I going to go?" he asked. "I can't swim."

Ella rolled her eyes and left with Liz.

The crowd comprised a variety of people, though all looked extremely wealthy. Many could have been audience members at the stadium. How many of their associates had been killed in the bot attack that night? Would those losses hold no sway over their perception of the incoming threat?

Some in the crowd, though similarly dressed, were more muscular, their hair not quite as well done and their clothes poorly tailored for their frames. They reminded Wil of Fry, as though they were trying to give the appearance of fitting into a society they weren't truly a part of. He shrugged. Who was he to know what was normal? Nobody else seemed to pay any mind to the differences in appearance. Everybody was dressed bizarrely compared to anything he had ever seen.

"Nice to see you made it." Kayla stepped out from the crowd, greeting him with a smile. Her burgundy dress flowed as she crossed the wooden floor. It was similar in cut to the ensemble she had worn in the stadium, though this was more of an actual dress than a costume, and the material was fabric rather than stiff leather. Wil couldn't help but notice how complimentary it was to the warm tone of her skin.

"Where else would we go?" Wil said. "The city gates are closed. It's not like we could leave."

Kayla shrugged. "There are always ways if you're resourceful. And I get the sense you are."

"We came here to convince your father to aid us in the fight against the bots," he said. "If our presence here could help with that, what do we have to lose?"

"I'm of the same mindset. Why refuse help if we're under threat? And beyond that, if our city is threatened, it is the responsibility of our City Guard to be among those fighting."

"So why not tell that to your father? He seems to listen to you."

Kayla's smile faded, and she looked around as if ensuring there wasn't anyone close by who was listening. "My father is a child," she said. "I can sway his decision, but I need to be crafty about it. The intended outcome needs to seem like his own idea, or he'll push back. Any sense of confrontation and he digs his heels in and refuses to change his mind."

Kayla stepped closer to him, her perfume stronger than ever. Part of him wished she wasn't so intoxicating. Did she know the effect she had on him?

Either way, this was a rare opportunity to talk to the woman alone.

"Your father doesn't seem too concerned about the SZ falling," he said.

"The ancients promised the field would grant us protection. He has to cling to that truth. But he is short-sighted in his approach."

"And what about the people in the Rings? Will you be able to convince him to offer them protection?"

"Father will bend to the will of the masses. He won't decide one way or the other until he knows his choice will be popular."

A server carrying a tray laden with a mountain of food walked by. Crab, fish, oysters, and cheeses decorated the platter. Wil thought back to the hall at the municipal building filled with carts, both full and empty, coming and going from the entrances.

"And how do *you* feel about it?" Wil asked.

She leaned in towards him, her scent overpowering. She was so close, for a moment, that Wil thought she was going to kiss him. His heart raced at the idea, but instead she leaned in and whispered in his ear, her warm breath sending a shiver through him.

"You have more allies here than you know, Bot Killer. Stay out of the way and don't do anything stupid."

What was that supposed to mean?

He wanted to ask a thousand questions, but the words got caught in his throat as he inhaled her lavender and honey scent.

The quizzical look on his face must have spoken volumes. Kayla moved her head so she could look him in the eye, her face mere inches away from his own. "A line is about to be drawn, Wil. Don't get caught on the wrong side."

22

Kayla walked away, her hips swaying purely for Wil's benefit.

"Getting a good look?" Ella's voice snapped him out of his trance.

Wil turned a dozen shades of red before Liz interrupted, cutting him off before he had a chance to deny it.

"We should find out where we're sitting," she said.

The other diners seemed to have had the same idea, as they set about migrating to the tabled area in the main atrium.

Three long tables outlined the room's perimeter and smaller circular tables filled the middle, leaving the entranceway to the rest of the boat clear.

Wil reached for Ella's arm to escort her to their seats, but she coldly shrugged him off.

Before he could react, an attendant pointed them to the far end of one of the side tables, and they made their way to their seats in silence.

The lights of the room reflected on the glass ceiling, rendering the windows useless. The faint green hue of the nearby force field was all that made it through.

At the front of the room, Director Sens sat at the center table, with Kayla to his right. On either side of them sat four officials. Wil guessed from their plain black suits that they represented the

Council. Others at the side tables also wore unembellished suits, but those dominating tables in the middle were all dressed in flamboyant colors.

Kayla was the only person at the head table whose outfit bore any color.

In the conversations he'd had with them, Wil couldn't recall either Kayla or Director Sens mentioning Kayla's mother. It seemed odd that she wasn't also present at the head table. There were several women around the table, but none looked to be close enough to the Director to fit the bill.

"Is the Director married?" he asked.

"His wife disappeared shortly after Kayla was born," Liz replied. "She hasn't been seen since."

Wil let his eye wander over the table, his mind drifting to Kayla's warning. It closely mirrored what Liz had told him a few nights prior. One of them, at least, seemed to realize the bots were a threat to the city. Maybe Kayla could talk some sense into her father.

"Be careful with that one, Wil," Liz said, keeping her voice low. "I've heard many rumors about her. She treads a dangerous path."

"Funny," Wil responded. "I've heard the same about you."

He shot Ella a glance.

Liz shrugged off the comment.

"Liz isn't trying to get into your pants," Ella scoffed.

"Says who?" Wil replied, a grin on his face, which earned him an eye roll from Ella.

Liz put up a hand. "Enough, you two! Not here. Ella does have a point, though. She wants something from you, Wil, but it's probably not what it seems. Don't trust her."

"Is this another one of your visions?" Wil asked derisively.

"I don't need visions to see what's as clear as the desert sky. That girl is planning something, and it isn't anything good."

Ella gave Wil a look of smug satisfaction. They hadn't talked properly since the stadium. It had been clear from the moment Ella had met Kayla that she didn't like the woman. He knew Ella wasn't one to talk about her emotions, but jealousy wasn't like her either.

He'd thought the two of them were close enough for her to at least talk to him about it.

A loud bell rang three times, and everybody grew silent. Director Sens stood, and all eyes were focused on him. Several uniformed guards remained at full attention, spread out around the atrium.

Were they ensuring nobody else entered, or that nobody could leave?

"Friends and supporters," the Director began. "As you know, our beloved city is under siege. The threat from the Rings has grown to new heights. Even as we speak, the Ringers are trying to break through our protective barrier. If they are allowed to continue, the sanctity of our City Center lies in jeopardy."

Nods of affirmation and quiet murmurs of approval filled the atrium.

Threat from the Rings? Wil raised an eyebrow. Was that truly what the Council believed?

"If allowed to continue, these people will bring their crime and delinquency into our streets. You know our opposition would love nothing more than to allow these people in, as they are supporters of their lawlessness and of their handouts. If she were elected, I wouldn't be surprised if Bhavika and her party would even push to give the Ringers a right to vote.

"As it stands, I continue to be the best chance the City Center has of maintaining the order we have all become accustomed to over the years. The Ringer rebellion could be the single greatest threat our city has faced since the ancients erected the force field."

Wil couldn't believe what he was hearing. Not only did the Director's words completely ignore the real threat of an incoming Guardian attack, but he was implying the real source of danger were people under his own jurisdiction.

He can't be serious.

"Starting tomorrow," the Director continued, "we will be deploying the Guard into the Rings to quell the rioters and bring justice back to our city."

A round of applause started as he uttered the words.

Before Wil knew what he was doing, he was on his feet. "What is wrong with you?" he roared. He knew it was impetuous, but he also couldn't believe the display of agreement from the Director's audience. The entire room was acting irrationally. Did they not know the actual source of the danger they faced?

Ella and Liz each grabbed an arm and tried to pull him back into his seat, but Wil was determined. Even Kayla looked at him with a warning glare, motioning with her hand across her throat for him to cut it out.

"The Ringers are citizens of *your* city," Wil continued, "and their homes are being destroyed as we speak, by the real enemy—the Guardians. Worry all you want about the people on your doorstep; the bots will kill them off when the SZ falls. Then you'll be forced to face the real threat, with the blood of your own people on your hands."

Gasps rung out across the room. The shuffling of chairs and murmurings among the guests filled the atrium. Kayla's mouth hung open, and Director Sens's face turned purple again.

Ella tightened her grip on Wil with both hands and yanked him down.

"What *is* your problem?" she hissed.

"He's blaming the *victims*," he raged. "Rather than addressing the real threat. We wanted support in fighting the bots, not the bloody farmers!"

Sens rested his weight on his knuckles as he leaned against the table. Though the color of his face betrayed his emotions, his cool demeanor remained intact.

"Friends and honored members, I apologize for this young man. I welcomed him here as my guest, but it seems I've made a mistake. Guards, please detain him until we dock."

The nearest guards took two steps toward Wil but didn't get any further.

Three individuals dressed in gray suits stepped past the guards and into the atrium. A woman led the group, her golden-brown wrinkled face indicating she was at least as old as Sens. A solid streak of dark brown ran through her silver hair from front to back.

The two men behind her, while not large, stood at the ready, eyeing the crowd for potential threats to their escort. They stepped right past the guards, who looked to the Director for instructions but didn't stop the trio. The three newcomers anxiously shifted their gaze around the room, as if expecting an ambush.

Though the guards made no offensive move, the half dozen Council members at the head table rose from their seats, drawing blasters.

The face of the newly entered woman betrayed no emotion, but she nonchalantly put her hands up in protest. "We're not here to fight," she said.

"Then what are you doing here, Bhavika?" Sens said. Unlike the rest of the table, he remained unfazed, cracking his knuckles absentmindedly. Having a dozen people with guns protecting you likely had that effect. "This is a private party. Invite only."

"Sens, I'm disappointed," Bhavika answered. She pulled on a finger of the dark gray glove that clung to her hand, making a show of the action. "I thought we were friends."

"You have two minutes to get off my boat. And you can take this Resistance fool with you." Sens motioned to Wil.

Wil stood, but Ella and Liz reached to pull him down again.

"This is not our fight," Liz whispered to him.

"You're not the one they want to haul off," Wil said.

"You need to show some self-control," Liz replied.

"Who is this woman?" Wil asked.

"Bhavika is the leader of the opposition party. She's running against Sens in the upcoming election."

The six uniformed guards that stood throughout the room now had a hand on their weapons, but none had drawn them yet.

The only other person at the head table to be sat motionless was Kayla. She had her hands folded in front of her, seemingly content to see how the situation played out.

"You thought wrong," Sens answered. "But I doubt that's why you're here."

"You've been ignoring my calls," Bhavika said. "I wanted to speak to you face to face about our situation."

"And you thought interrupting my party was the best way to do it?"

Bhavika lifted an eyebrow. "If I were surprised, Sens, I'd be insulted. I received the invite to attend this morning. Besides, what other opportunity was I going to get to speak to you and the Council all in the same room?"

Sens tapped his fingers on the table impatiently. "As kind-hearted as I am, I wouldn't dream of ruining my evening by inviting you."

Bhavika carried on, unaffected by the remark. "On our doorstep are hundreds of farmers who have had their homes and crops destroyed by bots, and how have you responded?"

"We've shut the gates to keep the chaos at bay." Sens waved, as if it were the most obvious response.

"You've left our farmers to die and cut off our food supply in the process!"

"Bhavika," Sens said smolderingly. "You can address your concerns during your campaign, not during my private dinner!" Sens's voice was raised, his face returning to its purple shade.

"Those farmers need a place to go *now*," she said. "Not a month from now. What are you going to do when the Silent Zone falls? Let them all suffer at the hands of the bots?"

"The Silent Zone *will not fall*," Sens said through gritted teeth.

"Haven't you been listening? It already has." A toothy smile crept over the woman's face. "Just ask your daughter. She was there."

Kayla's face turned a deep shade of red, but she still didn't move.

"Leave my daughter out of this," Sens retorted. But Wil couldn't help but notice Sens's eyebrow rising at the implication, and he guessed Kayla would have some questions to answer later.

"Fine, but all we're asking is for you to open the gates for the farmers to seek refuge. We have more than enough space for them."

"You're insane," Sens said. "We open the gates for these farmers now, and where does it stop? The Ringers will overrun us. There are three times as many of them as there are of us, and most are criminals. I won't have them wreaking havoc on what we've established.

"We'll have people from the entire west coast knocking on our door. Are you prepared to let *them* in? How about the bandits?

Prowlers? What happens when the Order seeks sanctuary after their robot gods turn on them?"

"You would let our citizens die?" Bhavika asked pointedly.

"We'll *all* die if we allow a free-for-all! We'd run out of food in a month."

"You're all going to die anyway!" Wil shouted at them both. "You think the bots are going to stop terrorizing your people because of an ancient force field? One by one, they won't stop until we're all under their control. And instead of working together, you're fighting with each other? We need to rise in unity and fight against them!"

Both of the leaders turned to Wil and looked at him as though he had two heads.

"How things are changing! Inviting the Resistance to your parties, old man." Bhavika smirked. "It's so off-brand."

Sens rolled his eyes and waved dismissively.

"A mistake, Bhavika. Clearly this one doesn't know his place."

Sens snapped his fingers. "Guards! Why is he *still* here? Take them upstairs until we're docked. *All of them.*"

Ella punched Wil in the shoulder. Liz shook her head, raising a palm to her face.

"You can't keep your idiot mouth shut," Ella muttered.

Guards moved behind them. One grabbed Wil forcefully by the arm while two others each grabbed Ella and Liz, lifting them out of their seats and pushing them down the hall.

Wil's guard was less efficient and held back, taking his time. Wil thought the guard was perhaps interested in the exchange that still continued in their wake. He scanned for a way he might use the man's delay to his advantage but found none.

"Why *did* you ask me to come here anyway, old man?" Bhavika asked.

Sens's face contorted in the first sign of emotion other than anger. "Why do you keep saying that, you old bat? I *didn't* ask you to come here. What kind of game are you playing?"

Kayla rose from her seat. All eyes, including Sens's, went to her.

Ella and Liz were already out of the room, but Wil's guard stopped in anticipation.

Wil shot an uneasy glance at Ella across the room, but her focus was on the guard that had her hands bound behind her back. The two women disappeared from sight.

The rest of the room seemed to have forgotten Wil existed.

Bhavika and her two companions appeared as confused as to what was happening as anyone else.

Before she could say anything, chaos erupted.

23

THE GLASS CEILING SHATTERED, crashing over the partygoers in a cacophony of sound. They scrambled as the shards rained down upon them.

The guard behind Wil shoved him to the floor, lifting his blaster in a reflex response.

The rest of the crowd hit the ground. The few who were armed also pulled out their weapons, instinctively pointing them at each other while wondering where the true source of the action had come from. Wil caught a glimpse of Kayla, who had a maniacal grin on her face as she brandished a blaster of her own and seemed to seek a way to exit the room.

Through the broken ceiling, a dozen masked intruders rappelled into the atrium. Attached to their ropes, the strangers were equipped from head to toe in protective gear and were armed with energy weapons. It only took moments for them to reach the deck and open fire.

Guards fired back, causing a blanket of blaster fire. Bhavika's guards unsheathed knives to strike at closer range.

Wil stayed low to the ground, watching everything unfold quicker than he was able to process. An overturned table provided him with some false sense of protection, but there was nowhere for him to go.

A line of guards now blocked the only exit to the room. They were fish in a barrel.

A fist fight broke out next to him. A masked assailant threw a punch at a middle-aged Council member. There was no contest. The masked man was twice the size and likely half the age of his victim, muscular, and covered in weaponry. The Council member scrambled in desperation. Fumbling for a hold on his attacker, he grabbed onto the man's mask and ripped it off.

Wil gasped.

"T'al?" he said, not loud enough to be heard over the chaos.

The revelation momentarily stunned him, but his friend didn't seem to notice Wil. T'al wound his arm back and struck the man in the jaw with an explosive punch. Teeth went flying and Wil was sure he heard a *crack* as T'al's gloved fist made impact.

T'al tossed the man aside as though he were weightless.

Who were these people? Why was T'al with them?

T'al drew his weapon and fired at an unseen target across the room.

Wil noticed the Director being hauled out of a hidden door with the assistance of several shielded guards. Nobody else seemed to notice the exit.

Kayla, too, was nowhere to be seen.

Wil wanted to help, but he didn't know how, or whom, he should be helping. His instinct was to help fight off these new intruders, but if T'al was with them, he couldn't tell if they were friend or foe.

Was this some sort of plan executed by the Resistance that Liz had failed to tell him about?

Wil regretted being separated from her and Ella, and the fighting completely blocked the path that led out of the atrium, though blaster fire and frenzied shouting indicated there was more fighting past the guards.

He jumped at a *thump* on the ground beside him. Bhavika lay on her belly, mere feet from where he sat. Her face turned toward him, her mouth open and the burn mark from a blaster discharge still steaming on the side of her head. She was completely lifeless.

One by one, Wil watched the suited individuals fall as knives penetrated their guts, blaster fire tore holes in their flesh, or a well-aimed punch knocked them out.

His hiding place wouldn't conceal him for long, and he was dressed no differently than half of the diplomats in the room. He had to make a run for it. If he could find Ella and Liz, they'd know what to do, and how to get off the boat in one piece.

There had been a lull in the action between him and the exit. He had to cross the space unseen.

Nobody appeared to be paying any attention to him, but he remained crouched, ducking behind pillars and tables. He had to step over several bodies and a lot of discarded debris, and he could do nothing to help the crunch of glass beneath his feet, but there was still enough shouting and blaster exchange for him not to have to worry about the sound giving him away.

He hadn't taken more than a dozen steps when a sharp pain struck him in the back of the head and everything went black.

WIL CAME to among the throes of rolling waves which tossed the boat back and forth. All around him was in darkness, and though his eyes were closed, he could tell that the fluorescent lights of the yacht were no longer operable. The sound of the water filled his senses, as well as a group of foreign animals barking in the distance. As he realized he had never truly heard the ocean before, Wil became lost in its all-encompassing sounds.

Then the pain at the back of his head came screaming through to him, and all sense of calm disappeared. The skirmish and the chaos that had broken out aboard the Director's vessel all came roaring back.

Wil fought to open his eyes, though they seemed to weigh a hundred pounds each. A black sky cut off by a green wall filled his vision.

He was outside the force field.

Wil pushed himself up quickly, causing the blood to escape his head, and he braced himself, closing his eyes once again as light-headedness kicked in.

"Whoa! Easy there," a nearby voice said. "You took quite a blow to the head."

A thick hand rested on his back and tried to guide Wil to lie back down.

Wil grabbed onto a thick, hairy arm and held himself up for a moment longer, trying to gather his senses.

When he opened his eyes once again, T'al sat next to him, a look of uncertainty and concern on his face.

"Wouldn't want to be you after a knock like that," T'al said.

Wil struggled to comprehend what T'al was saying, so he instead tried to focus on what lay around him.

He was indeed on a boat, though it wasn't the Director's yacht. This boat was much smaller. He was lying in the open air, and a small cabin was situated near the boat's center with a handful of people inside. Another dozen people sat on the deck nearby.

Wil had to brace himself against the ship's movement as much as his own unsteadiness.

"Where am I?" he asked. "What happened?"

Wil took a deep breath, trying to center himself. Everything around him seemed hazy, as if he were dreaming. The sharpness of the saltwater air betrayed his vision, though. Its chill cut through him with icy daggers. The rest of his senses needed to catch up.

"The Director's guards hit you on the back of the head," T'al said. "Kayla insisted we take you along, rather than leaving you with the others."

Fuzzy memories of the evening swirled in his head with the bobbing of his surroundings.

"Kayla? Others? I don't understand. Why were you there? Why did you attack the party?"

"We've grown tired of waiting at the City Center's indecision, Wil," a familiar woman's voice spoke into the darkness. "War is coming."

Through the haze, Wil tried to make out who was speaking. The woman was sitting behind T'al, her back facing them.

Short black hair with blue streaks that had been spiked and styled out to the sides, barely visible in the dim evening light. A bright white neck between her hairline and her dark outfit.

There was only one person it could be.

"*Voth?*" Wil asked. He didn't know how it was possible, but it made sense that if T'al was there, Voth would be by his side.

"You rescued her?" Wil asked as a smile crept over his face. The man had seemed so lost without his closest friend.

"I was never in need of *rescuing*," Voth said, now standing and turning to face them. The moonlight reflected off her pale skin. Her blue tattoo circled her left eye, searing down her face as though a lightning bolt had formed a geometric pattern and had then regathered itself to continue down her cheek. "The Prowlers didn't take me more than a mile before I slit their throats." She looked to T'al, as if for validation. "But it gave us both a chance to get out from Liz's watchful eye."

Wil studied her as the waves rocked them back and forth. The air blowing over the open water continued to send chills across Wil's exposed skin. The suit jacket he had been wearing had been discarded, and the short-sleeved button-down shirt he wore did little to keep the wind off him. His shirt was damp, more from sweating in his sleep than the seawater, which added to the chill in his bones.

"Do you want to explain what's happening here?" Wil asked. "Are you fighting *against* the Resistance now?"

"Fighting?" T'al asked, eyebrow raised. "No, of course not. But lately our leader seems to have forgotten our purpose. We formed the Resistance to fight the bots at all costs. Ever since Liz had visions of Vegas, she's lost sight of that."

"But her vision was right. She predicted the collapse of the SZ in Vegas."

"We had no business going there," Voth huffed. "In the end, your friend Sierra's magic handled the matter. If anything, we should have brought *her* back with us, but we didn't even manage that. So, what benefit did we get from Liz being right? We lost a lot of good people trying to defend that city, and now San Francisco is doomed to the same fate. We need to take action before it's too late."

"But why attack the Director and the Council? Surely there were easier ways to get Liz out of the picture."

"Liz wasn't the main objective tonight. The Director imprisoning her was only a bonus," Voth said. "Don't get me wrong, we have no ill-will toward Liz. She's a powerful fighter, and she has good intentions. But unfortunately, good intentions aren't nearly enough when you're facing an army of war machines."

Voth rolled up the sleeves of her black sweater, revealing the tattoos that lined her arms. Wil often wondered about the meaning behind them. One arm was decorated with stars; constellations that Wil had learned about in his lessons but had never truly seen until he had ventured out into the desert. Her other arm appeared to reference a map. He didn't recognize the coastline it depicted, but the two of them had never been close enough for him to ask where the place was —or if it still existed.

"We didn't know you'd be there," T'al said. "*Someone* failed to mention it."

T'al looked to his left, to the center of the boat. There were many people crowded on the wooden seats that dominated the boat's middle, but it was clear about who he was implying. In the center of their section sat a woman in a burgundy hooded cape, staring into the night. Wil didn't need anyone to tell him who it was.

"Do you want to explain this one to him?" T'al directed his question to her. "Since you're the reason he's here?"

Kayla stood and pushed her way across the deck, past men and women who seemed to be nursing wounds from the skirmish. She threw back her hood with purpose, approaching them as though as she was in command of the party.

And then Wil realized she had been. It was the reason she had risen from her seat before the fight broke out, and the reason she had disappeared once it began.

"You killed them all?" Wil asked. "Your father? The Council?

Bhavika? What about Liz and Ella? Did you kill them, too?"

Wil clenched his fists. What kind of psychopath would slaughter an entire room of people?

"Not directly." A sly smile crossed Kayla's lips. Though the force field distorted its light, the moon shone brightly upon them, tinting her light blonde hair and white skin a tinge of green. She found a spot beside Wil and sat next to him, pressing her warm body against his. "Let me ask you a question. Why did you follow Liz out here? Why did you ally yourself with a faction leader of the Resistance?"

Wil hesitated. He felt like he was being baited. Three people he had thought he could trust stood before him, but they had possibly killed two others he cared about deeply. If they had killed Ella, he would never forgive them. But mostly, he would never forgive himself for leading another one of his closest friends to their death.

Ella and Liz had warned him about Kayla, and he had ignored them. He didn't want to be proven wrong yet again.

Waves crashed against the side of the boat. As far as he could see in the distorted moonlight, the white foam-capped waves continued to toss the boat up and down. He wasn't sure if the nauseous feeling in his gut was because of the motion or the situation he found himself in, but he didn't have many options. He was stuck on the small boat, crammed full of the people who had led the attack on the Director's yacht.

Until Kayla answered his question about Ella, there was no way for him to know if he would support them or not. Only the curvature of the force field showed him they were outside of it. Even if he jumped ship, he didn't know which direction would take him to safety, and there was also the inconvenient fact that he didn't know how to swim.

His only option, for now, was to play along, at least until they made landfall. Once they reached their destination, wherever that might be, he could reassess his options.

"I lost someone," he answered. T'al knew the story anyway, it wasn't as if he was giving away any secrets. "The bots killed someone close to me. They lied to us and then they killed him."

Kayla spread her arms, her red robe floating gracefully through the air. "That's why most of us are here," she said. "If you knew you could stop the bots from hurting anyone else, that you could save lives, would you? What would you be willing to do to protect humanity?"

"Anything within my power," Wil answered truthfully.

"Would you allow one man to die in order to save ten thousand others from the bots?" she asked.

Wil lifted a hand to his chin. He had never thought about such a scenario.

"I suppose if it were to save so many lives, it would be hard to put the life of one man ahead of thousands of others."

"Would you allow twelve men to die to save a million?" she asked.

Wil saw where this was going, and he didn't want to play her game. "What are you getting at, Kayla?"

"The men and women in that chamber refused to keep their people safe. People who rely on them for leadership. Their inaction would have caused the immediate death of thousands, maybe tens of thousands, and the impact would have reverberated throughout the region. Removing the Council was necessary."

"And your own father? You sacrificed him in order to protect the city?"

"My father is the worst of them all," she said. "You saw how he reacted when you and your friends told him about the threat from the bots. There are rioters on his doorstep, and he *still* refuses to do anything. He'd rather kill the protesters than cure the disease. You said you would do anything within your power to protect humanity? I am merely doing the same. My father was the biggest obstacle to keeping the rest of the city safe."

"What about the rest of the City Center? Surely they'd be willing to help those protesting?"

"You really haven't been paying attention, have you, Bot Killer?" Kayla rolled her eyes. "You don't remember the spectators at the stadium? Those people are the rule, not the exception. The city has been cut off from the rest of the world for so long, they don't understand the genuine danger the bots represent. So much so that they'd pay to watch bots and humans fight. To many of them, the

Guardians are a fairy tale, and the Ringers are the dirty leftovers the ancients left behind."

"What about Bhavika? Didn't she want to help those on the outside?"

"She did, but she was just as clueless. Everyone in the City Center has been conditioned to believe this bloody force field will be their savior, but it's no better than putting a bandage on a broken arm.

"In some ways, my dad wasn't wrong—letting the Ringers into the city but not taking care of the bots would only make things worse. We'd all be trapped, and how would that be better? With our current supplies and population density, the Center could survive for six months, maybe longer if we ration. If those on the outside were let in, that supply would need to stretch further. We'd run out of food in a matter of weeks, even with strict rationing."

Torchlight from the city's Inner Ring slowly crept into their line of sight.

"So, you thought killing off the leaders would give you a better chance? If people are so ignorant of the truth, how will that help anything?"

"With my father, the Council, and Bhavika out of the way, I can seize power, at least for a short time. My father already had me heavily involved in the day-to-day decisions. It isn't a big leap for staff to accept my command in matters of security and warfare in a time of crisis. I can order an increased armed presence within the Rings—and allow the Resistance to prepare for battle. We can ready powered weapons to be deployed where the SZ has fallen and grant access to strategic positions in order to defend the city. We can evacuate affected sections of the city and make plans with neighboring districts."

Wil had to admit her reasoning sounded good, in theory—except for how willingly Kayla was prepared to commit murder.

"But killing your own father? A whole room full of dignitaries? There had to have been a better way to gain power. Couldn't you have arranged for the Guard to imprison them? Take control from the inside?"

"If you haven't noticed," Kayla replied, "we're running out of time. A coup would have taken too long to orchestrate, and too many things could have gone wrong. And who knows how many would support me while my father, the elected leader, sat behind bars? No, we had to act fast, and our actions had to face as little opposition as possible. With everyone out of the way, we were able to do what was necessary."

Though it didn't sound ideal, Wil was starting to see the logic. Liz had explained to him that, in this world, you had to choose the greater good over the individual. As cold as it sounded, this seemed to be an extension of that belief.

Sacrifice a few to save a city.

He watched the torches grow closer on the shoreline, bobbing with the ship's movements.

"So, why are we headed back to the Rings?" he asked. "Why aren't you preparing for the next stage of the plan?"

"Because we failed," Kayla said, turning back to look at the force field. "My father was hurried out of the room before we could kill him."

"We'll never get another chance like that," T'al said, rubbing his face with his palms and pulling his cheeks back momentarily before letting them go. He was showing signs of fatigue, and Wil realized the man had probably not slept since they had visited the stadium.

"Months of planning," Kayla continued. "All in vain. The Council is dead. Bhavika is dead. There is nobody left to oppose my father now. Rather than remove him, we have only strengthened his position."

"What about Elizabeth and Ella? What happened to them?"

"They're safe," Kayla said, her fingers rubbing her temple. "When my father's staff collects the boat, they'll be discovered and detained for a few days before being questioned. The City Guard will soon realize they weren't part of the attack. If your guard had done his job, you would have been with them, but you being in the atrium actually benefited us. We had hoped we could fill you in and have you join our cause."

"But why?" Wil asked. "Why drag me into this at all?"

"You don't realize what your power can do for us," T'al answered.

"After we saw what you could do, both in Vegas and on the desert road, we knew you'd be invaluable to our cause. The one thing Liz got right was bringing you back with her. You are the answer to turning this whole fight around."

"And you assumed I'd agree?"

T'al smirked. "Like you'd refuse an opportunity to fight the bots? You nearly got Cali killed so you could free Dagger and Sara. You followed a peddler in a strange city because he offered you the promise of a fight."

"Yeah, and look how well both ended," Wil said.

"It doesn't matter anyway," T'al said, his gaze resting on the Inner Ring ahead of them. "We failed. It's over. The best we can do is to gather the Resistance and protect those who want to flee with us. Those that believe there's a danger, at least."

Far in the distance, Wil could see lights flying through the night sky. Despite it being too far to see anything more than specks of light, there was nothing else they could have been but orbs.

"So that's it?" Wil asked. "You're giving up?"

"My father will be infuriated," Kayla said. "He's not going to take any chances. He'll double down on his efforts. If he doesn't decree the Resistance leave the Rings altogether, he definitely won't allow them to militarize. He'll permanently station guards at the gate and ensure the Center citizens believe the Ringers are the real threat, rather than the bots. And they'll believe him because it's easier to blame those they've viewed as dirty their entire lives than a concept that has been outside of their reality for generations."

Wil had an idea, but he cringed at the thought of it. If Director Sens was going to be the only obstacle to saving the lives of thousands of residents, they had to do something to save them.

"Well," Wil said, eyeing the force field now behind them. "There's only one thing we can do."

"Pack our bags?" T'al asked, deflated.

"We try again. Finish what you started. We have to kill Director Sens."

24

THE CALLOUS WORDS had rolled off Wil's tongue far too easily. The reality of his thought process frightened him, but if the death of one man could save the lives of thousands, it would be worth it—especially if it finally secured the support needed to take on the bots.

"It's too late," Kayla said. "My father knows, or will at least suspect, I was involved. We'll never get close to him. Once word gets out that I've gone missing, the trust I earned with his staff will be gone."

Part of Wil felt relief at her immediate rejection of the plan, but his persistence surprised even himself.

"That's why we need to take him out tonight," Wil said. He quickly calculated how long it had taken them to travel from the Renaissance to the yacht. "Assuming we haven't been floating in the bay for hours, he'll only just be arriving back at his quarters."

Others on the boat had begun to move. Their vessel was now approaching the dock, and the crew was taking the necessary steps to secure the boat and bring it in.

"We can't go back the way we came," T'al added. "By now, they'll have taken in the yacht and will be searching for us. We're lucky few remember the old entryways, but it won't take long before the Guard realize there's nowhere else for us to go."

Wil leaned back in his seat. "Why wouldn't they know about those entries?"

"The City Center used to be nearly twice the size it is now," Kayla said. "Over centuries, the oceans have risen and reclaimed much of it, and earthquakes have torn down sectors that were once well above sea level. But the gateways through the force field that the ancients installed are still there, if you know where to go. But it doesn't matter now, even if we got back in, they'd discover us almost immediately."

"Why does any of this matter?" Voth said. "If you want to stop the bots, send Bot Killer out there and let him unleash his energy burst. Problem solved."

"It doesn't 'solve the problem,' Voth," Kayla disputed.

"Why not? The kid wants to help. He's got more ability than any of us here. Maybe more than the entire Resistance combined."

The boat had docked, and the others stood to disembark.

"Because there's more out there than just these bots," Kayla answered. "If we truly want to win, we have to think long term. My father won't learn if the problem simply goes away; he'll retreat into his protective force field, and we'll be left waiting for the next wave. Instead, we need to expand our reach further.

"The citizens of San Francisco need to learn where the real threat to them lies," Kayla said. "We could be so much greater than what we've become. But the more I try, the more it seems like it's a hopeless cause."

Hopeless. Wil was tired of hearing the word. The monument that existed in front of them was a testament to the ingenuity of the humans of the past. *Hopeless* was what the bots wanted them to become, but Wil knew they could become more again—*if* they could stop fighting among themselves.

Liz had told him that the future would depend on the decisions he made. Was this one of those moments? Part of him wished she had said nothing to him about her premonition, as it had caused him to second guess every decision he had to make. He had no way of knowing if the path before him led to good or to ill, but doing nothing was a luxury Wil didn't possess. If the fate of humanity depended, even in part, on the decisions ahead of him, he had to step up and become who he was meant to be.

"No more excuses," Wil said. "You wanted me to join you, and I'm not giving up before I even start. There's got to be another way in."

The others stood silently. Wil wasn't sure if they didn't know where to go or whether there was something else they weren't telling him.

He had an ulterior motive for wanting to return to the City Center, something the others had glossed over: Ella and Liz were still being held captive there. Liz's visions of him and Sierra defeating the Guardians in the Battle for Vegas had proven she had a special insight into the future, and that alone was enough to know this was the right course of action to take.

"With Liz imprisoned," he said, heeding each word as he spoke it, "who now leads the Resistance?"

"Kayla was to take charge of the members within the city," T'al said. "Others further out mostly operate independently, anyway."

"And they'd listen to her? Why would they follow someone from within the Center? And the Director's daughter, no less."

"That's where T'al and I come in," Voth said. "And the others here among us. It wouldn't take many of us to convince the group that this is our chance to unite with the city's forces. We'd present a common goal for both the City Guard and the Resistance. The technology of the city, matched with our resolve, would aid our cause in a way that hasn't been seen since the ancient wars."

Wil carefully followed the others off the boat, fearing he would fall flat on his face as the boat bobbed next to the solid dock. The wooden slats of the dock boards were slick from the waves splashing against them, but he found his footing with the help of a Resistance member he didn't recognize.

"Come," T'al said. "We need to get to the safe house. It won't take long before the Rings are put into lockdown."

Most of the Resistance members took off, but Wil held his ground. Kayla, T'al, and Voth looked to him, encouraging him with their stance to follow the group, but also anticipating that he had something else to say.

"There's no time to waste," Wil said. "If we're going back there, it needs to be now."

Torchlight caused shadows to dance across Kayla's face. Wil fought hard not to be entranced by her beauty. He shook his head—there wasn't time for adolescent fantasy. Ella needed him.

"Kayla," he said, forcing himself to focus. "Are you sure your father knows you were part of the raid?"

The further word of Kayla's involvement spread, the harder it would be to convince the City Guard to join their cause. But if there was a chance her involvement was unknown, they had to take it.

Kayla shook her head. "I can't be sure. I intentionally didn't involve myself in the fight. But they will notice my absence."

"Perhaps that could benefit us," Wil said. "Surely they'd assume you were taken hostage before accepting you were involved in the attack?"

"It doesn't matter," T'al said. "The entrances were closed even before we attacked. Now, with the waters being patrolled, there's no way we'll get in."

"I'm not so sure of that," Wil insisted. "Kayla, you told me last night that the residents of the Center were at the stadium illegally. How do they get in and out of the city?"

Kayla's eyes lit up. "The tunnels."

"Tunnels?" Voth asked, skeptical.

"Abandoned shafts that run underground beneath the city. I don't know what the ancients originally used them for, but smugglers have been using them for years to bring people out to the robot fights, as well as transporting energy weapons and other devices. The tunnels aren't unknown to the guards, but they're rarely watched. It's not a perfect plan, but if there's a way to get in, that'd be it."

"We're not going to able to sneak our entire party through," T'al cautioned. "There's too many of us. We'll attract attention no matter which way we go."

"It's just going to be the four of us," Wil affirmed. "Kayla knows the way. You and Voth can provide protection."

"Who says I need protecting?" Kayla scoffed.

"You're going to take on a dozen guards by yourself? Having these two with us won't hurt," Wil encouraged. "This isn't going to be easy, but we know what we have to do. We find the Director, finish the job, and get back out before sunrise."

T'al and Voth both looked uncertain, but nobody argued.

"Good," Wil said, smiling. "That's settled. Lead the way, Kayla,"

WIL FOLLOWED Kayla through the city streets of the Inner Ring, T'al and Voth striding confidently a half-step behind them.

Doubts plagued him as they hurriedly walked through the alleys and backstreets of the Inner Ring. Was murdering the Director really something he was willing to do? Killing bots was one thing, but people? Regardless of the end, it was hard to justify the means.

Wil did his best not to stumble on the rugged stone streets of the Inner Ring, the surfaces of which were especially uneven in the side streets. Other than the small torches they carried, the darkness between buildings offered more protection than the main roads. The street lanterns barely licked at the edges of their path, and only the faint green luminescence from above offered them any guidance.

Several times, they needed to dart across main roads while attempting to remain discreet. Wil wasn't sure if it was his imagination playing tricks on him, but the Guard's presence had already increased from the previous night. There was nothing marking their small party as suspicious, but they did their best to blend in with others who lingered outside, despite the late hour. Merchants and sellers staggered along, likely making their way home from the pubs. The mob of farmers who had been shouting at the main gate had quieted down, though, with nowhere else to go, many had opted to camp on the sides of the streets.

Families had set up makeshift shelters made from carts; others had nothing but tarps for protection. Despite the calamity that had befallen those now seeking refuge, they appeared to be helping each other out. Families shared wares with each other, and those who hadn't brought anything with them during their escape were sheltered by families who had. Light from small fires lit at the roadside danced on the faces of the survivors, all waiting for a chance to reclaim their lives.

The sight of the people they were aiming to protect strengthened Wil's resolve. These people deserved a chance at life without the tyranny of the Guardians or the isolationism of the City Center, and humanity would have to work together if they were to stand a chance.

Their plight was swiftly helping him to come to terms with the decision he needed to make that night.

Wil's heart was beating ferociously as they continued, certain that around each corner would be a complement of guards waiting for them. Though Kayla didn't seem as concerned with the guards, they did their best to stay out of their way all the same.

Wil was blind as to where they were headed. Between being distracted by nearby guards and his racing thoughts, he realized he hadn't been paying attention to their route and likely wouldn't be able to find his way back if he needed to.

"This is the old district of the Inner Ring," T'al whispered, jolting Wil from his thoughts.

Buildings that half-stood from the time of the ancients lined the streets. The Ringers had painted many over in fresh white, barely masking that the tops of them had crumbled years ago.

"Only the bottom floors are stable," T'al continued. "The tops often give way, usually requiring massive repairs, but it's where the majority of the traders and merchants who deal with the City Center live."

"If it's that dangerous, why do they choose to live here?" Wil enquired.

"To live among the work of the ancients," T'al said. "It's the closest thing most of them will get to prestige."

Among the homes serving as luxury accommodations were an equal number in far too great a state of disrepair to serve as more permanent dwellings. Even as far as they were from the main gate, farmers who had lost their homes in the Guardian attack continued to be found tucked away in cracks and crevices of the painted buildings.

Entering yet another narrow back alley, Wil was met with a space so tight that they needed to walk through it in single file. Old cement walls lined either side, and garbage and debris indicated the alley wasn't used for much other than as a convenient dumping space.

Wil held his breath as best he could to keep from inhaling the stench, but it was no use. Every step he took was met with the alley's potent smell, as though every resident of the city had dumped their old fish guts there. Its tight walls contained the stench within the narrow space, causing Wil's eyes to water. It grew so bad that after five minutes he was about to ask if they could find another way when Kayla abruptly stopped.

A small metal door rested within the side of a decrepit gray building. Graffiti in a script Wil didn't understand decorated its side and looked as though it had been painted long ago.

A large rodent lay deceased a few feet away, cast on top of a collection of fish bones and seaweed, which didn't give Wil any confidence about the space they were set to enter.

Even T'al turned up his nose. "Kayla, are you sure about this? I can't imagine even the most eccentric Center dwellers traipsing through here, no matter what kind of entertainment they were promised."

"You're right," Kayla answered. She rubbed a hand through her short, spiked hair as she studied the door. "They wouldn't. But there are dozens of tunnels and hundreds of entrances. This one is lesser known and isn't used to travel to the games. That said, guards aren't immune to curiosity, so depending on how desperate things get, they may send a patrol to scour the tunnels. Most won't know about this one, though. Hopefully it'll give us some coverage until it joins up with others closer to the Center."

Wil put a hand to the back of his neck, feeling the tension that had built up there over the last month or so. Kayla pulled a wired tool out of her satchel and set to work on the lock.

"How do *you* know about it?" Wil asked.

Kayla flashed him a sly smile and a wink. "Some secrets I'll keep to myself."

The door popped open, and Kayla dipped inside, beckoning for the rest of them to follow suit.

T'al and Voth kept at the rear of the group while Wil entered on Kayla's heels. Behind the door, a concrete stairwell led beneath the street, and Wil wondered how many years had passed since it had seen regular use. It looked untouched, with cobwebs and dust the only sign that any time had passed. They descended until they reached a large, open room. Light from their small torches bounced off its walls, but nothing else filled the space besides a few rusted shelves that had long been stripped of whatever they had once held.

The silence of the space was uncomfortable. Each of the group remained wordless as Kayla strode to the far end of the room, the sound of her footsteps echoing through the gloom.

Wil moved hesitantly, watching where his feet went with each step. Bugs skittered along the floor, pushing dirt as they did so, which caused him to shudder. The insects scattered, appearing as tiny balls of dust as they moved. Nothing had disturbed their sanctuary in ages, and they seemed frantic that someone was doing so now. Wil pushed the bugs from his mind—creepy crawlies were the least of his concerns.

A small opening appeared in the far wall, barely wide enough for them to slip through, one at a time. Nothing but wooden panels separated their room from something beyond, and at some point, someone had discovered this and cut a makeshift door. Whoever that was didn't bother to make an opening any larger than was absolutely necessary.

Kayla and Wil slipped through with ease. T'al found it more difficult, his muscular frame scraping against the jagged wooden cuts in the wall on either side, dust billowing as he passed through. Wil thought he saw Voth give him a gentle nudge before he made it through.

Once through, a long hall stretched before them into darkness. The gray brick walls were damp and partially covered in dirt that had accumulated over the years. Water dripped from the arched fifteen-foot ceiling, the dripping noise like a blaring cannon inside the otherwise silent corridor. Their small torches touched the edges of the hall a short distance in front of them, but mostly, they walked forward in darkness.

Wil wrinkled his chilled nose. The sour stench that hung in the air was faint but wretched, and Wil feared it would only get worse as they headed deeper into the cave. He tried to push the thought from his mind as he pushed on.

At least it wasn't as bad as the fish guts on the surface.

25

It was hard for Wil not to marvel at his surroundings as they made their way up the stairs to the government building. Whatever the underground tunnel had been used for in the past, it led directly to the basement of the Renaissance.

Though she refused to say anything at all on the subject, Kayla must have discovered the path while growing up in the buildings.

The trip had been both long and tiring. It couldn't have taken more than a couple hours, but it had felt like days, a feeling compounded by the fact that lack of sleep was now taking its toll. There were a few times Wil had closed his eyes against the overbearing darkness of the shaft, only to catch himself jolting awake as he nearly dropped his torch.

Between the dankness of the tunnel and the party's sleep deprivation, they had walked most of the journey in complete silence. The only sounds had been the echoes of their own footsteps down the empty hall.

After endless walking, Kayla had finally opened a nearly identical metal door to the one that had led them into the abyss. Dim electrical lighting illuminated a stairwell that had led them to the building they were now within.

Despite it being the dead of night, the risk of being seen using the elevators was too great, and Kayla insisted on using the stairs. Even if nobody yet realized Kayla had been part of the coup, her sudden return would raise far more questions than it was worth, and it was best to save those until they reached her father.

Wil struggled to keep lifting one foot in front of the other and leaned heavily on the rail lining the wall, using his upper body as much as his legs to heft each foot into the next step. He kept reminding himself it had been his idea to come here right away, rather than after a night's rest. Fifty floors of metal stairs definitely made him question that decision, but they needed to find Director Sens and take care of him quickly.

Wil didn't dare let himself think about the journey back. He hoped there would be refuge in the Center for him. Perhaps Kayla would allow them to sleep in the tunnels. Despite the despicable odor, he was so tired he might be okay with that.

It couldn't have been more than twenty minutes before Wil dragged his body onto the final landing. He shook himself off as the party gathered themselves before continuing. None of the others seemed fazed by the effort, even though the bags under T'al's eyes were telling.

Light from the hall streamed into the stairwell as Kayla cracked the door open. Wil's heart dropped to his stomach, and all hope of a quick and easy mission fell away.

A uniformed guard held a silver energy weapon pointed at Kayla's head.

"You've got a lot of nerve showing your face here again."

AN ESCORT of guards led the four of them down a glass hall. Wil guessed they were being taken to Sens, as he recalled little else being on the penthouse floor other than the Director's office.

He was surprised, though, when the guards pushed them into a small room instead. With the push of a button, the hum and slight glint of an enacted force field closed the room off.

"Do you mind telling me what this is about?" Kayla asked.

The guards didn't answer. One even smiled, as if taking pleasure in imprisoning the Director's daughter. They left them there with no sign of how long they would be held for.

Cold white benches lined the brightly paneled walls. The depth of the seats was so shallow that there was barely enough room for Wil to sit semi-comfortably on one of them. T'al attempted to sit, but his back muscles pushed his bottom out farther than the bench would allow for. Wil knew T'al would typically have stood anyway, but the events of the last few days had worn him out to the point where he opted to sit on the floor. He leaned back against the bench and closed his eyes, apparently relieved to be taking a brief rest.

"This was a wretched idea," Kayla said, staring through the semi-transparent boundary that separated them from the hallway and resting an arm on the wall's small outlet. "We would have been better off resting tonight."

Nobody else spoke. Wil stared at the white walls of the room. At least the cell was clean. It was hard to know how much time had actually passed, but it had to be close to morning. Wil was sure T'al had fallen asleep sitting on the floor, while Voth resigned herself to sitting next to him and resting against his frame.

Wil allowed his eyes to close. Although the bench wasn't at all comfortable, it was the most reprieve he'd had in a while.

He did his best to push the thoughts of his botched plan deep into the recesses of his mind, but he failed miserably. Each second they spent locked in the cell was another they could use to help the Resistance to prepare. That didn't even factor what might happen to them once the guards came back for them.

Would Sens execute his own daughter? Wil guessed if the Director suspected treason, the man wouldn't think twice about it—especially as Kayla had no issue with taking his life if the chance arose.

"What's going to happen to Ella and Liz?" Wil thought aloud. His plan had been to free them, but what fate would they be subjected to now?

"Ella and Liz? Are you *serious*, Bot Killer?" Kayla scoffed. "Maybe you should worry about your own hide. And those you're currently with." Kayla crossed her arms and leaned back as she closed her eyes.

Wil rolled his eyes. "Forgive me for being worried about my friends."

"Quiet," T'al admonished, his eyes not opening. "Don't implicate our friends in something they had no involvement in. It might be best if you don't say anything at all from here on out."

Wil swallowed as his face went still and his jaw tightened. He was used to being reprimanded by Liz and Ella, but never by T'al.

Kayla sat down on the bench beside him, and Wil found himself thinking she wasn't nearly as close to him as he would have liked. Part of Wil wished Kayla would lean against him, reassuring him that the others didn't hate him for landing them in this mess. He knew he shouldn't care what the others thought, but it was difficult to ignore when every move he made seemed to work against him. He also couldn't suppress the feeling of guilt over longing to be cuddled up to Kayla while Ella was locked away elsewhere.

Besides, the warmth Kayla had shown him earlier had disappeared. So, instead, she sat curled up in a ball on the corner of the bench, her feet up and her head placed between her knees as she rocked back and forth. Kayla, at least, knew her father wouldn't hesitate in punishing her.

Wil shifted and squirmed in his seat, trying to find a more comfortable position. It was hard to tell how many hours had passed before a lone guard appeared in the hallway.

"Kayla," the guard whispered, looking over his shoulder.

She stood quickly, her posture stiffening as though she had been a picture of confidence the entire time.

The guard's pale face and unnaturally dark green eyes were accentuated by the deep green uniform he wore. His helmet sat slightly crooked, as though it wasn't quite the right size, and he seemed on edge.

"Nobody move," the guard said, the helmet's visor now lifting. To emphasize his words, he swung his weapon at the group, fixing it on Wil as he punched a few buttons on the wall panel. The hum of the force field disappeared, as did the shine it had projected.

Wil wondered how effective the guard's weapon would be if the four of them rushed him, but he quickly realized it would be a mistake risking the guard getting a shot off on even one of them.

"Are you taking us to see my father?" Kayla asked, straightening further. "I'd like to know why I'm being treated like a criminal?"

"We've been instructed to hold *anybody* trying to get into the building," the guard answered. "Nobody was to receive special treatment, not even you. Your father has been even more erratic than usual."

"Can you blame him?" Kayla asked. "The entire Council has been eliminated." She arched an eyebrow. "Why are you here?"

The guard reached to his belt, and everyone tensed as he pulled out a dagger. He flipped it around and handed it, hilt first, to Kayla.

"I came to give you a message," he said, motioning for her to take the blade while still keeping his blaster trained at the cell's three other residents. "You have friends in the Guard."

The questioning look never left Kayla's face, but she didn't voice her thoughts, so Wil decided to do so for her.

"What are you implying?"

The guard shot Wil an annoyed look, clearly not wanting to engage with anyone but the Director's daughter.

"If something were to happen to the Director," he said, his focus turning back to Kayla, "know that the Director's security detail would stand with you. You have been the voice of reason behind this administration for a long time."

Wil studied Kayla. Her expression changed so slightly that he barely caught it. She reached out and grabbed the dagger in a rapid motion, as if she was expecting the guard to change his mind if she didn't.

"I could turn you in for treason," she replied, flipping the dagger so that it pointed in the guard's direction.

It was only then that Wil realized the guard could have been framing her, using the offering as bait.

The guard's eyes went wide, and his hands went up, along with his blaster, which he pointed to the ceiling. His eyes darted up and down the hall to ensure nobody else was coming.

"I assure you, Kayla, this is no trick. There are rumblings among the Guard about your involvement in tonight's terrorist attack. A small circle of us realizes the importance of what you've been trying to convince your father of. We believe in your cause. Most of us will follow your command, regardless of your actions."

"You believe this enough to risk treason?" Kayla asked skeptically.

"I do, as do others. We know what needs to be done."

Kayla studied the man, weighing his words. The dagger she held bounced slightly, and Wil could tell by her controlled breathing that Kayla believed her time to act was growing short.

"What do you believe you're committing to?" she asked. "Why do you suppose I'd be a better leader than my father?"

"You know the bots are a threat to the city, while Sens denies their aggression. But more than that, word has it you're willing to unite the cities to the north and the south. With San Francisco's influence and advancements, we could make a push toward unity that we haven't seen since the wars."

Kayla squinted skeptically but moved to tuck the blade into her belt. At the last second, she stopped and turned the blade around, offering the hilt to Wil.

The guard relaxed with an audible sigh of relief.

Wil stared at the hilt of the dagger being offered to him. Its solid wood handle had the familiar-looking symbol of a sun and waves engraved onto it. It triggered a memory of Sierra. When they had fled the Sphere, her friend Greata had given her a medallion bearing a symbol that had been nearly identical to the one before him.

Wil shook off the memory. "Why are you offering me this?" he asked.

"When the time comes, I want you to do it. My father deserves to die, but I'm worried I'm not strong enough. No matter what, he's still my father. We can't risk the chance of me losing my nerve."

Wil nodded at the sentiment. He understood where she was coming from. Kayla could get closer to Sens far easier than he ever could, but if the roles were reversed, he didn't think he'd be able to follow through on killing his own father, either.

"What's your name, soldier?" Wil asked.

"Aros," the guard replied.

"What you've done here won't be forgotten, Aros," Wil responded. Perhaps Kayla should have been the one to say it, but she had handed the knife to him. "War with the bots is inevitable, and it's good to know who we can trust."

Aros nodded. "I've stayed too long already. When you speak with Sens, remember you haven't been accused of a crime yet, so say nothing to implicate yourselves. The Director is suspicious that you disappeared into the night, but he'll probably believe any credible excuse you come up with."

With that, Aros left the cell and reinstated the force field, leaving as quickly as he had arrived.

"Are you up to this, Bot Killer?" Kayla asked. "Killing a man isn't the same as deactivating a bot. When you look into a bot's eyes, there's nothing but lifeless circuitry and lights. When you stare into a man's eyes, you see their hope, fear, and a lifetime of regret."

"I think I'll manage," Wil said. "Whatever it takes."

26

THE SCENT of honey and lavender that had wafted from Kayla the past couple of days had dissipated, which was good because Wil didn't need anything else muddying his thoughts. Kayla's warning was causing him to consider the task ahead of him, and the steady realization of her words was eroding his confidence.

Wil had never killed a person, not even when he'd wanted to. The closest he had come was attempting to fire a blaster on a bandit back at the Outpost, but that gun had never fired, or at least not for him. The more he dwelled on the thought of his blade entering flesh, the less comfortable he was with what he had agreed to.

Liz had spoken so intently about the decisions he would make. Somehow it didn't seem fair to bestow upon him the weight of humanity's future. That his actions or inactions could determine the fate of the entire world was crippling. The only solace Wil gave himself was that he would amass more support to the Resistance's efforts. That was what Liz had wanted all along. This was just a different means to the same aim.

As they continued to wait, he let his mind drift to Sierra and the circumstances that had brought them both into this incredible unknown world. Wil had grown believing there had been nothing outside of their protected bubble, and here on the edge of an ocean lay a city that never went dark. Sierra wouldn't be spending her time locked away in cell blocks, awaiting an unknown fate. With any luck, she'd be working with Malachi and Terre to bring the people of the Sphere into the protection of the Silent Zone and the city of Vegas. For a moment, he was envious that his fate laid on the more difficult path, but it was one he had pursued.

Kayla remained standing after Aros had left, as if the knowledge that a faction of the Guard supported her had reignited her confidence. Her time working with her father had earned her more influence than perhaps even she had realized.

Which led Wil to wonder how old Kayla actually was. Surely she couldn't be that much older than Wil—perhaps twenty at most— but that would mean she had been commanding the City Guard when she was a young teenager. Not impossible, he supposed, but it was a far cry from the costumed girl he had met at the stadium.

Wil's eyes grew heavy once again as they continued to wait. He nodded off once or twice, though he was unsure for how long. T'al and Voth had also drifted off, and Wil was pleased his friends could at least get some rest.

Kayla eventually resigned herself to leaning against the wall, her arms crossed before her, content to bide her time for whatever fate awaited them.

"Is Sens a terrible father?" Wil asked her. The question surprised even himself. He hadn't realized his thoughts had drifted back to the Director and his task of putting a knife between the man's ribs.

Kayla smirked, her eyes never leaving the hall.

"That would make this whole thing a lot easier to stomach, wouldn't it?" she replied. "If he was mean or absent or even controlling, then this would all seem a little more justifiable."

Wil wasn't sure if she was being sincere or criticizing him, so he let her continue.

"Stories of the ancients are filled with tales of mistreated daughters growing up to take revenge on their fathers. But no, despite being a pitiful ruler, he is a good father. My upbringing was unconventional, but it was good. My father has trained well me in the ways of the world. In reality, he has groomed me to be his successor."

"But still you want to kill him?" Wil asked.

Kayla sighed and ran a hand through her short hair. It bristled back and then snapped into place, like running a hand through a brush.

"I don't *want* to kill him," she said, her voice lowered. Her blue eyes turned from the hall to gaze at him. "It's the very reason I can't be the one to do it. But it *must* be done. He may be a good father, but he will damn us all. And few within the Center understand what's happening in the world around them. The city has been closed off for too long. It's time to let it blossom into its full potential."

Kayla's words didn't put Wil's mind at ease. He'd have less of a problem killing a tyrant, but ending the life of a man whose only crime was poor insight didn't sit well.

"Couldn't one of the Ringers rise up and become Director?" he asked.

"Absolutely not," Kayla said. "The Director might govern the Rings, but that doesn't mean the Ringers hold status. They can't even vote under current law, never mind take the opportunity to run for office. Only those within the force field have the ability to choose the city's path. The City Center was set up in a time when the world was in chaos, and they've fought to maintain a level of order that the ancients had been accustomed to while the rest of the world has struggled to survive. The government in the Center at the time managed to organize and gain control of the Rings, but they did so in a manner that was heavy-handed. No surprise given the bands of looters and thieves fighting tirelessly to gain entry into the Center, but that doesn't fully justify their choices. After decades of hardships, this system came into place and has proven to be stable."

"The people fought for a chance to survive," Wil said. "As those in the Center were able to do."

"Perhaps," Kayla said. "But it was an ancient struggle that required decisions neither you nor I were involved in making. We can never understand, but we can overturn. We can't allow humanity to repeat their mistakes. Killing my father is the only way to ensure we learn from the sins of the ancients."

Four guards appeared in the corridor—three women and one man, all with bags under their eyes and frowns of fatigue. There was no sign of Aros, but if what he'd said was true, the Guard were on high alert, searching for the attackers and preventing anyone that might chance a second attempt.

The cell barrier fell and the guards entered, batons in hand, the smell of sweat and alcohol entering with them. Fatigue wasn't the only thing plaguing them.

"Let's go," one of them said.

Calloused hands roughly grabbed Wil from behind, and they shoved him forward into the hall with the others. He noticed that while Kayla was prodded, they did not push her around, and she was allowed to step out of the cell with her head still held high.

Kayla strode down the hall with the confidence of someone who ran the place, her guard merely walking next to her, as if she were being accompanied to their destination rather than coerced.

The end of the blaster embedded in Wil's back offered no such suggestion. The metal of its barrel dug into his flesh.

The corridor soon turned into the more familiar office space Wil recalled from last time he'd been here. The Director stared out over the city which he ruled, through one of the paneled windows that lined his office.

The sun had just crested the horizon. Oranges, reds, and yellows were dulled by the green hue of the Center. The buildings themselves reflected its green shimmer, giving the entire metropolis an emerald vibe.

Director Sens still wore what appeared to be the same suit from the night before. Either the man had multiple of the same design or he had not yet been to bed.

"Father! I'm so happy you're okay!" Kayla made a move toward the man but was met with the arm of the nearest guard blocking her path; the first sign of open aggression shown to the Director's daughter.

"It's all right, Reggie," Director Sens said, addressing the guard as he turned to face the group. "I know the City Guard has their suspicions, but let my daughter through."

Seeing Sens's tired expression, the bags under his eyes, and the hollows of his cheeks caused Wil to question whether assassinating the man was the right course of action. The dagger weighed heavily on his belt, the weight of its implication growing by the moment, but the man before him looked as though his mind weighed heavier.

Here was a man who loved his daughter and his city. His only crime was his inability to see the true threat that lay outside the Center, putting his own political interests over the lives of his people.

The guard moved hesitantly out of Kayla's way and the girl stepped forward with poise, not as an excited daughter, but as a diplomat of equal status.

Perhaps, Wil thought, her behavior was for the benefit of the guards. It felt as though every one of them held their breath, as if they were anticipating having to prevent an attack.

The woman stopped a few feet short of her father. The two couldn't have appeared more dissimilar: a long night had made Sens look far older than he had the day before. It was more evident today that his hair was graying, and his skin had lost much of its color. His suit had stretched and twisted over the course of the evening, making the slight paunch of his gut more obvious. Despite his aging features and expanding waistline, the man had once been handsome, but his ragged appearance in the early morning hours made it clear his looks had faded with his youth.

Kayla, on the other hand, was slender, yet muscular. Her time exploring the tunnels made her appear to be more ready to lead an adventure than to rule a city. It was her confidence that said otherwise. There was no mistaking the charisma and command she held with anyone she spoke to.

"Guards, step outside," Sens said. "Let me speak to my daughter in private."

The guards looked at each other and then back to Sens, shuffling uncomfortably.

"If I have to worry about my own daughter, then I'm really in trouble," Sens said.

Wil cringed.

"Leave us," Sens repeated. The guards nodded and tentatively complied.

"What happened to you, Kayla?" Sens asked. "I've heard reports you were kidnapped. Others suggested you were behind the rebellion. I hate to have to ask, but I've been up all night worrying about you. Which is it?"

"If you'd stuck around for long enough, maybe you would have found out for yourself." Her tone was icy, and her posture stiffened.

"My guards' duty is to protect me. They ensured my safety as soon as the threat presented itself."

"And they left me to be killed! I was fortunate enough to have Wil and his friends there to rescue me. Something your guards failed to do."

The Director's concentration broke, and he shifted his gaze to Wil.

Sens crossed the tiled floor, methodically and with purpose. Wil expected to see suspicion in the man's eyes, but instead there was something else. Something far more haunting.

Gratitude.

"So, I have you to thank for saving my daughter?" Sens asked, continuing to narrow the gap. "Even after your antics at my reception. Perhaps I was too hasty in my criticism."

The man was only a few feet away. Wil was going to have to act or lose his chance. Out of the corner of his eye, he could see Kayla nodding, encouraging him to take it.

The world around him seemed to fade as he focused on the man that could change the fate of the war that was to come; the man whose influence could save the lives of thousands of Ringers or allow them to be destroyed at the hand of the bots.

He had to give it one more shot.

"I did what anyone would do," Wil answered. "And I realize the city has suffered a tremendous loss tonight, but as terrible as that was, the

Silent Zone is poised to fall, perhaps at any moment. If nothing is done, many more lives will be lost."

The Director stopped and lowered the hand he had extended to shake Wil's. The smile faded from his face as his forehead furrowed.

"This again," he huffed. "As I said before, the force field will protect us. There has been enough for me to worry about tonight. Terrorists have killed the entire Council—and the opposition, as well. As much as she was a pain in my side, Bhavika was an excellent woman. We didn't agree on much, but she had good intentions. We need to find out who did this and bring them to justice."

"But doesn't that make the city's protection even more urgent?" Wil pressed. "The force field doesn't protect the Rings. Only your militia can do that. They must help to defend against the threat of the Guardians."

The aging man waved a dismissive hand in Wil's direction and scoffed.

Wil realized the man wasn't willing to listen—wasn't willing to even consider any alternatives to closing the gates and letting the Ringers be destroyed.

"There is no threat from the bots," Sens said. "You've let those Resistance women get in your head, boy! The only threat we face is from those behind the attempt on my life. The city is being put into lockdown as we speak, and our entire police force will dedicate their time to finding those responsible."

Lockdown. Wil paused as the word triggered the memory of Liz mentioning the point of no return for the city. Sens's refusal to act would have grave implications for what came next. It could mean the end of everything. This was his one shot.

The consternation on Sens's face made Wil realize his window of opportunity was closing fast.

"Regardless, sir," Wil said, changing tack. "I'm happy to have saved your daughter's life. But I believe my companions Ella and Liz are still being detained. Might you know where I can find them?"

"Of course," he said. "They are being held in the basement cells. I'd get a guard to escort you, but as I mentioned, the Guard have no resources to spare. Once things have settled down, I'll be sure they're handled appropriately." The Director took another two steps forward with a hand outstretched. "I truly want to thank you for keeping my daughter safe. She's a capable girl, but we were all taken by surprise."

Another step.

"She's a special woman," Wil answered, one eye drifting toward Kayla. "I'm very grateful to have met her."

He thought he saw Kayla blush for a moment, but she regained her faculties instantly. She gave him a sly smile, though it didn't quite feel genuine. She then gave him a slight nod.

"She's wise beyond her years," Sens said, his chest heaving a sigh. "Sometimes too much for her own good."

Wil took the man's hand and pulled him close as if he were about to embrace him. "I couldn't agree more," he said.

Wil reached behind his back with his free hand, grabbed the dagger that Kayla had passed to him, and thrust it into the side of the unsuspecting Director.

Sens gasped as he doubled over. Wil could feel the grind of tissue and bone sliding over the solid point of the blade, the weight of the man pulling at it. He pulled back instinctively, blood and flesh hanging from its metallic surface. Wil nearly dropped it in disgust, but instead wiped it off and froze with it clasped in his hand.

The Director collapsed, struggling to breathe.

Wil's stomach lurched in response to the man's suffering. It wasn't a quick death, and his muffled attempts at screaming only made the situation more unpleasant.

Kayla appeared remarkably unaffected by the act. She had simply walked to the window and gazed out onto the city below her.

"I'm sorry, Father," Kayla said, her voice firm and her eyes dry. "I've watched you hold this city back from its true potential for long enough. It's time for us to prosper."

Sens looked at Wil, his gray eyes pleading for help before growing distant as the man finally became still.

Wil let out a breath.

"Let's move the body and get the floor cleaned." T'al said, not missing a beat between the old man's death and his call for action.

Wil couldn't move. Blood pooled on the white marble tile around the fallen leader, and Wil still gripped the dagger that had caused it.

If the blade was heavy before, its weight now was colossal.

27

By the time T'al and Voth had moved the body, the sun had already risen part way into the sky. Wil wasn't even sure where they had taken Sens's corpse, but they managed to hide it before the guards could return.

The blood was another matter. Once the body had been removed, T'al ushered Kayla and Wil into looking for the appropriate cleaning supplies to hide the evidence of the murder.

Fortunately, Kayla knew where the janitor's closet was, and she and Wil worked to clean the mess. Kayla didn't say two words and Wil ended up doing most of the cleaning, but it didn't take long before there was no trace of the crime.

No sooner had they cleaned up the mess than two of the patrolling guards made their way back into the chamber.

"Where is the Director?" one asked. The woman held her blaster as if she expected to use it at a moment's notice.

Maybe she did.

"My father is finally getting some much needed rest," Kayla said, breaking the silence that had overcome her since the altercation with her father. "He's asked me to take care of matters until he returns."

The guard nodded, as though the request was nothing out of the ordinary. Kayla being heavily involved in directing the day-to-day tasks of city administration clearly had its advantages.

"Have we initiated lockdown?" Kayla asked.

"We are just about to activate protocol to do so," the male guard said. "We have deployed squads on the streets and we'll have everyone indoors within a few hours."

"Belay that," Kayla commanded, her tone suddenly fierce. "Cancel lockdown."

"*Cancel* it?" the male guard questioned. "But the Director . . ."

"The Director changed his mind," Kayla said sternly, her folded arms marking the end of the debate. "Keep the SFPD and the City Guard on standby. Have them make preparations to enter the Rings when I give the order. I want them ready."

"Yes, ma'am." The guards nodded in unison.

Wil breathed a sigh of relief. If killing Sens meant lockdown had been deferred, he had made the right decision. Liz mentioned it would be a crucial juncture. Perhaps the crisis had been averted. With Kayla in charge, the guards would be deployed to the Rings and the Resistance would be allowed to prepare for battle.

"Is there anything else the Director changed his mind about?" the female guard asked wryly.

"That's all, for now," Kayla replied, ignoring the guard's sass. "But please return here when you've completed the task."

The two guards nodded before leaving the room.

"Will it really be that easy?" Wil asked.

"No," Kayla said, shaking her head. "There will be questions, and I'll be challenged when my father doesn't return, so we need to act fast. All we have to hope is they'll go along with my orders long enough for us to be effective."

"What happens if they won't?" Wil asked.

"In the circumstances?" Kayla said. "I'm not sure. But they won't be, either. Normally, decisions would be deferred to the Council. Since there is no longer a Council, there is no clear chain of command. Others could claim to be the legitimate interim leader, which will slow down any decision making, or at least make things harder to implement. As I said, since my father kept me heavily involved, hopefully it won't be an issue until it's too late and my influence is secured."

"Who else could fulfil the role?"

"The Chief of Police, for one. Mostly, the police play by their own rules. I expect a challenge when I deploy them to the Rings. Others may follow suit."

"And what do you want us to do?" T'al asked. His clothes were soiled, but fortunately, the spots on them didn't appear to be blood. Voth had a similar appearance.

Wil imagined he looked just as worn. Kayla was the only one among them that did not appear to be affected by the evening's events. Her burgundy outfit looked as crisp as the last time it had been laundered and pressed.

"Head back to the Inner Ring," Kayla replied, "and mobilize the Resistance. Tell them the SFPD and the City Guard will be on their way to assist when the rest of the Silent Zone falls, then see if you can recruit any new members to our cause. With a slice of the Outer Ring gone, the bots will be on our doorstep before we know it and I want to make sure we have as many people ready for the fight as possible."

T'al and Voth both nodded. T'al looked to Wil and gestured for him to follow.

"You guys go ahead," Wil said. "I'm going to get Ella and Liz."

"No, you're coming back with us, Bot Killer," Voth said. "They're safe, and Liz will only want to scale back our efforts. We don't have time—the SZ could fall at any moment."

"There's nobody left for her to negotiate with," Wil said. "She won't have a choice but to allow the Resistance to prepare for battle. They're our friends. I'm going to get them. And it's not up for debate."

"Wil's right," T'al said. "There's no harm in letting them out now. Maybe Liz can make use of her visionary skills."

Wil shook his head. "Liz is the heart of the Resistance. She's saved us all more than once."

"Kid," Voth said. Wil rolled his eyes. The woman was barely older than him. "What impact did we make in Vegas? What impact did we *truly* make? And for what? The bots killed dozens of us, and we were only spared by your friend's ability. We served no purpose. In the meantime, we could have been here, making preparations."

"If it hadn't been for the Resistance, the devastation would have been much worse," Wil protested. "Thousands of people would have died."

"And how many more will die here because we weren't prepared?" Voth asked. The vitriol in her voice pushed Wil back a step. "We weren't able to defend the Outskirts because of our absence."

"Are the lives of those in Vegas worth less than the lives here?" Wil asked.

"Careful, Wil," Voth hissed. "You might mean well, but you haven't fought alongside those of us who have put their lives on the line for this fight."

"Enough!" Kayla said. "Voth and T'al, take the underground tunnels back. Start putting the wheels in motion for the attack."

"But Kayla!" Voth protested. The gritting of her teeth was telling.

Kayla held up a hand. "We can't change the past. And Wil's right— Liz has got nobody left to negotiate with."

T'al and Voth nodded, though Voth glared at both Kayla and Wil, her jaw clenched. Wil wondered if they realized they had deferred a matter for the Resistance to the Director's daughter. Despite any flaws she might have, Liz would never have done that.

Kayla grabbed a plastic card from her father's desk and made her way over to Wil, standing so her chest was barely an inch from his. Wil swallowed. Her scent had faded over the course of the evening, but with her so close to him, he could still detect its faint sweetness. It wasn't until she had gotten so close that he was suddenly aware of her lips, painted red with a coloring that somehow hadn't faded.

"Take this," she said, gripping Wil's hand with her own and placing the hard plastic card in his palm. Her hands were warm and soft, and not how he expected the hands of someone so fierce to be. "It will grant you access to the entire building. If a guard questions your presence, show it to them."

She used the grip on his hand to pull him against her, and she pressed her lips against his. His first thought was to push her away, but he couldn't resist the sparks that coursed through his veins. His mind tried to convince him to stop, swarming with thoughts of Marco and Ella, but the scent of her sweet perfume dissolved them. Kayla held her body against his and brought him in closer, as if to absorb him in the moment.

Wil wrestled with himself about how to react, but in the meantime, he did nothing at all, until Kayla stepped back and smiled sweetly.

His mind raced. He was unable to find the words to describe how he was feeling, and his heart was about to beat out of his chest. Everything about the exchange felt wrong. He had told Ella it was too soon after Marco's death to start anything, and it had been. Kayla's kiss confirmed it still was. Meanwhile, Ella was sitting in a cage in the basement, and he was fifty stories above her head, kissing the Director's daughter.

It wasn't fair to Ella. Kayla, standing before him in her burgundy pantsuit, set fire to his veins with just one look. He let the heat on his skin burn for a moment longer, but her eyes told him she wanted him to stay. Begged him to. So many emotions bubbled through him, and he couldn't sort out how he truly felt. Guilt, confusion, passion, duty, betrayal—all overwhelmed him.

It wasn't lost on him that he barely knew Kayla. Ella had proven more than once that she'd be there for him, no matter what. And those nights under the stars on their way to San Francisco were all he needed to know that what the two of them shared was too important to be shattered in a moment of passion.

Kayla saw an opportunity in his hesitation and tried to pull him in again.

"I think I should go," he said, taking a step back. "This isn't right."

Her face went wide before furrowing in frustration. "What?" she said. "You can't seriously be pushing me away in favor of that Spherian girl?"

"It's not like that," Wil said. "It's . . . *complicated.*"

Her face told him that had been the wrong thing to say.

"Please, Kayla. Don't take this the wrong way," he continued. "You have to understand, I owe her my life, several times over. But I'm not promised to anyone. I've lost someone and I can't just give away my heart. It's too much."

"I'm not asking for your heart," Kayla said, her mouth pouting, her eyes large and longing.

"I need time," Wil replied.

"And the Resistance leader? Are you in love with her, too?"

He hadn't said he *loved* anyone. "Of course not."

The smile returned to Kayla's face, but her eyes narrowed. She swayed her hips as she took the few steps back toward him and lifted a finger to his chin.

"You'll find your friends in the basement. Clear your head on the way down. This is more than about how right we are for each other. We could accomplish so much together. We can take on the bots and make humanity great once again."

Something still didn't sit quite right, but Wil breathed a sigh of relief at her reply. "Thank you for understanding."

Ella had seemed hesitant about his quest to defeat the bots. At least Kayla appeared to understand his desire. But the death of Marco still haunted his dreams, and part of him felt guilty for even entertaining being with someone else. What would Marco think of the two women vying for his attention? He'd likely punch him in the shoulder and wryly accuse him of letting the attention get to his head. Marco had never understood Wil's attraction to both men and women, and he'd always teased him when a woman had caught his eye.

But none had ever affected him the way Kayla did. It was staggering to Wil how intoxicating she was, and he struggled to understand the hold she had over him. Others, both men and women, who interacted with her seemed to be similarly affected—all except for Ella.

Wil turned to the exit as he reminisced about the short time he and Kayla had known each other. A thought crossed his mind, and he paused.

"Why were you at the stadium?" he asked. "The Director's daughter at an unscrupulous robot fight club? The cage suggests you weren't there to spectate."

Kayla turned her head, her cheeks flushed, and she smiled. "Who said anything about me being scrupulous?"

Wil waited, not willing to let her off so easily.

"I had a deal that turned south on me," she replied. The color returned to her cheeks. "But let's leave it at that. It's not relevant."

Sensing she wouldn't tell him anything more, Wil nodded slowly before turning to leave, his heart pounding. Whether it was from the kiss or out of fear for what was ahead of him, he wasn't sure. He double-checked the card in his pocket as he swallowed, his throat parched.

"Oh, and Wil? One more thing," Kayla said, as he was about to turn the corner out of the penthouse office. "Watch out for the jailer. He can get a bit grumpy sometimes."

28

WIL TIPTOED through the corridors of the Renaissance. The cool gray walls reminded him of some of the more important buildings in the Sphere, but the dark tile floor was enough to make the hallway feel both ominous and foreign. Everything about the city seemed to be an echo of the Sphere, but with its own sense of flair. Designed by the ancients, this building had been taken care of and accented by a human's touch.

He pressed the down button on the elevator. A nearby window let in light from the sun, emanating the full intensity of the morning. A haze of green still cast itself over the city, but not so much that it dulled the reflection of the sun's light as it glinted off the glass windows.

Nothing within the City Center showed the same damage from the wars that the buildings of the Inner Ring had. Each looked as pristine as the day it had been built. Far below, vehicles dotted the bustling streets, some on the ground and others airborne, hovering between docks attached to windowsills tens of stories in the air. Wil had thought the Sphere had been far removed from those that lived in the SZ, but clearly the people of the City Center were as technologically capable.

The elevator dinged, and he stepped through its doors into the tiny car. It was remarkable, and yet he had nobody to share his amazement with. He had caught the same bewildered look on Ella's face as they had been taken to the Director's office for the first time, but they hadn't had chance to discuss it between the party on the yacht and the attack. Even Sierra would have had to admit it was extraordinary, and he hoped he would one day get to share the amazing aspects of this city with her.

Wil pushed the button next to the letter 'B', as Kayla had instructed. There had been no buildings with a basement in the Sphere that he knew of, and the concept of burrowing beneath the surface of the Earth was more than a little intimidating. The only other time he could recall being underground was while he had been recovering in the infirmary during the attack on Vegas. His stomach flip-flopped at the thought of an entire building being on top of him. The Rio Grande in Vegas had only been a few stories high. Fifty stories now hovering above his head was unimaginable.

So much had changed in his thinking over the past few weeks. Even the past twenty-four hours had brought a dizzying amount of information and obstacles he'd had to circumnavigate. His friends, for instance, were potentially not who he'd thought they were. T'al and Voth being at odds with Liz was mind-boggling. She had done so much to further the cause of the Resistance; it was difficult to see why they wouldn't trust her. On the other hand, he understood the need for action, but he wasn't sure if he was in favor of their methods to get her out of the way. Had Liz's plan been brought to completion, he wondered what the result might have been, and where he'd be sitting right now.

The doors opened at the basement level, and Wil nervously peered out. The card in his pocket was supposed to be his access pass in case any guards questioned him, but part of him worried they'd shoot first and ask questions later.

A small room greeted Wil. Two windows within a large metal door stood between him and whatever lay on the basement level. The air was stale and smelled of must and grease, like it had once been an old mechanical warehouse.

Wil pushed his way through the set of doors and padded across the cold gray concrete floor. Dim lights flickered on the dingy brick walls, buzzing as they flashed, as if the bulbs were loose in their fixtures. Their illumination bounced off the concrete pillars lined in rows throughout the open space, casting long shadows across the floor. Along one side of the room lay an endless row of glass cells, the walls of which were transparent and solid, with no visible openings or insets for a door or even a window. There were about a dozen cells, and each cage was lit with its own cool glow from a single blue-white fluorescent bulb that lined its back wall, casting a clinical luminescence on the dejected person within. Long, matted hair and beards made it appear as though some inhabitants had been there for an extremely long time.

Wil immediately scanned the residents for his friends. Each face within the cells was gaunt and worn, and most sat in the corner of their units with their eyes closed. With the way the lights flickered, he didn't blame them. There was no privacy, not from the main chamber, and not from the other prisoners.

Nobody looked to Wil. Most stared out into nothingness, as if he wasn't even there.

Wil crept into the room, cautiously placing one foot in front of the other, afraid to make a sound. Kayla had mentioned a jailer, but so far, the room seemed unattended. Perhaps he'd gotten lucky. That was, if he could find who he was looking for.

A chill crept over him, and although he wore his cloak to fend off the humid air, Wil pulled it in closer in the basement's dampness.

A solitary woman caught his eye. She stood in the middle of her cube, staring into the chamber. Unlike the other prisoners, she stood tall and unbroken, ever confident.

Liz.

Wil walked to her cell and placed his hand on the glass. She didn't appear to notice his approach until he touched the glass surface.

Liz jumped as her eyes focused on him and then grew wide, her mouth growing slack.

"Liz," he said. "It's all right. I'm here to get you out."

She shook her head, and for the first time Wil could remember, the woman looked terrified. Her mouth moved, but the words disappeared through the soundproof glass.

"Where's Ella?" he asked, undeterred. "How do I get you out of here?"

He fumbled along the glass wall. There was no edge, no inset or panel to betray any sort of door.

Liz was waving frantically, trying to bring his attention to something, but he continued to feel the edge of the glass chamber for anything that would allow him to let her out. It was as though it had been constructed around Liz rather than her having been placed inside it. How any of these prisoners had air was incomprehensible to him.

His actions had caught the attention of the inmate in the cell next to Liz. The man looked to have been in the enclosure for months, possibly longer. He hadn't shaved in quite some time. His beard was greasy and matted, and bits of food were littered within its layers.

He pressed his bearded face into the corner where his cage met Liz's. His gaze cast into the distance, as if focused on something behind Wil.

At the same spot Liz was looking at.

Wil twisted around and dove out of the way, barely in time before the arms of the robotic giant came crashing down in the spot where he'd been standing.

Goliath towered over him.

Wil scrambled to move again.

The robot lifted both arms above its head, seemingly enraged that Wil had evaded its attack. He hadn't been this close to the monster in the stadium, having only witnessed the destruction it had caused from a distance. The beast didn't have a mouth, only a dark gray metal plate where a mouth should be, but a low rumble echoed from its head, like a wolf warning him he had intruded into its lair.

Wil's chest heaved. Was this the robot Kayla controlled? If so, why was it attacking him now?

The jailer gets grumpy. What kind of game was Kayla playing?

The other inmates watched the action unfold, some with looks of horror, others with maniacal grins of glee.

Wil gained his balance. He had nothing to defend himself with; the dagger Argo had given him still hung heavy on his belt—but it wouldn't be of any use against the bot.

He could test his luck and try to call on his power, but Wil didn't know how that would affect the surrounding building. He'd hate to knock out the lights in the already dim basement, or worse, decommission the elevator that would be his escape. And that all rested on whether he could call the ability at will.

The bot lunged at him again, swiping with his tree trunk-sized arms. Wil barely avoided his grasp for the second time. Metal limbs slammed into the concrete floor, shattering its surface and sending dust into the air, forcing Wil into a coughing fit. It seemed like the entire building shook above his head.

Wil scrambled to get behind one of the wide concrete columns that ran from floor to ceiling. Though they'd probably shatter if the metal bot attacked it, he reasoned they'd probably fare better than his head.

The bot studied Wil, in the same way as it had observed Dagger in the stadium before the roof had come crashing down, sizing up its opponent and wondering how best to strike.

This bot was not a Guardian, but it also wasn't the tame being Kayla made it out to be. She had claimed there were signals broadcast to the beast within the arena, but Wil was coming to grips with the fact that Kayla might not have been completely forthcoming with him. Through the haze, he could see the bot's shining yellow eyes taunting him, assured in its ability to win this fight.

Ever since the day he had left the Sphere, Wil had known his death would be at the hand of a bot. He'd just thought it would be while fighting Guardians on the battleground rather than a homemade bodyguard locked away in a basement.

Behind the bot, Liz stood against the wall of her cell with her palms pressed against the glass and a grimace on her face. She was rendered helpless, and Wil knew it was eating the Resistance leader up inside.

An idea occurred to him, and he whipped the yellow card Kayla had given him from his pocket and waved it to the side of the column so Goliath could see it. Perhaps the robot would honor his pass.

Liz shook her head, only slightly, while lifting a hand to her forehead.

I'm open to ideas, Wil thought.

Goliath pressed his shoulders back as he let out another loud mechanical roar. The force of the noise alone sent vibrations through the column.

Wil dropped the pass as the bot charged forward, and he pushed himself back from the column, tripping over his own momentum and falling flat. He braced himself to be overrun by a freight train of metal, but the impact never came. Instead, the building shook once again, and more dust rained down. The robot had missed its target and charged right into the column, unable to compensate for the structure that stood between it and its prey. The bot's shoulder bounced off the solid surface, and it, too, fell over from the pressure of the impact.

It was the sort of image Wil would have found amusing if his life hadn't been hanging in the balance. He scrambled backed to his feet, stumbling in his haste to get behind the next column.

A large chunk of concrete slab from the first column lay at its base. Wil coughed as dust coated his lungs, and the ground shook again. Fresh dust and concrete fragments dropped from the ceiling.

That couldn't possibly have been because of one column?

There was no time to worry about the foundation's stability. Unconcerned, Goliath hurtled across the floor toward Wil once again. Wil stood to one side of the columns, allowing himself to attract the bot. As Goliath closed the space between them, Wil sidestepped and hid himself behind the concrete pillar. He didn't think the bot would have enough time to pivot, believing it would bypass him completely, but he miscalculated.

The bot hadn't appeared to learn from the first encounter and dove headfirst into the column.

Once again, Wil dodged the collapsing pillar, but only just. The concrete slab caught the back of his shoe and sent him flying. He barely managed to get his hands out in front of him in time before landing on the stone floor, scraping his wrists and elbows.

Chunks of debris slid past Wil, and he scrambled to avoid some of the larger pieces.

"All right, Goliath," said a familiar voice. "There's no need to bring the entire building down."

Kayla stood over Wil with a grin.

29

WIL FIDGETED with the bonds Kayla had placed on his wrists as Goliath rested a hand on the glass in front of Liz. The robot's touch activated white and blue lights on the cell's surface.

Cell 02B. 67°F. Conspiracy.

An opening in the glass appeared. There was no sliding door, no door of glass; there was simply a hole in the cell where there hadn't been before. The walls appeared to be nearly six inches thick. There wouldn't be a way to smash their way through its surface by hand, or even by blade.

Other numbers and statistics flashed on the panel quicker than Wil could make them out before giant metal hands pushed him forward into the cell. Liz reached out and caught him, stopping his momentum.

Wil backed into the glass wall and rested his burning shoulders against them. He wished he could do the same for his scraped knees and bound wrists, but they weren't serious enough to be anything but an irritant. They were far less of an agitation than the woman in the tight bodysuit outside the cage. Wil cursed he had kissed her in a moment of weakness. He didn't know whether it had been her plan all along to double-cross him or if this was his punishment for not conceding to her advances. Either way, it stung just as hard that he had fallen into this mess.

He had killed for this woman.

"This was never about protecting the city, was it?"

Kayla's amused grin widened.

"Protecting the city is open to interpretation. My plan has always been to take back control of San Francisco from my father and his sniveling Council."

Wil glanced around at the other cells. All eyes were on them.

But someone was still missing.

"What have you done with Ella?"

"You really are quite taken with her, aren't you? Well, since you were having a tough time choosing who to be with, I made things easy for you."

"You think killing her will make me want to be with you?"

"Kill her?" Kayla's voice inflected. "You think so little of me. I've merely sent her out into the city. She's being held there, waiting for you. That is, if you choose to go to her. You could decide to stay here with me. I'll let both her and your other friend go, and you and I get to rule here together, no harm done."

"Wil," Liz hissed at him, her eyes narrowed. There was no question this was one of those important decisions she had warned him about. He could feel it in the adrenaline that coursed through his veins. Each beat of his heart screamed at him to choose wisely.

But which decision was the correct one? He looked to Liz for further direction, but she had clamped her mouth shut as if she had realized she had said too much already. So, what was he supposed to do?

Kayla was promising to let Ella go if he stayed, but how could he trust that she'd stick to her agreement? And what did that mean, exactly? Would he be stuck in this tower with her forever? Or would it be easier to escape once Ella was freed?

What about the Guardians?

With him stuck within the walls of the City Center, there wouldn't be anything he could do to help in the fight. The Resistance, the City Guard and the police on the front lines would all be slaughtered.

"You had no intention of fending off the robot attack, did you?" Wil said as the realization struck him. "You want those you sent out to die?"

"Pretty ingenious, isn't it?" she said.

Wil had once seen her grin as inviting, but he now realized what it had been all along—manipulative and sinister. He silently scolded himself for falling for her charms.

"There are too many in their ranks who were loyal to my father," Kayla continued. "With the army devastated and the Council dissolved, the city will now rally behind me with their support. I bring stability. A new hope for the future. I'll be able to lead how I want and bring San Francisco back to our days of former glory, before the floods and the earthquakes made us a shell of what the ancients designed."

She was planning something else, but Wil couldn't quite connect the dots.

"But what about the farmers and the tradespeople? You said the City Center will starve if the bots destroy the Rings."

She scoffed. "With my father in power, we would have. But we have the capability to grow our own food within the Center. We'll set up hydroponics on boats in the harbor and utilize the wetlands that overtook our city. My father couldn't see past centuries of tradition that made us reliant on the scum of the Rings."

"And then what?" Wil asked. "Surely you have more to offer than being locked within the City Center barrier?"

Kayla smiled and walked toward him. Wil had to consciously push aside the temptation she induced. It was Ella's sincerity and kind heart that had attracted him to her, and this woman was the complete opposite. Kayla, it seemed, was just as likely to throw him to Goliath as she was to kiss him.

"This is why we'd make an excellent team," she said, leaning in beside him and whispering in his ear. His heart raced as her warm breath brushed over his skin. "You and I are more alike than you think.

You want the bots destroyed, not out of the kindness of your heart, but to exact revenge for the death of one teenage boy. It's nothing to be ashamed of; it's a noble cause. But in the end, it's a waste of your talents. Think of the good that could be done for humanity if you put your mind to a more productive use.

"The Resistance hasn't changed their tactics in over two hundred years. You think they're going to win now, simply because the Silent Zones are nearing their end? They still fight a battle they can't win. We might not defeat the Guardians, but we can build our own empire and use our resources to unite the cities to the south. The bots divided us long ago; separated us from each other to keep us weak. Under our rule, humanity could forge a path toward unity once again."

Wil arched an eyebrow.

"And in order to do so, you'd let the Ringers be crushed by the Guardians?"

Her smile widened. "I haven't left them defenceless, remember? I've sent them the entirety of the SFPD, the Guard and the Resistance."

Liz swallowed beside him, but remained silent.

"You've sent them out to be slaughtered," Wil said.

"I've simply done what the Resistance asked of us. If they were wrong in their thinking, then why am I the villain?"

Liz's demeanor hadn't changed throughout the exchange. Her arms were folded over her chest, and her lips were pursed in irritation. She was clearly unhappy, but it didn't lend any clues to Wil. If the fight was doomed to fail, then what *was* the point of Liz's request for fighters?

"We also requested safe haven for those who reside in the Rings," Liz said. "You've twisted my request to suit your own ends."

"I won't have the City Center overrun by refugees. My father wasn't wrong about that. What happens when the battle fails? How are we to feed all these people with killer robots at our door?"

"If you think you'll come out of the war unscathed," Liz said, "you're dreaming."

Kayla snorted and turned to leave the cage. "The ancients designed this field to keep the bots out. I don't doubt it will succeed in doing so."

"What are you really after?" Wil asked.

"My goal is to expand our influence. There are so many resources left untapped in the Silent Zones to the south, traders and commoners that can't organize themselves enough to control their own commerce."

"You're not concerned about the bots?" Wil asked. "Once the Silent Zones fall, how do you plan to travel between cities?"

"That's where you come in, Bot Killer. You think it was an accident that Fry found you the night you went to the stadium? I *sought* you out. I had you delivered to me. I had hoped to see a display of what you're capable of. T'al had told me great things of what you can do. We can work together to take out the Guardians and restore humanity's great cities again. Your power could clear the paths we need to travel."

"I think you underestimate the Guardians' reach," Liz said.

"Think about it," Kayla said. "You not only get the revenge you want, but you'll also get to be the right hand of the most powerful leader in the land. The first empire since the wars."

"Why would I help you?" Wil asked. "You haven't exactly been upfront until now."

A smile curled at the edges of Kayla's mouth. The red of her lips hadn't faded since they'd shared a kiss. Her gaze made Wil's heart quicken.

"Consider this," Kayla said. "There is only one person in this room who is able to stop the Guardians from destroying all of your beloved farmers and merchants."

Wil's heart continued to pound as she took a step closer to him. Kayla lifted a hand to his chest, her wide eyes focused on his as she ran a finger between his pecs.

"If you want to save them," she said, her voice lowered to a near whisper, "then save them. Once you've done that, our actual work can begin."

Wil swallowed. The weight of her words did little to slow his pulse.

"Plus," she said with a mischievous grin, "there will definitely be added benefits for you."

Kayla removed her finger from his chest and stepped back to the exit.

"You want to use me?" Wil said. He hated to admit her offer was appealing, but it had nothing to do with him and everything to do with what she thought his power could accomplish. "Wield me as your personal weapon to expand your empire?"

Kayla's smile twisted briefly as she stood in the cell's entryway. "My poor Spherian friend. You think Liz doesn't want to use you? Why do you think she's brought you along, *Bot Killer?* Do you think the Resistance would fare any better if my father had agreed instead of me? You're her insurance policy as much as you are mine. But I'm offering you the chance to be part of something more. To rule alongside me. Would you still choose her over me?"

The worry had plagued Wil since they had arrived in San Francisco; that Liz had only brought him along as a pawn or, perhaps worse, a weapon. He had become someone of value. Just as he had been sold to the Prowlers, his worth had been tied to an ability he had only recently discovered and did not yet fully understand.

The thought of keeping the bots at bay so humanity could regain its position in the world was the entire reason he had left the Sphere. Perhaps Kayla was offering something Liz could not—a united human front, and action against the bots. Perhaps the path forward was an unconventional one he hadn't anticipated.

If only he could control his ability. Everyone was crawling over themselves to put it to use, but he still couldn't call it at will or stop it when it came.

"I'd like to see Ella," Wil said. Despite everything he could or couldn't do, he owed the woman who'd followed him out here an explanation. "If I'm going to believe you'll let her go unharmed, I need to see her. And I'd like to at least say goodbye."

Kayla looked back over her shoulder at him. "You'll get to see her. And I promise I won't harm her. She's protected for now, but her future depends on you." She stepped out of the cell completely before adding, "The guards will escort you out of the SZ. From there, you'll be free to do as you wish, but you won't be able to return until you're ready to fully commit to me."

"Outside the SZ?" Wil questioned. But Kayla had already put a hand to the cell wall. Lights on the wall's surface spun and turned red before the glass rematerialized.

The sounds of the chamber beyond the cell were instantly silenced. Wil hadn't noticed the hum the chamber had made or the creaking of Goliath's joints until they disappeared. Kayla strutted to the exit, presumably fully aware that Wil was still watching her. He cursed at the realization as the door closed behind her.

Goliath stomped off into the shadows. Wil guessed he was programmed to stay out of sight unless he detected motion in the chamber.

Until this point, Wil hadn't had a chance to take a good look at Liz. Her arms were crossed, and her dark hair hung limp, clinging to her pale face. She hadn't been mistreated, per se, but she definitely hadn't been well taken care of over the past twenty-four hours.

"What did you do?" she asked, her voice cold and unimpressed.

"Glad I'm still the favorite," Wil replied.

Liz pulled at his shirtsleeve. He hadn't noticed the blood that stained it until then.

"You killed the Director," she said. It wasn't a question.

"How do you know?" he asked, his eyebrow arched. It didn't matter, so he quickly continued. "I was trying to help. How was I supposed to know she had ulterior motives?"

"There was only one living member left in charge of the city, and you didn't think to ask yourself if the woman who refused to kill him herself might have something to gain from the Director's death?"

Wil crossed his arms.

"You're lucky she's attracted to you," Liz continued, "or she would have used you as the scapegoat for the coup. She obviously thinks she still has a chance at winning you over."

Wil sighed as he reflected on Liz's words. It made sense; Kayla didn't want to get her own hands dirty.

"What the hell were you thinking?" Liz asked. "Aid in the rebellion and help Kayla? You've doomed the city. You might have doomed us all."

"I was following the path I thought was right. T'al and Voth thought so, too," he said, before he realized the implication of Liz's words. "You know everything that's happened? You've seen this all take place? This was one of the decisions that alters the course of the future?"

Liz still held his shirt, and she swung him against the cell wall. "How could killing the leader of the most advanced city left untouched by the Guardians not alter the course of the future?" She bared her teeth in fury. "I've seen dozens of scenarios which could have occurred over the next twenty-four hours. But now, those options have dwindled. Every vision I've had where the Director dies before the attack proves to play out badly. And it's always worse when it's been by your hand."

Liz released her grip on him and sat down in the center of the cell, her eyes staring into the distance.

"You could have told me, you know," Wil said. "A little heads up that Kayla couldn't be trusted."

"You should have seen that for yourself. The only scenarios I've seen that are worse than the one we're in now," she replied, "are the ones where I gave you more of a warning. You might not believe this, but you don't like being told what to do."

Wil scoffed at the accusation. "So, now what? Are you going to fill me in on what happens next?"

Liz shook her head. "Even if I wanted to, I don't know all the pieces. The bots are coming, and the SZ may already have fallen. The Rings will be destroyed. I had hoped we could get the people into the City Center, into some semblance of safety, but I don't believe there's any hope of that happening now. The best we can do is to fight; help the army and the Resistance to hold off the Guardians for as long as we can."

"You knew T'al and Voth would turn against you, didn't you?"

She nodded, but only subtly. "Except I don't believe it's as bad as it looks. They haven't turned against me as much as they've sought to bypass me in order to do what they think is right. If Director Sens was still alive, their attempts wouldn't have mattered so much."

"The attack. You warned the Guard," he said. "That's how they were able to get the Director out so quickly."

"All I did was tell them to be extra vigilant."

"But if you knew the attack would happen," he pressed on, "why did you let the meeting happen at all? Why didn't you stop it?"

"I can try to sway people in the direction I think is best, but as soon as I try to force things the way I think they should be, I end up making it worse."

"Why did you bring me to the Director, then?" Wil asked. "If you hadn't brought me here, I would never have been sucked into the plan on the yacht."

"Sens had his issues, but at least he was willing to work with us. If he were still alive, he would have eventually given in and had the Guard help in the fight. Most importantly, he would have let the Ringers inside the Center gates. We could have saved thousands. Kayla doesn't care about us, and she doesn't care about the city."

"You should have told me," Wil said, leaning against the glass wall where the door had been.

"I tried to warn you about Kayla," Liz responded. "And it drove you closer to her. Would you have reacted differently if I had told you why? Would it have been a better alternative to this? Whichever way you cut it, you were to be either the Director's savior or his killer."

"Surely I couldn't have been the sole hope for the city," Wil said. "There's got to be another way out of this."

"You weren't just the sole hope of the city; you were the hope for *the world*, at least in part. But in all the scenarios I've seen where the Director dies by your hand, I haven't seen a path forward where you live past tomorrow."

30

WIL LOST track of how many hours he had been lying on the concrete floor of the cell before someone roughly nudged him awake.

After Liz had informed him of his impending death, she had suggested he use her legs as a pillow and get some rest. If he was doomed to fail, it was best if he weren't sleep deprived for it. It wasn't the most comforting of sentiments, but he'd nearly been falling asleep where he stood, so he'd agreed.

Out of courtesy, he'd offered Liz the first sleeping shift, but she'd refused, indicating she and Ella had already held the same arrangement the night before. Wil hadn't argued, instead melting onto the floor as weariness took hold of each of his muscles. The concrete held small reprieve, but despite the lack of frills, a few hours away from the madness of the last two days would provide him with some well-needed sleep.

When he awoke, it took him a few moments to reorient himself before realizing a uniformed guard was prodding him with the end of a baton. Liz had a grip on his shoulders and was shaking him. The act had either been too gentle to rouse him from his slumber without the guard's less sympathetic help or he had been so tired that his body had been too slow to respond for the guard's liking. Either way, the result had been the same.

Whether he had been asleep for fifteen minutes or all day was impossible to tell in the dimly lit basement. Nothing outside of the cell appeared to have had changed.

"Get up." A boot greeted Wil's ribs, kicking off any lingering effects of sleep.

Wil spasmed at the impact and scrambled to his feet, trying to get a sense of balance and allowing the enormity of his situation to sink in.

"Let's go." The guard motioned toward the cell's newly reformed exit.

Wil shook his head and complied with a sigh. He didn't know why the guards had been instructed to take them outside of the SZ. Perhaps Kayla's intention had been to have them destroyed by the bots all along. If Liz was right, he wouldn't live to see past tomorrow. Or today, depending on how long he had actually slept, but if his spinning head was any indication, it hadn't been that long.

The guards escorted them back up the elevator and out into the streets. He squinted at the sun's intensity as they left the Renaissance. Wil wished he could have held up his hand to shade his eyes. The sun peeking through the tops of the buildings intensified as it reflected off the glass skyscrapers surrounding them, indicating it was mid-afternoon.

It seemed he had only slept the morning. Somehow in the next day and half, he had to save Ella, possibly the city, and prevent his own death. The sweat on his brow was as much from the heat as it was from the pressure mounting inside him. Once again, he was at the mercy of a riddle Liz had given him. She had presented him with enough information to drive him crazy, but not enough to decide about what steps he could take. If any.

Wil didn't believe that knowing his life was about to end would be any less detrimental to the fate of the world than knowing exactly how, but according to Liz, knowing would only make it worse.

"Are you taking us to see Ella?" Wil asked the guard as they shoved him into the back seat of a black-wheeled vehicle. The black leather interior bore none of the warmth of the outside; like the buildings in the Center, it must have been cooled with air conditioning, something he had grown up with in the Sphere. The cooling sensation was surprising after traveling for weeks with no technological comforts.

"Oh, you'll see her all right," the guard said with a smirk, and he slammed the door in Wil's face. He had learned the guard's name was Mario, a heavyset man who enjoyed prodding Wil in the ribs. The guard assigned to Liz was named Annabelle, a petite woman who seemed a bit more apologetic about pushing Liz around. As bruised as his ribs were, Wil was appreciative he was taking the brunt of the abuse. Liz didn't need to suffer any more than she had already because of his missteps. He just hoped there would still be a chance he could right the wrongs he'd committed.

Many cars that drove past them on the street looked as though they could have been repurposed from ancient vehicles. Others looked as though they were more modern creations, but they were still pieced together with repurposed materials used by the ancients.

Buildings that touched the sky lined the street. Even after having been in the city for a couple days now, Wil found it hard not to stare. His mind drifted to Ella, to his future, and how only a few short weeks ago, he had lived in a bubble. It was in that bubble that he had watched the Guardians murder Marco. How far away that all seemed now. In reality, only a few months had passed, yet it felt like a lifetime.

Pedestrians ambled along the sidewalks, their eyes focused ahead, intent on completing their daily duties. There was no concern about a Guardian attack here; not even a concern about Ringer refugees or if the shops would have enough supplies to get them through the week. Without the call for lockdown, it was business as usual. Most of the populace wore outfits similar to the late Director and the other Council members; business suits, gray, blue, and black mainly, though some sported other colors. But there were some who wore the more eccentric outfits. Feathers, sequins, and ribbons; flashy hats, gloves, and canes.

If Kayla was to be believed, many of them had no clue of the hostile intent of the Guardians outside their gates or that the protective Silent

Zone surrounding their home, protecting their crops and merchants, was in danger of collapsing.

Wil wondered if the same people had any clue that their leader, their Council, and his opposition had been killed in a coup orchestrated by his daughter. The streets were eerily unconcerned for a city that had lost its entire leadership.

The handcuffs the guard had placed on them were constructed of glowing bands of energy, yet they constrained Wil's hands tighter than any metal. There was no room for his hands to move; no give at all. He even struggled to understand the technology that wrapped itself around his hands, holding them still with nothing but electrical current.

The bonds were unnecessary. There was no point in them causing further disruption to the City Center. His only goal now was to find Ella and to ensure she was safe. If he could stop a robot invasion without getting himself killed, it would be a bonus.

The car drove through the city streets, passing storefronts that appeared as if they had been ripped from a photograph of the past. "It's like the ancients never left," Wil said. "Everything preserved, just as it was."

"The ancients built hardly any of what is here," Liz said, staring out the car window.

Wil looked at her, bewildered. "I thought they put the barrier in place to protect the ancient city?" he asked.

Liz closed her eyes, as though trying to fight off a bad memory; something she had no interest in sharing. "Most of the ancient city was destroyed *before* the wall went up," she said. "What you see here has been built by their descendants. Those who refused to believe the time of the ancients had come to an end."

Their ride meandered through the city's streets for what seemed like an eternity. As they drew closer to the force field, the skyscrapers didn't seem to stretch as high, and brick began to replace glass. Wil imagined that if the wall didn't exist, the outside of the City Center and much of the Inner Ring would be indistinguishable.

The streets also became more and more congested. The vehicle was all but crawling by the time the guards stopped the car and opened the door.

"Wait here," Mario said, as if they had any choice. Wil had tested the door handle with his loose fingers multiple times. They had no way out.

Wil pressed his nose against the window to get a better glimpse of what was happening. He couldn't see much past the sea of bodies standing before the giant concrete wall that separated the market from the rest of the City Center.

"What's going on?" Wil asked. It didn't appear as though the crowd was getting anywhere, and the guards weren't letting anyone in through the main gate.

"The gates have been closed for over a day now," Liz said. "My guess would be the stalls are running low on stock."

Wil could only catch glimpses of the contorted faces among the crowd. Many appeared to be yelling, but Wil couldn't hear anything through the vehicle's soundproofing. Uniformed guards pushed the crowd back from the market entrance, but there weren't enough to keep everyone at bay.

"They sent most of the guards out of the city," Wil thought aloud.

"Thanks to your friend," Liz said. The windows of the vehicle were tinted, but sunlight still filtered through, casting a contrast of light and dark shadows on Liz's face. The woman somehow seemed both unfazed and utterly annoyed at the situation that was playing out.

"How much do your visions reveal?" he asked. "Do you know every step we take from now onward?"

Liz sighed and fidgeted with the hem of her jacket. "If I could, it would either make things infinitely easier or more frustrating. But no, I actually see very little that takes place. All I see are snapshots, specific moments in time. For instance, for every time I've seen you stab the Director, I also see you lying dead in the city's streets shortly after. I have no insight into the events that happen before, after, or in between. I couldn't have told you before today what actions led to the stabbing. I also can't tell you what will happen between now and your death, only that the two events are linked."

"So, it's a certainty, then?" he asked. "There's no changing the outcome of what I've done?"

"It's impossible to predict when a seemingly small action might change the course of history," Liz replied. The car shook as some of the civilians bumped against it. Liz carried on as if nothing was occurring. "Kings have lived or died because a driver led their procession through an unscripted route. City walls have fallen because of the misspoken word of a leader. Mistranslations have changed the course of history. The future is never written in stone, even if the odds are stacked against us."

Wil's door opened, and a pair of stubby hands grabbed him and pulled him out. One guard had a firm grip on his arm and dragged him through the crowd. Bodies pressed against him, threatening to tear him from the guard's grip. Wil wasn't sure if he should be more worried about his escort or the crowd.

Waves of noise crashed over him, along with the swarm of bodies, yelling and chanting mixed with unintelligible noise. At this rate, the City wouldn't hold together more than a couple days, never mind months.

Wil's head felt as chaotic as the street around him. Kayla had set him up to kill her father, yet was offering him a chance to rebuild a link between the cities on the west coast. Her motives might be convoluted, but he couldn't argue with her appeal to rid humanity of the bots.

Despite Liz's insinuation that it was his attractiveness keeping him alive, he suspected it had more to do with his reputation for destroying bots. He hadn't been about to tell Kayla that he didn't know how to control the ability, nor would he tell her it incapacitated him every time it flared up.

He'd worry about that later. His goal now was to get out of the Center and find Ella.

Kayla had implied they'd have no problem finding her, and to Wil, that meant she was probably back at the Resistance safe house.

Wil tried to get a sense of the crowd surging around him, though it was difficult to focus on any individual person in all the disruption.

Those he saw seemed to be dressed in a similar fashion to the merchants of the Inner Ring. Their clothes imitated what he had seen at the Council party and within the stadium, but like Fry, they were ill-fitting and sometimes misshapen for the person wearing them. These were mainly merchants, traders, and their families, but since they were on this side of the marketplace, Wil guessed they, too, lived in the City Center.

A fight broke out between two of the more wide-eyed among them. An overweight man appeared to have grabbed a live chicken out of an older woman's hands, causing a younger man, possibly her son, to take offense and throw a punch squarely into the burly man's jaw. They haphazardly dropped the chicken to the ground with a squawk before the man wound up a basketball-sized fist.

The blow never landed. Mario released his grip on Wil and grabbed the metal baton from his belt. A blue electric current radiated from its tip as he swung it. On impact, it sent the man into a fit of seizures, dropping to the ground and convulsing from the current discharged into his muscles.

In response to Mario's intervention, the crowd surrounding Wil and their vehicle retreated, creating a ten-foot buffer around their escort. The roar of their yells faded into the distance, and the street grew disconcertedly quiet for the size of the crowd. Wil shot a look at Liz, who he could now make out with the horde no longer separating them, and Annabelle escorted her over to where Wil stood.

The guards exchanged an annoyed look with each other. Mario, still holding his pulsing baton, waved to follow him, and the crowd parted, creating an open space for the four of them to travel through.

Lined against the wall, before the entrance to the market, were a dozen other guards, holding their batons at the ready, stationary at their post. Behind them was a twenty-foot archway, which marked the general entryway into the market.

"Tigen," Mario said to one of the guards standing watch. "Why have you allowed things to escalate?"

Tigen, an athletic-looking woman in her mid-thirties, intently surveyed the crowd. Her gaze remained firm, but a slight movement in her eyes revealed apprehension. Whether it was because of the crowd or Mario's stern undertone was impossible for him to tell.

"Sorry, Mario," Tigen replied, drawing out her words in a nasal voice. "They were peaceful before you arrived."

"Peaceful or not, we can't have this kind of disturbance clogging the streets. Chase them home, and beat the ones that don't comply."

"Sir?" Tigen's hard resolve dissolved at the command. Her eyes narrowed, and her mouth hung slightly agape.

"Kayla's halted the lockdown, but in exchange, she's authorized the use of force to maintain order. With the Council dead, we can't allow the streets to descend into chaos. We need to bring this under control."

"Is Kayla the new Director now?" she asked.

"For all intent and purposes, she seems to be. She basically ran the show before, anyway. Now, get this crowd out of here!"

Tigen waved a hand at the guards behind her, and their batons lit up in unison. She grabbed a megaphone before addressing the crowd, instructing them to disperse back to their homes.

There was a moment of confusion, but eventually the crowd trickled away.

"But we need food!" shouted a man with graying hair and darker stubble on his face. "If we can't get to the market, what will we eat?"

"There are still supplies at the grocers. There is no need to congregate here."

"We can't afford those prices!" the man protested. "And how long before they run out of food, too? We need to know more will be coming. When will trade begin again?"

"Please move, sir," one guard said to the man. "We need to clear the area."

Mario and Annabelle continued to push Wil and Liz forward. Wil couldn't hear the man's reply or see the guard's response, but he heard the charge of the electric baton and the groans of the man as it made contact.

That act electrified the crowd further, who all now scrambled to leave.

31

THE MARKETPLACE, which had been packed with merchants and traders the previous day, was now silent. A handful of vendors still sat behind their now empty tables. They had dissembled most of the decorations that had given life to their tents, but some banners and flags still clung to what was left, hanging onto hope by a thread.

A swirling wind, initiated by enormous fans that lined the streets, tossed printed pamphlets and other garbage, the only evidence that several thousand people had crowded the facility the day before. The road might have been paved, but a thick layer of dirt covered its surface. Wheel ruts from carts exposed the concrete surface beneath. Hundreds of footprints from those who had walked over it in recent days packed the dirt down everywhere else.

"Where did everyone go?" Wil asked to no one in particular.

"Back into the Rings, where they belong," Mario replied. "We let too many of those dirty merchants in here, if you ask me. Caused more harm than good. Our crime rates will go down once people get used to the idea that we'll be growing our own food."

Mario's thick hand pushed Wil forward, and Wil tried his best not to trip over the litter on the street. The concrete ceiling and wall that separated the market from the Center felt a little more ominous after the guard's comments. It hadn't dawned on Wil before that the walls were meant to separate the Ringers from those in the rest of the City Center, despite relying on them for food. He didn't push the matter any further, though; he wasn't in a position to argue with the guards.

"What will become of the market?" Wil asked instead. "Will it sit abandoned like this?"

"Our people will finally get a chance to sell their own products without being undercut by the Ringers. Can you imagine if those outside the gate had overrun us? Our peaceful Center would have been destroyed."

As if placed to emphasize what the guard was saying, Wil noticed a poster which clung haphazardly to a metal post.

Someone with a shaky hand had scrawled the freehand message: *Keep the Ringers OUT!*

As he scanned other nearby surfaces, he realized they had hung similar posters throughout the facility. The desire to keep the City Center gates closed appeared to be held by more than the Guard and the now-deceased Council.

It was a physical manifestation of what Director Sens had been hoping for. It only took a swell of upset farmers, proving how unruly they could become, for the people of the Center to reveal their prejudice.

It didn't take long for Wil, Liz, and their escorts to cross the emptied marketplace to the main gate. Mario and his accomplice tapped on their bonds with a small handheld device to release them, and Wil breathed a sigh of relief. He immediately rubbed his wrists, trying to regain feeling as the blood rushed back into them.

"Don't get too comfortable," Mario snickered, holding out a set of metal cuffs.

"Come on." Wil rolled his eyes. "Are those really needed?"

"The electronic ones won't work outside the Center," Mario replied. "Kayla doesn't want you unrestrained until you're on the other side of the SZ."

"Why take us through the SZ?" he asked. "Do we have to stay out of the Rings as well?" That would make the task of finding Ella more difficult. He was sure she would have returned to the safe house.

"You'll see," Mario chuckled. Wil looked to Liz for understanding as to what was going on, but the furrow in her brow indicated she knew as little as he did.

"What are you going to do once we get back?" Wil asked Liz as they resumed their march. He eyed the guards warily, but they didn't appear to be concerned with them speaking to each other. "Will the Resistance still listen to you?"

"The majority will," she replied. "T'al and Voth are outliers. Others may be restless, too, but they'll respect my position. I've worked hard to build the Resistance into the movement it is today."

"So, what's the plan now?" he asked. "Sens is dead. And it sounds like Kayla won't help willingly."

"There's only one thing left to do. Ironically, it's exactly what T'al and Voth wanted all along."

"And what's that?" he asked.

"Fight."

Two guards stood in front of the small entrance the group had entered when they'd first arrived. They stared off in the distance, as if bored with their duty. It appeared as though everyone trying to get to the market had been halted before they'd reached the pair, so there was nothing for them to monitor other than loose leaflets blowing in the wind.

They gave their party a quick nod, and a few quick turns later they were past the force field.

Upon exiting, the scene that met them wasn't anything like Wil had imagined.

The City Guard had forced the crowd back. Guards carried their batons in hand, but with no ability for their electricity to function in the SZ, they were merely blunt sticks.

Protesters had been moved back several hundred feet and were now lined around the Center's wall in an evenly distanced ring that matched its perimeter.

Their numbers had grown exponentially from the day before, and as Wil lifted his gaze, he realized why. Dozens of gray orbs criss-crossed the sky, hovering above the Rings. They looked to be nearly as close to the Center as the refugees.

"It's happened," he whispered. "The SZ has fallen."

Mario grunted, but the two guards were relentless in their push forward.

They followed the sidewalk that led from the main gate toward the crowd. A low barrier lined the sides of the path, turning into a short wall that circled the outer edge of the force field. It made it difficult for anyone to approach it directly without funneling through one of the intended entrances.

The atmosphere of the thousands that now lined the streets had turned from anger to dejection. Hope for change had now turned to fear, as their attention was less on a place of refuge and more on the threat that flew overhead. All eyes were to the sky, and Wil guessed that these were the first Guardians many of these people had ever seen.

The gray orbs were only Scanners. Wil remembered from their assault on Vegas that these bots were only present to map the area that had lain hidden from the Guardians for centuries. Whatever the ancients had done to this land had kept technology from entering or functioning within the space, and that included the bots' ability to map what lay within. They were seeing the land for the first time in two centuries and gaining a sense of what the land held and how many inhabitants there were to be extinguished.

Wil was unsure how they were going to break through the mass of the crowd, but he was surprised when four other guards joined their group. The crowd parted without hesitation. He wondered what the guards had done to break the crowd's resolve and to push them from the gates. Mario and his colleague received looks of both fear and contempt as they approached, which told Wil all he needed to know.

The Silent Zone's failure must have extended into most of the Outer and Middle Rings, forcing the inhabitants onto the road before them. The SZ appeared to be failing in stages, unlike the Vegas SZ, which had all dropped in an instant. The bystanders were relying on the integrity of the remaining section of SZ, and Wil wondered how long the effects would linger where they stood.

He feared it wouldn't be long before they'd find out.

Murmurs and cries echoed from the people surrounding them, but overall the mood was deflated. Children clung close to their mothers and fathers as the guards pushed Wil and Liz past them. The two of them walked on in silence; there was nothing for them to say to each other.

The Ringers were being forced to confine themselves to the remnants of the Silent Zone, afraid of what might come next. Wil had seen a glimpse of that in Vegas. The devastation here would likely be worse. Vegas had already been crumbling when the Guardians had arrived. Even the Outer and Middle Rings of San Francisco were thriving by comparison.

"These people should be preparing to fight," Wil whispered to Liz.

"They'll be forced to fight regardless. Most of them won't last long."

Wil swallowed at the dire revelation and scanned the crowd. Men, women, and children not so different from the faces he would have seen within the Sphere swarmed around him, even if they were a bit dirtier from their night spent out in the open.

"When did the SZ fall in the Outer Ring, Mario?" Wil asked his guard. "How long have these people been stuck here?"

"You think I care what the Ringers do?" Mario scoffed. "Keep moving."

Wil stumbled as Mario jabbed him, and Wil wondered how much bruising his ribs could take.

The sun was making its descent, and he wondered if the safe house was still within the SZ. If it wasn't, would anyone still be there? Would they all be out in the streets preparing for the inevitable fight that was brewing? He also wondered if the Scanners would continue into the night, and if the Sentinels, Onyx, and whatever other attack bots might be in the area would come before morning.

The now familiar half-repaired buildings of the ancients lined the paved streets of the Inner Ring. Businesspeople peered out of office windows three and four storeys high that overlooked those gathered below, their noses turned up in disgust, more concerned with the sojourners on their doorsteps than the bots in the sky. Women and children nearly spilled out of the windows of multi-storey residences, their eyes to the sky, watching the Scanners cross the skyline in the distance.

The crowd thinned as they reached the Middle Ring. Other than the lack of people in the streets, it was difficult to tell where the SZ now ended. Trepidation seemed more severe on the faces they passed. Regardless, the guards didn't halt their march, and they stopped answering the questions Wil threw at them.

Liz had retreated into herself, as she sometimes did, which was just as well; the guards also reprimanded Wil when he tried to speak to her. So, they marched in silence as the sun continued its descent toward the horizon.

Signs of preparation against the coming attack were becoming more and more apparent. Uniformed guards ran through the streets, fully equipped with weaponry and armor. The Resistance had set up stations atop several of the taller buildings, fully prepared with double-handed energy weapons as well as full-scale ground laser cannons. Wil had seen one such piece of artillery in the Battle for Vegas. It had been fairly effective at taking out Onyx until it had overheated and was rendered useless. Hopefully, these would prove more reliable.

Other members were fortifying reserves of blasters and other powered weapons, choosing strategic breakpoints in between the buildings. The Middle Ring dwellings were much squatter than those of the Inner Ring, and though some buildings appeared to be revitalized structures, even more appeared to be newer constructions. But the older brick buildings provided perfect strongholds for the Resistance fighters.

Dozens of Resistance soldiers occupied the streets, far more than Wil had realized were present in the city. Wil knew the space they'd marched through was only a fraction of the vast cityscape, and that there would be many more fighters in districts he hadn't even seen.

The scale of the battle was going to be epic, and it was Kayla's intent that none of them were to survive it.

Unless Wil could do something.

Others involved in the preparations appeared to be residents of the Middle and Outer Rings. The clothes they wore identified them as farmers, merchants, and tradespeople who weren't experienced in battle but were eager to help. Several were receiving last-minute lessons on firing a weapon or swordsmanship. Wil wasn't close enough to make out what was being said, but he recognized some of the lessons he had received from Ella during their training.

Some stood with newly forged blades, others with makeshift weapons that couldn't have been anything but the remnants of old buildings; rebar, pipes, anything blunt that could be swung at an aggressive Sentinel. They weren't the best equipped army, and Wil knew that for many, their first battle would also be their last.

Mario, Annabelle, and the newly arrived guards seemed unconcerned with the orbs that grew ever closer to their location, and Wil wondered how prepared they were for what was coming. Did they understand the danger the city was in? Kayla had sent most of the City Guard's resources into the Rings to fight alongside the Resistance. She at least understood that most of them wouldn't make it through the battle alive, but she had men and women loyal to her that she was keeping close. Those guarding the gates, for instance, were unlikely to see battle unless she sent them out to join the fight. Wil didn't see that happening as long as Kayla intended to keep the City Center separated from the Rings.

They were more than halfway across the Middle Ring before Wil realized they would not be stopping at the safe house. Kayla had told Wil they'd be free once they had left the SZ, which they were well beyond now. So why were the guards still leading them? Why were they still bound?

Liz offered no sign that she was having similar thoughts—or any thoughts at all. Her face remained unreadable, despite her people running through the surrounding streets, preparing for what seemed to be inevitable combat.

It surprised Wil that none of the surrounding Resistance members intervened, but they appeared to be too involved in their preparations to notice the guards hauling a couple of captives down the road.

"Where are we going?" he asked. "I thought we were to be freed outside the Silent Zone."

"We'll let you go when *we* decide." Mario pushed him once again, causing him to stumble. "Keep your mouth shut!"

Wil's chest grew warm with anger, but he bit his tongue as he regained his footing.

He turned his vision skyward and tried to discern where the Scanners were and how much of the SZ remained. As he did so, something else caught his attention. A ball of green glowing light, similar to that of the force field around San Francisco, hovered high in the sky.

At first, he thought it had to be a Guardian. He studied the object, intrigued by how it stood out against the evening sky. A figure stood within the sphere, arms and legs spread out like a bird.

His heart sank.

It was Ella.

32

IT WAS hard to make out Ella's features from where Wil stood, but he couldn't mistake the frame of his friend. She was being held by bonds he couldn't see, and she must have been hovering a mile in the air.

"Ella!" he yelled, trying to push forward. Mario chuckled, as if this had been the joke they were leading him toward all along. One of the other guards swung her baton into his gut with a *thwack* as he tried to break from the group, knocking the wind out of him. He stumbled and fell under the effort of trying to catch his breath. Gritty hands grabbed him and set him upright as he gasped, while the guards laughed at his efforts.

"Why?" he wheezed. It was all he could manage to ask.

Kayla had lied to him. Ella was being held prisoner, not patiently waiting for his return to the safe house. How would he even rescue her if she was suspended in the sky?

Kayla's words struck him. *You'll get to see her. And I promise I won't harm her. She's protected for now, but her future depends on you.*

Suddenly all the feelings he had been holding back for the woman suspended above them bubbled to the surface. He had been hesitant to allow himself to feel them because of Marco. He had lost one person he'd loved—he hadn't wanted to lose another. But in order to shield himself, he had denied his emotions, causing nothing but frustration for Ella—and now it was too late. He could still lose her, anyway.

Liz was quiet beside him, her eyes downcast as they resumed their march. She had seen this taking place in her visions. She had known all along things would be this way.

Wil scanned the skyline, hoping for an answer; hoping for a solution to break away from the guards and bring Ella down safely. But he couldn't think of any way to reach her. Had Kayla planned this march out into the Rings so that he'd crawl back to her? Beg her to bring Ella down in exchange for himself? He would surrender himself if he had to, but it wouldn't make him loyal to her.

There was no question now how foolish he'd been for letting Kayla's charms influence him. He had been so quick to put his guard up when it came to Ella—someone he truly had feelings for—but he'd allowed Kayla to break down his wall—and for what? He had allowed himself to be manipulated, and he had once again put the lives of those he cared about in jeopardy.

Kayla didn't expect him to leave Ella. She had planned it out so he had no choice. She didn't care if he came to her by choice or by force, only that he'd be available to her when she required.

Wil sunk to his knees, only to earn a boot in the back from Mario.

"Get up!" the guard barked viciously.

Wil didn't care. They could kick him to a pulp if they wanted. If he had any worth, he wouldn't continually send his friends to death's door.

Through the glaze in his eyes, Wil happened to get a glimpse of the dark dots in the distance. He didn't have to be told that it was a mass of black orbs beginning their approach. The Scanners must have relayed their information to the central network. Would they hold off their attack until the morning? The Onyx in Vegas had waited until one of the Resistance members had fired on them prematurely. They had been calculated in their aggression.

The first wave of the attack on Vegas had been small; a preliminary salvo to test their defences while the Guardians gained their bearings. The Resistance had taken down the first wave, but they had sustained heavy damage in the process. The second wave had been overwhelming—a ground assault of Sentinels that the city had been forced to fight through hand-to-hand combat. If it hadn't been for Wil and the explosive power that had emanated from him, knocking out the machines, they likely wouldn't have been able to hold the city. He had held the destruction at bay long enough for Sierra to ignite the device that had finally ended the assault and preserved the Vegas Silent Zone.

And then it dawned on Wil, Ella's imprisonment wasn't simply a clever set up for him to choose between her and Kayla.

Kayla was trying to force his hand. He could use his power to stop, or at least slow, the robot invasion, disrupting the power to the device and releasing Ella. If he refused, the bots would overtake the city in a fight that the Resistance and the city's uniformed services wouldn't be able to defend on their own. Not only would the Rings be destroyed, but Ella would die as a result.

What other choice did he have? Could he ask to be taken back to Kayla to beg her to free Ella? The problem was, he didn't trust the woman to do as he asked. He'd more likely be forced to watch Ella plummet.

His heartbeat was deafening. He hadn't even realized he was back on his feet, marching toward whatever destination the guards saw fit to take them. Perhaps they'd just kill him.

Not yet, though, Wil reminded himself. *Kayla needs my ability.*

Beside him, Liz kept her eyes on the path before them. She knew what was to come, and she also knew that no matter what she said or did at this point, it wouldn't stop what was already in motion.

Wil was being forced to either do nothing and allow the Guardians to kill Ella, or to act in the interests of the city and have the woman he loved die by his own hand.

Wil collapsed again as the weight of the thought struck him anew. His escort lashed out at his crumpled body, picking him off the ground and tossing him forward. He stumbled as he was involuntarily cast back onto his feet. Wil had lost the will to stand as the brunt of the realization ripped his heart from his chest. Having enough of his antics, the guards grabbed him by each arm and practically dragged him onward.

Unless he could think of an alternative, Ella would die, and with Liz's prophecy still ringing in his ears, Wil knew his own death was in the cards, too.

I haven't seen a path where you live past tomorrow.

Liz had seen what would happen, but she wouldn't tell him. *Couldn't* tell him, was what she'd claimed. Wil didn't know how she could make this decision worse. He glared at the Resistance leader now, her face cold and still downcast, but not because she was hurting. She was avoiding his accusatory stares; avoiding having to answer his questions about what would come next.

Or perhaps trying hard not to relive it.

Wil tried to feel sympathy for her, but all he could muster was anger. Liz knew he'd have to watch another person he loved die. She had known he would be the one to kill her. The excuse that things might turn out worse was thin.

Things can't get much worse.

And this was all based on the assumption that he'd be able to trigger his power to take down the machines. It had been unpredictable in the past. How many more bots would descend on San Francisco? If there were Silent Zones and Spheres all the way along the west coast, would their numbers be that much stronger? Would he even have the ability to take them out?

Kayla's intent, Wil realized, was to leave him without options. If he fought against the bots, he would be free to join her in her further crusades, and Ella would be out of the picture. Of course, this was an unreasonable expectation; he'd rather slit his own throat than help her to expand her empire.

But if Liz's prophecy became reality, it might not matter; whatever was about to happen would lead to his death. Perhaps there was a way he could end his own life to save hers.

There had to be a way.

"You could have told me!" he hissed at Liz, not caring about the guards. What was one more bruise on his side? "You could have warned me I'd have to choose."

"Would it be any better if I had?" Liz snapped, her purple eyes turning on him for the first time since they'd left the City Center. They were fierce and burned deep into him. "It only would have caused you to do something rash. Something that would definitely have doomed us all."

"In your visions, have you ever seen a scenario where she lives?" His heart was in his throat as he asked the question. He didn't think he wanted to know the answer, but he *needed* to know.

Liz sighed, turned her head, and continued her march.

Bile churned in his stomach, and Wil thought he might retch.

"Once," she answered. "Of the dozens of times I have seen this play out, she survived once."

"But I didn't?" he asked. He would be okay with his own death if it meant Ella would live. He would give himself up to any scenario.

"No, you didn't."

The blow was a bigger punch to the gut than he had expected. He tried to look past the guards, past the Resistance and the officers running through the Middle Ring, making preparations for the incoming fight. He took a deep breath, and a sharp pain struck his chest as he inhaled. The beatings were taking their toll.

The air was still warm, but it was cooling quickly, and for a moment, his thoughts drifted to the life he had left behind in the Sphere; the times he had spent in the hills with Marco; the time he had spent in the classroom, being spoon-fed lies by the Guardians, ignorant yet safe. Eighteen years of believing the world he now stood in was uninhabitable. And now, by the cruel force of irony, he was about to die, having only known for the past month that there was more to life than what the Guardians had told him. He only wished he could have made a bigger impact in the fight for humanity.

He took another deep breath, which sent him into a fit of painful coughs.

Perhaps he could still do something. Perhaps all was not lost. If there was one way to save Ella, there was one path forward he had found. He could find it again.

He had to compose himself. There was more at stake than his own life.

The guards had gone back to ignoring them, but Wil noticed their pace had quickened and their attention had turned to the surrounding sky. They didn't want to be out in the open any more than anyone else did.

"How can I save her?" he asked. "I know you don't want to risk making things worse, but if there is a way, I need to know!"

Liz sighed and shook her head. "I don't know."

"Quiet!" Mario admonished. "We're almost there." The scolding was only half-hearted; his focus was on the orbs coming their way.

Nevertheless, the constant waves of nausea his bruises invoked were enough for Wil to stop. He had to focus. If there was a version of the future where he had figured out how to save Ella, he would do everything in his power to replicate it.

The surrounding buildings were once again becoming familiar to Wil. They had long ago passed the safe house, crossing the bridge into the Outer Ring. The Scanners hummed loudly above their position, removing any lingering doubts that they had long left the SZ's protection.

The black dots of the Onyx had bloomed on the skyline. He expected they'd be descending upon the city within the hour. If they attacked at night, he wondered how much worse it would be for the residents who called the Rings of San Francisco home.

Wil had been so focused on his thoughts of Ella that he had completely missed the dark-robed man who stood on the street before them.

"Well, *Oathbreakers*, we meet again."

Wil snapped his attention to the imposing figure, taking a moment to realize who it was.

His odds of freeing Ella became exponentially more difficult.

"Oculus," Mario said. "Just as we agreed, the one they call Bot Killer, and one of the two Spherian witches who accompanies him."

33

WIL STRUGGLED to compute the turn of events. Had Kayla set them up to be traded with the Order? Even after all she had done, that outcome seemed highly unlikely.

So much had happened since they had last seen Oculus that it took Wil a moment to place the burly man with the glowing red scar running down his cheek. Not enough time, though. Wil still remembered the interrogation the Order had forced his Resistance friends to endure.

"Sergei and I will take things from here," Mario told the crew behind him. "Leave us."

The remaining guards shared a confused look with each other, but they didn't verbalize their inquiries. A group of soldiers that were readying supplies quickly caught their attention, and they hurried off to help.

"Where's the other one?" Oculus asked, ignoring their departure, his low growling voice rumbling through Wil's core.

Mario lazily pointed skyward to Ella's suspended frame. They were close enough now that Wil could make out her face, but he could not gauge her expression. A sharp pain shot through his chest. It seemed the odds of discovering a small window of opportunity to save her were rapidly diminishing.

"You can get her if you wish," Mario said. "But if you want to cause the boy additional misery, it seems you're better off leaving her there for the bots to deal with."

Wil wondered at what point everything had turned to the disaster it had become. Was killing the Director the catalyst? Or should he not have trusted T'al after they'd crashed the party? Did T'al know about this arrangement with the Order? Or would things have been better if he and Marco had never picked up that radio within the Sphere? The Guardian wouldn't have dropped out of midair, Marco would still be alive, and they'd be none the wiser that an entire world existed outside of their bubble.

Would it have been better if he had never known? Was it better to live a lie or to die at the hand of truth? He wouldn't have met Ella, but the fate of her life wouldn't be in his hands.

"Elizabeth," Oculus said. "You left so suddenly, we didn't get to say goodbye."

"I didn't think you'd miss me," Liz replied. She lifted her head to meet the gaze of the Order member towering over them. As annoying as it was, Wil was envious of her ability to stay collected and appear in charge, even when the odds were stacked against her.

Oculus unsheathed a dagger from beneath his robes and held it out. He made the blade dance across his fingers before taking hold of its shaft and pointing the tip at Liz's throat. "I always miss you, love," he said, his mouth uncomfortably close to her ear. Wil cringed, yet Liz didn't so much as flinch.

Wil turned to Mario. "Kayla put you up to this?"

Mario let out a quick burst of laughter. "No, boy. Kayla told us to take you outside the SZ so you could see your girlfriend in her flying prison. But she didn't specify we couldn't make some coin in the process."

Oculus took that as his cue and waved a bony finger at a man who stood behind him. He stepped forward, brandishing a cloth bag jingling with coins as payment for the exchange, and handed it to

Mario. The guard tested the bag's weight before opening it and peering inside. Apparently satisfied, he closed it again before nodding and pushing the two captives forward into arm's reach of Oculus.

It was clear as the Order members took over their march that their situation had drastically deteriorated. Liz had the good sense to remain quiet, but Wil tested his luck more than once and ended up with a stick to the head or to the knees, adding fresh sets of bumps and bruises.

"You don't learn, do you, Oathbreaker?" Oculus chided after Wil's latest attempt to ask about their motives. "We ask the questions, and you answer. Next word out of your mouth and Elizabeth takes the beatings for you."

Wil hadn't thought to ask Liz before their abduction if things could turn out worse than he had imagined. He thought he had to choose between saving the city and saving his friend, but at least in those scenarios, he was still the one making a decision. But now Wil started to feel as though that choice was being ripped from him. If the Order was still camped in their previous location, they'd be too far from the city to do anything. He might die at the hand of the Order instead, or be kept alive while they continued to beat him.

There were eight members of the Order accompanying them. Two held pointed sticks to the ribs of both captives, and two bore red flags fringed with gold. Wil recalled Ella once telling him that each of the colors stood for a purpose. Red was the color of warriors; those who fought on behalf of the Guardians. Laughable for a technology that made him chant the mantra: *"The Guardians Protect Us."*

The final four, including Oculus, marched around them, intent on shepherding them securely to wherever their destination happened to be.

As they reached the Outer Ring, the chill of the evening air was taking hold, and Wil hoped nightfall might slow the impending Guardian advance.

Wil smelled the devastation before he saw it. The acrid scent of burnt grass, crops, trees, and homes accosted his nose, followed almost immediately by a faint haze that the setting sun highlighted in deep orange light, giving the scene an eerie feeling.

The few orbs that had attacked the farmsteads had caused so much damage. Many of their unsuspecting residents had fled to the city, but how many had sacrificed their lives trying to stop their homes from burning?

Among the ruins along the road, Wil could make out the smoldering remains of bodies. Most were hidden well enough that he didn't have to try too hard to avoid looking at them, but others were strewn across the landscape, the sight and smell of which turned Wil's stomach. Many of the corpses were livestock, but the smell of both cooked and rotting meat did nothing to ease his nausea.

Wil instinctively tried to look behind him to ensure he could still see Ella. He tensed as he expected a blow of a baton on his backside for his efforts, but he was surprised when the impact didn't come.

The green glow of the distant force field was still visible. Wil wondered what must have been going through her head; how she was coping with being suspended a mile in the air. Ella was typically cool and collected, and she was the only person Wil knew who could have handled the pressure she must have been under, other than perhaps Liz.

Then he saw the reason the Order had allowed him to stop. They had wanted to watch, too, but their focus wasn't on Ella. The dozen Onyx had reached their destination. The blue lights dancing across the Guardians' bodies were evident, even through the haze that surrounded the city.

They were headed straight for Ella.

Wil stopped breathing. The black orbs were set on a collision course with his friend. He wondered if they would shoot her out of the sky or crash into her and send her tumbling. At this distance, there would be nothing he could do, regardless of what happened.

Wil cursed every decision he had made, including leaving Vegas. If they had stayed and helped Sierra with reintegrating the citizens of the Sphere, he wouldn't have to watch the murder that was about to take place.

He wanted to look away; he couldn't watch the death of someone else he loved. But this was his doing, *his* fault that Ella would fall from the sky, and he *needed* to see it to allow the consequences of his actions to sink in. It was to be his penance for following the path of revenge.

Liz had mentioned witnessing a way for Ella to survive. Perhaps he had missed his opportunity. Perhaps a decision he had made previously was coming back to haunt him and he had passed the point of no return long ago.

There was no way to tell now, and there was nothing he could do about it.

Every muscle in his body tensed. Each Onyx dwarfed Ella in size and it was apparent from Wil's vantage point how devastating an assault from the machines would be, not just for Ella, but for the entire city.

Light spun on their surfaces, acting in unison as they tried to lock onto their target. It appeared as they were going to take her down with firepower, to blow her to pieces in the sky for all to witness. A public display of his failure.

But the Onyx held their fire. The bots passed over Ella, not even coming within yards of collision, and then, once they had passed her incarceration bubble, they unleashed their fury on the city below.

Wil gasped for air at Ella's momentary salvation, not allowing the tension that grasped every one of his muscles to release. The Onyx fired on homes and businesses that were no longer being protected by the embrace of the Silent Zone, much as they had done to the farms and shelters where he now stood.

Blue light pulsed from their shells before erupting into concentrated beams of light and fire. Most of the residents of the Middle Ring had long moved on, but Wil knew there would be some who wouldn't have left easily, including members of the Resistance and the City Guard who stood to protect the city. How many still lingered in the streets and had just been torn to shreds?

The ground shook from the impact of the blasts. In the distance, the screams of men and women was interspersed between the blasts of firepower. Shouts of the Resistance traveled over the terrain, audible but incoherent from where Wil stood.

He should have been there with them, fighting against the destructive monsters that threatened humanity. Behind the battle, the light glow from the ancient force field stood strong, mocking Wil and those who fought for their lives. Its residents were safe, at least for now, hiding within its protective boundary while allowing the residents of the Rings to fight and perish on their behalf.

The last bit of sunlight edged out of the horizon. The faint green glow surrounding Ella remained visible in the distance, as did the blue lights spinning frantically on the shells of the Onyx, providing a perspective of depth in the fading light. Blaster fire from both the bots in the sky and the soldiers on the ground lit up the sky in a spectacular display of fireworks.

The surrounding Order members cheered as homes burst into flames. Wil raised an eyebrow at Oculus, doing his best not to spit on the man.

"You cheer for their deaths? You realize you're human, too? Or at least you were, once."

"The Guardians are making way for the future they've designed. A *better* way forward. It is a task worth celebrating. There will be necessary casualties along the way, but it will all be for the greater good. I won't let you interfere with that vision again."

More blaster fire and the whine of laser cannons warming pierced through the chill of the evening before a wide pulse of light erupted from the ground and into the row of orbs, knocking more than one out of the sky. The damage to the city would be great, but at least the Resistance here seemed better prepared than the defenders of Vegas. This first wave of a dozen Onyx would be taken down, maybe even as the SZ remained intact within the Inner Ring. But how many more robots would come? How long would the Resistance be able to hold out?

Oculus waved to the other Order members before spinning Wil back toward their original direction.

The sounds of battle raged late into the evening. Wil wasn't sure how long they walked for, but each step of the way, he could only think of two things: escaping and saving Ella.

He had been so lost in his own thoughts that he hadn't noticed the encampment until they were on top of it. The Order had moved significantly closer to San Francisco since they had last parted ways. Wil could have sworn they had been heading east toward Vegas, which could only have meant they'd followed Wil, Ella, and the Resistance after they'd escaped.

Torchlight lit the encampment, and dozens of Order members stood on the sidelines watching the light show from the battle occurring miles away. There wasn't much visible except for flashes of light in the night sky, but it was enough to brighten their faces with pure ecstasy.

A boot kicked Wil from behind, knocking him down and pushing his face into the dirt. Rope cut into his skin as it was wrapped around his legs. He grunted as a thick beam of wood dropped onto his backside, also striking him on the head. His face was crushed deeper into the dirt by the impact, and a flash of light filled his vision, warning him he might lose consciousness.

He fought through it. He had to stay awake if he was to have any hope of getting free. Gaining a bit of movement once the board had landed, Wil tried to narrow his focus in on Liz, who lay in the dirt beside him. She was face down as well, a thick wooden beam also across her back. Wil couldn't tell if she had been knocked around quite as heavily as he had. Oculus seemed to have had zero patience for him running his mouth off. Or perhaps it was his nickname, *Bot Killer*, which had drawn the Order leader's ire.

It was a nickname Wil was beginning to wear with pride. He would take down every last one if he could, and if he managed to free himself, he would do his best to live up to the name.

A dark boot stepped directly into his line of sight, and Wil's nose crinkled at the scent of leather and putrid sweat that radiated from it. He didn't have to see its owner to know it belonged to Oculus.

"String them up," Oculus said, though he wouldn't have had to, as the beams were already rising off the ground.

It wasn't until he was upright that Wil fully understood what was happening. They faced the city. The beams would hold them upright, forcing them to witness the destruction of San Francisco. The Order members carried them several feet and erected each of them in the middle of a pyre. Either after, or perhaps during, the attack on the city, they were to be burned alive.

Wil had a hard time making out Liz's face. How much of this had she foreseen? Did she know if there was a way for them to escape? Or were they doomed to burn?

There were so many questions of what might happen in the coming hours, and Wil didn't have a clue whether he would live long enough to see any of them answered.

34

As if there had been any doubt surrounding Oculus's plans, he ordered an enormous bonfire to be built adjacent to the pyres where Wil and Liz had been put on display as a visual reminder of the fate that now awaited them. Either that, or it was for the benefit of the Order members, who were now intent on celebrating the inevitable destruction of the Rings of San Francisco.

Their aerial restraints had been raised on the outskirts of the encampment, and two Order Guards had been designated to watch over the prisoners. The cracked pattern of their uniforms both glowed red, but more colors were present within the camp; greens, blues, and yellows glowed softly within the party grounds, roughly a hundred yards from Wil and Liz.

The Order members discarded most of their robes as the night wore on, revealing drab gray pantsuits underneath. All pretence of propriety disappeared as alcohol flowed and excitement over the battle taking place miles in the distance doused all other sense of duty. Skulking by himself at the edge of the party, Oculus and the two guards delegated to guarding Wil and Liz were the only people not partaking in the festivities.

The guards couldn't have been more disparate in appearance. One would have given even Oculus himself a fair fight if they were to spar, standing nearly seven feet tall and as wide as a redwood tree. His partner kept his head down and was slight and short. The second individual had kept their hood up the entire time they had been keeping watch.

"If you wanted to join the festivities so badly, you shouldn't have signed up for the watch," the smaller guard said. With their hood masking their features, Wil was uncertain if the second guard was a man or a woman. With their slender physique and soft voice, it was difficult to say—perhaps the guard was a teenager—but then Wil was certain the first guard had referred to them as Angel.

"Sign up?" the giant responded. The contrast in his voice was near comical, so deep and rough that it likely could have sanded furniture. "You think I want to be here? This was my punishment for letting them get away the last time. 'Cept this time, I had to be out in the open so everyone could see if we screwed up. Could have been worse, I guess."

"We've got it easy, then. Oculus has done worse for far less." The guard spat, wiping her mouth on her sleeve as if she hadn't quite cleared all of it.

"'Tis the way it is, I suppose. I'm just happy we're out here, rather than with the rest of the blasphemers in the city."

"Don't worry, Jason. We'll have more chances to celebrate," Angel said.

The banter between the two guards continued, and Wil attempted to tune it out. He was getting a headache, but at least they were leaving him and Liz alone.

The night pressed on, and Wil would have gladly slept within his confines were it not for his muscles feeling as though they had been raked over the coals of the bonfire that still blazed beside them, and the discomfort of the ropes that held him to the pole.

Liz, on the other hand, appeared unaffected. She had slumped over, her head hanging down, the only sign of life the rise and fall of her chest as it struggled to push against her bonds as she breathed.

For hours, the revelers remained awake, laughing and dancing long into the night. The distant flashes of laser fire had died down within the first few hours, and Wil hoped their cessation meant the Resistance had successfully brought the Onyx down. But even if that were true, he knew that legions of Sentinels wouldn't be far behind.

Eventually, Oculus must have retired to his quarters, leaving the guards he had entrusted with the prisoners to maintain their compliance.

Angel and Jason eventually quieted down as well. Jason appeared to be bored with his assigned duties, and as the night progressed, he seemed to be more jealous of those who could rest in their beds than of those still celebrating. It was impossible for Wil to get a read on Angel with her face still hidden.

Wil's arms blistered under the pressure of the rope. He had subconsciously been shifting his arms, trying to find a weak spot. There had been none, and he knew that the several layers tied around his midsection would need a blade to cut through them.

Or fire.

The bonfire on the edge of the outcropping had waned in the early morning. It would only be a couple of hours until daybreak, and Wil imagined most of the Order members in the camp would be nursing sore heads well into the day.

Wil wondered at what time the Order planned to roast them. According to Liz's prediction, it would be sometime later that day. How many hours would he have to watch men and women celebrating the downfall of humanity?

"What are you doing?" Jason quipped, interrupting his thoughts.

Angel had sat down on the grass beside the stakes. "We're supposed to keep watch all night, and not get a chance for a rest?" she replied. "My feet are killing me! I'm going to sit for a few minutes. You stay standing and we'll switch. It's not like these two are going anywhere."

Jason stifled a yawn and nodded. He had been shuffling his weight from one foot to the other for about an hour already, and it surprised Wil that Jason hadn't been the first to crack.

"You better hope nobody spots us," Jason replied, nervously eyeing the residual festivities.

"Just keep watch," Angel insisted. "It's what we're *supposed* to be doing, anyway."

Jason stifled another yawn and nodded. "All right, but only fifteen minutes each. Oculus will skin us alive if anything happens."

Wil rolled his eyes. He had forgotten how incompetent the Order Guard had been during their first visit to the camp. He and Liz must have had been strung up for nearly eight hours, and the fact these guards hadn't taken a break for that entire time wasn't lost on Wil. Hopefully, their fatigue would play into his hands.

The celebrations had all but ceased, and the explosions in the city had ended long ago. In the rare moments of absolute silence, Wil was sure he could hear hammering and the occasional shout in the distance as the residents of the Middle Ring began repairs and braced themselves for the second wave.

The first indications of dawn were appearing on the edge of the horizon, a thin stroke of light promising that morning was coming. Wil ignored the depravity around him and decided he would watch the sunrise. It was likely the last one he'd ever get to experience.

As reds and oranges lined the horizon, Liz still lay slumped over on her post. She had slept for most of the night, but Wil imagined she'd have an awful crick in her neck from the way she'd been positioned. When compared to being burned alive, though, Wil figured it hardly mattered.

The ground shook with the dawn. Ella had told him that this area had been prone to earthquakes, and Wil's first thought immediately tried to reconcile this with the ground moving beneath them. But movement in the distance caught his eye. If it wasn't for the glowing blue panels and lifeless eyes, Wil likely wouldn't have been able to see the Sentinels that marched along the road from the south. The second wave of the attack on Vegas had seen dozens of Sentinels descending upon the city, and Wil knew there was no way the newly exposed Rings of San Francisco could withstand that kind of direct assault.

Below the rise, hundreds of bots all moved in unison, bits of blue lights and a muted reflection of the first hints of daybreak reflecting on their paneling. Whatever army the Guardians had managed to assemble for their assault on Vegas, they had amassed ten times that number to march on San Francisco.

The few Order members who remained conscious must have felt the vibrations as well. More than one vomited at the sensation before turning their sights to the source of the disruption. Smiles grew as they realized they would now be privy to the second round of the fight.

Despite the increased assault, there were far more Resistance and other fighters than there had been in Vegas, but Wil didn't know if they would be enough. He had no way of knowing how many Resistance members stood on guard in the city. From everything Liz had told him, though, it wasn't going to end well.

Additional movement along the horizon caught his eye. Hundreds of black dots peppered the skyline. The Onyx were coming, and they were coming now.

There would be no third wave.

The Sentinels and Onyx were going to launch their assault simultaneously. Wil wasn't going to live to see the end of the day, and neither was the city.

Wil inhaled deeply, his chest pushing against the bindings wrapped around him, and he fought to ignore the excruciating pain the pressure spawned in his ribs. His limbs had gone from fatigued to numb as a result of rubbing against the harsh bindings all night, and as Oculus had predicted, they would now be forced to watch the city's destruction.

Angel stood. Fifteen minutes was apparently up.

"You'd better take your break now." Angel motioned to Jason. "Probably your last chance before those Guardians reach the city."

Jason shook his head. "Nah, it'll be hours before the fight starts. They're further away than they look."

Wil took another look at the Sentinels coming from the south. It definitely didn't appear as if they were hours away, but he wasn't as familiar with the landscape; perhaps the guard was correct. In reality, it made no difference to Wil. Even if he wasn't currently being held captive, he didn't believe there was anything he'd be able to do against an army of such great numbers.

"But," Jason continued, "I wouldn't mind a few minutes off my feet. You'd better watch out for Oculus. If I'm caught because of your stupidity, I'm going to make sure you suffer, too."

There was nothing Wil could do but watch the Sentinels advance. His heart was heavy with the thought of the impending devastation. His thoughts turned to Kayla, and he pictured her watching her people burn. All she had to do was open the gate, and thousands of lives would be saved. But instead, the people of the City Center would rather guarantee the Ringers be slaughtered than potentially make their own lives slightly less comfortable.

Barely a minute had passed before Jason was snoring loudly enough for Wil to hear. Wil rolled his eyes again. He didn't blame the man; he would have jumped at the chance to sleep if every bone in his ribcage and legs weren't screaming at him, but clearly having a rest in the middle of his guard duty hadn't been the smartest idea. Wil wondered if Angel was going to wake Jason, but he then realized Angel was no longer at her post.

Wil whipped his head from one edge of the campsite to the other, but the Order guard was nowhere in sight. A tug on the ropes of his bonds startled him.

"Keep quiet!" a voice behind him admonished. "We don't have much time."

Out of the corner of his eye, Wil caught a glimpse of the slight figure behind him. He thought it was Angel, though he didn't know what the guard would be doing tugging at the ropes that bound him. Only when the figure moved into Wil's line of sight did he realize the guard hadn't been a woman at all, but a teenage boy. In that moment, all the anxiety of the past twelve hours left his body at once.

"Dagger!" Wil whispered. The boy had let down the hood of his cloak to reveal his true identity. "You sneaky sandfly! How did you get here? What are you doing in that Order robe?"

"Shut up!" the boy repeated. "If Jason wakes up, I'll be strung up on a stake next to you."

Wil nodded and let the boy use his knife to work the bonds. Wil couldn't help but feel a pang of guilt; somehow, the boy had tracked him and Liz down after he'd been abandoned at the stadium, and while Wil had wished nothing but the best for the boy, he had hardly given him a second thought after they had lost track of him.

That had only been two nights ago, but it felt like another lifetime.

The sun was now cresting over the horizon, and those in the encampment who had not been celebrating through the night began to stir. They were a couple hundred yards away, but Wil could make out the robes of Order members going from tent to tent, making preparations for their day. The glowing lights of their colored robes stood out in the dim morning light. Unlike the red of the warriors, Wil spotted mostly the orange-accented robes of healers and the green-accented robes of administrators. After the night they'd had, Wil didn't doubt that today the warriors would rest and leave the other factions to keep the camp operational.

But if Wil and Liz were going to escape without being seen, their window of opportunity was quickly disappearing.

Wil slid down the pole as his bounds loosened. His feet touched the ground for the first time all night, and he winced as the blood came rushing back to his extremities. He nearly crumpled as his legs protested at bearing any weight, and he leaned against the pole to help him keep his footing.

Dagger gently roused Liz from her slumber. The woman was momentarily startled, then confused to see Dagger's face looking at her, before she finally settled on being relieved.

She handled being released from her bonds with more finesse than Wil had managed. The woman didn't have to be scolded to be quiet, for one, instead looking to Dagger for direction as to where they should turn next.

Jason still sat slumped over in his seated position, his snores only faintly audible beneath the rumble of the earth caused by the advancing Sentinels.

Dagger motioned them away from the encampment and toward the road. Once they descended the hill from the outcrop, they could slip in between trees in the more wooded area and wouldn't be as easily spotted by Oculus or his guards. They likely wouldn't have much of a head start; once Jason woke, the Order would follow them. They wouldn't abandon a prize they had paid such a healthy sum for.

The three clandestinely slipped into the night.

35

WIL TRAILED behind Dagger and Liz, stumbling over the hilly terrain a few miles from the Outer Ring. The wind had picked up, moisture from the ocean caught in its grasp, clinging to him as if attempting to find a warm body to lay claim to.

The three ran until they reached the trees of a small protective forest, separating them from the Rings and the now defunct Silent Zone. Even with the cover of the trees, they only slowed their pace; they had a lot of ground to cover before they reached their destination, and it would be best if they arrived before the fighting resumed.

"How long have you been following us?" Wil asked Dagger once they had slowed and he had caught his breath. "How did you know where we were?"

"Ever since you took off with that girl and her bot," he said. "I knew she was up to no good, so I lingered behind."

"You had better instincts than I did. But how'd you know?" Wil asked.

"She was pulling that stupid bot with her when you fled. Of course she was up to no good!"

"You were there when Goliath met up with us?"

"I was still chasing the bot!" he exclaimed. "I thought I might overtake it in the confusion. It was a stupid thing to do, but I was angry. Angry that Sara had been killed. Angry that I was too powerless to do anything about it.

"When the bots attacked the stadium, I thought I could at least take out Goliath. I knew it wasn't possible, but it seemed to be as confused as everyone else. I saw the way it slaughtered the champion before me. I thought destroying it would make me feel better."

"Kayla said the fight organizers were emitting some sort of signal in the arena; something to make the bot kill."

Dagger let out a sharp laugh. "If you believe that, you'll believe anything." The boy's eyes found Wil's. "I saw what you did to the bots that killed Sara. There's something special about you. Somehow that woman knew it. It was like she had been waiting for you. She wanted to test you."

"The kid saw it," Liz said. "Somehow you're the only one who didn't figure it out."

Wil huffed.

"When it joined you, my plan changed from killing Goliath to helping you," Dagger continued. "So I followed you back here."

"But I've been all over the place since then," Wil said. "I went in and out of the City Center twice. How did you track us out here?"

"I've had to follow people and find my way into all sorts of places my entire life. Once I saw the Order take you, I knew I would have to help. So, I snuck into the camp, stole a robe, and volunteered to watch the prisoners while the rest of the guard celebrated the attack."

Wil shook his head, a wide grin on his face. The little brat was crafty. "But why?" he asked. "Why risk your neck to rescue me?"

"You did the same for me. Even though you couldn't save Sara, you saved *me*. You destroyed the bots on the road just by thinking about it. They don't call you Bot Killer for nothing. I heard the rumors that the Silent Zone was going to fall, and I knew that if you could take them out in Vegas, you could do the same for San Francisco. I knew the city needed you."

"That's very brave of you," Liz said. Her eyes showed as much astonishment as Wil's. Dagger's rescue effort, it seemed, hadn't been something her visions had predicted.

"Wil was willing to save me and my sister when nobody else would," Dagger replied. "Nobody else has ever stuck their neck out for us. *Ever*. We'd been cast aside our entire lives by everyone, even our own father. I owed it to Wil."

Every decision will impact how this ends.

If he hadn't saved Dagger back on the road to the city, they'd still be tied to the pyres, awaiting execution. Would it be enough to save them? To save Ella? Wil didn't have an answer. If he were to judge by the wide-eyed glances Liz shot his way, he'd guess she had not seen this play out in her visions.

In Wil's mind, that meant one of two things. This could be one of those situations that had been skipped over in what she saw, an event so trivial it made no impact on the outcome, or it was part of the scenario where Ella made it out alive. Perhaps, somehow, this was the way that event was supposed to unfold. It wasn't much to go on, but it was enough of a sliver of hope to give Wil the motivation he needed to carry on. Perhaps in saving Dagger and Sara, Wil had introduced a new variable that Liz hadn't envisioned.

"Liz?" he asked, hesitant to push any further. "In the scenario where I saved Ella, does the rest of the city make it? Do I have to choose between Ella and the Ringers?"

Liz sighed. "There will be much destruction, no matter what happens," she answered.

"You know that's not what I mean," he persisted. "The robot assault, will it be stopped?"

"Honestly, Wil, I didn't see much else beyond Ella's survival. Remembering my visions is like trying to recall a dream, and the more likely the outcome, the more I remember, and the more solid the dream feels. I'm sorry, but the scenario in which she lives was extremely vague."

Each time Liz spoke of Ella's death, Wil felt like she was stabbing him in the chest. He tried not to let himself be discouraged. There was at least one outcome where he was able to save her, and he had to hold on to that possibility.

But if there was only one successful scenario in however many times Liz had seen the day play out, perhaps it would be best for him to think of the least likely thing he would do.

The problem was, Wil didn't even know what his *most* likely decision would be. He kept running through his options, but it was like trying to grab at sand in a windstorm. He could do his best not to unleash his power, therefore not deactivating whatever technology held Ella suspended in the air. It would at least prevent her from plummeting to her death. But the city would be destroyed, and just because the first dozen Onyx hadn't shot Ella down from the sky, didn't mean the next hundred wouldn't. He'd also likely die fighting in hand-to-hand combat, along with everyone else in the Rings, as the Guardians overran the city and the Resistance fighters became outnumbered.

The second option was to let his power take over. If there was one thing that had remained consistent, his power seemed to activate itself when those around him were under threat. That made the first option implausible, as he didn't know if he had the control to contain it. So far, he hadn't successfully kept it at bay.

So that meant the option he was most likely to pursue was to unleash his power, taking out as many bots as he could, and therefore sending Ella hurtling to her death in the process.

When he'd used his power to take out a mere seventy-five Sentinels in Vegas, the action had rendered him unconscious. At least ten times as many bots were converging on San Francisco. In the few times he had unleashed his power, the impact it had on him seemed proportionate to the size and number of the bots affected. He routinely discharged blasters without notice. Taking out the handful of bots on the way into the city had rendered him unconscious for several hours; in Vegas, he had been bedridden for nearly a full day. Hundreds of bots were now descending into San Francisco, and he felt in the core of his being that confronting so many bots at once would take more strength than he possessed.

His own ability would likely be the death of him.

In either scenario, he was dead. Just as Liz had predicted.

The three pushed on as the sun's light crept higher in the morning sky. So far, there was no sign of pursuit from the Order, but Wil kept a watchful eye over his shoulder. More than once, he thought he heard a rustling in the bushes or the shout of an Order guard, but every time they stopped, the woods were as tranquil and peaceful as ever.

They wouldn't be under the cover of the woods for long. They'd soon have to cross the fields of the Outer Ring and then continue on through the devastation.

Perhaps that was where Oculus would wait, knowing their chances of being detected would be easier.

They neared the tree line and stopped to catch their breath. They had been running for close to an hour, and the brush underfoot made it difficult. Given Wil's legs weren't doing well after being tied overnight, he figured he wouldn't be able to keep the pace for much longer.

"What's the plan once we get to the city?" he asked.

"Don't look at me," Dagger said. "You're the Bot Killer. My goal is to get you there."

Wil sighed as he peered through the last remnants of the woods, trying to sense if anyone was waiting for them in the adjacent fields.

"Well then, I guess we pick up blasters and start shooting." Wil shrugged. "That is, unless I can unleash my power on those Sentinels."

"An effort that great is going to kill you," Liz warned. "You need to learn how to control it; to target your efforts."

Target his efforts? It hadn't been a thought that had occurred to him. So far, it had seemed like an all-or-nothing situation, but perhaps discharging little doses of power could be just as effective while being less draining on him.

"What does it matter?" he asked. "No matter what, you said I'm dead by nightfall."

Liz didn't argue, which didn't provide Wil with any additional hope.

From where they sat, the swooping Onyx were now clearly visible.

The bots had covered a fair distance in the early morning hours, and it appeared they were ready to strike at any moment.

As if reading his thoughts, the blue lights on a single orb lit up and unleashed its fury on the city. The beam sparked an explosive fireball from the ground, which erupted into a ball of flame and smoke, ballooning skyward.

The fight had begun.

36

DESPITE THE ACHE in his legs, Wil broke out of the brush in a full sprint. He could hear Liz and Dagger trailing behind him, all pretense of stealth now evaporated.

Wil didn't care.

He kept his momentum going for a short sprint before he realized how much more he actually had to travel. They didn't have enough time.

The Onyx hung ominously over the city, a cloud of black casting spheroid shadows on the ocean to the west, threatening to overtake the city.

A familiar warmth was growing within Wil's chest. He did what he could to press it down, deep within him. It was much too soon to dispense his power. He had to get to the city and ensure he did whatever was possible to keep Ella alive.

The bots held their position. Wil had expected the shot to be followed by a volley of hundreds more, but they remained still. Lights continued to spin on their giant frames, but there were no further shots fired.

The Sentinels would arrive soon, and the Onyx were assumably holding off because of the incoming land-based assault.

It didn't feel like much longer before they were passing through the Middle Ring.

"We need to stop at the safe house," Liz said. "We need weapons, and the Resistance needs to know I'm still alive."

Liz was barely labored in her breathing, and Wil couldn't help but be a little resentful. Her sleeping position couldn't have provided a restful slumber, but it must have been better than nothing.

Wil had finally recovered the circulation in his legs, but each step was like running through sand, each pounding step more tiresome than the last.

Ella still hung where she had been imprisoned all night, suspended above the city in her front-row seat to the mayhem about to be unleashed.

Screams from the Inner Ring echoed through the streets, and Wil surmised the last of the Silent Zone had fallen. Even blocks away, the sound of motorized movements and the blaster fire of the Sentinels was unmistakable.

Suddenly, they met a crush of residents fleeing the Inner Ring, seeking to get out of the line of fire. They were civilians who had likely never even seen a blaster, weapons which would have been non-functional for their entire lives within the Silent Zone, and were either unable or unwilling to fight. Families with children were among those attempting to flee.

These were the people the City Center had abandoned. They had nowhere to go and no way to protect themselves.

This was the future Kayla envisioned, Wil thought.

If she was unwilling to protect even the most vulnerable of her own people, how could she possibly hope to unite humanity under her charge?

The streets filled far quicker than Wil and his companions had been prepared for, and it wasn't long before they were pushing their way through a sea of people who were desperately scrambling to get past them, heading in the opposite direction.

"We've got to get to the safe house!" Wil yelled. "Off the main road!"

The chaos threatened to bowl them all over. He would have hoped those who were more able-bodied would help those who struggled, but with no coordinated evacuation, many were simply pushing past those who could barely stand.

He broke out of the madness into an alleyway that was quieter than the main road and looked behind him, desperate to ensure Liz and Dagger had followed him.

"Come on, Bot Killer." Dagger's voice caused Wil to whip around. The boy and Liz had already made it through. The kid had a slick smile on his face. Wil rolled his eyes, and they pushed on.

They wound their way through the alley, the pristine condition of its ancient red brick acting as a reminder of the years the SZ had protected the city's dwellings from the disaster they now faced. Dust fell from their surface each time an explosion hit and shook the earth. Wil occasionally looked over his shoulder to see if the Onyx had continued in their fury, but for the time being, it appeared they were content to let the Sentinels do the dirty work for them.

They had yet to face the Guardian vanguard. The Sentinels would have come up the Peninsula on the eastern side of the city and marched straight to the Inner Ring, where the citizens had been hiding. Blaster fire sounded to the east of where Wil and his party scurried; Resistance fighters were attempting to slow the bots down before they reached the crowds of people. If they hadn't already.

The only hope for the citizens would be for them to wind their way westward, along the coast. But it was only delaying the inevitable. The Onyx would soon target the groups the Sentinels had missed.

It took a few twists and turns, but eventually they made their way to the safe house. Though they were anything but safe within its confines, Wil breathed a sigh of relief as they crossed the threshold. It had been the closest thing to home he had had in over a month.

Two Resistance members stood in the entryway, fully equipped and ready for the fight. Both soldiers were of average height and build once their makeshift armor had been removed. Panels scrapped together from pieces of abandoned ancient tech would offer them some protection from both blaster fire and melee weapons, but they must have weighed a ton.

One guard was a young girl who couldn't have been much older than Dagger—fifteen, at the most—but she held herself as if she had been equipped for battle her entire life.

The second guard was a dark-skinned man that looked old enough to be Wil's father, with salt and pepper facial hair that sprouted from his chin. Wil wondered if the hair beneath the man's helmet matched, or how much of it remained.

The fact that the Resistance had left anyone behind to guard the safe house was surprising to Wil until he saw the stash of weaponry sprawled out along the floor and against the walls. What had been a cozy meeting hall only a couple nights prior had been turned into a full-scale armory. The stairwells and mezzanine above confirmed there were several more guards waiting, guns at the ready in case any wayward soul decided it would be worth the effort to attempt a raid.

Quartermasters were hurrying around, furiously cleaning and readying weaponry. Other fighters lingered in the corner, warily gearing up for what was to come. Despite the buzz that filled the house, nobody spoke. They had prepared for this moment, likely for centuries, and unlike the Order camp, none of these folks were celebrating its arrival.

On sight of Liz, the eyes of the two guards widened, unabashedly dropping their fierce demeanors as they realized their leader had returned.

"T'al told us you were dead!" the woman exclaimed.

"Well, I'm not," Liz stated, her voice steady and firm. "At least, not yet. What else has T'al been saying?"

"T'al and Voth have taken command in your absence. He seemed intent on taking the fight out of the city at first, but then the Silent Zone fell to the Inner Ring. We've followed standard procedure ever since."

"How long ago did the Inner Ring fall?"

"Only this morning. A handful of Onyx fired on the Middle Rings last night and took out a good number of our frontline, but we managed to bring them down. The Sentinels marched in this morning, straight to the Inner Ring where the bulk of the citizens had been taking refuge. It's been chaos on the streets ever since."

"Where are T'al and Voth now?"

"The last we heard, they've gone to the Center to try and convince the Director to open the gate and allow these people inside," the older man piped up. "They said there had been a deal made to let the refugees in. There had been thousands of them lined up, waiting for the Center to open its main gate, but it never happened. Then the Sentinels marched right to them. More have died trampling each other to get away than the bots have killed. All hell's broken loose."

"You said you were following protocols? Is that still the case?" Liz looked around the entryway and into the common area, as though looking to determine if specific actions had taken place.

"Once the bulk of the SZ fell, we enacted the battle protocols you established," the man said. "I think T'al had something else in mind, but there was no time to deviate. Everything has happened just as you laid out."

Liz nodded and her face relaxed, as though relieved. Wil couldn't imagine the stress she must have been feeling with the weight of the Resistance on her shoulders. She had shown much more fortitude than Wil ever could.

"Elizabeth! You're not dead!" a familiar voice called out from behind them.

Ice, Buzz, and Cali all stepped off the street and into the safe house, each one of them sporting a wide-eyed grin and eyes that were grateful for some good news.

The three ran to Liz and embraced her. Each of them started speaking at once, trying to outdo the others in a bid for the resurrected woman's attention.

The ground shook again, interrupting their reunion, and cries from the street simultaneously rose in volume and intensity.

"You've got to get out there," said Cali, her dark eyes flitting between the woman and the door. "The rest of the troops will draw hope from seeing you alive and well."

"Agreed." Liz nodded and turned back to the guards they had greeted upon entering. "Get me and these two suited up."

There was a mad rush of activity as they rushed to arm the trio. Wil refused the armor. Deflecting blaster fire wasn't going to help him if he couldn't move under the weight, but he reluctantly accepted a pair of blasters and a blade.

"We've got more blasters available here than we did in Vegas," Liz said with a smirk. "But I would still appreciate if you didn't destroy too many of them. They're still difficult to come by."

Wil rolled his eyes as he fastened the weapons to his belt. She wasn't wrong, but he hoped he wouldn't have to use them.

Dagger had undressed and was being helped into his armor by the young guard. Rather than the bulky paneling, they outfitted him in a much more pliable, sleek gray material.

"The City Guard brought us a stash of these tactical suits," the girl explained, blushing as she helped to suit the boy up and brushing a strand of silky black hair from her face. "They're supposed to deflect blaster fire better than our makeshift ones. We didn't get enough for everyone, but you looked to be the right size for one of the few we had remaining."

The girl flashed Dagger a flirtatious smile as she helped him to adjust the suit and handed him a weapons belt.

Wil had to admit the newly adjusted suit made Dagger look the part of a soldier, despite his youthful face. Wil knew the lad was more capable than he could even surmise; he had seen more hardship in his short life than Wil had even dreamt of over the last few weeks.

"What's your name?" Wil asked the girl.

"Alice Cho," she said without hesitation, though her eyes never left Dagger.

"Make sure to look after this one when this is all over," Wil said.

The girl grinned, and Dagger's eyes went wide in a petrified stare. He glanced between Alice and Wil as if unsure what had prompted the remark.

Wil grinned to himself as he turned to ready his own gear. It was people like Dagger and Alice who reminded him he couldn't shy away from what he had to do. They still had so much life to live, and there were thousands of them in this city. Even if it cost the lives of those closest to him, even if it cost him his own life, how many more could he save? Maybe he couldn't save the world like Liz wanted, but he could at least save those here.

Though his thoughts were noble, Wil caught himself; he was stalling, and by doing so, lives were being lost.

From the moment they had stepped into the Rings, Wil had felt his power building within him, eager to boil to the surface. It had been the first time he had sensed it without it threatening to be released immediately. Its warmth called to him, beckoning him as though it knew it would be put into play soon. If he could use it, if he called upon it as he had in Vegas, he wouldn't need the blasters. Part of him didn't want to hold the weapons at all, but the power that manifested itself through him was so unpredictable. Even now, only a hair's width out of reach, he wasn't confident in its reliably.

I haven't seen a path where you live.

Liz's words still weighed down upon him. Wil was certain that if —*when*—his power unleashed, it would be the last action he ever performed.

He had to be sure he was ready.

They stepped outside, back into the tumult of disarray.

Shadows were cast over the brick and concrete buildings of the Middle Ring as the Onyx overhead blocked out the sun, still awaiting the opportunity to unleash their destruction.

Meanwhile, Sentinels were doing their best to thin the crowd. Even from the alley, they could see bodies already littering the main road. There was no opportunity to move those who weren't able to make it out of the Sentinels' grasp in time. The white machines stalked the main street back toward the Outer Ring, meticulously following those who had fled.

Blue light pulsed from the surface of the closest Onyx unit which hovered over their heads.

A beam pulsing from its surface released fury into one of the taller buildings in the Inner Ring. It exploded on impact, and a plume of fire, rubble, and ash was tossed into the air. Laser cannons from nearby buildings returned fire on the machine and brought the offending bot free-falling to the ground. The ground shook again with the impact of the massive electronic ball as it collided with the dirt.

One down, a hundred or so more to go.

Buzz, Ice, and Cali rushed off without saying another word. Wil watched them as they ran through, headstrong into battle. He did his best to keep his emotions in check. He'd never see his friends again.

Any of his friends.

From the alley in front of the safe house, Wil could make out Ella's face as she floated above the city in her technological prison. To his dismay, she was conscious, a look of horror on her face as she was forced to watch the city beneath her descend into chaos and ruin.

Wil cursed Kayla. It wasn't hard to believe that the woman who had so willingly sacrificed her father for her own gain would also believe stringing Ella up would be an effective means of manipulating Wil.

Except, according to Liz, no matter how this played out, he wouldn't be around to help anyone. He thought back to the promise he had made to Sierra when he had left Vegas; a promise to find her again. It would be another promise he would be forced to break.

More Onyx unleashed their blue firepower, collapsing more buildings and causing more screams to erupt through the streets. Wil ducked as a piece of the ancient wall beside him came crashing down from the tremors. Sentinels marched only a block away, winding their way through the streets, firing upon the citizens as they went.

The bots were barricading the humans within the Inner Ring. Hundreds of Sentinels blocked the roads toward the bridges, including the way by which Wil and his group had entered the city.

The Onyx, now springing to life, appeared to be aiming primarily for those who had been corralled by the Sentinels. This was a much more coordinated attack than the bots had employed in Vegas. Those who sought refuge in the Inner Ring were being targeted for slaughter.

Blaster fire from windows and roofs rained down on the bots as Resistance members gained visuals on the invaders. But when one went down, there were another two to take its place. There was a never-ending flow of robot soldiers and their flying counterparts.

If Wil was going to act, it had to be soon. He reached out for the warmth he had felt before. The fringes of his power still flirted with him, dancing like a flame he couldn't touch. When he couldn't quite grasp the spark that was being held out to him, panic flowed over him, and he struggled to catch his breath. What if he couldn't bring it under control in time? What if stray blaster fire blew a hole in his chest before he had time to act?

"I've got to work my way through to some of our primary strongholds," Liz shouted above the chaos. "Are you coming with me or are you going it alone?"

Wil couldn't see straight. His gaze shifted from Onyx to Sentinel; from explosions to dying men and women on the side of the road.

"Wil!" Liz yelled. "Snap out of it!"

Wil shook his head, but something about her gaze brought him back to reality.

"Focus on what needs to be done."

That was precisely his problem; he didn't know what needed to be done. Just that he needed to do *something*.

"Go ahead; you're needed elsewhere, and I'll only slow you down. I've got a plan."

He had no idea, never mind a plan, but Liz had other people to worry about than just him.

She nodded and took off, leaving Wil and Dagger to stand in the alley alone.

Wil positioned himself against the red brick of the building that lined the alley. The rough stone dug into his skin, and he prayed the Onyx wouldn't obliterate the structure as he stood beneath it.

It was time to change tactics. Whether he died attempting to kill one bot or a hundred, it didn't matter; Ella *had* to survive. If there was only one small way for that to happen, he needed to think of it quickly.

As Wil shifted his focus, the warmth began building in his belly, as if it were jealous that he had turned his attention away from it. The power, it seemed, was now coming to life. It would soon spread, and once it did, he wouldn't be able to master it.

Wil urged himself to get a grip. If he hesitated for too long, it would only be a matter of time before one of those Onyx blasts targeted the safe house or a Sentinel turned down their alley. He was going to have to decide, and the clock was ticking. Every second ticked by as he struggled with indecision.

Gut instinct, what do I do?

Kill the bots. It had been his whole motive for venturing out to San Francisco in the first place, his reason for following Fry to the arena, and the reason he had trusted Kayla when he shouldn't have.

As the thought swelled within him, the itching heat made its way into his veins and he knew he wasn't going to retain the ability to decide for much longer. He held the reins as if it were a horse champing at the bit, desperate for freedom. Everything in him wanted to take out the bots, no matter the cost to himself. For each and every lie the Guardians had told him, for killing Marco, for attacking a city of thousands, for keeping humanity on the brink of extinction for centuries.

The wall of the City Center's force field acted as a backdrop to the carnage that spilled through the Rings. The ancients had succeeded in hiding from the rest of the world while it burned, while their brothers and sisters had been slaughtered or hauled away to the Spheres. History seemed destined to repeat itself. Once again, the Center sat back and watched as the panicked cries of the Ringers filled the streets. Was this what it had been like during the wars?

But no matter how badly he wanted to enact his revenge, no matter how much he wanted to stop the bloodshed of thousands of innocents by surrendering to the fury building within him, the last thing he wanted was to be the cause of Ella's death.

Wil paused.

The earth shook as an explosion echoed in some far-off corner of the Rings.

Kayla knew the last thing he would want was for Ella's downfall to be caused by his actions.

The last thing I would want.

As he inhaled deeply, Wil settled on a thought so outlandish that part of him thought it had to be the answer; something he wouldn't do unless all other options were off the table. And even then, it could only be in a moment of clarity that he would have the audacity to make a move that would go against every instinct in his heart.

Wil lifted his blaster to the sky.

"What are you doing?" Dagger's voice called out behind him, but Wil barely heard it. The youth had already been halfway to the nearest street, where machines were hunting down unarmed civilians, their protectors unable to keep up with the carnage.

From his current vantage point, Wil could make out the two black strips of what appeared to be metal encircling Ella's prison, the green force field glowing between the artificial beams. Attached to these strips, two small devices jutted out from the otherwise spheroid shape. Wil assumed these were keeping it afloat, like engines of some sort. If both of them were knocked out at the same time, Ella would come hurtling to the ground, but what if he took out just one? Her fall might be dampened enough for her to drift down rather than plummet.

He had to try something, and it wasn't like he could make the situation worse.

I hope.

Out of time and out of ideas, he pulled the trigger. His aim landed far better than he could ever have hoped for; the shot landed true, striking one of the black outcroppings that powered Ella's cell. Sparks flew from the engine and the ball spun. Suddenly, Wil worried he had made a grave error; that the remaining engine would propel her into the ground faster than if she had free-fallen.

Although Wil couldn't hear her, Ella's widened eyes and open mouth suggested she was screaming.

The cell spun several times, but eventually it righted itself and the orb drifted downward, swinging from side to side like a piece of paper that had been dropped rather than a giant ball hurtling to the ground.

The fire burning inside of Wil wouldn't be held back for much longer; he was about to erupt, and there wasn't anything he could do now to stop it. He prayed his actions had been enough to save Ella. The ache in his heart hoped that, for once, his rash actions wouldn't end in disaster.

With one eye to the orbs in the sky, Wil pushed his way past uniformed fighters and Resistance members, doing his best to avoid paths the Sentinels had already claimed. He clawed his way through the sea of citizens scrambling to find a place to hide that would offer some shred of safety from the butchery.

Smoke filled the street, making it difficult for Wil to navigate. Dust and debris cut loose from the explosions made the already thick air heavy in his lungs, and Wil choked on its grit. The earth shook again, and pieces of buildings that had remained intact for centuries crashed to the earth, scattering those the ancient stonework threatened to crush.

Finally, he saw her.

The cell sphere had landed in the middle of a side street, one that had yet to be occupied by the advancing Guardians. Its shield had dropped, and Ella lay on the ground, sprawled out on the roadway. It wasn't until Wil was next to her that he could see the rise and fall of her chest. She was unconscious, with a few cuts on her face and arms, but otherwise she appeared to be in one piece.

He wrapped himself around her warm body, even as the energy within him pushed its way through his extremities and out into the world around him. Whether the force of the flame was caused by his attempt to hold it back for so long or the immensity of what was needed to stop the surrounding conflict, he had no way of knowing.

He let out a gritty "I'm sorry," to Ella, before the screams took over. Ella squirmed in response, and Wil would have breathed a sigh of relief if he could, but every ounce of effort he could muster was being put into not breaking apart at the seams.

The force upon him was so extreme that he eventually had to let Ella go, and his back arched so far that he wondered if he would snap in half with the pressure. Everything around him disappeared. He could see nothing, feel nothing, except for the intensity of the sun that was exploding from within him. The sounds of war disappeared, and a loud buzz took over his senses. He felt as if he were spinning, falling uncontrollably, as if everything solid around him had dematerialized, as if it had ceased to exist except for the white-hot heat that was both himself and the universe around him.

The world came crashing back. The last thing Wil sensed was Ella sitting and wrapping her arms around him. Then everything went black.

EPILOGUE

ELIZABETH RUNAR STUDIED the remnants of the Inner Ring. During the hours the Guardians had barraged the city, they had inflicted a massive amount of damage. Buildings had been leveled and thousands slaughtered. If it hadn't been for Wil, there would have been nothing left. They still had so much work to complete, and it would only be a matter of days before the Guardians returned to assess what had happened to their fleet. With that in mind, the survivors were pushing their luck already.

Shells of the machines littered the streets of the Inner and Middle Rings. The collapse of the Onyx had caused more damage than their actual assault. Hundreds of giant metal and glass spheres had rained down from the sky. It was a miracle more men and women hadn't been killed in the volley. Too many had, but it could have been far worse.

There was no time to grieve, and there was barely time to gather the survivors and try to move out. They were so far from the nearest Silent Zone, and who knew how long it would be before the people of San Francisco were protected from the Guardians again.

The crunch of metal and glass behind her told Liz that someone approached from behind. The scraping of one leg across the earth, being dragged behind the other, meant she didn't have to turn to know it was Ella.

Liz had honestly not believed Ella would make it through the battle. The odds of what Wil would pull off were nearly impossible. Not only delaying his urge to enact revenge on the bots, but also opting to shoot at the woman he had wanted most to protect, he had grown far more than she had given him credit for.

She turned to greet Ella. The woman's dark eyes were determined, despite her deeply tanned skin being battered from the fall and the bruises from whatever treatment Kayla's guards had given her. The woman had so far refused to talk about what happened after she had left the cells beneath the Renaissance.

"Dagger tells me you're planning for us to move out tomorrow morning," Ella said. She stood on her good leg and leaned against the partial wall of a building that had mostly collapsed. Liz eyed the structure, uncertain it maintained the integrity to hold the woman, but the odds had favored them so far. Ella had done a remarkably good job of putting on a determined face since the battle, and Liz wasn't about to coddle her now.

"Yes," Liz said. "We've lost far too many men and women already. I won't stand to lose any more just so we can secure supplies."

"But what about the cache of weaponry and tech?" Ella began. "It would be a shame for bandits—or worse, the Order—to lay claim to all of this. This much supply would be a great benefit to the war effort."

Liz smiled. With everything Ella had gone through, her primary thought was still for the good of the people. But Liz also didn't miss the woman's change in tune about the Resistance's mission to fight. Perhaps Ella had realized the time for choice in the matter had come to an end.

"Don't worry, I've got it covered," Liz replied. "We'll have members stationed here. The Resistance holds claim to San Francisco now, and these reserves are ours. I don't think anyone will challenge that for the time being, but any non-essential personnel need to be cleared out of here before another assault occurs. The Guardians will be drawn to our numbers. If I leave a skeleton crew behind, it's more likely the bots will leave us alone, at least for a bit longer."

It had been three days since the attack. They had already stayed in the city for longer than Liz would have liked, but Ella was correct in her line of thinking; the resources in the Rings alone were enough to give the Resistance a leg up it never would have dreamed of having before.

And that was only from what remained in the Rings.

The high-rise buildings of the City Center, once impressive, now seemed ominous, towering in the distance. They seemed out of place without the green force field surrounding them.

Liz had purposefully neglected to inform Wil his actions would cause the field to fall. She didn't want to add another layer of complexity to his decision, and she had already feared she had told him too much. She had assumed he would have worked it out on his own, but he was so focused on rescuing Ella that if it had crossed his mind, he'd never mentioned it.

This time, it seemed, was one of the rare instances where she had revealed the perfect amount of information in order for things to not end in the worst-case scenario. She'd told Wil enough so that he knew he had to deviate from the course of action he was likely to take, but not enough to make things catastrophically worse, though she'd had her doubts after Wil had assassinated the Director. Ella surviving may have been a personal victory, but the real achievement was keeping as many of the citizens alive as possible.

Most of the surviving Ringers and City Center residents had already been evacuated, sent along the coast for the long trek toward South Angeles and the Silent Zones that hopefully still stood along the southern coast. With any luck, they'd be halfway there by now, but it was nearly a weeklong journey at the best of times. With families, elderly, and those wounded in the attack, it would be much slower going. Thankfully, there was a Silent Zone or two for them to rest up in along the way. It was the best she could hope for. They had to get past one obstacle at a time.

The sojourners would face bigger hurdles, such as finding enough to eat, never mind where they all would sleep. Thousands of residents from the City Center had likely never seen a day of discomfort in their lives. Even with the obstacle of the bots removed, many probably wouldn't survive the grueling trip. Water, food, fitness levels, and mental preparedness would all play a role.

"He's not going to make it, is he?" Ella's question caught Liz off guard, ripping her from her thoughts. It took her a second to realize that Ella meant Wil. Though Ella had worn it on her face since the battle, it was the first time she had voiced her concern for the friend who had saved her life.

Liz shook off her surprise, knowing that with Ella, there was no appropriate way to sugarcoat the answer. "No," Liz said. "The Healers have said he might have a couple weeks, but he won't regain consciousness."

"We'll be leaving him here, then?" Ella asked.

"There's no point in hauling him on a two-week journey if he's only going to die on the way. I'm sorry, Ella."

"He knew what he was doing," Ella said, her voice firm. "He came here seeking revenge, but in the end, he gave everything to save us."

Ella's voice pitched just enough for Liz to catch that she was trying to control it. She offered no condolences; Ella wouldn't want them.

"Still no word from T'al or Voth?" Ella asked, changing the subject.

Liz shook her head. "No. And still nothing from Kayla. They either snuck out with the rest of the inhabitants or they're hiding somewhere in the catacombs of City Center. Either way, it's none of our concern right now. They'll eventually be found."

"What will happen to T'al and Voth? After their part in the coup?"

"The Resistance knows what took place. If they attempt to come back, they'll need to answer for their crimes." It was a shame that two of her best fighters had acted so foolishly. She had no doubt T'al had wanted nothing more than to do what he felt was best, but insubordination could not be tolerated, and mutiny needed to be dealt with swiftly. She didn't feel the need to tell Ella that she had scouts looking for the pair.

"We journey south with the others at dawn?"

"Unless you plan to join the Resistance, you can go wherever you please."

Liz studied Ella. The woman's dark hair elegantly framed her naturally tanned skin, and it was a wonder to her that Wil had had such a hard time making up his mind about his feelings for her. Although Liz knew his reticence had stemmed more from his own past, she also knew the two would have made an excellent couple had they both been destined to survive. It seemed, however, that in fate's cruel irony, it was not meant to be.

Ella was quiet for a moment, staring at the final efforts of those loading caravans of goods to be hauled south, as if contemplating her next move. As if there could be any decision for the woman other than the obvious. Liz had to stop herself from smiling. People had far less free will than they imagined. Circumstances tended to pull you in one of two directions, and usually you were heavily weighted in one. Wil, for instance, could never have possibly run away from the attack on San Francisco. Every part of him would have sought to bring the bots down. He could have brought them down out of nobility, out of revenge, or out of self-preservation, but no matter how he tried to justify it in his own mind, fate would always lead him to the thing he was meant to do.

Just as Ella was meant to go back to Vegas. She could start a new life and perhaps even fight for the Resistance now that she knew they were more than a group of vigilantes insistent on revenge. Despite what had happened with T'al and Voth, Liz was certain those she had placed in command would be more steadfast in their purpose. They had to prepare for the next wave of fighting after securing the travelers' safety.

"I'll think about it and let you know," Ella replied.

"We leave at dawn tomorrow," Liz replied. "You have until then to make your decision. If you're unable to walk, we'll save a spot on a cart for you."

Ella gave her an appreciative nod and excused herself, hobbling back inside the safe house.

Liz set out on the long walk to the waterfront. After the past week, she needed a few moments to clear her head.

Sea lions cried in the distance; even as far as she was from the City Center, they were still audible. She had seen photos of what the city had looked like before the wars, bustling and full of life. Though they were built after the wars had destroyed much of the original city, the skyscrapers that now stood in the Center were unlike anything else she had come across, at least on the west coast. Travelers claimed cities still stood to the east, though abandoned or fully within Silent Zones.

She had hoped she could have kept the force field from falling. The City Center, despite all of its problems, could have been a great resource in the war that was coming. A working city of the ancients equipped with the ability to construct weaponry, advanced armor, and more. Despite his stiffness, with enough prodding, the Director would have eventually let the Ringers inside. His daughter was much colder and more calculating. In her mind, the Ringers weren't worthy enough to keep alive.

Liz sighed again. Bleached white buildings remained standing along the waterfront. Someone had tagged all the buildings with the same mark Liz had seen throughout the city, but she was still unsure where it came from. The image was familiar to her, a sun setting over three wavy lines, but she couldn't recall where she had seen it before. Regardless, she didn't have the resources to be too concerned about a little graffiti, but this seemed more orchestrated. The last thing the Resistance needed was more terrorist groups or rogue militias impeding what they needed to do.

Kayla had been right in one regard; the people of the west coast needed to unite in a way they hadn't seen since the wars. Humans had been too spread out, locked away in their Silent Zones, cities, and Spheres to be effective. The path they had to take would be difficult, but she knew it was possible.

Liz turned back toward the Middle Ring. There was much to be done before she could turn in and get one last good night's sleep.

An arm grabbed her shoulder, and she jumped. She rarely let her guard down enough for someone to sneak up on her, but between the crashing waves and the distant gulls and sea lions, she had missed the sound of whoever had approached her.

A young woman stood before her with dark hair and purple eyes. For a moment, Liz thought she was staring at her own reflection. The woman before her was beat up, scraped, and bruised. The outfit she wore was a sleek black suit that hugged her slight curves, but it looked as though it would be easy to move in if necessary.

Sierra.

Liz stepped back, her heart racing, her eyes darting around as though the foundation of the city might collapse beneath them. She wasn't supposed to be with her younger sister, not yet. The end always started when the two of them met, regardless of when or where.

Sierra put a hand to Liz's shoulder and gave her a light shake. "Izzy, it's okay. I'm not really here."

Liz blinked and took a deep breath. The nickname wasn't something anyone had called her in the eight years since she had been forced to leave the Sphere. Forced to grow up that day, she had left the childish name behind.

Her sister smiled a knowing grin and gave her a pat on her shoulder.

"What's happening?" Liz asked. "Why are you here? Or . . . not here?" Liz furrowed her brow. "I don't understand what you mean."

"I don't have much time to explain. You can't travel south with the rest of the Resistance. It's time to journey to Vegas. And you need to take Wil with you. The fate of the world depends on it."

"Wil's all but dead," Liz said, slow and calculated. Had her sister somehow transcended space and time to deliver this message? If so, it would be a first, and she didn't doubt her sister was taking a significant risk in doing so. Liz had not been able to master any control of the things she had seen.

"He needs to make it there *alive*. There's no other option if this is to end well."

Suddenly, Sierra began to . . . *fade*. It was the only way Liz could explain it; her body simply became transparent, as though she were a ghost.

"Where are you?" Liz asked. "How are you doing this?"

"There's no time," Sierra said, her image nothing more than a faint reflection. "I love you, Izzy. Keep Wil alive at all costs."

And then she was gone.

The End

ACKNOWLEDGMENTS

A huge thank you to everyone who made Sins of the Ancients possible.

Thank you to my wonderful editor Pete Smith at Novel Approach for taking the extra time and effort to help me through several rounds of cleaning up the manuscript.

Thank you as well to Miblart for the cover design.

An enormous amount of thanks to Aime Sund for jumping in at the last minute to give the manuscript a final proofread, and the entire Rebel Author group who has provided me with much needed motivation and comic relief.

To Margie Viers, and my beta readers, thank you for your initial insights into the early manuscript.

Again a huge and overwhelming thank you to my wife, Nettie for your support, encouragement and putting up with my hours behind the keyboard.

I also want to thank you, faithful reader, for continuing to journey with me through the world of the Guardians I couldn't have done it without you.

ABOUT THE AUTHOR

Herman Steuernagel is a crafter of dystopian worlds and dark tales, including his debut, internationally bestselling Lies of the Guardians series.

Herman grew up with a love of story and of writing. That love has never waned and led to a Bachelor of Arts (English Major) from the University of Calgary. His past titles include entrepreneur, financial branch manager, and journalist. He currently works as a web developer.

Herman lives in British Columbia, Canada where he wields his stories of robots, vampires and other fantastical creatures. He can often be found cycling, running and enjoying time with his wife.

Lightning Source UK Ltd.
Milton Keynes UK
UKHW010109230921
391042UK00007B/382/J